JETT HARROW

POSITIVELY LETHAL

Love has its place, as does hate.
Peace has its place, as does war.
Mercy has its place, as do cruelty and revenge.

-Meir Kahane

PROLOGUE
THE BLADE MAN

The orange glow of a tepid afternoon filtered into the office through half-drawn blinds.

The sun was vanishing behind the peaks of Los Angeles skyscrapers soon to completely disappear below the horizon and stay hidden for quite some time. It was just another scene from just another day in the West Coast city of opportunity.

A man with piercing brown eyes that seemed to be a perfect fit for the sallow complexion of his face regarded the very tip of the knife he held up in one hand mesmerized by its cold, minacious shape. Just over six inches, its butt lined with four decorative holes and both its edges that met at the tip, gleaming in razor sharp beauty. It was a simple, but effective masterpiece of metalwork.

The man suddenly flipped the knife upwards. It did a full somersault a foot above his hand and he caught it in the same position it had been in before.

Again, he stared at the summit of the blade and though his eyes were ritually fixated, something behind them gave off a pleasured glaze. The corners of his lips were curled ever so slightly and he let his top row of teeth bite softly into the sponginess of his lower lip.

"Where are you goin', boy?" he whispered softly under his breath in a Southern accent. "Who's gonna be next in line?" It was a deep moment, like a father talking to a child and the way he was holding the thing gently, looking at it, was similar to the first moments with a newborn, eyes in awe of creation. It was an odd sight.

He was reasonably tall with skin that looked as if it had acquired a slight tan some years ago, the kind that never fades completely. A few stray wrinkles disturbed the features on his gaunt face and his dark hair was short and greased up into curling fronds at the fringe.

His black suit fit him perfectly and made the red tie that hung down stand out in contrast to its charcoal background. The shirt beneath the suit, though not clearly visible, was also black.

Lysander Shades was still looking at his knife when the noise of a heated argument from below disturbed his concentration. It wasn't unnatural to hear such things going on in the Holden Tower. As long as it ended in a fistfight and not gunshots, then he didn't see the problem, although some real peace and quiet would be nice once in a while. It didn't seem like there were many truly quiet moments anymore. Not for him. Things had gotten ridiculously huge in a short amount of time, like a sudden boom in criminal enterprise had struck.

He stood listening to the muffled noises below for a while, then lifted the right side of his suit jacket revealing a custom-made armory within.

Knives, all identical to the one in his hand lined the purple interior, held in by tailored strips. He had about twelve holsters in that side and twelve in the other. One was bare. He replaced the knife as if he were slipping a credit card into an ATM and then pulled the side of the jacket back over his chest.

Times like this were few and far between, when Shades stood alone and just thought to himself- so he enjoyed the moment.

Walking over to the window he parted one of the strip blinds letting orange light cover his features completely, but it didn't cause him to squint as he looked at the shadowy buildings against the skyline.

He hated the city. Hated it more than anyone would ever understand. He was raised a country boy and had liked it that way, but he went where the work was.

Far below people would be walking to and from stores, arms laden with groceries and such. Men would be cheating on their wives and women would be cheating on their husbands. The life of the ordinary really did sicken him.

He would remember to thank fate later that he wasn't sitting in some trashy trailer watching CNN on a small T.V. while two children bearing his eyes played Monopoly on the rug.

Even so, the cheap and often carefree life of the country still called to him, however if fate believed it appropriate that all the events in his life led him here, to this moment in time, then it was only fair he made the best of it. He was, after all, making good money. 'Too bad he had no urge to share it with anyone just yet. If he was still in Stellaville maybe he'd have some woman on his arm.

The thought made him frown and he shut his eyes momentarily hoping that when he opened them the towering structures of concrete and steel would be gone, but when his eyelids lifted again his vision had not become a reality.

Shifting his jaw slightly, he put a flat palm on the window pane and tried to see the ant-like pedestrians far below, but the angle would not permit it.

Without warning the door behind him opened and Gordon stood on the threshold. He was an older gentleman in the same attire as Shades. He had liver spots on his neck as if it descended into the body of an old leopard and the marks adorned his hands too. His hair had vacated the top of his head and hung down to his neck in greasy, gray strands. Wrinkles were most prominent on his forehead and around his thin lips. As well as the suit, the man also wore dark, circular glasses that a blind person might sport, but Shades knew for

3

a fact the old man wasn't blind. The coot was actually a dangerously good shot.

"The envoys of the Tagliano Family have arrived. They're coming up now. 'Boss wants you in his office," Gordon said in his croaky voice that never exceeded a loud whisper.

Shades had turned to face him and left a smudged handprint on the glass. He looked at the floor for a moment and then nodded.

"Okay," he said in confirmation.

Gordon returned the nod and made to leave. Shades followed him purposefully after pressing his suit into a more crisp position with his hands.

'Wouldn't do to look unkempt for the boss.

He shut the door behind him and the room was left silent. The only things still to desert it now were the stripes of vermillion from the setting sun outside.

"**W**e know how many?" Shades asked as he strode behind the senior gentleman.

"Why?" Gordon replied in a flat tone.

"Oh, you know me, Gordon. 'Always like to analyze the situation and know all the details."

"Funny, I always had you down as the shoot-first-ask-questions-later type."

The way he had said 'funny' was so unconvincing, Shades almost laughed. Gordon never found anything funny. He must have been in a good mood, which still resulted in no smile whatsoever.

"There are three."

"Mr. Tagliano must have tremendous faith in old school mafia rules of engagement, huh?"

Gordon didn't reply. They continued for a while down the hallways.

Subtle opera music being played on a loop drifted in the air, but apart from that, the only sounds were vague conversations going on in the rooms that they passed. On this level of the Holden Tower, people kept quiet. Ray combated stress by surrounding his office with men who whispered and a somber theme tune that never exceeded the volume level of 3. It seemed to work, but Shades found the setup unnecessarily creepy.

"'Too bad Ray is as far from old school as it gets."

"'Gives us a certain edge, Lysander."

Shades winced. He didn't like people calling him by his first name. Not even his father had called him Lysander. It had just been Sander and that was that, but his conversations with Gordon were rare so he would let it slide.

One thing that was on his mind at that moment was his boss, Ray's, prior history of negotiation. It wasn't exactly exemplary. A particularly nasty incident involving a Mexican drug cartel and a lot of bullets sprang to mind.

Ray certainly didn't have the best people skills; however that did make things more interesting in a way.

Shades had become increasingly office bound of late waiting for action that never came so if the whole thing blew up then all the more thrill and kill for him.

He smiled as a shaft of amber from a window flashed across his face.

"Enjoyable," he said.

CHAPTER ONE
THE SNIPER AND THE STONER

"Check your shit at the door, Dean."

That was what he kept telling himself. Those words kept his aim steady as he lay on his belly on the roof of the Casa De Coffee.

The steel butt of his customized sniper rifle (that could be mistaken for an SR-25) dug into him harshly, but he took no notice. All of his concentration was split between keeping his left eye tightly shut and his right eye looking steadily through the yellow-tinted sight that he had fitted himself. The crosshairs were centered on the door of a cab as it opened and the fare got out onto the sidewalk of a freshly constructed park square flanked on all sides by roads.

Minimal traffic trundled past.

He didn't usually like to be this close, but it was becoming a frequent and necessary occurrence.

The kid who stepped out of the cab looked just as he had in the picture, a tall, pale youth with a green vest top and some baggy jeans. His sneaker laces were untied and a mop of red hair hung down from under an upside down sun visor.

How sporting headwear like that had ever come into fashion Dean Cottrell would never know. The cab pulled away and the kid, no older than nineteen, stood static on the sidewalk for a second reaching into his pocket and withdrawing a blunt before lighting it.

His name was Jake Bentwood. Some small-time drug peddler from Glendale. What his business was in Echo Park, Dean had no idea. That was of little or no importance. What was important was the fact that the upstart stoner had opted to put one of Thomas Bentley's affiliates out of business; the fact that Thomas Bentley had not taken too kindly to this; the fact that now he had sent someone to deal with it.

With great confidence that nobody would catch him with his joint, Jake Bentwood set off along the path that led across the small park.

He had his hands in his pockets, gold bracelets too big for him clinking as he walked past other people who were going about their business. He had no way of knowing that a cross of thin, black lines within a yellow circle was trained on his head.

Dean focused and almost let himself squeeze the trigger.

Burnout, grade-A screw-ups like Bentwood were in abundance. They did nobody any good whatsoever. Taking one off the streets was practically a civic duty. It was almost a treat for a boy like him to be taken out by someone of Dean's caliber, because chances were he would get shot by cops in the near future anyway.

Unfortunately this particular burnout, grade-A screw-up disappeared behind the foliage of a tree and Dean was forced to curse the bad timing.

"Fuck."

Dean was practically invisible peering over the edge of the coffee house roof, beneath its large sign. The shot would come as a complete surprise, or rather the mess that it made would. The long, silver suppressor that choked the barrel of his gun would make sure that the location from where the shot had been fired would remain secret. It would only be worked out after the police had done diagnostic laser alignments, which they wouldn't bother with and even if they did, by the time they got around to it he would be long gone.

The target appeared again strolling with no obvious purpose. Dean trained the sight on Jake's head once more and traced his movements.

It was all too easy. He really hoped they would start giving him some more leash after this. 'Let him take on something more important. Thomas had to be at least marginally crazy to have someone like him kill a guy like Bentwood when any bum would take five dollars to stab him in an alley.

His calm finger pressed on the trigger and at the last second, when everything lined up in Dean's head, he fired.

The muzzled bang came out as a barely audible '*poom*', and the rifle jerked slightly.

The lanky form of Jake Bentwood passed on the pathway in front of two picnickers and at that precise, unlucky moment a medium caliber round punched through his head just above his left eye. It powered through skull and brain as if there was no difference in density, and left an exit wound the size of a small fist, before slamming into the base of a tree and sticking. The couple and their picnic blanket were assaulted with a splatter of crimson, and reflexive recoiling was followed by screams.

Jake's body collapsed in a heap. The shot had been powerful enough to cut through him without making him fly backwards and he now lay on the pavement, blood pooling around his head as if eager to escape from the self-abused body.

The picnickers were both screaming and bundling away from their blanket. Other pedestrians were also crying out and shouting. Some had just stopped and stared, hypnotized by the unfathomable occurrence.

Mission accomplished.

Dean ripped the rifle apart and threw it quickly into its specially designed metal case. He closed it and then stood up behind the sign hidden from view. At the back of the roof, he thundered down the flight of metal stairs that led to an alleyway where his pristine, black BMW M5 Sedan waited. He jumped inside throwing the case onto the passenger seat.

The sound of distant sirens became audible causing Dean to look up sharply before turning the key in the ignition and speeding out of the alley, making a hard right to the annoyance of the Pontiac he had cut in front of.

His car rolled along, one mile an hour over the speed limit, and checking his watch, he saw that the time was 4:44. That had been what he had expected. Sighing, he checked his rear view mirror just in case. Nothing apart from regular city cars. His body relaxed and he let down his window to feel the stale, late afternoon air on his face.

The sun was dipping below the skyline. This was his favorite time of day. It always had been. A true West Coast sunset was a sight that resonated with him on a personal level. Watching it made him forget about the job and for a few seconds, who he really was.

Dean Cottrell had a peachy complexion and a tidy husk of blonde hair. His green eyes were particularly captivating and he had a set of perfect teeth. He was rather well built, although nothing too special when compared to some of the real brutes that the Red Dawn employed. He had always thought that name kind of extreme. Either the 'man upstairs' had some sort of communist agenda, or he had watched too many action movies as a teen.

Dean wondered whether Ray Bentley's guests had turned up at the Holden Tower yet. News of an important meeting had filtered down to him, but of course, that was no business of his. He was paid to shoot not to sit down at mahogany tables and talk money and respect with people who had Italian last names. That wasn't his job.

In this world, if you concerned yourself with tasks that weren't your own, you ended up face-to-face with some really dangerous individuals and the man on the throne certainly had a lot of those individuals at his disposal. Dean had had the displeasure of meeting some of them. Definitely not people he would call friends. In fact, there were very few people Dean called friend in this life. He guessed that came with the territory. There was of course Williams, who was a true friend, despite his tendency for getting Dean into trouble. All kinds of trouble.

Still, 'couldn't be any worse than the Middle East. He used that as an excuse way too often and he knew it, but it was true. At least here he had some security. Idiots such as Bentwood had no idea about what was coming. They were living in an ordinary world where war was far away. Out there on foreign soil, the enemy was hunting you most of the time ready with traps and a desire to cause pain and suffering. The world out there was hell compared to L.A.

The haze of the declining sun took Dean back momentarily.

As the only source of light ducked behind mountains in the background of Taliban rocket nests, in shelter before the conflict, Dean viewed enemy targets through infra-red binoculars, and the guy next to him ground his teeth.

Both had known about the helicopter that had taken four men on its flaming descent through the air in the form of shrapnel and body parts. Both had known what needed to be done.

On this day, in what was probably the most developed area of Echo Park, Dean had done what needed to be done. He hadn't held back and he hadn't choked.

CHAPTER TWO
A MEETING BETWEEN RIVALS

Three men stood in the fast ascending elevator. Each was wearing a gray, pinstripe suit and black leather shoes. The eldest of the three had a gray Fedora on his similarly colored hair.

He was Luga Tagliano, Godfather of the Tagliano Crime Family, set up in '55. It had only been a week since the death of his beloved mother so he was still in a pretty distasteful mood. His father had died ten years earlier of food poisoning and now it was just him, his one sister, his one brother (who had not been able to attend this particular shindig due to illness), and his son who stood behind him.

The boy, Vito Tagliano, was twenty-seven years old and was a fast learner. He handled business appropriately just like his father. He was also the one set to inherit the family's fortune and power once Luga and his brother had fallen to Father Time, or the bullet of a rival gang's sniper. Vito was shorter than his father and had a shaven head to top a rather flat and boring face. The other man in the elevator, Yeltergio Maroney (or Yelton as he was more commonly known), was the tallest of the group with a slender build and jet black hair that he hadn't bothered to grease.

Luga had been getting strange, twitchy feelings deep within his head the moment they had entered the Holden Tower and couldn't shake them loose. It was as if a light bulb inside his brain was shorting, fizzing in and out. To make matters worse he would then have to go home to Mrs. Tagliano, who would complain about how he didn't appreciate her cooking. Luga allowed himself a sly smile. If he could just make this alliance work the Tagliano Family would have a powerful ally on board when the Goto-gumi yakuza branch in Little Tokyo made another move on their warehouses.

The Red Dawn was the fastest growing crime syndicate in Los Angeles. Nobody knew where they had come from. They had just shown up. As far as Luga could tell their ties to Italy were minimal, but 'boy' were they organized... Italian organized.

The elevator shuddered to a halt, and the doors opened.

Lysander Shades walked slowly and methodically behind Gordon down the red walled hallway to their destination. As he neared the office of Ray Bentley things changed. Whereas most of the floor was a modern labyrinth of thin partition walls and windows this part had a very different look and feel. The color scheme remained constant the walls adorned with art that Ray had either bought or stolen - all labeled and well-lit. The quiet trill of the opera music was ever flowing.

They turned a corner and came out into a wider hallway culminating in a large, ivory white set of doors. Gordon opened them carefully and both of the men went in.

The large office of Ray Bentley was twice the size of the room Shades had come from. Opposite the doors was a large, rectangular window that looked out onto the skyline on the side of the tower best placed for viewing the sunset. A mahogany table dominated the space, but wasn't the only piece of furniture as an antique desk was situated at the furthest end to the right everything on it neatly arranged. Behind it was a comfy massage chair and behind that was an oil painting of a snow swept plain. On the same side as the doors there was a large fish tank almost the length of the window,

12

embedded in the wall. Yellow tangs swam within the clear, blue water and lights at the back of the tank made aquatic patterns dance across the table. This was even more noticeable as the sun was obscured completely and left the room now lit only by the lights behind the water and glass.

The chairs were set up differently to how Shades had last seen them. The ones at the side had been removed and now three sat at the end closest to the door. One resided directly across. None were meant for him.

Ray's organizer, Valentino, was leaning against one of the walls near the desk. He too wore the black suit and red tie, but he was a large man with a wide girth and his chin had lost itself so it maybe didn't work so well for him. A small amount of gray hair perched on top of his head like a bird waiting to fly south. The comparison wasn't so farfetched. What bird wouldn't want to fly away from the fat, bureaucratic know-it-all? Shades had never genuinely liked him.

With his back to them, staring out through the window at the city which had so quickly descended into night, Ray Bentley was shifting his fingers near his mouth as if in deep consideration. Dressed identically to everyone else, Ray was tall with handsomely clipped features and ink black hair that he had permanently slicked back in greasy streaks behind a small quiff. He had deep, rich, brown eyes and always carried himself with a posture that showed dominance, control and vanity.

The man put both his hands in his pockets and arched his back putting a deliberate strain on his thighs.

Shades took up a position directly across from the door and Gordon marched over to just beyond the fish tank and lingered quietly against the wall. They watched their boss with anticipation, but he just stood there, staring into the dark city. What he was thinking - they didn't know.

High above the sprawling metropolis that served as their playground, the boss, his brain, and his two closest hands waited in the darkness. It was serene and special and a moment that Ray would look back on. It was times like these when he felt truly in control.

There were footsteps close by and Ray turned to greet them as three suits were shown into the room by one of his henchmen.

For a moment Ray stood staring at the three men who stared back in turn. He liked to keep people on edge. Slowly, his blank mouth curled into a warm smile.

"Please, gentlemen. Sit." He motioned to the three chairs. Yelton sat down closest to the window, and Vito took the seat near the door while his father sat between them.

There was a brief silence while they expected Ray to take his seat at the opposite end, but he didn't. Instead, he put a hand on it and gave the three men a thoughtful look. Vito shuffled slightly under the man's gaze.

"I must thank you for taking the time to attend, gentlemen," Ray said finally, a jovial aspect manifesting itself on his face. "We have a lot to discuss."

"My sentiments exactly." Luga Tagliano had a very thick, Sicilian accent, whereas Ray's was a hospitable, East Coast drone.

At this point, Yelton (who was a very powerful and influential figure in the Tagliano Family) spoke up.

"The Goto-gumi are moving in on our drug operations. They're shipping in firearms from a well known dealer in Spain. I assume you realize how important an alliance between our two organizations would be to all of us," Yelton said.

"We've already tried conversing with the Gambino Family over at their Long Beach estate, but they don't want trouble with yakuza. Nobody does. I don't get it. The States is our turf. Fucking Japs show

14

up and everyone runs for cover." Luga had a dry look about him and Ray picked up on it. It was the look someone had when they desperately wanted something, but were trying to be casual. His ability to read people was something Ray was secretly proud of.

He stood opposite the three men taking in every detail about them and then he shot a look at Shades.

"Scotch, gentlemen?" he said tactfully giving a nod to Valentino behind him, who moved over to the desk where a large, crystalline decanter of scotch and four glasses stood. He popped the glass stopper off and poured the four drinks, the amber colored swill filling the glass containers. He handed the beverages to his employer and Ray set them down on the table expertly sliding three of the glasses to his guests, keeping one for his own consumption.

Luga looked down at the drink in front of him and narrowed his eyes. He had built a picture of the man he would be meeting that day, and flippant generosity was not in his profile. Nevertheless, Luga took a hefty swig and his companions did the same.

"Mr. Bentley, we need some assurances. Now, you obviously want this to work otherwise you wouldn't have agreed to these talks. We know you have the means to help keep us in business, but you're still fresh, am I right? I mean, you're limited players on a big board here. We've been running our shit for years now. The name of the family is cemented in crime everywhere. There is a lot we can do for you. We work together and this could be great for both of us. Help us defend what's rightfully ours from these Japanese carpet salesmen and in return what's ours is yours. Safe passage during overseas transactions, our contacts in Bolivia, all the details you'll need on triad shell companies in Zurich." Vito's words were to the point and driven with enough force to make it home. He was the spitting image of his father.

"The yakuza aren't gonna roll over just because I get involved. Like you said, I'm a limited player and they probably wouldn't give me a second thought," Ray said simply, taking a sip of scotch and a fleeting look at his fish tank where the yellow tangs darted around excitedly.

"We don't expect them to," replied Yelton. "You'll have to get your hands dirty, but I'm guessing you already have. 'A lot of strange things happening in L.A. at present."

Ray considered this for a moment, his lips pursed in thought.

"You're an astute man. If we're optimistic, it's not long before I'll have enough assets to make the yakuza disappear from L.A. forever," he said suddenly.

"Weapons?" Vito raised an eyebrow.

"My brother handles all that. We have deals with sympathetic sources inside defense contractors from all across the continent. I could gather enough firepower to level Little Tokyo if I wanted."

Vito and his father smiled at this. Ray Bentley was exactly the ally they needed. More so than he would ever guess.

In reality, they were in the tightest squeeze they ever had been and this really was a golden ticket. What's more, Yelton had done some digging on Red Dawn assets beforehand and he knew that Ray wasn't talking about hot snowballs. These things were real. He would be damned if he knew how Ray had what he had, but it didn't change the fact that he had it.

"If we wipe these guys from our map for good it benefits us all. It's time to stop all this aggravation between the families. We should be working together now to turn a profit. It's the twenty-first century after all and though you're not exactly the most traditional group, you are a Western syndicate," Yelton added for good measure.

"I couldn't agree more. A united criminal front here in L.A. would prove to be in the interest of generating a stable cash flow in these

16

harsh economic times. 'Just a few conditions I think we should run through though. I mean, I am taking a risk here, kind of pulling your asses out of the fire in a way. There has to be some level of control with this thing, am I right?"

CHAPTER THREE
TAGLIANO, GOODNIGHT

Dean pulled his car into the underground parking lot of the Holden Tower. It was a huge building, large enough to challenge the skyscrapers of legitimate businesses.

The car halted in the first available space as in the cold light, Dean watched shadows fall across the support columns and the elevator off to the left. He stepped out and felt the arresting temperature of the place immediately. The elevator doors chimed open before he got to them and a man wearing dark sunglasses trotted out. Taking little notice, Dean stepped inside and hit the button marked '3'.

The first and second floors of the Holden Tower were mainly just administration, several offices and filing centers. He had only visited them on rare occasions, because it was the third floor that was a recreational level for the business' less mundane employees, and where he spent most of his time.

The doors hummed apart and he stepped out. An oriental style bar stretched ahead of him. Booths separated by fretwork ran along the edges. Aside from these features there were restrooms and a shutter window where Huan took peoples' jackets, but it was the bar that took pride of place stocked with every drink you could want. Double doors at the end of the room led to a maze of saunas, lounges, and a swimming pool. There was also a thick staircase leading up to the fourth floor which included more saunas, another bar and a 24/7 disco with a surround balcony, neon lights and a 70s style dance floor.

Taking a seat in one of the fretwork booths he rubbed his forehead. Images of Jake Bentwood's skull as it was punctured by the bullet replayed in his mind's eye. It didn't disturb him or make him upset in any way. It was just a thing that he couldn't control.

Realizing he was hot, he walked over to the window with its metal shutter pulled up.

"Good afternoon Mr. Cottrell." Huan's English was very good, yet still slightly fragmented reflecting his Chinese origin.

"Hey, Huan," replied Dean, taking off his black jacket and handing it over to the smiling Asian man.

A few other people occupied booths. Most were Red Dawn men with women in revealing dresses. It was the usual crowd alright. Dean frowned. He walked back over to where he had been sitting and took a long time deciding what kind of drink he was in the mood for. Unbeknownst to him, upstairs on the forty-first floor the deal between the Taglianos and Ray Bentley was turning sour.

"Let me get this straight," Luga Tagliano said firmly. "You want me to hand control of the family over to you so you can protect it?" The disbelief in his voice was thick.

Ray nodded in affirmation.

"We aren't asking for a merger…" Vito began, but Ray cut in rudely.

"The yakuza are calling in assets they have in Chicago and New York. You're in a lot of shit. What I am saying is that you have to hand the reins over to me now so I can save your asses." Ray was no longer smiling. In fact, he looked to be moving rapidly towards being pissed off.

They hadn't expected this in a million years. Yelton had had an inkling that Ray might ask for money, however what he was proposing was insane. No crime lord in their right mind would agree to it.

"Yeah, hand over the reins and all of our operations. 'You think we're stupid enough to grant you control of the family, you 'got another think comin'." Yelton had downed the rest of his scotch and was glaring at Ray. It was obvious the bastard was taking them for a ride. It wasn't the first time some jumped up asshole had tried it either.

"You'll still be within the family of course, but think of it like this; you'll be working for me. It's like you said, a united crime front working for mutual profit. You need preservation and I can give it to you." Ray said it as if he was making the obscure very clear. He walked closer to his fish tank. "Consider the pilot fish. It swims under the shadow of sharks and larger predators for protection, and then feeds off of the host's scraps to survive. I'm taking you under my wing. It's an opportunity of epic proportions. I am offering you a seat at my table, my future. All that I ask is that you sit."

"The Tagliano Family doesn't feed on scraps you prick. You have no future. You'll be a memory in less than a year and I can see that now I've met you in person," Luga concluded. "Come on, we're leaving." He started to get up.

"Mr. Tagliano, if you don't grant me control of your organization, then I'm gonna take it by force. You think old man Taiki can fuck your shit up, wait till you see what I can do."

There was a deathly silence. Ray Bentley had both of his hands on the mahogany table opposite the three men. Vito looked slightly worried, but his father and Yelton were just staring maliciously.

"Oh, you think so, huh?" Yelton pointed an accusing finger. Ray smiled and slowly nodded in confirmation. Behind him, Valentino was frowning. He now stood upright beside the desk.

Jesus, what was Ray doing? He was literally asking to get blown away the stupid fuck. Valentino didn't normally carry a gun with him so if things got really nasty he wouldn't get out alive. This wasn't what the Taglianos had been expecting. He could tell. Old school Cosa Nostra didn't do this. They just didn't. There was a vague code of respect that everyone followed, but Ray wasn't old school. He was new wave and outright dangerous.

"I don't want anyone to get hurt. Compliance is a powerful thing," Ray said simply.

"Compliance is surrender. 'You think because you have some guns and a fancy building, that makes you a real business? Not even close. You're the cardboard cutout of some wannabe's imagination. You're not a family. You're dirt. A dolled up street gang and at this moment, you don't know who you're fucking with," Luga spat. Suddenly Ray's eyebrows furrowed and he stood up straight.

"No, you don't know who you're fucking with!" he retorted, his voice full of menace and threat.

"The hell I don't!" And with that, without any kind of warning, Luga Tagliano reached into his pinstripe suit jacket and pulled out a Steyr TMP.

Things seemed to slow down from Valentino's point of view. The patterns of the water in the fish tank danced across the surface of the table in spectacular fashion, just as Luga Tagliano was about to pump Ray Bentley full of lead. Suddenly there was a loud bang, however it didn't issue from Luga's gun.

Gordon, Ray's aged bodyguard had a Ruger P-85 Mark II pistol in his hand and the single bullet that had made a bloody spot on Luga's suit was followed by another.

21

He jolted, and the small submachine gun fell from his hand and hit the table as he lolled forward with two red patches on his chest and a pained expression on his face. The other two Italians were on their feet in seconds. Yelton couldn't believe it. He had been getting a strange hint of a confrontation before they had even entered the room and with what had gone down he had half-expected the hotheaded Luga to pull a gun, but for him to get shot... Jesus.

He reached into his jacket for the pistol sheathed within. Ray was still standing in the same position, unmoving, confident, and brooding.

Before Yelton could withdraw his gun in response a hand reached around his neck. The man who had been standing in the corner had appeared behind him as soon as Luga had pulled out the weapon. Something glinted below his field of vision and there was a surge of immense pain as the hand snapped back. The blade of a knife cut cleanly through his carotid artery and then severed his windpipe before leaving his skin. Blood surged out violently and Yelton was forced to abandon his grope for the gun in his jacket and reach up for his sliced throat. His hands were covered instantly with the sticky mess and he fell onto the table before pulling back and landing in a heap on the floor, leaving a streak of bloody handprints over the mahogany surface.

Vito Tagliano had been carrying a weapon, but he was too panicked to think of pulling it out. He made a mad dash for the double doors that remained open. His dad was dead. His dad had just got blown away! He didn't have a spare second to take the blow in any kind of emotional context, nor think of anything beyond escape.

No guards stood in the hallway. He had a clean exit. The image of those bloody spots appearing on his father's suit flickered in and out of his head like an old movie reel. They would pay for that. They would all pay. He would tell his uncle and they would pay.

Shades, still holding the blood streaked knife, turned methodically and reached his free hand back to pull out one of the two Desert Eagles that were tucked into his pants. As he withdrew it he threw the knife with deadly accuracy and force. It span with an almost unreal quality through the air, nothing but a blur and then when the barrel of the gun was brought around, he fired a single bullet that went chasing after the knife. Both projectiles impacted points on Vito's spine simultaneously and he stopped and embraced the intrusions before flying forward and hitting the carpeted floor with a thud.

The assailant looked down at his smoking weapon. So beautiful.

He turned to face Ray and noticed that Gordon still had his gun drawn.

Their employer was smiling gently and looking at the body of Luga Tagliano sprawled on the table. Observing his cold, dead hand that was home to a wedding ring. Nobody knew whether he had planned the meeting to end this way all along. Nobody ever would.

"Great job, Shades. You got blood all over my table," Ray said flippantly.

"Sorry, boss," Shades replied. Those words unapologetically betrayed his Southern origins. The upbringing his single father had given him in Stellaville, Alabama. He took note of the smeared blood on the table and also the small pool that was emerging from beneath Luga Tagliano's corpse.

Ray turned to Gordon who was putting his gun back into his jacket.

"Get someone to clean this shit up," he ordered.

The old man nodded and walked briskly out of the room.

Valentino had never liked gunfights. They got his heart pumping too fast for him to keep tabs on. He slowed his breathing finally, realizing it was over.

"Are you serious, Ray? Are we going to take their business?" He seemed nervous. Ray turned to him, sipping the last of his scotch with a satisfied gleam in his eye.

"'No use taking a business that's at war Val. You should know that. We'll deal with the yakuza first. By the end of the year I want to own this fucking city. Then everyone will know who they're fucking with."

CHAPTER FOUR
A MESSAGE FROM THOMAS

He had stayed for much longer than he had anticipated and bought a few drinks, but not enough to screw him up. After doing some work on the eighth floor, he had returned to the bar and waited for a while in the hope that someone he knew might drop by and provide company. They didn't, and eventually Dean had returned to his car and driven off.

The BMW came to a steady halt at the traffic lights and he checked his watch. It was coming up to 10:00. Yuki would probably be asleep. Great.

The lights changed to green and he took the next left as his cell phone began to ring. Wrestling it from the confines of his pocket, he flipped it open.

"Hello?" he said, keeping one hand on the wheel.

"Hey, Dean. It's Williams. 'Just got word about Bentwood. Great job."

"Yeah, well, you know me. I aim to please."

"No, you aim to put a bullet in their skulls," chuckled Williams. Dean couldn't help but let himself smile.

Williams was his best friend. Someone within the organization he could always trust. They had met during a collaborative mission to rid Los Angeles of the Guccini Family, and since then, they had been close. Williams' first name was Harry, but everyone just called him

Williams. It had always been that way. The reason Dean liked Williams was that he was the sort of person who never tried to stand in the way of what you wanted to do. He didn't try to understand your actions, he just accepted them.

"You did good Dean. If Thomas doesn't give you some bigger stings now I might have to shoot him myself," the man on the other end of the line said carelessly. If anyone else had heard him say that he would probably be dead before he hit the floor. Another thing Dean liked about him. He had guts.

"Don't worry. He should. Last time we spoke, he seemed at least a little more lax than Ray. 'Always a good sign. Then again, Ray's not exactly the most level person out there." Dean was forced to halt again at another red light.

"You don't like Ray?"

"Nah. The guy's a total nutcase. You could run this shit better than him."

"Well, thanks for the compliment... I think. Anyway, I 'got some files I need to get organized. See you sometime tomorrow?"

"You 'got it, buddy." Dean closed the phone with a quiet slap and then continued his journey along a well-lit road at the end of which, he turned into a side street and parked in a small lot.

When he opened the door to his apartment, Dean noticed that the red digital clock on the wall read 10:14. Yuki had yet again forgotten to chain the door when it got late. Her safety was everything to him even if it meant waking her up at night to get in.

Dean flicked on the lights and the room lit up instantly. The door to the bedroom was closed, indicating that he had been right about Yuki not waiting up for him.

Dean Cottrell's apartment was spacious with laminate flooring. It was open plan with the only doors inside being the one to the bathroom and the one to the bedroom. The kitchen was cordoned off by a marble worktop on the left.

With another flick of his finger, Dean turned on the lights in the reasonably sized kitchen area. He worked his way around the countertop and reached into the wine rack to withdraw a bottle of Layer Cake Malbec.

Walking with heavy steps past the couch, he took a seat in one of the leather armchairs. His orange juice from this morning was still on the glass coffee table. Yuki had not moved it, which was unusual as she was a meticulous housekeeper. From under the chair he pulled out his laptop and set it up.

Yuki didn't know what he really did. As far as she was concerned he had a mundane office job at the Holden Tower and it didn't go far beyond that, but even though this was the easiest thing to believe it didn't mean she was stupid enough not to have at least a few niggling doubts at the back of her mind. Once she had found his Berretta after he had distinctly said he didn't own a gun and for a few weeks after, she had seemed suspicious of him. It was more than possible that she had a vague idea that something shady might be going on, but hadn't once openly interrogated him about it. She loved him and he loved her. That was all that really mattered. Even so, (though Yuki had her own laptop) Dean had three separate passwords required to access his.

RED DAWN – For obvious reasons.

JENNIFER – His birth mother's first name.

DE OPPRESSO LIBER – The motto of the Special Forces, from which he had discharged himself.

He was now thirty and that all seemed a long way behind him even though it really wasn't. The computer loaded up and with what seemed like coincidental timing, the light cut out. He looked around. It had been playing up for weeks now. It would, at random intervals,

27

cut out and come back on again after an unspecified amount of time. He hadn't yet found time to fix it.

Not tonight. He cracked open the wine and poured himself a stiff glass of red knocking it back like it was beer. His face was now lit only by the blue glow of his computer. A message window popped up indicating he had recently received an email he would need to read.

Dean Cottrell

I have been very pleased with your work. Jake Bentwood won't be a problem anymore thanks to you.

It has come to my attention that your record of problem solving is very impressive and I feel that we may not be using you to your full potential, if you get my drift.

It is my belief that you have earned the right to know what the business is going through, as it may prove useful to you to have background information on what you're doing.

My brother has recently sealed a deal with the Tagliano Family, and we are set to expand, whichever way it's sliced, but first we need to clear out the yakuza who have operations in Little Tokyo and around Los Angeles. Certain hits will need to be carried out, and I have selected you as one of the people qualified to get the job done. I know it's soon after your last assignment, but this is of paramount importance right now, as I am sure you will understand.

The first thing I need you to deal with is a guy called Yoshikuni.

He's a computer hacker living here in Los Angeles and he's working for the yakuza helping them in their endeavor to have some sort of insight into goings on within the police department. This would prove extremely advantageous to our Japanese cousins and so it is therefore necessary to have him removed.

He works in the UBS Electronics building across from the Strickler Corp. place. We don't know much about him. 'Don't even have a photo to show you, but intel' says he works on the twenty-ninth floor facing the Strickler scraper, and the description we have says he has recently dyed his hair blonde and apparently does jack-shit at work, so he shouldn't be too hard to find.

Just locate a secluded room at a reasonable distance and then send him a present from the Red Dawn. No witnesses. If the yakuza get so much as a clue as to who killed their precious computer nerd, then you'll bring hell down on a LOT of people. Good luck.

And there'll be a nice bonus for this one. You've earned it.

Thomas Bentley

Dean leaned back and read the email over and over again. Thomas had a habit of writing more eloquently than he spoke in real life. In fact, even though he wasn't as highly strung as his older brother, he was downright unpleasant to converse with. Something about him made Dean's skin crawl. Fortunately, most of their contact was electronic. Maybe Thomas would be more personable if he was a computer... No, too weird.

Sighing, Dean took a moment to consider. On the downside, he would have a lot to get ready tomorrow. On the upside, there was the fact that he was finally getting some recognition *and* a bonus. He would just have to see how it went.

Closing down the laptop and throwing back the last of the wine he replaced everything making sure the apartment was almost exactly how it had been when he had walked through the door. He made his way through to the bedroom, took his clothes off and crawled into bed next to Yuki, who was sleeping soundly. It wasn't long before he fell into a deep slumber to the pleasant rhythm of her breathing.

CHAPTER FIVE

THE FOLLOWING DAY

"**F**ried?" asked Yuki after cracking two eggs into a bowl.

"Yeah."

Dean was on the couch, sifting through the local paper. There was an article on how some kid had gotten himself shot in Echo Park near the Casa De Coffee. No picture was shown for obvious reasons. He flicked through to another page about how Governor Dalton wasn't too popular as of late. Another boring issue.

His ears picked up the sound of the sizzling in the pan and after a few moments Dean began to smell the wonderful scent of fried eggs in the morning. *Her* fried eggs in the morning.

Yuki Nakamura was slightly shorter than Dean and also slightly younger at the age of twenty-six. Asian girls had always been something of a lust for him and she had been Dean's diamond in the rough of the women he had been with. They had met not too long ago in a bar somewhere in Los Angeles. That night, Yuki's boyfriend had left her there and Dean had offered her a ride. She had looked so beautiful. She still did. Her luscious, black hair tied back in a neat bun. Her eyelashes always long and seductive. Her figure that of a small hourglass, but an hourglass nonetheless. She had an olive complexion, reasonably sized breasts and firm buttocks to go with it.

Dean couldn't help but admire her as she came over and placed his eggs on a small, foldable table in front of him before she took a seat herself.

"I have no work today. The manager says that all the people in administration got the flu so he's declaring a day off." (Yuki worked for a small office firm called Neeson Affiliates.) She didn't seem too happy about missing a day. That was another thing Dean loved about her. She was a go-getter. She knew the manager wouldn't deduct the day from her paycheck, but she had a desire to work.

"Lucky you. The office wants me to fire some lazy guy today." (This was true)

"Oh, no." Yuki looked at him with her sweet features.

"I know. I hate to do it, but I suppose it's like they say, with great responsibility comes great shit you don't like, but you have to do."

"How is work going at the moment?" she asked, her big eyes ready to suck him in. He licked some stray yellow from the corner of his mouth.

"It's going fine. Yeah, just fine. My supervisor promised me a bonus sometime soon, so that's good. Things are going... great, you know? Just great."

"I'm glad to hear it."

Dean then felt her tender hand on his thigh and she had her famous 'intense' look on.

"It's all for you, baby. I'd give everything I own. You do know that, right?" he said.

She nodded, yet there was a slight sadness in her eyes.

"I would never ask it. I love you."

There was a long pause during which Dean felt a strong need to fuck work and stay home, but he repressed it. Thoughts like that were foolish. Thomas Bentley was putting a lot of coin in his pocket and he had to be glad of every dime.

Smiling, he wolfed down a forkful of fried egg white.

Yoshikuni's time grew short. Little did he know that soon LAPD would be zipping him into a body bag. What did he care? What did anyone care? The kid was scum. He hated to say it, but it was true. Dean had no major problems with taking out an innocent man when necessary, however when it came to gangsters, hackers, and potheads, it was like throwing back a glass of wine. It was nothing.

Judging by how the movies portray things one would envision Dean having to sneak around corners, break a suspicious office worker's neck and then abseil down the side of the building to get into the room he needed to be in. Unfortunately for Yoshikuni, businesses never made it that difficult.

Dean didn't invest time finding out what Los Angeles based companies did. Strickler Corp. seemed to be some kind of financial holdings firm. The suit and metal case probably helped him to blend in and look like just another mindless keyboard drone, as he roamed the halls and elevators. Not once was he stopped and asked to present his identification badge, or told that the area he was exploring was off limits. Not once did he see a security guard or even a surveillance camera.

As Dean navigated the blandly colored hallways of the twenty-ninth floor, he only passed one women carrying a bunch of papers. That had been it. Most of the doors were closed and behind them he could hear either silence, soft clacking, in depth conversation, or the sound of pacing footsteps. It was moments like these that made him glad that he had not taken up a desk job or something boring. He couldn't fathom how people could waste their lives like that.

He was now certain that he was in the right corridor. The eastern wall of the Strickler building. The twelve rooms that ran down his right were the options. Any one of them would provide a decent enough vantage point to eliminate the target. He was already aware that all the windows of the Strickler building were slide-ups, so it would be an easy in-and-out job. No hiccups. At least he hoped there would be no hiccups.

He listened closely at each door. The first held within it the sound of fast typing, as did the second. In the next room two participants were engaged in conversation and Dean couldn't help but listen in.

"Honest to God, the fucker had me up against the wall and I'm thinking 'That's it. You blew it. He's gonna fire your ass right now. Then he just walks off and doesn't say another word."

"'Serious?"

"Yeah, I mean, I should consider myself lucky, right? Innocent, old Bill got canned for just looking at him in the wrong way. Now he says he's gonna burn the place down. "

"Innocent? Really? I heard he was sleeping with the guy's wife."

"No. If that was true half the fucking building would have had to pack up their shit and go home." Both of the men laughed raucously.

Morons. Boring simpletons trapped in their own affairs. Dean smiled a little before checking the next room.

Laconism emanated from behind the door. He waited for a few seconds to be sure, straining his ears to hear even the slightest squeak of a wheeled office chair, but the room was silent. Slowly and methodically he opened the door and peeked in.

A single window was framed in the wall opposite him. A pretty bland office setup. The single thing worth any attention was a picture of what Dean could only assume was the Los Angeles skyline at night hung on the wall that it shared with the timber veneer door. As his ears had informed him the room was devoid of life.

He crept in shutting the door quietly behind him. He then walked over to the window. Directly opposite, if not slightly lower, was the twenty-ninth floor of the UBS Electronics building where his target resided. The structure's white exterior was a harsh contrast to the battleship gray of Strickler Corp.'s tower.

Dean casually slid the window up and it moved without a grated, metal complaint. He then spent a minute observing and double checking he had the correct floor. He did.

Just as he had done when he had silenced Jake Bentwood near the Casa De Coffee in Echo Park, he was wearing his suit and leather gloves. He had no criminal record, but even so, he never left a trace. It was all well and good when you were ridding the streets of drug peddlers like Bentwood. Nobody cared, including the victim's relatives and least of all the police, but when it came to office workers and the general public you had to drop 'risk' from your vocabulary.

Dean pulled one of the chairs in the room over to the door and propped it under the handle just in case.

'Risk' was not an option.

CHAPTER SIX
MISS AND HIT

The clasps on the steel case were snapped open and its top was flipped up. Inside was a specially vacuformed interior that held the barrel and the chamber as one component and the stock, trigger and magazine well as another. It also had a place for the suppressor, a bipod, the yellow-tinted scope, plus two magazines. It didn't take a lot of effort snapping the pieces together and tightening a few integral screws here and there. Dean's custom rifle was an optimal weapon for such a mission and had been his constant companion for some time now. He felt a fondness towards it as strange as that was.

There was a loud click as he hammered the magazine into its appropriate place before ducking slightly and with the barrel just over the sill, looked down the scope.

Kyoichi Yoshikuni was rather short and never bothered to dress formally. How in the hell he still had a job with UBS Electronics was anyone's guess. On this particular Tuesday he was wearing a dark green shirt with a faded image on the front, along with some cheap pants. That day he hadn't done much but swivel around in his chair and play computer games. He had also sent an email virus to one of the girls on his floor who he detested, but he didn't like to think about that out loud.

Walking down the carpeted hall and taking in large bites of a sandwich, he was thinking about how he could get an advanced payment from Motobuchi for the job he was running. The yakuza's errand boy wasn't paying him nearly enough. He was world class and they knew it. As he was about to turn the corner into a hallway on the west side of the building, ending at his office, a door opened quickly behind him, and he turned in response. It only then occurred to him how many Japanese co-workers he had.

"Hey, Kyoichi. Did you get my email?"

Kazu was the exact opposite to Yoshikuni. He was hard working, positive and dull as shit. The lesser employee considered the question momentarily then remembered that he had junked that email an hour ago.

"Umm… uh, no. I don't think I got that one," he said convincingly.

"'You sure?"

"Mmm. Definitely." He was now walking slowly backwards down the corridor as his colleague regarded him with suspicious eyes.

The next hallway ran left. It was lined on the right by a continuous row of windows looking out onto the ugly Strickler Corp. building.
He really didn't like to look at the place for too long. 'Reminded him of how he could be earning the big bucks dealing with other people's money instead of their computer software.

Just then, dryness in his mouth became noticeable and he stopped at a water cooler. Ripping out a conical cup, he watched the bubbles surface as he filled the paper container. He had no way of knowing that he had crosshairs trained on him the whole time.

Dean was prepared to take the shot. The rifle quivered uneasily in his hands as if warning him of something, but he took no notice. The window behind his target was slid wide open making it a perfect hit.

The man's slightly crouched posture meant that the bullet would rip the top of his spinal cord to shreds before traveling through.

"I 'got you now, you piece of shit," Dean murmured.

The sniper rifle made its usual sound as the bullet exited from the end of the suppressor, however just at the wrong moment the target moved from where he was.

The bullet missed him by an inch, tore effortlessly through the plastic of the bottle atop the cooler and out the other side, creating a tiny spray of dust as it embedded itself in the wall.

All of this went unnoticed by Yoshikuni who, taking gulps of water walked on to his office not knowing that an inch had separated him from death.

"Shit!" hissed Dean. He had missed! He had actually missed! The mark had moved and the bullet had gone wide. Water was now trickling from both of the punctures in the cooler tank like a weak hose. The shooter concentrated again, noticing his quarry was now in his office sitting down and doing something on a computer. Dean lined up another shot, his mind elsewhere, preoccupied with how he had missed his mark. He wouldn't do that again.

Yoshikuni checked his email while perfecting his 'bored' face. He had definitely deleted that message. Screw it. 'Probably just an invitation to one of Kazu's team building conferences. He gulped down the last of his water unaware that it would be the final thing to ever enter his body that wasn't cold and metallic. A new email announced itself, and he stared at it with contempt. As he had suspected.

'Team Building Conference!'

Asshole! It wasn't that Yoshikuni was jealous of Kazu. The guy was just one of those people he couldn't stand. He sighed. If it wasn't for the Goto-gumi, people like that would be his only company and what would he do then?

The idle worker was not allowed to answer that question even in his mind.

The bullet from a sniper rifle made a neat hole in his office window, the penetration mark branching outwards in thin lines. It then went all the way through his head as if it was being shot through warm butter. He felt very little pain. In fact, the pain that he did feel didn't even register properly as the brain was violated. The mess was nowhere near as bad as that which had emerged after the Jake Bentwood assassination, but Yoshikuni's computer screen was splattered with an amount of thick blood that wasn't underwhelming. He slumped forward onto his desk noisily, with two bloody holes on either side of his head. Funnily enough, it almost seemed as if he had fallen asleep on his desk. His laziness at work summed up in one ironic gunshot. Dean was thankful he was able to see such ironies. It brightened his day sometimes. Relaxation washed over him.

"He died as he lived. Slacking."

With a short-lived smile on his face, he took apart the rifle quickly, disassembling each part without fumbling, and then packed it away in his case. Taking one last glance out of the window and seeing that nobody had walked in on the body yet, he returned the chair he had used against the door to its original place and left quietly, wondering when somebody would make the discovery. That was another reason for not working in a tightly packed office block. Everything was done by email, so you could theoretically just die and then not be found until the night watchman snuck in to steal stationary.

While Yoshikuni had paid for his chosen side-career, Dean was going to get paid for what he was doing. What you put in was what you got out. Still though, he sometimes had to consciously try and fight his moral compass which was like a fly that kept bothering him. Luckily, he could forget about it if he tried. People lived and died in L.A. every day. The latest victim was no different.

This secret, stone-cold thought showed on Dean's features as he walked into the atrium of the building and to all who regarded him with faces hollowed by monotony he was just another of the city's businessmen. He was just like them.

CHAPTER SEVEN
TALKING TO WILLIAMS

It had just turned half four when Dean came into the bar on the third floor of the Holden Tower. The barman, Bert, had a sturdy look about him. The bastard also charged a lot more than anyone would be happily willing to pay. Dean didn't usually drink until later in the evening so just ordered a cola. He was glad to be away from the scene of his crime. It felt... cleansing.

Turning he noticed his friend Williams drowning in a beer. He smiled to himself. Some friends in life, you saw, you smiled and you walked over. Williams was one of these characters.

"Hey Williams, you look like shit," he said, swinging himself into the seat opposite his colleague. He wasn't joking. Williams was slightly shorter than Dean with richly dark, brown hair that's style often reminded him of Adolf Hitler. One side seemed to just have more strands that would sometimes fall over his face without warning. Today however, both sides of his coiffure looked disheveled and unruly. He had blue eyes and a slightly crooked set of teeth that he had inherited. To Dean, he always seemed to look slightly ill, like his complexion had been messed up during his teenage years.

None of this affected what he thought of Williams. The guy was one of the best people he had ever had the pleasure of meeting. He was in a black shirt and pants, but his jacket and tie were nowhere around.

"Well, thanks for that assessment Versace." Williams' Italian/Brooklyn roots showed through when he spoke, and his reply was typical. Always wisecracking no matter who he was talking to.

"Where have you been?" he asked.

"Thomas emailed me last night. 'Had to take out some guy working for the yakuza."

"Really? Did it go okay?"

Dean was debating whether to tell Williams about the miss that had occurred before he hit his mark.

"Yeah. Just like every other one."

"I 'got something to get done later today. Some of the yakuza are planning to hit a warehouse in Culver City. 'Gotta play shooter for some rocket jockeys." Rubbing his eye Williams made a disgusted expression as if he had just eaten something that didn't agree with him and then shrugged and put away some more of the beer.

"So, Red Dawn are moving in on the yakuza." Dean seemed to be deep in thought and for a moment, Williams was debating whether or not to let Dean in on the fact that he didn't feel up to making it back to his apartment in Santa Monica, let alone picking off Japanese mobsters from a distance. In the end, he thought that was something best kept to himself.

"'Seems so, but when you think about it after the Taglianos got whacked, it's the next logical step."

Dean stopped drinking his cola and paused, his eyes narrowing. He set the glass down.

"The Taglianos got whacked?" he asked uncertainty in his question.

"Yeah. You didn't know? Thomas didn't mention it in the email at all?" Williams was treating the information as if it were something that had been on every news channel for days.

"He said that Ray had sealed a deal with them."

42

"Yeah, well… with Ray, getting killed is probably the best kind of deal you can hope for," Williams chuckled sipping more of his beer. "I do feel sorry for the other brother though."

"What?" Dean was still slightly stunned by the fact that the Tagliano Family had suffered losses from their command circle. He had taken out many of their men in the past. 'Had once had a sit down with Luga Tagliano at a fixed drug deal. A good man really.

"Luga, his son and some family friend. Only the last brother left in charge now. They found the bodies early this morning. All of 'em wrapped in plastic and floating under a pier at Paradise Cove. Now the family's weakened, 'looks like Ray's gonna pull the yakuza off their back so he can move in and swallow them whole. Plus, it seems like he's looking for alliances with a new triad base of operations in New York. 'Got a meeting with some big shot on the 19th. Helix Hotel. 'Looks like Ray's throwing his money around." Williams frowned into his drink and even Dean was slightly shifted by what he had said. There was no use dwelling on it. The Taglianos were a rival gang. They had to be eliminated. Ray was only doing what was best for his precious organization.

"But, hey, it's all good, well, for us it is anyway." The man opposite Dean looked slightly less like a heroin addict going cold turkey now.

"What's the latest on our Japanese friends then?" asked Dean.

"Well, they aren't going without a fight, I'll tell you that. Goto-gumi have their teeth in the Taglianos now and they aren't going to let go any easier than we would. Going on info that's filtered down from the top, they're calling in reinforcements from their bases in Chicago, New York, Boston and someone told me there's increased activity in San Francisco. They're on alert now and you killing one of their boys here in Los Angeles won't have helped. I am deadly serious Dean. These guys are bad news and have proved the nail in the coffin for a lot of other organizations. 'You wanna hear something else? A contact in Poland also told me that some of the

43

larger skinhead groups over there are helping get weapons through Europe and shipped right into the hands of those bastards."

"I'm sure we don't have to worry about that little hacker I killed today. He wasn't even a member. Regardless... This shit ain't gonna be easy." The round face of Yoshikuni floated in and out of Dean's thoughts. Had he been found yet? Did the yakuza know?

Not that he was worried. The yakuza didn't scare him and like he had said, it probably wouldn't even register with them.

Seven minutes must have passed with them just sitting and trying not to think about what would happen in the days to come and then Williams saw fit to break the silence.

"I was up at the disco an hour ago." He smiled and put on his most conversational tone.

"Oh, yeah?"

"Yeah. 'You know that chick from Ray's personal staff. The blonde one with the legs that go all the way up?"

Dean strained his memory. So many blonde girls he knew had legs that went all the way up.

"Oh... I think I know. Christa or Christina or something like that?" He had a vague idea of who Williams might be talking about.

"Well, I got talking to her for a minute or two." Williams was nodding confidently like a real player and then his expression dropped and he leaned forward.

"Be honest... 'you think I have a shot?" he asked. Dean considered this for a moment.

"No. I don't," he replied simply. Williams didn't get annoyed or upset. He shrugged in acceptance and drank the last of his beer.

Just at that moment a man with a tall, blocky build sauntered up to their table. He wasn't wearing the black suit and red tie. Instead, he was wearing some cheap pants and a plain, black T-shirt covered by a creased leather jacket that looked as if it had been worn by many people of different sizes over the course of a few years. He had a pair of shades over his eyes and the slightest trace of a goatee teasing the area around his mouth. His hair was short and spiked, dark blonde much like Dean's.

"Kruge. What's happening, my man? 'You learn to count yet?'" asked Williams, doing a bad imitation of streetwise. Kruge looked at him blankly for what seemed like forever before replying with a short laugh.

"Good joke." He then glanced at Dean.

"Hey, Dean. I just got asked to give you this message. Thomas Bentley wants to see you at the zoo tonight."

The man's voice was notched with what sounded like the symptoms of a bad throat, but it was always that way. He just couldn't help speaking through a permanent growl.

"What time?" Dean asked.

"Somewhere around half nine."

"I'll be there." Dean really wished he wouldn't. The zoo, on the outskirts of Los Angeles was the last place he wanted to be tonight. Surrounded by Thomas Bentley's goon squad while the jerk patted him on the back and congratulated him on bringing Yoshikuni's existence to an end. He really didn't want to go, but like most things in life it was something he had to do.

Kruge nodded and then floated away towards the bar. He was somebody Dean had only met a couple of times and he seemed like a total moron who overrated his own potential.

"Well, well, well. 'Looks like somebody has a date."

"'Looks like it. God, anywhere but there."

"Hey, look at this as an achievement. Thomas wants you in front of him so he can tell you just how good you are."

"Believe me. I don't need a confidence boost."

Dean could see the argument, but he still didn't want to go. It was going to be dark, cold and uninviting. He could think of many other places he would prefer to be. In bed with his lover was one of them.

Noticing his disconcertion, Williams gave him a thump on the arm to get his attention.

"Stop your moping. Nobody likes going out there. Thomas's boys are fuckheads at the best of times."

"Yeah, well, 'got a few fuckheads here as well."

"What? Kruge? Fuck him. The guy still uses his thumb and index to check which way's left. He'll be gone soon enough."

45

"How are you so sure I wasn't talking about you," Dean quipped, a grin on his face.

"Because I'm your fucking hero," he said matter-of-factly. "Harry Williams, God's gift to sharpshooters."

Dean laughed and looked up at one of the globe lights above. Joking aside, he really didn't want to go to the zoo tonight.

CHAPTER EIGHT

AT THE ZOO WITH A JOB IN MIND

Yuki had been glad that Dean had returned from work after running a few errands, despite saying he would have to leave again later. They had watched some T.V. and eaten a slightly early dinner and he was forced to treasure the seemingly fleeting minutes he spent with her in the knowledge that soon he would be keeping a different kind of company. One that would no doubt put him into a state of disquietude for the night to come.

As Dean pulled up alongside the stone wall on the western side of the zoo, he promised himself he would make the time up to Yuki. She would be asleep when he got back so it was important to him that he was with her tomorrow. Why she put up with him, he didn't know.

He smiled, stepped out and shut the car door. After a moment of consideration, he also locked it, mainly because he didn't trust the man at the side gate. He was one of the many huge enforcers that Dean encountered in his daily routine of delivering packages, sending messages and of course killing people. The man had a gray beanie over a very large, round head that was kept snug between two mountainous shoulders. He was much taller and wider than Dean, and could probably snap him in two without a second thought. Dean guessed that *snapping people in two* was his special talent as he wasn't armed. Through small, narrowed eyes he glared at the new arrival making him stop before continuing on through a metal gate in the wall.

Located in close proximity to the rough terrain of the San Bernardino Mountains the zoo had been erected five years ago by some wildlife institution in order to capitalize on the declining interest in the animal sanctuary near Big Bear Lake. This place was smaller than the zoo in Griffith Park, but perhaps more fantastic. It was like whoever had originally built it had poured all their time and money into it making waterfalls and Aztec-style steps. The place was impressive to say the least

The gate creaked closed with a silence-shattering song. Inside, darkness had settled and hung over the enclosures. Many of the animals were inside small shelters or holes, having turned in for the night. Unfortunately, the real animals were wide awake.

As Dean trekked over the cobbled ground past a cage, a man sitting on a wall nearby cocked a Kalashnikov and puffed on a cigarette all the while watching him intently. None of the men at the zoo, save Thomas Bentley, were members of the Red Dawn. They were hired thugs used to obtain weapons, pack them, ship them where they needed to be, and guard the place. Dean had been to the zoo many times before and knew exactly where Thomas would be in the menagerie of slimy individuals. Heading down a small flight of stone steps he came to the pathway that was flanked on the right by shrubbery and on the left by the side of a huge greenhouse.

A Mexican man, Cheo, who Dean knew as the head of the zoo operation's security, stepped out suddenly from a strip curtain door with such good timing it was enough to make anyone recoil. He always wore the same creamy colored shirt with patterned border work and brown pants. After all, they complemented his greasy, dark hair and slick mustache so well.

"You. Come," he said, nodding behind him. Dean followed him through the strip curtains.

A pathway wound through the wild, humanly maintained jungle that Dean traversed, droplets of moisture in the air making his face damp. They passed through another set of strip curtains and walked by a pair of metal doors that Dean knew led down to where Thomas kept the shipments of weapons. The hall finally opened out onto a large area scattered with crates. On his first visit, Dean had thought them to be full of guns, but it was all animal food and other odds and ends. All legitimate, so it looked out of place amongst the grimy-looking figures propped up against the walls wielding various firearms and cheap clothing. A set of metal stairs led up to an office. Thomas stood at the top of them looking down as his underling led the man he wanted to see to the bottom of the steps.

"Dean. Glad you could make it," he said happily. On this occasion, the man who gave the orders was radiating positivity. Regardless, he was still a creep.

"What's this about, Thomas?" asked Dean, putting his hands in his pockets and not bothering to wipe the moisture of the greenhouse's humid climate from his face.

"Come up. Let's talk." Thomas smiled down at him and then turned back through a wooden door into his place of work.

Suppressing a sigh, Dean mounted the steps and dragged himself up into what Thomas treated as his office. It was a square space that held the ambience of a cigar club, furnished with his desk and some paintings of elephants. Thin, wooden slat blinds covering the overlooking window allowed him to keep a discreet eye on the voluminous space inside the zoo's central building. The man had a penchant for wanting to know what was going on 24/7. With casual grace, he sat down in a comfy looking chair behind the desk leaving a cheap wooden one for Dean to take.

49

Thomas Bentley looked quite different from his brother. His hair wasn't greasy or styled in any way. It was still jet black, but slightly longer around the sides and at the fringe. He also had a more well-rounded face that lacked Ray's angular quality and his eyebrows seemed to be more prominent. Dean had always thought Thomas had a shorter, but slightly more thickset physique than Ray, however now that he took the man in again, he realized there was little difference between the brothers.

With a sharp glance from his ice blue eyes Thomas quickly did something on his computer before he started to speak. Tonight, he wore the typical attire for Red Dawn members under a black jacket that reminded Dean of one a security guard or a ranger might wear.

"Great job with Yoshikuni." Thomas nodded to himself. "That fucker won't be worming his way into any criminal records for quite some time, huh?"

"The thing was easy enough. Why am I here?"

"'Thought it would be better if we talked face-to-face. You're improving hit by hit and emails can only take you so far. I've got another job for you."

Dean's heart sank. He knew what was coming next. Though he wanted this (the chance to prove himself a little bit more), it would come at the cost of doing what he really wanted to do.

"I need you tomorrow. Nine P.M." Thomas had his head low and was staring up at Dean which made him look rather sinister. "This isn't some filler task either. No I.T obsessed assholes, no drug dealers. Big league stuff."

Dean had taken out more important individuals than those mentioned, but he kept his mouth shut as Thomas reached into his desk and withdrew some photographs from a drawer.

"This guy right here." Thomas threw down a Polaroid of a nondescript Japanese man in his late thirties, walking across a road.

50

"This is Ryosuke Motobuchi. He's a big hitter with the Goto-gumi in Little Tokyo. Intel' says he has a staked poker game tomorrow with some low-level criminals."

Dean stared at the photograph for a while, before Thomas dumped down four more.

"These are the other people attending his little shindig. None of them are important to us. Linderman Zwinkoni. He's just a common street peddler dealing in firearms and stolen goods." The photo showed a large, bald man with a blue bandana. "Arthur Faubus, enigmatic host of a pirate radio station." An elderly gentleman with a mane of white hair and a snowy goatee. "William Hutch, an agent of the Gambino Family." A middle-aged man with a gray hat and tie. "And Milton Corks, a member of the Caligula Gang." A bulky, black man with a shaven head and a stern face.

"What do you want me to do?" Dean scratched his neck and tried to avoid eye contact with Thomas. Having the man stare at you was a little like being stabbed in the face. It wasn't pleasant.

"They're playing in a room above the Misty Drink night club Downtown. I'm sure you know it. The parking garage will give you a good view. Third floor. Make sure Ryosuke bites it and I'll increase your flat salary by twenty-five percent."

"What about the others?"

Thomas considered this for a moment then flashed a genuinely amused, gleaming white grin. For a moment his eyes seemed slightly crazy and unreal. He was obviously a person who got off on having control over life and death, to be able to snuff someone out with a few words. The smile actually managed to disturb Dean and almost made him lean back before he told himself to remain firmly unaffected and rigid on the seat.

"Kill 'em all."

"That's a risk. There are a lot of guys here. Whatever I do, yakuza are going to know someone with a grudge shot their man. I might as well leave the others."

Thomas smiled again and seemed even more amused, his eyebrows raised.

"Don't think, Dean. Kill. That's what I'm paying you for. Let me deal with the mental side. You just keep your finger on the trigger until these guys are all in the ground. Are we clear now?"

There was no hint of anger in Thomas's voice, and that was what pissed Dean off the most. That stupid look of mirth as if the man were watching some animal do a trick. Thomas hadn't considered the operation at all. It was on a whim that he wanted the other men dead. What was more annoying was that he was taking hours that Dean would have rather had than not, and wouldn't even consider his opinion.

"We'd be wiser to make Motobuchi our sole target. Like you said, Gambino Family, Caligula Gang. We could benefit from not taking risks when it comes to them. We have nothing to gain from killing these guys. I think…"

"You don't think!" Thomas yelled in a sudden flash of anger. "You do. You do as you're told. I pay you a lot of money for your work, and it's far from your place to start asking questions."

"But I thought you said I was coming into my own now and deserved more…"

"Money, Dean. More money… and I'm giving it to you. Now, that'll be all."

Dean nodded solemnly and stood up. Thomas seemed to study him with regained beguilement as if considering something important, but at the same time entertaining.

"I really am impressed with your work, you know?" It didn't sound like Thomas was saying it with full conviction. Bastard.

"I give what I can to every assignment. What would I be if I gave anything less?"

"Exactly. What would you be?" Thomas continued to smile. "You have the potential to go far in this world, Dean. Give it a couple of years of pristine hits; you'll be working with Valentino on a day-to-day basis. A few more, and you could be on Ray's personal staff."

Dean didn't reply. That wasn't really what he needed to hear, not to mention the fact he sensed Thomas was talking out of his ass, which seemed to be one of his hobbies, right up there with bad decorating and being a prick. Finding an excuse to look away, Dean scanned one of the elephant portraits on the wall. It wasn't even an original. Cheapskate.

"Just concentrate on getting the job done. That's all that matters."

"Sure thing, Thomas," he said quietly.

"Now, I'm glad we had this little talk." Thomas grinned warmly.

Dean turned and left.

While walking back through the zoo, he couldn't help but visualize himself guarding Ray Bentley as the man brooded in his office. That wasn't what he wanted. For the time being, he had only one thing to focus on. He needed to kill everyone at this upcoming poker game and make no mistakes. It was like Thomas had said. This was big league stuff. When you had more than one isolated target, things had to be contained very quickly. Nevertheless, the more he thought about it, the more he was sure he could handle it.

CHAPTER NINE
UNCONDITIONAL LOVE

The sounds of Yuki cooking filtered in from the kitchen to the bedroom where Dean was getting himself ready. After having taken one suit to the dry cleaners he was putting on another. He belted up the black pants and fastened the top buttons of his shirt. This routine was becoming increasingly similar to putting on a heavy suit of armor. Dean was longing to stay home and eat a late dinner with Yuki, but it was not to be. Slipping the tie around his neck he prepped it expertly before slipping into his black suit jacket. He looked at himself in the mirror on the wardrobe and didn't like what he saw. It was as if it was not the person whom he had seen nine years ago. Not even two years ago. He touched his cheek. Maybe it was just aging.

Walking out of the bedroom he saw that Yuki was frying something, but it definitely wasn't eggs. A content look formed on his face. Coming up behind her, he ran his fingers through her hair and with a look of exuberance, she turned to him and he snaked his arms over her shoulders and kissed her passionately. The exact motive for the random act of sensuality was unknown. Maybe he was trying to get the image of himself in the mirror out of his head or maybe he just needed to get a grip on a life that wasn't full of violence and snarling maniacs.

"Are you sure you're okay with me being gone tonight?" he asked.

"Yes. You need to work." This was correct. Thomas hadn't been lying about the extra money for getting rid of Yoshikuni; however there was something that Dean picked up on, deep inside Yuki's words. She had been raised in Japan and had been taught to be dutiful and faithful, but those teachings were at war with her personal feelings. The desire to spend every waking moment with Dean. He knew this. She wouldn't say what she felt. She would just go with the flow, a sailboat being blown about by Dean and his work. Part of him wished that things were different for he also pined for more time with the one he loved. He wished he didn't have to kill five men tonight. Those precious hours of preparation and execution could be spent making up for the workaholic boyfriend he had saddled her with. For a moment he felt something sting in his eye and tried to convince himself it was whatever Yuki was cooking. She drew him into another kiss and he hugged her close.

Shit. He would have to stiffen up before tonight. She let go.

"It's okay. Things are busy at the moment. I understand." Her eyes seemed more beautiful than Dean had ever seen them and he suddenly felt the stinging sensation intensify. He had to try and think about his targets. Now was not the time for feeling sorry for himself. He breathed in deeply through his nose.

"I love you," Yuki said, running a finger over the top of his left ear. "You're committed to your job. I could never ask for anything else."

But she didn't know what the hell Dean did for a living. She had no idea how many people were in the ground because of him, because of the business. She never could. It was too dangerous. That was why nobody Dean knew had his home address, not even Williams. Things were just too unpredictable. He nodded and looked at her with admiration.

"And I couldn't ask you to be more selfless." He touched her cheek and she leaned into it closing her eyes like a cat being fawned over. He kissed her one last time and then headed for the door.

The trunk slammed.

With the briefcase in hand Dean walked around to the front of his car and hopped in slinging the case on top of its much larger, steel counterpart. He shut the door and started up the engine.

The drive to the Misty Drink night club wasn't a long one. All the way, Dean could not stop thinking about Yuki and how patient she was. They had not had sex in a good three weeks due to the sudden rise in jobs that the business had needed him to do. This was good for his career, but bad for his love life. Somehow, the two never went hand in hand. He would have to make damn sure he treated her well the following night. If Thomas came out with another job he would just have to say, "Sorry, but you'll have to get someone else." With the new cash bonuses, maybe he would plan something special for winter. Maybe a vacation. Dean relaxed slightly at the thought and let the car take him around the next bend.

The Misty Drink night club was one of those extremely popular, yet sufficiently seedy places, occupying three floors. The lot beside it was like a huge beast bearing down on the plaza of poor dancing that jumped to Ibiza-style music. People were flooding in, some giving the bouncers a hard time, all watched by Dean. It was at moments like this that he felt out of place. He was sure every killer felt out of place a lot of the time. Here were people having the time of their lives and then here he was driving past, a mobster with a high powered rifle sitting right next to him, on his way to make a killing.

He would just have to remember that amongst the partygoers were a dirty street peddler, a brutish thug, a gangster, a pirate radio mogul and a high-ranking yakuza agent.

Passing the club Dean headed straight for the parking structure. The first level was packed. The second was dotted with two dozen vehicles, all probably owned by attendees of the Misty Drink's after dark rave. The third level was all but deserted. Dean drove around for a while on the side of the building that overlooked the third floor of the club. Many rooms could be seen through the windows of the place, but he eventually found the only one that anyone would play poker in. It was actually a rather small room. A door was opposite the window and in the middle was an oval shaped, oak, gaming table side on to Dean's car that ground to a halt, one big drop away.

A man was sitting at the table already and even though he was not too close, when Dean lowered the passenger window, he recognized the old face of Arthur Faubus from the photograph he had been shown.

The seating arrangement was perfect. Nobody had their back to the window so those on the other side of the table wouldn't be obscured. Three seats were set up on the wide part of the oval with one on each end giving a total of five. Faubus was sat in the fourth seat from the right reading something and drinking a glass of amber colored liquid.

Dean sat in silence for a moment just watching the old man who was wearing a dark windbreaker and navy colored clothes beneath it. His eyes were narrowed and surrounded by wrinkles, his mane of white hair even more snowy now that Dean was viewing him in person.

The assassin opened the leather briefcase and withdrew the Beretta 92, which was of course, silenced. He slipped it into his jacket holster. You could never be too careful in public places. Anyone could sneak up behind you while you were aiming. Putting the briefcase down at his feet, he opened the steel case and took a good, long look at the sniper rifle.

Thoughts of Yuki drifted into his mind at the worst possible moment. Her smile made him melt inside and that wasn't what he wanted at a time like this. He tried to shake her from his head, but found he could not. Why had he gone out tonight? Because Thomas had told him to. Was that a reason? What the hell was she still doing with him anyway? She was at home watching television and he was in a cruddy parking lot looking down at the sleek, black form of a rifle.

He smiled and stroked the weapon lightly. He supposed it just went to show how important they were to each other. He supposed it just went to show that he really was a two sided coin. On one hand he was a lover, full of all the passion and teary-eyed joy that you would get from a husband of twenty years and on the other, a monster who could kill those with wives, children, dreams...

Tonight however, he was putting an end to some less than innocent individuals. All he had to remember was that what he did with this side of the coin could never cross over onto the other side. The vile murderer in his blood could never seep into the man Yuki had made love to so many times. They were two separate people. Worlds apart.

CHAPTER TEN
POKER FACES

The door behind Arthur Faubus swung open on its hinges and three men entered the room. Arthur turned in his seat to address the tall form of Ryosuke Motobuchi who nodded to him. He returned the gesture. Never one to change a style that worked, the yakuza agent had a streamlined, black suit that fitted perfectly. A dark purple tie hung down over it and the man's eyes were covered by purple-tinted sunglasses probably to hide anything they might give away. The players would be betting big tonight, after all.

"Arthur." Bill gave him a pat on the back and occupied the seat next to him as Ryosuke took the one on the end, to Arthur's right. Bill was wearing his usual gray ensemble capped by his trademark Fedora. The third man, large like a grizzly bear, was Milton Corks. His shaved head glistened in the overhead light and Arthur took note of the fact that his muscular arms were visible, sloping unrealistically from his black vest top, an obvious attempt to intimidate his competitors.

"Wassup, Faubs?" he said, smiling and offering a hand over Bill. Arthur shook it and smiled back before Corks took the seat next to Bill, his huge form making it creak. The five men had been having poker nights for a long time and were all reasonably comfortable with one another.

"'You dealin' first Faubs?"asked Corks, brushing something from the top of his boulder-like fist.

"'Probably for the best." Arthur reached over and grabbed the deck from the center of the table, shuffling it expertly. "'Wouldn't want Bill stacking the deck in his favor too soon."

Bill chuckled uneasily and clasped his hands together. He was banking on being able to pay off his mortgage soon and get a new car. Either that or his wife was apparently leaving him.

"All we have to do now is wait for Mr. Zwinkoni," announced Arthur, still shuffling the deck.

"Yeah, where the hell is Zwink?" Corks said in response. It wasn't like him to be late. Almost on cue the barrel chested peddler burst into the room. He was wearing some old denim jeans, a blue vest top and his usual blue bandana.

"Sorry I'm late, guys," he stammered taking the seat opposite Ryosuke, across the table.

"We were getting worried," Arthur joked.

"'Had to empty the tank. 'Been drinkin' all day," Zwink explained apologetically.

The beat of the club music two floors below was muffled, but you could still hear it pretty clearly. 'Maybe not the best place to be playing a game where concentration was everything. Regardless, Arthur could think of worse. He finished shuffling the deck and started the deal just as a man in a red dinner jacket came in with a tray of drinks, (most likely ordered before the men had come up.) A green cocktail was set down in front of Ryosuke, Jack Daniels for Bill and a can of beer for Corks.

"I took the liberty of bringing your usual, Mr. Zwinkoni," said the waiter and Zwink nodded in appreciation as a second beer was put in front of him. Arthur took another sip from his scotch on the rocks as

Corks cracked open his beer and the waiter left them in peace to play.

Dean began piecing the rifle together clipping each component into its corresponding segment.

Kill 'em all. That was what Thomas had said. 'Couldn't be too hard. Just had to be quick about it. Take out one, then the next and so on. Even if they were packing it wouldn't make much difference. With a light weapon it would be nearly impossible to nail him at this range in the night's visibility. His car was just a shadow in the darkness to these men. They wouldn't know what hit them. He could have killed them there and then, but he decided to wait for a while. The suppressor twisted onto the barrel with the sound of a bottle cap being screwed in place. He would see how things went for a couple of minutes; let the men ease into the game. That way the first bullet would come as more of a surprise, plus, he hadn't watched poker in a long time.

The game was giving Bill a good vibe. Faubus had just dealt him the king of diamonds and the three of hearts.

"One hundred, Mr. Big Blind," Ryosuke said, pulling out two fifties from his pile and shoving them into the middle of the table. Each man had his available cash beside an upside-down hand. Zwink pursed his lips and nodded. Both he and Ryosuke had matched Corks' one hundred.

"One eighty." Faubus put in, evidently confident with his hand.

"Here's your one eighty." Money stacked up in the pot and Bill had his eye on it, but was playing it cautious. Anything could turn up on the flop. After a long look at his hand Corks put up the one eighty and so did the other two.

"So we have no folders. Let's see what tomorrow brings." Ryosuke looked expectantly to Arthur who quickly set down the burn card and three face-ups.

The king of clubs, the two of diamonds, and the five of spades. Bill had a double. Enough to make him go for another round.

"Okay. Let's put in two hundred," he said.

"I'm in," Corks chimed immediately after making Bill slightly cautious. He obviously had something he thought would get him somewhere.

"Me too."

"Fold."

"Well, you can count me in," Faubus said, hoping his enthusiasm would drive the others away.

"What 'you got up in there, Faubs?" asked Corks.

"Ah! A wise, old man never reveals his secrets."

"Yeah, but you're not a wise, old man Arthur. You're an asshole," Zwink joked. Everyone laughed including Faubus. A calm atmosphere was settling in.

Another burn card was put down and then the two of clubs followed. Bill looked for a change of expression on any of the gamblers, but didn't pick up on anything. He didn't have enough. A double and that was it. Something urged him to continue however and he had never been one to ignore his instincts.

"Two fifty."

"KK I'm with ya."

"Fold."

"Two fifty it is."

"Two thousand four hundred and fifty. That's a lot of cash." Bill gave a short whistle. Faubus burned another card then showed everyone the river card. The king of spades. Three of a kind. The question was, did Arthur or Corks have anything better.

Zwink scratched the back of his neck. He had his money on Faubus. The old man could really pull out the numbers when he needed to. They were without doubt an unlikely gang, but the combination of character made for a good poker night between thieves. In the end they were all on sort of the same team. Bill adjusted the position of his gray fedora. Fuck it. Bring it on.

"Five." He slid five hundred dollars into the pot.

"I raise you to six." Corks put on his *'don't fuck with this'* face, but after the ninety-third time, it wasn't so scary.

"Six." Faubus put in, and Bill decided that it was worth chasing. Corks and Faubus had bluffed before.

"Let's see your cards gentlemen." Ryosuke said, eager to get onto the next round and win his cash back. Faubus revealed nothing but a pair. In his hand a spare ten of diamonds and the five of spades. Not much to go on. Bill smiled and put down his two cards.

"Three bastards." He looked at Corks whose expression had gone very sour. The larger man threw down his cards.

"Shit," he murmured, revealing them to be the five of diamonds and the two of hearts. He had also had three of a kind, but unfortunately they hadn't been high enough. Bill chortled at his win and reached his arms out, raking the pot towards himself.

"Come to papa."

CHAPTER ELEVEN
DON'T SHOOT THE DEALER

Three more rounds had passed and Bill Hutch had somehow come out on top each time. Dean had never fully appreciated just how entertaining a good game of Texas hold 'em could be. He had been watching it all very carefully through his sniper scope. In fact, he had become so absorbed in the game that he had forgotten all about the fact that he had to put the five men away. The killer shuffled in the car slightly, laid out across the seat, uncomfortable on his front with the rifle pointing out of the open passenger window. The four losers were not happy about relinquishing so much money. He had watched their expressions carefully. The big, black guy was especially pissed. Four rounds was a miracle for a game where it wasn't a pro against a group of five year olds. The game had much to do with luck and Bill had been given the whole of Ireland. There was of course, a different way of explaining it. Dean knew more than one way to cheat at poker and when it came to sleazy mob types, it was an even more likely possibility.

Corks had been dealt a high card, but nothing special yet. He had the ace of spades and the three of clubs. The three cards on the flop were the nine and seven of diamonds and the jack of hearts. He had lost a shit-load of money. How the hell had Bill won four rounds in a row? How could someone be so lucky? He had to be cheating somehow. He had to be. He was taking them for a ride and they were falling for it. Corks shot the man an angry look. He wasn't usually the paranoid type, yet there was a different side to every person and an addiction to the game coupled with losing continually did not sit well with him.

"I'll raise. One K and five," Bill said. He had been dealt an excellent hand by Ryosuke. The queen of spades and queen of hearts. His luck tonight was something special. Four rounds! He had not counted his total winnings yet, but he was without a doubt, a rich man.

"Well, Corks. What will it be?" asked Ryosuke who was pretty confident with his own cards. Corks was sweating from his forehead. The guy didn't look well and it was about time too. The thug had won the last two poker nights. Corks shuffled in his seat eyeballing his hand. It didn't feel right. Damn! Why was his luck so bad tonight? The asshole, Bill, was using some kind of devious chicanery. That was why. He was cheating Milton Corks out of his money. Out of money that he had borrowed and promised to pay back to the famed owner of the Misty Drink night club, Ryan Westwood. The weird-ass fucker would give him years to pay it back thanks to his relax-don't-do-it attitude, however Milton Corks never wormed out of a payment. He was a man who stuck to all promises, deals and I.O.Us, and God help the man who prevented him from doing so.

"Well…" Zwink said from his left. He had folded early in the previous two games, but didn't look perturbed as he hadn't lost too much just yet.

Corks kept staring at his hand and kept sweating. Not only did he not look so good, he didn't feel so good either. He didn't like being cheated, but where was the proof?

Who needed proof? He smelt a rat.

"The table's no place for hesitation, son," Bill chuckled.

Without warning, Corks reached into the back of his pants and pulled out a blocky handgun aiming it loosely at Bill's head.

"Shut the fuck up!" he yelled.

"Hey! Holy shit!" Bill recoiled, almost falling off his chair.

"What the fuck?!" cried Ryosuke. Corks now held the gun firmly with intent.

"This fucker's been cheating. He's cheating me out of my dough!" yelled Corks. He had worked himself into such frenzy; he was totally convinced he was right.

"Come on, man, calm down," Zwink said. He was letting out tense breaths between heavy swallows. If Corks blew Bill away then poker nights were officially over.

"You know me, Corks! I wouldn't cheat you!" Bill's eyes were wide, and he was pale with fright. In the Gambino Family, he handled accounting and monetary transactions. He had never fired a gun or indeed had one pointed at him.

"SHUT UP!"

"Corks! For Christ's sake man, think about this!" pleaded Arthur from behind Bill. He was currently leaning forward, just in case Corks did fire and the bullet went all the way through Bill's head. Ryosuke casually sipped his cocktail for the first time since it had been placed in front of him. Perfect moment for it. Corks was going nuts.

"How'd you get so lucky anyway, Bill, huh?!" The man had menacing eyes. Crazy eyes. It was now Bill's turn to sweat. He hadn't been cheating! He hadn't! Was he really about to get killed for something he hadn't done? Damn his stupid luck!

The whole thing had unfolded so fast; it took Dean a while to register it all. Corks had pulled a gun on Hutch for some reason or another. He suspected that it had something to do with the scumbag's good fortune. Squinting, Dean got a perfect line up. This nutcase was about to end the party. That was his job, and he'd be damned if he'd let some burly street thug blow one of his targets' brains all over the wall. The suppressor on the end of the gun quivered like a canine's nose sniffing a trail, then stiffened before Dean took the shot.

"I swear! I swear! I didn't!"

"Corks! Come on, man! This is ludicrous!"

"Corks!"

"Look at me, Corks. You don't wanna do this."

"Please! I have a wife! I wouldn't cheat you, Corks."

"YOU 'PLAYIN' ME, FOO!" Corks yelled the words with such finality that Bill prepared for his skull to be rudely violated, but it didn't happen. He closed his eyes; yet all he heard was a small, sprinkled crack, like glass being shattered.

Corks jolted as Zwink punched him in the chest.

He blinked and looked sideways, yet the man with the blue bandana tied around his shaved head was just staring at his poker buddy's chest. Zwink hadn't hit him. Then who had?

He looked down. A clean, circular hole had been made in his ace of spades, and a stain was growing on his black vest top. His face screwed in combined pain and confusion. How had that happened? Just then another smashing sound filled the room for less than half a second and another patch began to spread on Corks' front. His gun arm faltered and fell, everything slowing down as the weapon hit the floor. Cork's head lolled forward and he let the scene slip away from him. Things didn't only slow down for Corks. They slowed down for everyone. Two, sugar crusted holes perforated the window and Bill's gaze dragged from the slumped body of Corks to them. He was in shock. What had happened? Why? How?

"What the fuck?" he asked nobody in particular.

A third bullet was pumped into the room. It hit Bill directly in the forehead and splattered the wall behind with dark blood. His head whiplashed back and then forward and then back again. He slumped like his neighbor, blood dripping in a long string from the hole in the back of his head. It was then that the remaining three men understood what was happening.

Faubus went for a silver revolver in his jacket and managed to withdraw it, aiming wildly at the window just as he was hit right in the heart. He convulsed and cried out in agony with no last thoughts. Arthur Faubus then fell forward onto the poker table his gun clenched in his old, dead fingers.

"NO!" Ryosuke yelled. This shit was going down too fast even for him to keep a lid on. His much needed entertainment was now all but finished. His only remaining player was about to let loose with a fully automatic which would no doubt alert the police to the location and result in him getting screwed.

Zwink was up on his feet, the Micro-Uzi from his pants gripped in his hand. He let out a harsh war cry and dived across the room behind the three bodies firing insanely at the window. The rough and inaccurate shots did not reach Dean or his car, but did bring the entire window crashing down in tortuous shell-like chunks. Three shots came sidling towards him. One barely missed his leg and slammed into the door. The second hit him in the stomach and the other burst through his lower jaw and into his brain stem. He hit the ground with a vociferous thud and lay still.

"Don't shoot!" Ryosuke had just decided that it would be a good idea to run, but he didn't get a chance to rise from his seat as a round found its way through his temple and out of the other side. Blood splashed into his green cocktail, turning it a cloudy, muddy brown. The last man collapsed onto the table, crimson spilling from the holes in his head.

Someone inside was bound to have heard the shots. There was also shouting from below, where some of the glass from the window had crashed down into the alley and where early leavers from the rave had ducked to the sound of gunfire.

Dean recoiled. He would have to make this quick. He took the rifle apart faster than usual and slammed the case shut on the disassembled parts, which he hadn't taken the time to place in their vacuformed insets.

The engine revved and he sped off, doing a one eighty and then pulling back to the slope that led down to the second level. When he exited level one he heard the sirens coming from the direction he intended to take. He drove casually and inconspicuously as the LAPD rushed past him in response to a quickly placed 911 call. That had been way too fast for his liking. Someone must have called the moment the first shot was fired from Zwinkoni's gun. It was possible that the cops had been nearby anyway. Very possible. He should have guessed that the peddler would have been packing automatic. No matter. He had gotten away, again. LAPD were useless when it came to hitmen of his caliber. He smiled to himself. That had been done well. Thomas would be pleased. He questioned himself on the drive home as to why that had even crossed his mind. Thomas had been giving him jobs for some time now, and though the guy was clearly no longer playing with a full deck, Dean couldn't help but feel happy that he had carried out his task with unquestionable efficiency. The more heads he brought to his employer, the less dismissive and condescending the man could be when he next required Dean's deadly accuracy.

"Note to self: stroke ego more often. It feels good" Dean said out loud before turning on the radio. He really didn't give himself enough credit, and nobody else gave him any whatsoever. Then again, that

69

probably came with the territory. He wasn't working for the Goodwill after all.

CHAPTER TWELVE
BUSINESS AT THE HOLDEN TOWER

"He's been performing well. Almost too well. Any more success and he might start giving Shades a run for his money." Thomas smirked. Shades, who stood at the window of Ray Bentley's office, shot him a look of contempt then went back to gloomily staring through the clear plate glass. If he cut Thomas into tiny pieces, would Ray hold it against him? Perhaps.

"So, 'you think he's the one?" Ray asked from his seated position behind the desk.

"Oh, yeah. 'No question about it. He's skilled and obedient enough, but he isn't one who would put two and two together. At least not until it was too late."

Gordon shifted slightly from his position at the side of the desk. His liver spotted hands were clasped in front of him and he appeared to be gazing at nothing in particular through his dark spectacles. Valentino was sitting on the desk to Ray's right and Thomas was pacing around the large table that had recently been cleaned.

"This is a big game, brother. You better be right," Ray said, pouring himself some scotch.

"I always am. With Valentino's plan we should be able to bring the yakuza to a shuddering halt and eliminate their ally within the authorities. You have to break an egg to make an omelet. Dean Cottrell is our egg. Plus... I don't like him. He feels like a liability."

Dean had received an email the morning after the multiple assassinations at the Misty Drink night club. It had congratulated him on such a successful hit and had told him that another mission was lined up for him. He was to attend a meeting at the Holden Tower because this was a big operation. Bang and burn. They were going in hot.

He sipped from a glass of orange juice and flicked through the paper.

'FIVE DEAD IN GANG SHOOTOUT'

Gang shootout? Is that what they were calling it now? He read on.

'The bodies of five men were found by police just above the Misty Drink night club, Downtown. Only two of the victims have been formally identified. Arthur Faubus, wanted for radio piracy, and Ryosuke Motobuchi, who one officer speculated may have been a member of the yakuza. The same officer went on to say the killings were gang related. Officially, police have stated that the victims were killed while engaged in a game of poker, and they believe the men were picked off at a distance by a sixth individual, but have made no comment on beliefs that these murders may be related to other similar killings in the Los Angeles area, including the deaths of Police Chief Cheech Higgins or more recently, those of Jake Bentwood and electronic software programmer, Kyoichi Yoshikuni.

Cheech Higgins had not actually been his work. Someone else had carried out that hit, but many other names made it onto Dean's list. He threw the paper down onto the coffee table and stood up.

"Yuki," he called. She came in from the bedroom, all ready for work in smart clothes. His body warmed at the sight of her as if her image activated his heart's most intense fire.

"Yeah?"

"I know I've been neglecting you these past few days. Tonight, it doesn't matter if the business is going down in flames. I'll be back before dark." He put so much conviction into his voice he forced himself to believe it. She nodded and smiled at him.

"That sounds good. Listen I'm late, but it would mean a lot if you kept your word." She came around to kiss him.

"I will. I promise."

She turned from him and left the apartment.

It wasn't long before he had to think about leaving too. He knew how these things worked. Any big op was pre-planned so there was no chance it would be going down tonight. Maybe tomorrow, or the next day. He grinned with an aura of tangible satisfaction.

And he was in on it. He clapped his hands together. All was well. In fact things were better than well. Things were excellent.

Dean checked himself in the mirror and then left the apartment.

His car stood in the small parking lot waiting for him like a trained dog. Still carrying his contentedness he jumped in and took off down the busy streets of Los Angeles, windows down, and the radio tuned to a station that lurched between Bruce Springsteen and Metallica, in a dissonant fashion. As he hit the first set of traffic lights his cell phone started to ring.

"Hello?"

"Dean, where are you?"

"Williams? What? I'm on my way to a meeting at the Holden Tower. Where are you?"

"At the Holden Tower, waiting for you."

"'You involved in this too?" Dean was surprised, but slightly elated. He hadn't done a job with Williams in over two months.

"'Sure am. Hurry up. You've got eight minutes."

"I'll see you in seven." He hung up and hammered on the gas pedal as the light changed to a luminous green. The Holden Tower wasn't exactly close to his apartment complex; however he knew all the short cuts and was an accomplished driver.

Williams was waiting in the underground parking lot his arms folded full Red Dawn attire clinging to him.

"Come on, come on!" he said annoyingly as Dean pulled himself out of the door and slammed it before locking the BMW.

"Alright. I'm here." He jogged over as Williams darted towards the elevator.

"'Meeting's on the seventeenth floor."

The elevator ride was a silent one and when they hit the floor both of the suited men walked quickly out and down a hallway that offered no choices as to where to go.

"'Any idea what this is about?" asked Dean curiously.

"Hey, I just work here," Williams replied.

"Mr. Cottrell? Mr. Williams?" inquired a man on their right as they hit a fork at the end of the long corridor.

"Yeah?" Williams replied. Dean recognized the wrinkled face of one of Ray Bentley's body guards. The man with the liver spotted hands and dark spectacles with a small amount of gray hair trailing down the back of a head that's top was as bald as a plucked chicken. His voice was croaky and whispered as if speech was a trial.

"Please follow me." He turned from them down a winding, red walled corridor. Dean had never been on this floor and took in the artwork hanging on the walls at ten second intervals. The hallway ended in a widened area where there was a set of vermillion doors. Dangerous-looking men stood on either side guarding them, red ties dazzling in the light from a fixture above. Dean took note of the fact that both were holding Ruger MP9s. The old gentleman opened both of the doors, and Williams and Dean were ushered into a large room that had a very traditional and classic feel, like the lounge of a rich land owner. Red carpets, a roaring fireplace on the right hand side, a couch in front of that and a big, dominating table.

Five men were on or around the couch, drinking beer and Thomas Bentley along with his Mexican chief of security, Cheo, were standing beside the fireplace with their arms crossed.

Kruge, the man who had told Dean to meet with Thomas at the zoo was in the corner, a cigarette between his teeth and at the far end of the table standing, were Valentino, Shades and Ray Bentley.

"Gentlemen. Glad you could make it."

Everyone sat around the king size, cherry veneer table their attention fixed on Ray who sat at its head. Dean noticed a change on this occasion. A change in Ray's mannerisms. He was more confident and sure of himself than he had been previously and he wasn't exactly a shy person to begin with. A feeling of deep satisfaction swum in his irises and his words were commanding and echoless.

"I would first like to say that I am amazed at how well our organization has progressed. The reason you have all been chosen for this is because you have all contributed such brilliant performances. Miles..." He addressed a short, stubby man on the opposite side of the table to Dean. "Our racketeering operations were well planned and could have been something great, but thanks to your dedication and ruthless terror tactics. Well... It's become something much, much more." Miles smiled weakly. "Hollins. Who could forget your actions in Panama, and Cottrel... the hits you've carried out recently were those of a seasoned pro."

Dean couldn't stop himself from smiling as weakly as Miles had. Ray Bentley just had this irresistible radiance that made everyone around him seem so insignificant. It didn't matter how old you got, to be praised was something that every person relished, especially when it came from someone on a higher plane. If he had thought about it Dean might have been cognizant of the fact that this concept of true superiority was merely a self-spun veil covering Ray's egotism and arrogance, yet he was in such a positive mood that he didn't pick up on how his boss complimented the assembled lackeys as one might compliment a pair of shoes or a witty turn of phrase.

"But don't for a second think we're done, oh no. The Taglianos' operations have crashed, but the yakuza are still going strong."

Dean thought Ray was speaking rather dramatically, but then he had always been that way. He really was a character lifted strait from *The Godfather*.

"I have certain individuals in place who tell me that their lead man is having a meeting with none other than Police Chief Orion tomorrow."

There was universal muttering. Even Dean was taken aback. Orion was the replacement for Cheech Higgins and now chief of the Los Angeles Police Department. Despite saying he would bring his predecessor's killers to justice, Orion had never found them. Dean wondered for a moment whether the force would ever get a chief who was just straight up, because unfortunately for the people of L.A., Orion was almost as bad as some of the city scum. It was like Chicago's politicians had all gone into Californian law enforcement. The corruption was out of control and people either shirked responsibility for it, or just covered their ears and pretended that it didn't exist. That was probably the reason why crime syndicates were fighting tooth and nail over the cesspool the city had become. It was just such a great place to do business, all at the expense of the citizens who were powerless to fight back. The fact that the police chief was dealing with the yakuza was no great surprise. You just couldn't trust anyone in today's world.

CHAPTER THIRTEEN
OPERATION HEAVY STORM

"Ishimaru Taiki will be meeting with the bastard at the Starcross Motel. You might not know it. It's one of those places where cheating husbands go to do their thing and police officials go to pick up their dirty laundry." Valentino had stood up and was coming around the table, placing his hands periodically on the backs of people's chairs. He had definitely put on weight. It amused Dean how the man played the part of the intellectual finding solace in the fact that he committed his crimes in a *smart* way. No wonder Ray had chosen him to do all the brain work.

"Don't be fooled. Orion isn't the only filthy fucker in the police department. He might be bringing protection, mainly because you can never trust the yakuza as far as you can throw them. These are cops people. You kill a cop in Los Angeles you either better be good at what you do or be able to disappear fast. Thanks to our sources we know which room he'll be in and we have some knowledge of the yakuza's plans."

Dean let his mind wander for a moment. He couldn't deny that he was elated to finally be sitting at the table. It was a sign that he had moved up into a class where he was trusted with important, collaborative tasks such as this one. Why the hell Kruge, a jarhead with aspirations of being one of Ray's right-hand men was there, he didn't know.

"Here's how it's gonna work. Tomorrow, 10 A.M., we'll converge and then we'll head over to the Starcross Motel. Williams, we've got a good point for you. 'Need you covering our guys on the ground." Williams nodded and Valentino continued.

"Now, before things get underway, Shades is going to take out Orion in his room. He'll also deal with any officers guarding him there. Cottrell, you'll deliver a package to the billiard room and make it out of the back window in the store room. Kill anyone who gets in the way. Kruge, Hollins, Miles, Freddy, Gimble, and Diệm, you'll move in on the hotel lounge where Taiki and his goons will be. God knows he's going to be bringing a whole army so you need to push it and corner them into the billiard room, at which point..." Valentino smiled and made an explosive gesture with his hands. Dean tried to make sense of it all.

"Umm. Excuse me, but what is the package," he asked. Before Valentino could open his mouth Thomas cut in.

"The package is a bomb. A time controlled explosive device. You'll have four minutes to get to the billiard room and plant it and then four more to get the hell out of there. After that, Taiki and the rest of the scum'll be vaporized in the blast."

"Sir, I'm a sniper with varied experience in close combat and driving. Isn't there a task more suited to me?" Dean directed the question at Ray, who had his elbows on the table and seemed to be in deep thought.

"A good soldier is never one thing, Cottrell. I'm broadening your experience. Bomb delivery is one of the easiest things you'll ever do, I promise. Plus, it has to be done and if someone tries to stop *you* I feel you can be trusted to execute them without issue."

Those words resonated with Dean for some odd reason. He guessed it made more sense. The bomb was integral to the plot. 'Couldn't trust an idiot like Kruge to do it right.

"The operation is called Heavy Storm. If successful, we can hope to not only have an open playing field in Los Angeles, but it will be a huge blow to Goto-gumi. Gentlemen, if this thing plays out the way we expect it to; we have the potential to dominate the entire region." Valentino shot Ray a look of assurance and was returned a smile.

Dean was considering his role. The idea of holding a timed explosive made him feel kind of sick. He had seen firsthand their effects on the other side of the world. Dean would much rather have been picking off anyone who tried to escape the building. Heck, he would rather have been going in with Kruge and the goon squad, but unfortunately that wasn't the job he had been assigned. He had to make the best of what he had.

Just then, a thought struck him like a stone to the head. He had gotten what he wanted. Well… In a way. The operation was to take place tomorrow morning. Tonight was his and his alone, after running a few errands that he had scheduled for that day. He was already starting to plan it. He would be picking up some more wine on the way home for sure. A night of rough and tumble with Yuki was just what he needed to relax himself out of the tense state he was in. God, he was going to apologize heartily for his neglect.

Ray stood and looked at those around him. His expression was one of security with an unbreakable shield of aplomb. He took a darting look at the roaring fire away to his left and saw in it his destiny, kindled by this large step.

With the fire crackling away and the room looking like the last one you might find in a place like the Holden Tower, Shades took a quick peek at the collection of identical throwing knives concealed within his jacket each with their own mercury-like complexion.

He had already given it some thought, but now was forced to let it flow through his mind once again. How would he get it done?

It was not a question of how in the hell was he going to complete such an enormous task as offing the chief of the Los Angeles Police Department and his predictable entourage. It was more a question of which methods he would prefer to use. Thinking, he relaxed into the soft, Sarouk-patterned seat fabric of the chair. Getting Orion to open the door to his room was going to be a problem, but he was sure he would be able to figure something out. As for the man's pinhead escort…

Well, he would spare no expense in making sure he stained their uniforms with red.

He wasn't fond of police. His profession meant that he couldn't be, but dirty cops were worse than all the other hated professions in his eyes.

Out of nowhere, Shades heard his own father's voice in his head.

"Motherfucker! That's bullshit! You know it and so do you!"

The younger officer by the car looked at the space between his feet as the older one put the cuffs on Mr. Shades.

"Dad! Where are you going?!"

But his father was not listening.

"'This what you do with your spare time, huh?! That isn't mine!"

The older officer threw the bag of white powder to his partner who failed to catch it and had to bend awkwardly to snatch it up from the uneven road.

"Dad! Where are you going! Where are they taking you?" Lysander Shades stood stupidly on the front lawn, an old skateboard under his arm.

"Sander, get back in the fucking house!"

The older cop shoved his father into the car and slammed the door. BANG! BANG! BANG!

He would never forget that echoing noise for as long as he lived.

He had holed up with his grandmother for a couple of months and then Mr. Shades had returned to the house, only something was slightly different about his father when he returned. He had never been a model parent. In fact, looking back on it, he had been an abusive son of a bitch, but after that set up orchestrated by local officers that day, Mr. Shades lost the will to go on. He would sit for hours on end in front of a blank T.V. and drink beer that hadn't been refrigerated. Six years later, he had put both barrels of a shotgun in his mouth and that was it.

BANG! BANG! BANG!

Lysander Shades wouldn't forget that noise for as long as he lived.

CHAPTER FOURTEEN
SAVE TONIGHT

The errands Dean needed to run had taken more time than he had expected, but his evening was by no means ruined. In fact, it seemed to be building itself brick by brick into a night he would not soon forget.

He looked at the seat beside him. The bag labeled 'Buick Jewels' sat as a silent passenger. Maybe he was rushing things. Maybe she would take it the wrong way. Maybe it was too soon. It was only coming up on a year now. Maybe she didn't feel the same. Maybe she wasn't ready for that kind of commitment. Her parents certainly weren't the problem. Her mother had died in an accident when she was sixteen and her father was in a hospital back in Japan, receiving treatment for some kind of terminal illness. They hardly ever spoke...

But was she feeling the same things he was? Was she just as eager to make their partnership a fixture, sworn to by oath? He swatted these doubts away trying to concentrate on the slow traffic ahead. He had been planning to ask at some point. Some point soon, but he knew if he didn't swallow his pride and do it tonight, then he never would. It was after all, a night of change. The business (despite certain moral flaws) was making headway and he finally felt like he was along for the ride. He had money, he had satisfaction. This next step was logical. He just hoped to God his recent dive into the lowlands of poor reliability wouldn't influence her answer in any way unfortunately he couldn't say he would blame her if it did.

Yuki messed with the CD player, unable to get it to work. Why was it being so much trouble today? So much for Japan's marriage with technology. She frowned. If Dean was here he would fix it for her. Dean. Where was he?

She had had dinner and was going to bed in about twenty minutes, but was really hoping he would be home before that. She was longing to have him next to her while she was conscious; in fact, just thinking about Dean made her feel warm and secure. In his arms she was safe from the troubles of the world. Safe, even from whatever it was Dean did for a living. Though not entirely certain of what it was, she was pretty sure that office work was only half of it. Maybe he was doing dirty deals or something, but it was definitely more than he ever let on. Not that it mattered in the slightest because if there was a shady aspect to his work he never brought any of that home with him. Every time they saw each other he was the same Dean that she had met the night that her previous boyfriend had officially ended their relationship. What she had with Dean was so much more than she had ever had before. Her mother had told her when she was young that you can have many relationships in a lifetime, but when you find the right person you experience a kind of feeling that no other can give you. That was how she knew that Dean was her soul mate without question.

She smiled. God, she wished her mother was still around to give her more advice like that.

Yuki remembered the day that her mother had died. A truck had lost control and crashed headlong into a café. A freak accident. It was fortunate she hadn't been there. Her father had told her, quiet and emotionless.

Suddenly, the CD player burst into life and began to softly play Eagle-Eye Cherry's 'Save Tonight'. It was one of her favorite songs and its album was one of the few she owned on CD. With pride in her ability to accidentally fix things she went over to the coffee table with the intention of clearing up.

Just then, there was a clicking noise from the door and she turned expectedly to see Dean stepping in. His face was a lustful smile and made her own grin grow even broader. He shut the door behind him tearing off his suit jacket quickly and throwing it onto the hat stand where it stuck. Yuki abandoned the task and with an undeniable sense of compulsion crossed the room to him in seven, light steps. They embraced and it didn't seem strange that the feelings were so intense. Dean had kept his promise. She had secretly known that he would. Dean was the kind of man who didn't make promises he could never keep.

With Yuki in his strong embrace, Dean was asking himself what the next step of the evening would be. Well, the tie had to go. He pulled it off and let it hit the floor before he gave Yuki a long kiss. They both found themselves staring into each other's eyes longingly. Dean forgot to scold her for not chaining the door. She had to start doing that, but at that moment, it failed to matter.

"I want you," Dean said tenderly rubbing her neck with his hand. She smiled and nodded, both eyes shut.

"I've been waiting to see you all day," he continued and turned the CD volume to just below maximum before they both made for the bedroom.

Dean finished up rolling off of her and lying there, still and sweaty under the covers.

She lay next to him panting quietly, still enjoying that wet feeling of him between her legs. The CD had gone all the way to the end and was now back to '*Save Tonight*'. She looked straight up at the dim ceiling. Nothing came close to making love to Dean. She felt him next to her reaching down onto the floor where his crumpled pants were. He then rolled back, but she didn't look away from the ceiling. She had to wait for the sensations to pass before she looked at him again.

"Yuki?" His voice was barely a whisper. She waited and then replied.

"Yes?"

"I need to ask you something. Your answer means everything to me." His voice was still quiet and soft like velvet sheets. She froze. There was only one thing that a man ever asked a woman in that manner. He couldn't? No... Would he? Excitement rose like a soaring bird within her. It was happening. It was really happening.

"I'm so afraid you'll say no." He now sounded genuinely sad. She resisted the urge to look over at him.

"I won't," she replied. Her smile was not one of happiness or pleasure, but one of desire. The desire for that all important question that would bind them or break them.

"Yuki, will you marry me?"

Her lungs drew in a breath of hot air. He had done it.

Yuki paused, wondering whether leaving him hanging was the best option. She finally turned her head on the pillow and looked him dead in the eye. He had a serious look. One of expectation and slight stoniness. He didn't want his emotions to show at the moment. 'Didn't want to influence her in any way. The answer had to come from her heart and nowhere else.

"Yes."

Her reply was soft like velvet, quiet like the breeze, and the fact that she followed it up by drawing her naked body against him once again and bringing his mouth to hers was ample confirmation for him. 'Save Tonight' played on as though nothing was happening. He withdrew his tongue.

"I love you more than I can say. You know that, don't you?" He put his fingers through her hair and enjoyed the texture. "We can talk about it all you want tomorrow afternoon. I have that part of the day off."

"Where are you going in the morning?" She asked this with such sincerity that he was hard pressed to lie. God, it hurt not to tell her. "The business has a job for me. Real important. More important than anything before. I have to be there."

She nodded as Dean suddenly pulled his hand from beneath the bed covers. A Persian green box, small and weightless, rested within it. He opened it to reveal a ring inside. Gold, with a perfect diamond atop its beautiful form. She gasped and took it out taking a close look at it. This certainly was a surprise. It wasn't a cheap ring. Not that that made any difference. She would have loved him just as much whatever the ring's value.

"Dean, I don't know what to say," she whispered. Why she had said that, she had no idea.

"I don't need to know any more than what you've already said," and with that he kissed her again.

CHAPTER FIFTEEN

FIRST OFFENSIVE

In the back of the unmarked van Dean sat on a steel bench. His smile was one of off-world contemplation. Williams sat opposite to him, a conspicuous case cradled in his arms. The thoughts of yesterday were like stars hanging in Dean's head against the background. The background being the most important mission he had ever taken on.

"What's got you so perky?" Williams asked. Dean had been waiting to tell him and now seemed like the right time.

"I proposed last night," he said confidently. His friend raised both of his eyebrows. The conversation was between the two of them as the other plotters were discussing different matters and double checking their weapons.

"Really? Holy shit. What did she say?"

Dean left him hanging, that same smile still on his face. He nodded. Williams lit up and gave his crooked grin.

"Great going. I was wondering when you'd shackle yourself to that chick," Williams joked. Secretly he was thinking, 'lucky bastard.'

Dean double checked that his Beretta was fully loaded (though he knew for a fact that it was) and relaxed. It was good to get that off his chest and telling his friend was the final release.

A driver who Dean didn't know was directing the van with the speed of an expert down the road. The motel wasn't too far away and when they got there Dean was going to make sure he did the job right.

Adrenaline coursed through his veins ready for when it would be needed most.

Valentino was sitting in the passenger seat while everyone else (minus Shades) was in the back. It seemed strange to Dean that Valentino would actually come on a mission, but he supposed it needed some sort of field coordinator. 'No doubt Ray was in his office at the Holden Tower, hands clasped in front of him, waiting for the call to tell him that the mission had been a success. Thomas was probably at the zoo running his fingers over a shipment of RPGs while Shades (the man of the hour) was already at the motel readying himself for the signal to move on Orion.

The police chief was of medium height with a tidy husk of seal brown hair. The sideburns that hung about his ears came around and met under his nose and also under his bottom lip forming an awkward-looking goatee. His eyes were like fogged glass close to translucency and weren't complemented by his snappy, brown suit to which he was applying the polyester tie.

Three men, officers Barrow, Clemm and Lewis were stationed around the maze of corridors outside his room. He felt that there was only about a twenty percent chance they were doing their job right. Jarheads. He cursed under his breath and looked at himself in the mirror. It was almost as if a different man stood there now.

In this suit his look was very antithetic to its usual counterpart. This was a good thing.

The yakuza had arrived five minutes ago and were waiting in the closed off lounge for him. It was a rather simple plan. Offer what he had to offer and take what they were willing to give. Seven yakuza of high importance to Taiki were in jail, and with a few words and

89

misplaced files, he could put them back on the streets. He also had the power to make cops in Little Tokyo something of a rare occurrence. All he needed was money; something he was sure the yakuza had plenty of. He smiled to himself. To have some real green between his fingers would be good. 'Just had to make sure they understood each other. The fact that Goto-gumi had actually agreed to a little get together was something of a miracle, so they had to be interested.

"Money... Show me the money," he whispered to his reflection. He needed cash. That bitch Madeline had taken more than he could bear in the divorce court. Maybe the yakuza could remove her from the picture. He smiled at this dark and dirty thought that was hidden within his psyche. If that whore turned up dead he would be a happy man.

The van pulled up not a block from the motel. All the men who were going in hot had trench coats to conceal their weapons and to Dean they looked rather like some sort of satanic cult. The back doors were flung open by Valentino who jumped inside closing them behind him.

"This is it," he said, surveying them all. Most picked up on his rushed tone and the few beads of sweat that hung on his forehead. This was his plan. His responsibility. Ray would not be happy if it went up in smoke.

"Shades is in position. After I get word from him that Orion's takin' a dirt nap, Cottrell, you'll move in with the package. As he goes, everyone else will bust the yakuza in the main lounge and force them back to where the bomb is. After that, everyone clear the area pronto. 'Got it?"

Most of the men nodded.

"Williams, you know where you 'gotta be. I want any escapees taken out. Go now."

Surprised that the time had finally come, Williams stood up, case in hand and exited through the back doors giving Dean one final wink before slamming them after he was safely on the road. Valentino could see the pieces all coming together like blocks in a game of Tetris. *His* game of Tetris. Damn he was good.

Some began talking excitedly about how they were going to riddle the yakuza boys with lead, but Dean sat quietly on his own staring at the floor. His smile of pre-marital elation had fallen to an expression of worry and concentration. He looked up to see Valentino in front of him.

"'You okay, Dean? You look paler than my mother... and she's dead," he said, his Italian origin just about coming through.

"I'm good. Ready to go." Dean said, but even he didn't believe it.

"That's good to hear. Now, listen. You're the most important piece in this thing. 'Side entrance is your way in. Just keep straight. There should be signs. 'Think you can find the room?"

"Yeah. 'Shouldn't be too much hassle." Dean let a weak smile form on his lips.

"Perfect. Now, there's a store room in the back. It has a window. After you're out, run your ass off. I don't want a good man like you getting yourself grilled. Any stray men wanna fuck with you, you know what to do."

"I got it." Dean was thinking about that word, grill. How would it feel to have the force of an explosion blow you away, searing off all the layers of your skin, stripping it away like gray latex on a scratch card? He paled even more, but took a deep breath and told himself that everything would be fine. He had handled explosives before. The only difference was that they were military-grade devices, and the thing he was about to be given was probably held together by rubber bands. Valentino kept his eyes fixated on Dean for a moment then turned and dialed a number on an expensive-looking cellular.

Shades was beginning to get bored when the phone in his pocket began to chirp a cacophony of beeps. He answered it immediately, not greeting whoever was calling. Valentino's voice came through clearly.

"We move now."

The tall figure hung up the phone and slapped the clamshell closed. He had a dry and annoyed look on his face for a solitary second before pushing open the door and strolling into the building. A flight of stairs on the right led upwards to the second floor.

Shades could smell the rat from here. He could smell the kill and a desire to make the scent stronger filled him. His black, leather shoes made relatively little noise on the Tabriz carpet as he mounted the top of the staircase. Dark, wooden baseboards and handrails for the stairs gave the place a classical feel, but were alone in doing so.

The sound of cursing came from somewhere ahead, and Shades stopped dead to listen, creeping forward when he was sure he was hearing correctly. The wall caved on the left where a vending machine stood and with his back to the assailant a black officer in full uniform was bashing a fist against the machine.

Shades' kills were of a high caliber and nobody saw them coming. He had driven a blade into the first man's spinal column and left him on the ground. The second officer had then come to look for his friend and Shades had stabbed him in the side of the head not allowing him to even scream. Now walking at the pace of someone with a purpose, Shades rounded each corridor of the motel until he came to the one he needed to be in. With the bloodied knife, now varnished in a cocktail of juices, still in hand, Shades took in the guard posted outside the room. He had both hands on the belt of his police uniform and looked older than the first two sporting gray hair and a wrinkled complexion.

Officer Barrow saw the man coming, but didn't have time to react as something came hurtling in his direction.

The knife, quick like a bullet to its target, slammed into his carotid artery and he went down instantly in too much agony to cry out. Blood poured from his neck and he raised his hands in an attempt to staunch the flow from his uncomfortable sitting position. Shades came fast at him. With what could only be described as a low, *savaté* kick from Shades, Barrow's neck snapped upwards, and he flopped. The offending object was ripped from his neck, blood still spilling, and its owner wiped both sides on the navy police uniform before getting ready to dispatch Orion. The whole thing was like a sick cocaine rush, blood pumping, pupils blown. His fetish for violence was insatiable. It couldn't be cured, and even if it could, Shades wouldn't have wanted to end his addiction. It was just too sweet a thing. Now the only task left was to execute the real target. He sheathed the blade and pulled out the silenced handgun he had favored for this particular mission.

Knock. Knock. Knock.

The sound was patient and slow. Orion turned to it suspicious of everything. Was it Barrow or somebody else? He slowly walked towards the door, the sound of his footsteps traveling ahead of him, loud as a weighted thunder to Shades' trained ears.

"Barrow?" he enquired as he got up close and personal with the cheap door. He put an eye to the peephole. Strange. Nothing but black outside...

The silenced bullet punched through both circles of thin glass and ruptured Orion's eyeball splattering the bed behind with a shower of skull shavings and assorted offal. He fell back his arms giving the illusion that he was clutching for something and hit the floor with a thud. Outside, Shades lowered the smoking barrel and put it away again.

Flipping open the clam phone, he dialed the memorized numbers and put it to his ear.

"It's done.

CHAPTER SIXTEEN
NO WAY OUT

Valentino led Dean around to the front of the van and swung the door open urgently.

"Eight minutes," he said, hauling a silver case from the seat he had ridden in during the journey. At least it looked safer than what Dean had been imagining. Valentino tipped it on its head and the bomb's delivery boy was made aware of a small piece of metal poking out just past the first hinge. Valentino gave him a conflicted look and the mixed emotions flowing over the portly man's face made it impossible for Dean to read what he was thinking.

Without warning, the large man slapped the widget and it receded into the case with a double click. A high pitched beep emanated from within and Valentino shoved it into Dean's grasp.

He had it. He had the case. The bomb was in his hands. The vital component of the mission clutched in his sweaty fingers.

He turned on his heels immediately and began a brisk walk towards the motel at the end of the road. It's a weird thing, carrying a bomb. You feel a great sense of control and power, but also a sense that you threaten your own existence. Primal urges told him to drop the case immediately; however Dean had learnt how to override these instincts that had been passed down from generation to generation. In the modern world they were dated and useless.

The case didn't seem too heavy duty for one made of metal, but had enough weight to be taken seriously. He just needed to stop thinking about what it contained and start thinking about how he was going to deal with any obstacles he encountered when he got inside.

"This is it! Move!" Valentino yelled.

The men stood up and jumped out of the van, trench coats hanging off of them like capes.

"Don't hold back boys. I don't wanna get shot because one of you dipshits lost his balls. Once we're inside the lounge is on the left," Miles reminded, a little nervous himself.

Kruge paused to put both of his hands up making dual 'L's with his digits.

"Left. Got it," he growled.

From a distance, at the top of a small block of apartments, the eye watching over them stared through a sniper scope, scanning each of the assailants individually. Kruge was wearing his cheap, black sunglasses and usual annoyed look. Williams tried to remember what the man was packing. Heckler & Koch MP5A5. 9mm Parabellum. He was bound to put someone away with that. The bulge of the concealed weapon was just visible and most of the other men had similar questionable, raised spots in their jackets. He turned the rifle slowly to focus on Dean who was approaching the motel.

"Play it smart, Dean," he muttered.

The goon squad started their walk, attracting some attention, but not enough to warrant any action. This was going to be one hell of a firefight and it would all end with one, huge bang. If successful, there would be cash bonuses for all involved, and Williams was torn between the new dishwasher for his apartment or a night of alcohol-fuelled fun. In the end, he would probably choose the latter.

The rifle's crosshairs turned back to Valentino who seemed to be rubbing some sweat from his forehead. The guy was obviously nervous. If he was going in hot, he would in all likelihood get clapped like an Oscar winner, so it was good that he had opted to stay behind and *'monitor'* the situation.

Dean came to the side door and mentally admonished himself for taking so long to get there. He should have walked faster, but he was sure it wouldn't be a problem. All he had to do was traverse a few hallways and he was there. He took a deep breath and just as he was reaching for the door it flew open almost making him double back.

Shades did not look at him or even acknowledge his presence. He simply walked on by and out of view. Dean stared after him for a few seconds, wondering what had taken him so long to leave the building. He shook the thought away and entered the motel.

The first words that came to mind were bland and sleazy. Valentino hadn't been joking when he said that it was where cheating husbands went to do their thing. Nobody was around. The air had a certain musty quality to it and it seemed like somebody had put quite a lot of effort into covering the smell of tobacco ash with an equally obnoxious, floral air freshener.

What a shithole.

His cohorts were probably trudging there way over the blacktop of the parking lot, weapons heavy on straps around their shoulders. How many of them would get out alive? Dean would put money on less than went in. Luckily he was safer. It seemed like he wouldn't encounter anyone and bringing his gun had been unnecessary. He only hoped that was how it played out.

About ten men in suits that had no desire to mirror each other sat around in the main lounge.

The supposed *main* man of the Goto-gumi in L.A., Ishimaru Taiki, was not the sort of person you would expect to hold such a prominent position in a high-ranking criminal organization. He was short, with rather obviously bleached hair and an almost tanned complexion. He was also about forty and smelt of cheap cologne. At present, he was talking to two slightly younger-looking members and the last thing he was expecting was for six men in dark trench coats to burst through the double doors, whipping out automatic weapons and shouting something at them.

The room was swamped with the sound of gunfire and the air became firmly gripped by the choking stench of smoke.

Unfortunately for those who were crashing the party, Goto-gumi weren't unprepared. It was never good to be unprepared in the criminal underworld. Even allies hated each other. You never could tell when you were going down and the fact that they were executing a deal with crooked cops (the worst criminals in L.A., as Ishimaru thought them) meant that they hadn't taken any chances.

Two of the yakuza were gunned into silence where they sat and almost immediately the tall Vietnamese assailant named Diệm received a bullet to the face and flew backwards; smashing into the wall and hitting the carpet, limp.

"Shit!" yelled Miles, diving to the floor and dodging the fire of a Micro-Uzi. At the far end of the room, three more yakuza hit the floor and it looked like Taiki was retreating, maybe trying to find ground that would be advantageous to him. Using the chairs as cover and shouting something in Japanese, the remaining yakuza moved back. They hadn't been unprepared, however that didn't mean they had been waiting for a full-scale war.

Heavy fire ripped through Hollins and he spat out a spray of blood as his lungs were shredded and he crashed down.

More non-descript Japanese words that Kruge supposed were curses flew around. Boy, would it suck if he died here. 'Had to play it smart even though that had never been his strong point. He looked up over a chair and blasted another one in the chest. It wasn't as easy as Ray had made it sound. He looked over at the body of Hollins who now lay on the floor, blood oozing from the holes on his front. He had said they might need some additional men, but no... Ray didn't give a shit whether they lived or died. Chips of wood flew over his head from a table under fire. He peered over and shot aimlessly.

"KRUGE, MOVE IT!" Miles hollered from somewhere nearby. Was he insane? Moving it would probably tempt fate a lot more than was safe during a dangerous situation like this one, but fuck it. That was what Kruge was good at. Fucking it and going in all guns blazing. And nine out of ten times, fucking it worked.

Dean could hear the commotion from the room behind the double doors on his left. A few bullets even sprang from it through the doors and into the wall on the other side.

'Now or never', Dean told himself.

He sprinted past the threshold and straight to the big doorway at the end of the corridor. Nobody was inside the room, which was in his mind larger than the motel really deserved. The billiard table looked less than flimsy and several smaller tables sat around with chairs flanking them. At the end of the room was a door to what Dean assumed to be the store room. Perfect.

The case seemed a little lighter now and Dean threw it carelessly under the billiard table. Damn, it felt good to be rid of it. That hadn't been so hard. He would possibly consider bomb delivery as a decent fallback for semi-retirement.

He opened the door to the store room and stepped into the cramped space flanked by shelving units. It only took a few seconds for Dean to realize what was wrong with the room.

There were no windows...

None at all. Not even the small rectangular ones you sometimes find near the ceiling.

"Perfect. Now, there's a store room in the back. It has a window."

Valentino's lip movements were slow in Dean's memory. It had to be here. The guy never made a mistake.

Frantically, Dean ripped items such as bulk packs of toilet paper from the shelves, but it was useless. The room had no windows. There was no escape route. It was a fucking casket!

He turned and exited, his head whiplashing from side to side in momentary panic. The unexplainable deviation from the plan he had gone over numerous times in his mind had shaken everything out of place. Thousands of thoughts bolted through his brain with enough force for a migraine to ensue. Only one conclusion was left to Dean, but it was one he couldn't accept.

Wanting to know if the bomb had reached the four minute mark yet, he walked over to the case under the billiard table, bent down and flicked the latches off, starting to calm himself with the knowledge that he still had enough time to backtrack and make it out alive. He would just have to be quick about it.

The bomb device filled the case and looked exactly like the ones in the late night action movies Dean had watched as a kid. Lots of wires. The rule was never to cut the red one, but in this case there were so many wires that weren't red, that even Keanu Reeves would have had his work cut out for him. Green, blue, white, brown, orange. Heck, there was even a burgundy wire. What the hell did that mean? Dean's eyes flitted to the L.E.D screen in the middle.

His heart stopped.

0:11

0:10

0:09

0:08

His eyes widened. A tear of pure terror escaped and he let go of the case and stood up his motion fast, but at the same time slowed down. The fear he was experiencing, the knowledge that the thing was about to blow and he would either be dismembered by shrapnel or incinerated in the blast, was overpowering.

In the hallway access to the billiard room, the doors to the lounge burst open and six yakuza, blood splattered and disheveled burst forth, back first, firing their weapons towards their pursuers. One was gunned down a second later.

Now out of range, Ishimaru ran towards the billiard room not acknowledging the presence of a man inside. He yelled something, and his remaining men followed.

Dean dived over a table and flipped it with him to cover himself. It was the best thing he could think of. There was not a high chance it would work, but it was the best he could do with the given time. These logical thoughts were the only ones he would allow to be processed because if he gave way to what he really wanted to think it would include a lot of cursing and thinking about all he was leaving behind. Yuki...

"WAIT!" Miles shouted.

Kruge and Freddy rushed out into the hallway to take out the cowardly yakuza who were fleeing, but before they could send a full salvo of speeding bullets towards them, a white and orange light engulfed everything.

The bomb blew with the intensity of a hurricane and sent a tidal wave of fire towards the yakuza who stood in the doorway.

Their coats flapped in the presence of the inferno and their screaming forms melded with the blaze as they combusted. Even creatures with the most salamandrine of qualities would have had trouble standing up to the frontal assault of bitter, searing heat.

In the hallway, Miles grabbed Kruge and tried to haul him back. It ultimately saved his life, but not the right side of his face as shrapnel was fired as if from an air cannon, down the hallway. Small shavings of metal embedded themselves in his right cheek and part of his forehead. He yelped and fell back with Miles.

The goon named Freddy wasn't so lucky. One of the legs from the billiard table came spinning through the air at him and a shocked expression was all he could muster as it tore through his stomach and impaled him. He flew back under the force and landed on his side.

The yakuza were all dead. The chief of police and his guards were also dead and three of the hit squad sent in by the Red Dawn had been killed too. The survivors got out as fast as they could. Williams, who hadn't got to shoot anything, had seen the explosion and then he had seen Gimble and Miles hauling Kruge between them out of the place and towards the van.

He whispered to himself.

"Shit... Dean..." He then came to his senses and left his vantage point as quickly as he could.

Valentino could not get the van started up fast enough. A crowd was starting to gather although it was clear they were going to get away. The large man breathed an uneasy sigh of relief.

'Shame about Cottrell, but in war everyone was collateral.

CHAPTER SEVENTEEN
THE ROOTS RUN RED

One of the yellow fish in the tank in Ray Bentley's office realized it had reached the end and turned around to explore what lay on the other side.

With less light than he would have liked coming in through the window Ray only just shifted in his seat, but was otherwise still, seemingly in deep contemplation. It wouldn't be long before Valentino would call to tell him whether the mission had been a success or whether he had fucked it up. If the answer was the latter, Ray was thinking about getting Shades to silence him for his incompetence. Then again, if Shades had been the flat tire in the operation he would have to get someone to silence him.

He sipped from a glass of scotch.

It hurt his head to think about killing them. They were probably half the reason the organization was where it was right now. Well, more like a quarter. Of course, the driving force was Ray's charisma and flawlessly meticulous mind or at least that was what he liked to think.

The phone on the desk started to ring and Ray picked up quickly after putting the glass down.

"Is it done?" Ray had decided to skip 'hello' just to be edgy hoping that it was Valentino who had called.

"Yeah. 'Worked out pretty good. None of 'em'll be walking any time soon and that includes Orion." Valentino's voice sounded slightly distracted, but relieved.

"Great news. How many have we lost?" Ray took down some more scotch to prepare.

"Freddy, Diệm." That didn't matter to Ray much. They were disposable people who could be replaced easily.

"Hollins." Ray winced. Hollins had headed the takedown of some major drug dealing competitors in Panama, but again he could be replaced.

"Cottrell, of course... and Kruge got injured, but he should be okay." Leaning back in his chair, Ray weighed things up and it was still a big success. Heck, even if they had lost Miles it would have been one. A shame about Cottrell. He sounded like someone with potential, but if Thomas didn't like him then he had to go. Ray had come across his type before and he would continue to in the future.

"Okay, get back as soon as possible. You did good Valentino." He hung up before the man on the other end of the line could reply and allowed a gratified expression to wash over his visage. It easily could have gone worse.

Dialing the number of his brother's cell phone, Ray took down the last of his beverage. Thomas picked up. In the background, Ray could hear machines whirring and guessed it to be forklifts moving shipments of weapons around.

"Ray, talk to me." Thomas had energy in his voice that immediately told his brother he was happy.

"Tom, 'got great news. Things came out just like we wanted."

"Perfect. Tell Valentino he's one skillful S.O.B."

"You mean lucky S.O.B. If he fucked that shit up I would've killed the bastard."

"Kind of harsh, but you 'gotta do what you 'gotta do, right?"

104

"You know it."

"Hey, 'told you Dean was our guy, huh? Stupid fuck."

"I'll remember next time to trust your judgment without hesitation."

"Yeah? 'You know why you trust me? Because I'm trustworthy. It's all falling together now. Let's not screw it up."

"Never."

"Alright then, Ray, listen. I gotta go. That shipment from SA came in a little early."

"Sure thing, Tom. Bye."

"Bye." Thomas hung up first and then Ray let the phone slide from his grip. He was frowning when he should have been smiling which was never a good sign. Putting the phone on its cradle he leaned back as far as the chair would go. Unlike the yellow tangs in the fish tank he could recall specific memories and some of them were ones he would rather forget.

Ray was sitting on one of the low walls near the side of the building with two of his friends. He was barely thirteen and just starting to hate school and other things with a passion. Things changed in a dramatic way that day, when he saw his eleven year old brother traipsing across the playground some way away. Thomas was alone and didn't look so hot. He was wiping his face with his sleeve and his head was down.

Ray jumped down from the wall and jogged to him.

"Tom?"

When he got there he was shocked to see that Thomas had a black eye and a bleeding nose.

"What the fuck?!" He grabbed Thomas by the shoulders. His brother had clearly been crying at some point and had wiped away the tears.

"Tom! Tell me what happened. Who did this to you? Who was it?! Was it that fucking Corman kid again?!"

Corman was a classmate who, one year ago, had tripped Thomas up in the lunch hall and in return, Ray had tripped him up on a flight of stairs and put him in hospital for two weeks. An accident as it was concluded by the clueless principal.

Thomas stared at him vacantly. Ray got angry and shook him.

"Who did it, Tommy?! Tell me!" he yelled. His idiot friends were a few paces away now and could tell what was going on. Thomas wiped his face again and then said in a quiet but defiant voice, "Charlie Strouvelle."

Without another word to his brother, Ray walked away towards the area of the blacktop where the eighth graders played basketball. Charlie Strouvelle was a basketball fiend during gym so Ray knew where he was. Behind him, he heard his friends following, and talking excitedly.

"Hey! Ray's going to beat the shit out of someone again!"

Ray ignored them. Only one thing was clear in his mind. He was going to mess up Charlie's face. Mess it up so bad that he wouldn't dare go out without wearing a ski mask. The expression on his own face was enough to make younger kids stare as he stalked through the crowds of people. There was a game in progress as Ray stepped onto the court. He saw Charlie, smiling as he called for the ball. The blonde prick was about the same size as Ray and probably more muscular, but he had never had a real fight with anyone who wasn't younger than him.

Before one of the players passed, Ray snatched the ball away and continued walking towards Charlie who now saw him and had one of those sick looks on his face. He hadn't thought of this when he had punched Thomas twice because he walked on the court and was now *wondering what he was going to do. The kid's brother was a psycho freak that most people stayed away from.*

"You think you're real funny, Charlie, huh? Is it funny now?!"

With a lot of force, Ray threw the ball at him. He wasn't prepared for it and the impact broke his nose. He fell backwards onto the floor holding his face and making exclamations of flaring agony. Ray didn't stop there. It wasn't over yet. He jumped onto the crippled form and started punching him in the face over and over again. A huge crowd had now gathered. Almost everyone was drawn to the fight like ants to a dropped sugar cube. Through the punches, Charlie could be heard pleading for Ray to stop and apologizing, but Ray didn't stop. He just kept punching. He broke Charlie's jaw and blackened both of his eyes. His face was covered in blood and the only thing the boy could think of was why his friends weren't helping him. Nobody intervened. In fact, Ray's two cohorts cheered him on.

When Charlie's face was sufficiently pulped and teeth were circling the pool of blood in his mouth, Ray punched him hard in the throat making him cough it all up over himself. Just then, two strong arms hauled Ray away. If they hadn't, he might just have killed the boy. The next day, he was formally expelled and had to attend a different school, feeling extremely lucky that he hadn't done time in juve. Thomas came with him.

Ray never let anyone get away with hurting Thomas. His brother wasn't exactly an outcast, but he was always such an easy target and the amount of times he got wailed on and never told Ray for obvious reasons were plentiful. What Ray had been trying to prevent became apparent in Thomas too fast for him to keep track of. He became hateful towards people just like his brother. This resulted in Ray getting angrier about everything and becoming more hateful himself. His last years of education had been lonely. People kept away from him for fear of being put in hospital if Ray became stressed, but he got by, hating the world a little more each day.

Ray and Thomas were born to a mother and a father who didn't have much time for them and the results of their neglect were evident to anyone willing to look. Fortunately, they did find some true company with their uncle. Though their mother discouraged contact with her only brother, whom she blamed for all the problems in her past, she could not prevent him from giving Ray and Thomas their future.

Giovanni Trapenzi was the head honcho of an old L.A. crime syndicate looking at its final years, with their Godfather unable to have children and nobody else willing to replace him. He cared a whole lot more about them than their parents did and soon he was Ray's only family. In adulthood, Ray became a respectable member of the organization and was unable to stop his brother from following in his footsteps despite the desire for Thomas to have a better life. Whatever happened, Ray always had one thing in mind. He wanted it all for himself. Viewed by his uncle as the intelligent, uncaring criminal he was, the old man named him as his successor a few days before his fatal stroke.

The Trapenzi family had ended. The line was dead. Ray Bentley tore down the walls and carved what was left of the relatively small organization into his vision. He murdered the creditors who were trying to seize the syndicate's holdings. He preyed upon disenfranchised and vulnerable thugs to make up his elite. He made his own rules and didn't take an ounce of shit from anybody.

Of course, certain benefactors had helped with financing purchases such as the Holden Tower. Benefactors Ray didn't like to think about. Benefactors, who if Ray fitted into one of his childish fish analogies would be much bigger than even him.

He rubbed his thigh just above his kneecap. The only time he had ever been shot. There was a strange, sharp withdrawal like he was afraid of being caught doing something bad.

It was without doubt that the men who had invested in him were dangerous and they had proven it, but he didn't care about any of that. It was trivial. A means to an end.

With his brother at his side, he had begun the process of bringing his own dream into reality. A dream where his was the name people feared. A dream where everybody was forced to listen to what he had to say. A dream where nobody said no.

CHAPTER EIGHTEEN
AFTERMATH

Dean opened one eye. Things dimmed then became bright again. Then dimmed then became bright again. His lungs were full of smoke. He coughed and felt a burning pain in his chest. Was he still alive? Something told him yes. Did he still have his extremities? He looked down and was relieved, not only because his head didn't slide off of his shoulders, but because he had both arms and legs and wasn't on fire. The table had shielded him from the blast. A good move there on his part. His head was throbbing like the skull had ruptured and blood was being forced through his scalp. What was more he kept seeing blue dots. Big paint splatters on the coating of his eyeballs.

The case was there too. Shades walked past not even recognizing Dean's presence. Valentino gave him a worried look.

The images faded to black and he came to his senses. He stood up and peered over the table at what was left of the billiard room. Devastation. Flames tangoed in the stale air the debris of the furniture their stage.

He hauled himself to his feet and put a protective arm over his mouth to keep the smoke out. Nothing was recognizable anymore. It was all destroyed. Dodging the flames, Dean made it to the doorway. The din of emergency vehicles could be heard not too far off now. 'Had to get away before they found him. That was all he knew.

On the floor a few feet ahead were the char-grilled and still alight bodies of the yakuza. One of the goons from Red Dawn lay further down the hall with a large table leg through his stomach. Dean had no sympathy for the man and walked past him. Instead of heading for the way he came in, he thought a window a more optimal choice and found it some way down the corridor.

Escape from the building wasn't hard when he compared it to the fact that he had just survived an explosion that was no doubt intended to kill him. It had been a suicide mission. They had used him.

Fleeing from the hotel, Dean looked for a place to stop and think things over, which would be hard due to a sudden migraine he had developed. Coughing again he checked his pocket and found his phone still intact. That was lucky. It had cost him a small fortune. Taking refuge in an alleyway not far from the tail end of the motel and blockaded at one end by a chain link fence, Dean leaned himself up against a wall and slowly began to clear his lungs of the smoke.

The bastards had tried to kill him, literally used him as a pawn in their game, and much like a pawn, he was disposable. Everyone, Ray, Thomas, Valentino. They had all deceived him. For a moment he thought of Williams, but cast the suspicion aside. His friend wasn't like that. It had been his employer who had deceived him. There had been no escape route. He was sent in to the dead end of the motel while Valentino's men had closed the trap on the yakuza.

Before he could process any more he threw up violently all over the concrete. Thinking of what to do next was hard. Really hard. So many things came at him at once, but at the core of everything was one emotion. Hatred. Strong hatred. So much hatred he could strangle the last breath out of Ray Bentley. They wouldn't get away with it. He wasn't going to let them. He was going to kill them all. They'd be sorry. They'd all be sorry.

111

Dean threw up some more. His chest burnt, and his mouth was slicked with the stinging taste of acid and abandonment. It was only then that he realized his face was peeling like he had been in the sun too long. It was no wonder. The room would have been a furnace when the bomb went off. Thomas's bomb. He would kill him too. He was going to kill him slow and make sure he enjoyed every second of it. Just then a strange and misplaced longing for Yuki hit him from nowhere. He couldn't go back to her yet. Not yet. Not like this. His emotions were out of control. If he went running to his safe haven now he would walk through the door as the Dean Cottrell who killed people. The Dean Cottrell who was so bitter he could kill whoever pissed him off next. He didn't want her to see that man. Not ever. He would call and tell her that something had come up and he might not see her for a while. God, everything was crumbling around him and it was all their fault!

Noticing some flecks of ash on his red tie, Dean brushed them off. Though his suit had been relatively undamaged, it was covered in a thin layer of dust and would have to be cleaned. He couldn't believe that thought even went through his head.

Sirens blared through the air along with shouting and what was no doubt the gushing sound of fire hoses. He could barely think with the noise and to think was what he needed most. 'Needed to plan what he was going to do. He was going to get revenge, but that was something that seemed insurmountable now. There were so many questions and no answers to match them to. Time was essential. He needed to find a good motel. Hopefully one that wasn't on Ray Bentley's 'to-bomb' list, and he had to do it fast.

The sheets of the bed were crinkled, but had a homely feel.

112

Dean had had no trouble finding a good roost after a short and stealthy trip from the Starcross Motel. This one was less tacky, but smaller, like a trucker outpost.

Room twenty-eight. One thing in his mind. Killing.

He desired Ray Bentley's soul with such ardor that he was currently willing to take it by any means necessary. He wondered how long he would feel this, concluding that the need would not subside until the deed had been done. He not only wanted to kill Ray in the end, but he wanted the man's empire to come crashing down around his ears. To destroy him inside. He wanted those who Ray relied on for support to be snuffed out.

For some reason Dean kept worrying about his car and then remembering that it was parked at a private lot. He and the others had been picked up directly by the driver of the van. Dean had his gun on him and his sniper rifle sat in the trunk of his BMW.

At least he wasn't at a huge disadvantage. He still had a fair amount of money stored in his bank accounts not to mention his advantage of anonymity. That was something Dean had thought of immediately. By all accounts, as far as Red Dawn was concerned, Dean was a flash-fried corpse. Ray would probably not give him a second thought, and Dean was pretty sure Valentino would have far too much on his hands to watch the rescue teams extracting bodies from the place. There was something in 'The Art of War' about suffering defeat if you didn't know your enemy, so if Chinese military literature was anything to go by, Ray had a lot to be worried about

He got up and went over to the window. It was closing in on the 17th of November now. It was starting to get late and outside leaves weaved through the air currents on a light breeze. People had only just started to prepare for the colder temperatures that lay ahead as the hot and humid environment faded. At present, it didn't look like the upcoming winter would bring snow like it apparently had in

1962; however they were in for an unusually cold back end of the year according to meteorologists. Dean couldn't help but feel that the warm morning he had experienced would be the last for a long time, both inside and out.

All of a sudden Dean remembered Williams saying something to him after he had picked off Yoshikuni from an office block.

"Plus, it seems like he's looking for alliances with a new triad base of operations in New York. 'Got a meeting with some big shot on the 19th. Helix Hotel. 'Looks like Ray's throwing his money around."

It was remarkably sobering to remember his friend's voice after all that had happened.

The 19th. Ray was going to try and gain allies in the east to bolster his position of power. There was no doubt that he wanted to go completely national and perhaps multinational with not only his operations, but some sort of physical presence as well. The triads were an almost perfect ally for him. Relations between them and the yakuza were shaky at the moment and some sectors of the main organizations were now splinter groups. They would also provide a useful connection to the Far East, which was essential for drug operations. Ray thought he was being smart about his moves, but unbeknownst to him, the mob boss had made a prodigious mistake. He had tried to kill Dean.

The 19th. That was when he would stab the Red Dawn while its back was turned. A knife in the dark. A knife that could not possibly be held because a dead man can't wield a blade.

His main aim wasn't to kill Ray there and then. He would put that on the shelf for a while. He wanted to relish the man's discomfort and to cause that; he would first make relations between Red Dawn and the triads impossible. Then he would move on to more personal things…

114

Dean had the sniper rifle in the trunk of his car, which happened to be close to his current location, but for a long distance massacre through the obligatory, large window of a pre-booked meeting room, he felt that he would need something with a little more kick.

CHAPTER NINETEEN
A NEW RIFLE

Dean hugged his recently purchased jacket to his form as he traversed the street. Maybe he had underestimated Mother Nature. The change in temperature was extremely violent for somewhere like California. Pathetic fallacy was the term that Dean was thinking about. A storm was coming in the next couple of weeks or sooner and in a way, it reflected Dean's aspirations to strike Ray Bentley at his core right after he had pissed away the man's chances of adding the triads to his wall of people he could double cross in the future.

His phone call to Yuki the previous night had been an agonizing one. She was worried at first, but he calmed her down and told her that things had become very complicated at work and that his boss was in some serious trouble (which was no lie). He had however, been forced to lie in the end telling her that he could not see such an honorable man sink and had to be away for a couple of days to stabilize things. Any other woman would have probably huffed and hung up, but Yuki accepted it and then told him how she was thinking about wedding preparations which lifted his spirits instantly. He had almost forgotten that his significant other had recently become his fiancée. After that, he had hung up and fallen asleep dreaming of her. In his mind she fended off the bad thoughts. The bad thoughts that in his sleep he was unprepared for.

'*Big Bob's Sports Store*' could definitely have been named more accurately. Something along the lines of '*Big Bob's Gun Store Where You Can Also Buy Fishing Gear*' would have been closer to the truth. Dean had only ever bought a gun once and that had been one hell of a long time ago. His Beretta and sniper rifle had been supplied by Red Dawn demonstrating their '*good will*'.

Dean pushed the door open. It was about three in the afternoon. Not gun shopping time for most enthusiasts it seemed. The store was empty. Even the counter was deserted.

His eyes flew over two display racks noticing fishing poles, harpoon launchers and Kevlar helmets as he approached.Running his fingers over the countertop he let out a cold breath and scanned the guns that lined the wall, very much out of reach. He could not identify all of them, but he recognized quite a few. A modified SAR 21. Two M4 Carbines. What looked like a PGM UR Intervention. A now discontinued, Franchi SPAS-12 and even a single replica of the legendary, but never circulated, Pancor Jackhammer that was probably more for show than anything else. Looking down Dean saw that a thick, glass plate in the wood covered a modern-looking pistol. It had a flashlight and a laser sight and looked very attractive, but that wasn't what Dean had come for.

Slapping the head of a gold bell instigated some shuffling from the doorway behind the counter. A man who Dean presumed was the aforementioned 'Big Bob' appeared stepping out to serve him. The salesman was wearing an outfit that could only be described as 'casual safari' and looked to be in his very late forties. He had an almost completely bald head ringed by a small amount of well-kept golden-gray hair. A walrus mustache sat proudly atop his mouth and his eyes were watery stone.

"Afternoon, friend. What is it I can help you with?" He rested his stretched arms on the counter like balance struts on a fire engine.

"A gun," Dean said firmly. He injected his eyeballs with a look that said he meant business, but was by no means a threat to the shopkeeper who smiled warmly.

"I didn't think you a fisherman. What kind of cannon 'you looking for. Pistols, semi-auto conversions, shotguns?"

Dean tried to identify the man's accent and narrow it down to a single state, but didn't have much luck. It was deep and possibly had a hint of German hidden in it, but only a hint. Pennsylvania perhaps.

"Listen, I need something... special."

"Oh?" A mischievous smile spread across the mustachioed face and a hushed tone ensued. "Something special, huh? You're looking for an automatic bitch."

Dean had never heard a gun called a bitch or a whore or anything similar. Williams used to call his old car a bitch and Dean had no idea why objects were almost always female, a gun especially.

"You catch on quickly, Mr. Bob."

"Any assault rifle you can see here I've got in fully automatic mode just out back. I also have a nice selection of machine guns if you really mean business."

"I mean serious business. I'm searching for something specific. I need as close as I can get to a fully automatic sniper rifle for long distance, heavy put-down." Dean felt the time had come to cut to the chase.

The shopkeeper raised an eyebrow and for a second, Dean thought a sneer had started at the corners of his lips.

"An automatic sniper rifle? I don't think there's even a government license that'll get you one of those."

Dean was prepared for this. Every man had a price and gun salesmen were not people who usually occupied the moral high ground. From his jacket he pulled two, sizable elastic band wrapped wads of cash, fresh with the smell of the bank. Big Bob stared at them. It was a large sum. More than this customer would need to buy any gun currently in view.

"How's that for a license?"

For a moment the shopkeeper hesitated, then he leaned in a few inches closer.

"Follow me," he said quietly. Grabbing the cash from the counter he headed right, flipped up the partition and disappeared through the door. Dean slipped through behind the counter following Big Bob into his cave of wonders.

It was a den with enough firepower to level Cuba. Guns lined the wall like plaster. Dean even spied a couple of rocket launchers he was sure weren't legal. Something rested on a dusty table in the middle of the stone room covered by a gray sheet. Stacks of metal, army style crates sat in a corner a silver case on top of them - open revealing eight grenades in Styrofoam cups.

Big Bob rounded the table as Dean stared around trying to take it all in. He had never seen so many firearms in one place.

"'Knew someone like you would show up sooner or later. 'Got this baby off a friend of a friend. I think she'll do your job just fine."

He ripped the sheet from a beauty of a weapon that would make any gun enthusiast drool. Dean got closer to marvel at it.

"Meet the ARI-90. Close to fresh off of the assembly line. French company, Aiser International is behind this monster. 'Hasn't been circulated officially yet, but there are a few out there. The bitch will rip through a chest cavity no problem. Think of her like a cross between the M1919 and the AR-10. She's got a beast of a telescopic sight with illumination capability. 'Holds one hundred, 30 caliber rounds in the drum. Adjustable stock and... after nights of fine work I've managed to muzzle her with this." Big Bob held up a large cylindrical object that had been lying next to the gun.

119

She was sleek, black, with all the details that the now quite animated gun salesman had described. The sight was tinted green and the magazine was a large drum, much deeper than that of a Tommy gun. If old, it would not have been so beautiful, but its pristine state made it the most gorgeous rifle Dean had ever laid eyes on. He ran a hand over the jutting barrel supported by a bipod and suddenly realized why you might compare a gun to a woman.

"It's perfect," he said finally. Looking up he realized Big Bob was leafing through all the bills he had handed him.

"'Comes with a case and an extra drum. I can get more when you run out and need to use it again, although it might take a few days. Easy disassembly much like any other rifle. She's a fucking beauty."

Dean was tempted to bring up the fact that mere seconds ago Big Bob had referred to the ARI-90 as a bitch, a whore and a monster, but didn't. Instead he kept his eyes on the cash that the salesman was seemingly very satisfied with. It was easily enough to cover buying a gun like this with extra for the fact that Big Bob was breaking the law by selling it to him. In fact, owning the gun was probably breaking the law.

"I'll take her. How's my credit here?"

Big Bob smiled at him as he totaled up in his head.

"She's all yours."

It was the night before the 19th. In the time since Dean had bought the rifle he had occasionally gone out to his car (which was now parked at the motel) and looked at it, considering, calculating. Now, he was less than a day away from the big event the first link in the chain of his revenge against Ray. However, on this particular night it was Ray who came to Dean in his dreams and even thoughts of his fiancée could not block him out.

Dean struggled to pull himself from the black sand that sucked at him, trying to drag him under. Ahead of him a man ascended a flight of stairs towards a red light.

"No!" yelled Dean. With almighty effort he hauled himself out of the pit and onto the first step. He panted. The aching seemed so real to him: the sense of desperation and hopelessness. The shadowed figure climbed further and further away at a steady pace.

"No!" Dean cried out again. He brought himself up onto two feet and tried to follow the shadow up the stairs. He got close. Almost close enough to grab his shoulder then was forced to stop. The unmistakable shape of Thomas Bentley's body lay sprawled on the dark staircase.

Blood, bright crimson contrasting terribly with the inky shadow pooled on the step near his head and flowed down onto the ones below. Dean shook the image away. The figure was ahead again. The red light was a doorway at the top of the staircase. Darkness enveloped everything.

Dean ran this time, straining every muscle he could to try and stop the figure from getting to the light. Again, he was cruelly halted just before he could get close enough, but this time it was more horrifying than he could imagine.

A shadow with a red tie. No features. No clothing bar the tie. No eyes. No mouth. A pitch imitation of Lysander Shades' haircut. The figure grabbed him by the collar and threw him back.

He damn near broke his neck on the stairs and rolled over before coming to a stop on his front. He looked up. Shades was gone. The strange smell of fine wine like Dean sometimes drank filled his nostrils along with the smell of decaying flesh. He turned his head. He tried to scream, but could not. In place of Thomas was Yuki, not shadowed at all. Her body was very real. Blood streaked her face. Her eyes were dead. All of a sudden something grabbed Dean's leg

121

violently. He turned and looked down. Another crawling apparition in a red tie was pulling him back down the stairs. He tried to break free, but his attempt was futile. Looking up again he saw the first shadow was now at the doorway, arms spread out in the red light and now Dean knew who it was. Ray Bentley.

He was dragged backwards, now under the charcoal colored mannequin that assaulted him with its snaky arms. His eyes took in the face of a dead man. Dean could not even think about what the thing looked like, but it was dead. So dead, but very much alive at the same time. A gun was raised to his skull; the cold barrel's touch fully opening his eyes to the hellish vision that had engulfed his world. His breathing slowed.

"Nothing ever changes."

Dean awoke to the sound of the gunshot in his mind.

A single tear rolled down his cheek. He had no clue whether it was one of sadness or pure fear. That had been his worst nightmare and he had had his fair share of bad ones.

A very light shower streaked down his window. Things were so unstable at the moment he didn't know what to think; 'didn't know whether he was being a fool or not; 'didn't know what that dream had meant. Even the shivers now performing their dance along his back seemed alien, although he had experienced them so many times prior to that night. Everything had changed. He couldn't pretend it would go back to how it was before. He had been cast out, and dealing with that reality was in some ways the hardest part.

In spite of all the turmoil, he knew that he had to ignore it all. He had one purpose and couldn't stop, or the strange world he now resided in would swallow him whole like a raging ocean. Now was the time to apply the game face. Now was the time to discover just how much vengeance he could channel, and now was the time to teach Ray Bentley that it didn't matter how dangerous *he* could be, Dean was more dangerous still. By the end, Ray would regret his betrayal. He would wish he could go back and change his mind. He would wish he had picked a more surefire way to kill the man who would become his downfall.

CHAPTER TWENTY
THE 19TH

The room that Ray Bentley had pre-booked for the 19th at the Helix Hotel was a fine piece of art indeed. The hotel itself was relatively new and in addition to having many overpriced, luxurious rooms where honeymooners could spend long nights. It also was home to several spaces that were specifically tailored for business meetings where potential partners could discuss things over a table and enjoy doing just that. These rooms ringed the hotel's structure on the thirty-second floor. Apparently, discussing profit forecasts was more interesting with a good view of Santa Monica.

At present Ray had very little interest in the view. He was seated on a comfortable cream couch, hunched over with his elbows on his knees, holding his head. The room was exactly what he needed. He had not wanted a long mahogany table with everyone sat around. He simply required a chilled environment with a mini-bar and a place where they could just sit and talk. Ideally, he would have wanted Valentino there with him, but the deal wasn't the only thing on the to-do list and his advisor was needed elsewhere.

Ray turned to half-look at his brother who was admiring a piece of art on one of the bamboo green walls.

They were nine, all appropriately dressed; himself, his brother, Shades, Gordon and five of his high-level goons. Ray anticipated that Jun Heng would bring a similar number. The yakuza, not the triads were the ones who usually overestimated how many men to put in the wagon.

"Say, boss. If we're gonna land this deal what's the organization bringing to the table?"

Ray turned. Shades was behind the bar violently mixing liquids in a cocktail shaker. In response Ray pulled a case from its position beside him and set it down atop the surface before opening it.

"Four million. It's a small price to pay for what I want," he said flippantly.

The case was too small to hold that amount in dollar bills. The cash was in a stack of bearer bonds. Shades raised an eyebrow and filled a glass to the brim with the pink elixir he had concocted.

"That sure is a lot of mazuma in that there case boss. Just what makes the chinks that important, huh?" He sipped at the drink obviously content with the taste.

Ray gazed at the case thoughtfully for a moment and before he could answer his brother cut him off.

"Why so many questions, Shades? Something on your mind?"

"I believe that's two questions Tommy boy." Shades came around the bar drink in hand and stood confidently on the laminate flooring while Thomas came closer to Ray and stared at his redneck henchman with hateful eyes.

"I'm just curious. 'Already had enough trouble with those of the narrow-eyed variety. 'Not quite sure why we need to associate ourselves with a ragtag group of yellows."

It wasn't uncommon to hear Shades spouting racial slurs. Ray knew the guy was a confederate through and through. He wore a suit and could kill a man without a pickup truck, but he was a poster child for the worst side of the Deep South and it showed. He was as bitter as Ray himself and the fact that he took it out on those of foreign ethnicity didn't bother Ray in the slightest. People could

125

believe whatever they wanted for all he cared, however right now he wasn't in the mood. He put the case back on the floor.

"Shades... Shut the fuck up. This is important. We get the triads in our pocket and it opens up one big fucking door."

"Yeah, well, if anything funny or even mildly amusing occurs... I'll liquefy the sons of bitches."

"I'd expect nothing less." Ray closed the case and smiled jovially at the assassin.

A phone on the wall started to ring and one of the Red Dawn henchmen answered it to find that they would soon be receiving their guests.

"They're on their way up."

Ray immediately shot a look at Gordon who was standing against a wall with his arms clasped together as usual. The old bodyguard nodded and opened the door to the room, stepping out into the hallway. Ray then turned urgently to his henchmen who were standing behind the couch, scattered between the mini-bar and the wall in which the door was set.

"No sudden movements unless a weapon comes out. You keep the guns away and play nice. Unless a shot is fired you don't pull the trigger, understand?" he said in a hushed tone. Most of the men nodded robotically.

Thomas took up position right behind his brother, placing both hands on the back of the couch. They gave each other reassuring looks and just as they had drawn strength from one another in their youth, they did the same now.

When Jun Heng showed up from the elevator he and his men were ushered in by Gordon and Ray quickly counted ten men. One more than he had. He logged that piece of information for later analysis. Jun Heng himself was a smiley figure with a shaved head and was wearing what looked like an expensive navy suit. His

126

henchmen were dressed similarly and took up residence on the other side of the room in a haphazard formation. Ray had heard from Valentino that they called their enforcers 'Red Poles', yet he had no idea why. Perhaps they were all half Polish, or maybe they beat their enemies to death with red poles. Did people do that? On cue, Ray got up to shake the hand of the man he wanted to see and was warmly received.

Now he sat opposite the triad boss and a man who appeared to be his accounting advisor. A small guy with horn-rimmed glasses and greasy hair.

"Mr. Bentley, we are honored by this arrangement."

"Oh, it's no trouble at all. We're glad you could join us"

"I am a direct man, Mr. Bentley. I would like to get straight down to business if possible. As we understand it you are looking at our branch as a potential investment partner."

With an overly chipper demeanor, Ray mulled over his first impressions about Jun Heng. He was direct and had a mean streak. People who had smiles like that always had a mean streak.

"Mr. Heng, we have a lot of things in motion right now. My organization specialist, Valentino, can't join us today to get in depth; however I think that working together we can help secure control over the drug import market for California. 'Tall order, but a few days ago the man behind the yakuza operations here in L.A. fell victim to a rather unfortunate explosion at a motel in the city."

Both men grinned at each other enjoying the humor of ambiguity.

"The Tagliano Crime Family, one of the big hitters here are also close to breaking thanks to me."

"A successful businessman. I respect that. How have you managed to weaken Tagliano?"

"I'm currently moving in on their operations. With only one man steering the family their warehouses are falling like dominoes."

127

Fuck Shades and whatever he thought. Jun Heng seemed to be a likeminded professional who Ray predicted he would enjoy working with.

"And what of the Gambino Family. Are they pulling out of the West Coast?"

Thomas came around the couch and answered the question for Ray.

"The Gambino Family have no allies. They aren't posing any threat, but they aren't shutting down their rackets either. They seem to be under the assumption that if they don't get involved with us we'll leave them to their own devices."

"A foolish move on their part," Ray finished. He was giving Heng confidence in the Red Dawn. The man needed to be convinced that they were major players and not just one hit wonders. There were a few brief seconds of silence that to Ray seemed to last for hours.

"Mr. Bentley. I understand that your organization is advancing quickly and it would be foolish on my part to turn down an offer of alliance, however..."

Ray knew this was coming. He could have anticipated it at the age of ten. Heng needed money and held his own organization in very high regard. A pact of common interest was going to need payola to get the ball rolling.

"Things have not been going as well in the east as they have here. For one, my operations in New York are under scrutiny from NYPD. Last week alone I lost four shipments of heroin. We are at never-ending war with the yakuza. My own men even seem liable to desert me at times. Our profits are down, and we have lost a lot of territory in the south. You can see my dilemma Mr. Bentley. In Honk Kong things are slow. The government is still trying to shut us down. I think you know that our alliance could be a huge breakthrough for both parties, but I am forced to require remuneration. You understand."

128

Ray nodded understandingly and put the case onto the table. He opened it and slid it over the surface for the mob boss to get a good look. Heng then said something in either Mandarin or Cantonese (Ray couldn't tell the difference) to his advisor who withdrew one of the papers, holding it up to the light. He adjusted his glasses and Ray guessed he was an expert in spotting fakes. Heng was a careful man. Again, another plus for his potential partner.

"Four million dollars in bearer bonds. You hold them, you own them."

Thomas spoke up again to bolster Ray.

"Untraceable. No records of their possessors. We use them for big deals. 'Makes things easier. Think of them like…"

"I know what a bearer bond is." Heng shot Thomas a look that Ray could not identify. His accountant who was leafing through the stack of bonds (presumably counting them), said something else and he and his boss had a short conversation before Heng slowly turned his head to Ray. A look of contentedness was evident, but Ray could see that behind it was a lot of excitement. The man seemingly needed the money quite desperately for some venture or another. Much like the Tagliano's had needed Ray's friendship. Hopefully, Heng would not find himself meeting a similar fate.

For a moment he became distracted and began to daydream. He saw in his head the triads swimming before him, bright, colorful fins and flashing scales, the dangerous, oriental criminals as fish in his tank. The more he owned, the bigger the tank became until the glass would crack and he would flood everything as far as the eye could see. Flood the cities and the screaming lungs of everyone in his way and stain the sun red with the bloodied sea of his…

"The deal is good."

129

Ray was refocused by Heng's voice and shivered slightly. The shiver was not caused by the sudden awakening from a daydream. It came as an animal sensing that something was about to happen.

That was when the huge window exploded.

CHAPTER TWENTY-ONE
SHOOT 'EM UP

Through the green hue of the enhanced vision, Dean counted targets. All were in view. Ray and his brother, the triad boss and the man next to him, Shades, the old body guard, a selection of five goons from Red Dawn and eight from the triads. Surprised that Valentino wasn't there, Dean only had two men he would try not to kill: Thomas and Ray, ironically the people that deserved it the most. Nobody else was safe. Even Shades could die. Dean had no qualms about killing that particular S.O.B.

The events that had taken place to get him to where he was now (lying on his front on a bed next to the window of a hotel room with a rifle pointed in Ray's direction) were too mind-taxing to think of.

The hotel in which he resided was not face-to-face with the one his targets were in. It was across two roads and a stretch of small businesses. He had been to the Helix prior to Ray's arrival and found out from the concierge whose names were on the business floor rooms that day. Dean had gotten the information he needed and hadn't even had to present I.D. After that, he had checked himself into a corresponding room in another hotel within range, opened a window, moved the bed and watched things unfold.

"'Got you now, motherfucker," he muttered. It was hard to resist pumping a few rounds into Ray's head there and then. He was vulnerable. So very vulnerable and oblivious to the fact that the crosshairs were on him. With calculated accuracy he targeted the chest of one of the triad men who was leant up against a wall.

They would pay. They would all pay.

The window shattered immediately as a hail of bullets forced their way through. One of Heng's men convulsed as the rounds passed through him and into the wall behind.

He fell to the floor, dead.

No.

Ray could not believe it. How had that happened? Was it possible? But who? Why? Thomas was staring wide eyed at the body, too stunned to react. Before a second could pass, Heng yelled something in his own language and from his tone of voice, Ray could guess what it meant.

"NO! WAIT!!!" he screamed, but it was too late.

A triad withdrew a revolver and sent a shot the way of one of Ray's men. It punched through the base of the glass he was drinking from and then blew off the back of his head.

He fell with a thud and Ray took the cue to duck down below the table line. Gunfire filled the air around them.

The accountant and Heng himself also ducked to let their goons fight it out.

Shades, who would not refrain from saying "I told you so", if they got out of this, threw a knife at one of the triads before diving behind the couch. It sliced its target's throat wide open and writhing, he dropped his gun to rip the knife out. Blood splashed all over the wall and he subsequently hit the deck.

One of Ray's men was laying down heavy fire with a magnum from the cover of the bar and with a few shots, another triad was felled. The fire from the outside source began again and Gordon was plastered to the wall, a wretched expression on his old face.

"SHIT!" yelled one of the Red Dawn thugs.

Thomas made a run for it, but saw that one of the Asians had clocked him with a pistol. He reflexively grabbed one of his own men to use as a human shield, and the round ripped a hole in the new target's chest sending both of them flying to the floor.

"FUCKING KILL 'EM!" Shades hollered at the goon by the coach letting rip with his own gun, but before he could respond a stray bullet blew apart the end of the man's foot and splattered the floor with red. He fell back, shrieking and a return gunshot he managed to let off hit another one of Heng's men in the crotch area taking him down in a cacophony of pain. A few rounds towards the writhing figure on the floor silenced Ray's wounded man.

More shots from the unknown source.

The man behind the mini-bar was taken out.

Two more triads fell.

Trying to avoid getting shot, Heng yelled to his accountant over the noise.

"GRAB THE BONDS!"

The man nodded in return.

Standing up from behind the couch Shades fired with one of his guns, forcing the two remaining triad thugs to duck for cover. Rapid fire barely missed the back of his head as he rounded the couch on the window side. He hit the floor with a grunt, the bullets poking holes in the table. For a moment, Shades thought he had been deafened by the chaos, until he heard Heng yelling again.

"GRAB IT NOW!"

"NO!" Unable to do anything, face pressed against the couch in an uncomfortable position, Ray tried to turn. Why was this happening?

The accountant reached over the table, not really looking because he didn't want to put his head in the line of fire. He groped for the case, but accidentally closed it and knocked it onto the floor. The

133

Chinese curses he yelled fell to anguished yelps as, in a risky move; Shades violently reached up and stabbed one of his throwing knives through the money man's hand, its blade protruding under the table. Crimson started to soak the surface. The accountant vehemently tried to pull his hand free, causing horrible pain and more screams.

Ray finally managed to maneuver himself and saw the case on the floor, not far from reach. He grabbed at it; however Heng was already onto him. The Asian mobster managed to get a hold on the handle and then continued to awkwardly kick Ray in the face and chest, making him retreat.

"AHHH! FUCK!" The anger at the situation was more than Ray could cope with.

Shades was now under the table, the triad accountant wailing and thrashing about to his right. His movements were those of a cockroach scuttling quickly to pursue Heng who was almost up on his feet ready to make a mad dash for the door with the case of bearer bonds.

Ringing cracks and gun smoke still permeated the atmosphere. The triad enforcers overcame what Ray had left and his two remaining thugs crashed down against each other. Before they could do anything else the rapid fire was upon them and the first man was torn to shreds, falling into the arms of his partner who's head was then carved into something closely resembling a jack-o-lantern by a couple of 30 cal. rounds.

Heng ran for it.

Shades lashed out with a blade.

"AAAAAAAAAAAAAHHHHHHH!!!" Jun Heng fell to the floor on his belly almost immediately. The Achilles tendon on his left foot had been sliced cleanly in two just above his shoe and below his pants. A torrent of blood was unleashed and Shades foolishly put a hand in it for support and slipped in the most maladroit, childish way possible.

Now in plain view on the floor Heng's back was reduced to a bloody mess by the secret gunman. His eyes went glassy and a mixture of leaked internal fluids dripped from his horrified mouth as yet another crime lord perished in L.A.

That was it. Shades could live… for now. Tricky bastard.

With automatic and pre-practiced efficiency, Dean ripped the bipod off of the rifle, its silenced barrel smoking like… well, he supposed Big Bob might have said something like 'a Brooklyn whore'. He disassembled the rifle and fitted each piece into the case. The man had been right. The assembly was in some ways easier than his usual rifle. This baby was a keeper.

He was counting on Ray to be able to get himself out of the building fast. If he was in jail then it would be harder to get to him in the end. From what Dean had seen Thomas wasn't dead, which was perfect for what he had planned for the fucker. At his end, Dean would have no trouble getting out of his hotel all thanks to Big Bob's toiling over a suppressor. He had avoided looking directly at cameras within the hotel and it would take the eggheads at the police department over a week to realize that his shots had come from someone who hadn't been in the room. Unfortunately for Ray, the skills Dean had honed within the organization would now be used against it, and they had not diminished in the slightest. The attack had gone almost exactly to plan. Thomas would have been proud.

"Is it clear?" Ray asked urgently. Shades had been in the line of fire for some time now, firmly believing the gunman had fled. He was right.

"I think we're good," he said.

Ray got up. Heng's accountant was groaning, trying to pull his hand off of the knife. He looked up at the now standing figure. In a moment of frustration, Ray pulled out his gun and blew apart the triad's head. Blood and an unidentified liquid spat out and hit him in the eye.

"Ah, fuck!" he hissed, smearing the mess across his face as he tried to rub it away. No wonder he always got other people to do the shooting.

"Tom? Tom?!" He came around the couch expecting the worst. There was no movement for a second, then a lifeless body was hauled aside by someone beneath. Thomas, who now had a large red stain on his suit, got up and brushed himself down. Ray nodded at him, yet couldn't smile. Looking around at the carnage, he realized how lucky he was to be alive. Shades was checking Gordon's pulse, but the old man was dead. He then swiftly recovered the knife on the table and the other on the floor.

"We've gotta get the fuck outta here," said Thomas, stating the obvious.

Snatching up the case of bearer bonds the three men exited into the hallway. An unarmed security guard was coming towards them from the direction of the elevator.

"Hey, you there! Stop!"

Shades didn't even pause before sending a kill shot his way as his boss casually straightened his suit. They all headed for the stairs that led to an emergency stairway exit and Ray noticed Thomas was holding his left hand as they went. Two of his fingers were bent hideously and he winced with the pain of movement.

"How the fuck did that happen?" enquired Ray as they descended the stairwell quickly with Shades leading, gun ready.

"When I fell. 'Got it twisted. Fuck, it hurts."

"Cry us a river," Shades muttered under his breath. Ray didn't hear him.

"We'll get it fixed, Tom, just as soon as we get back"

"Who the fuck, Ray? Who the fuck?" Thomas was still dazed from the events that had unfolded and he stumbled a little, his brother steadying him.

"I don't know. But when I find out... I'm gonna make them regret it."

CHAPTER TWENTY-TWO
WHO WAS IT?

"Gordon?"

"He didn't make it."

"Just you, Thomas and Shades?"

"Yeah."

Valentino stood with his arms folded in what served as a treatment room on one of the lower floors of the Holden Tower. Ray was having a small cut on his head treated by someone with medical knowledge, while a man with a little more experience was on the other side of the room trying to fix Thomas's fingers. Shades had been unharmed and was elsewhere, probably cleaning his knives. 'Had to be pristine for that asshole. Ray tried to calm down. It wasn't Shades' fault what had happened. In fact, he had helped in a lot of ways.

"Who was it?" Valentino asked, knowing that if Ray knew he would have told him by now.

"I don't know. If I knew don't you think I would've told you by now! Ow! Fuck! Be careful!" The man looking at his head took a double take. "But I wanna know. I wanna know who the fuck is responsible for this."

"So what happened exactly? You were meeting with Heng; things were going well and..."

"Someone packing automatic shot up the room through the exterior window." Ray's tone was heightened in a combination of anger and condescendence.

"I don't know who, I don't know how and I sure as shit don't know why! The triads let loose and the place turned into a bloodbath."

"But you got the money out, right?"

"I told you, yes!"

Valentino wasn't great at dealing with his boss when he was like this. He was difficult to deal with most of the time, so this situation was nightmarish.

"Someone's playing a game with me, Val. Someone knew exactly where I would be and tried to kill me! I wanna know who. I wanna know where they live and I wanna know who they are working for!" Ray's anger reached breaking point for a second.

"Okay, calm down. I'll look into it, but I think I have an idea." Valentino made calming hand gestures then Thomas's voice cut through the air like a knife from across the room.

"Then would you care to share with the rest of the class!" At that moment the man looking him over made his finger click loudly. "AH! FUCK!"

Valentino ignored him and focused his attention on Ray. As irrational as his boss was, the man's brother was a trial to even acknowledge.

"Look, we left bodies of our men at the Starcross Motel. Their corpses probably survived the fire and if so it wouldn't have been too hard for 'yakuza to put two and two together. Word of the meeting probably got around via some loudmouth, low-level jackass, and they put a hit out on you, but the point is you're alive. The plot failed. You, your brother and your trophy assassin got out. Everyone lives happily ever after."

"That's not how it works. 'They find out I'm still alive they're not going to stop after one attempt. I want them closed down, Valentino. I want the schedule brought forward. I want you to find Taiki's replacement and I want him whacked. Then you find the one who's going to stand in for him and you whack him! Whack 'em all!" Ray bubbled over again like a pot of water on the stove.

"There's one other possibility, Ray."

"What?"

"Tagliano. You killed his brother and his nephew. They've slowed, but they aren't in the ground yet. I'd put money on..."

"No."

Valentino was rudely cut off.

"It was the yakuza. We blitzed 'em on the 16th, they blitzed us on the 19th. We should have anticipated something like this. God damn it!"

Inside, Valentino was trying to calm the panic that had arisen within him. That had been a bona fide disaster. The triads were out of the equation now. It was fucked. Red Dawn would be lucky if they now didn't have some Chinese hitmen knocking on the doors of the Holden Tower. He had way too much on his plate at the moment. Without that tie with the triads it was going to be one hell of a struggle to push through. Losing six of their top men, including Gordon, was not going to help matters. Ray had no idea how hard it was to make everything work. Bastard.

"Are things prepped for our move on the Gambino's territory?" asked Ray, now waving away the sorry excuse for a doctor.

Valentino winced. That knock on the head must've been harder than Ray had allowed himself to believe. He was crazy if he thought they were going to move on the Gambinos without triad reinforcement.

"That's not going to happen, Ray. We were relying on backup from the Chinese. Now that's been thrown to the wind we can forget taking Gambino turf any time soon."

"What?" Ray did not speak in anger yet under the surface was a kind of threatening growl.

"It's impossible. We don't have the manpower to keep all of the operations locked down."

Ray stood up. He was taller than Valentino, but didn't dwarf him. Without words he was giving his advisor a very stern warning not to tell him anything he didn't want to hear.

"It's not possible Ray. I'm sorry. We keep what we have at the moment, slow ourselves down a little and finish off Tagliano first."

Ray seemed to be resisting an urge that told him to do something he would regret.

"If we lose momentum our enemies will regroup. Our plan requires speed. Things need to unfold quickly or we lose."

Thinking that now was the time to hammer it into the guy's skull that it just wouldn't work, Valentino looked him dead in the face.

"We don't have the manpower! Listen to me Ray! I have never told you wrong before so for God's sake listen! We move any faster then I swear to you the bottom's going to fall out of this whole thing faster than I'm going to be able to fix it!" Valentino prepared for a violent reaction which never came. "Rome wasn't built in a day."

With a quick glance of defiance Ray stepped past Valentino who remained motionless. His brother was having his hand bandaged.

"Thomas. Where are we on weapons?" he asked distantly.

"Things are going well. 'Just need the men to hold them." Thomas was still in a lot of pain. It was evident from the way he spoke, voice hissing like a ruptured steam pipe.

"Valentino, I need replacements. Move people up. 'Should boost morale. I want the best on high level detail. Put effort into recruitment. We have the money. I want people who know how to handle weapons. Try to snare fallout from the Tagliano Family."

Giving an unenthusiastic, "yeah," Valentino turned to look at them both. Ray had his eyes fixed on him.

"And find out who tried to kill me."

CHAPTER TWENTY-THREE
A COMMON ENEMY

The parking lot of some non-descript office block was where Dean's car now sat, its lights off. The driver was just returning to it after a deeply satisfying late night meal from his favorite noodle bar on the outskirts of Little Tokyo.

Dean wiped away a trace of the odd tasting, Asian, alcoholic drink he had just tried on a whim. His car unlocked with two deep clicks that disturbed the night air.

Climbing inside, he looked at himself in the rear-view mirror. He didn't look well, very pale. Maybe because he was thinking about what he had done the previous day, although that hadn't been an unpleasant experience. In fact he had enjoyed it a lot.

"That's round one," he muttered, leaning back in the comfortable driver's seat. Taking out his cell phone he began to dial the number he had written in black ink on the back of his hand. It had taken all of the previous evening and all of today to find, but he finally had the contact number for the man he wanted to talk to. It would be impossible for him to do this all alone. What he needed was somebody who hated Ray Bentley as much as he did.

He cursed himself for forgetting to call Yuki that day. He just hadn't gotten around to it, although it was something that should have been at the forefront of his mind. She'd be asleep by now. Damn it!

He hated living like this. Fuck Ray. Fuck that maniac for screwing his life up!

Dean squeezed his cell and then eased off for fear of breaking it. Once everything had been fixed, once he had put them all away, then he could get on with his life. The question was what was going to be left of it by the time he came out of this.

He sighed heavily.

It was approaching ten P.M.

A quaint house sat at the doorstep of the beach in Pacific Palisades, lit beautifully by exterior ground based lights much like tourist resorts in Barbados. A few men in suits stood around the property obviously guarding it against intruders. In the background a yacht on a late-night pleasure trip glided past on the horizon.

Inside the house, a man sipped at some whisky. Occupying a particularly luxurious red armchair and dressed in his monogrammed bathrobe he seemed bored and depressed. In front of his sullen form a widescreen T.V. was informing him of something it had informed him about yesterday. In addition, his contacts had also told him about it. A gang related shootout at the Helix Hotel. A shootout that had left sixteen mobsters dead. The victims had been some triads (who really had no business being in L.A. at present) and a number of goons from the Red Dawn. Ray Bentley's men.

He had spent most of his spare time mulling over the event, trying to pull something useful from the mess. Red Dawn affairs were things that were very close to heart for him now.

In the corridor outside the lounge the phone on the wall began to ring loudly. He himself gave it no heed, but a lackey who held a lounge lizard's posture answered it with a peeved, Italian-American accent.

"Hello? Who is this?" The man's eyes seemed to make movements akin to reading a long text and he played with a button on his gray suit.

"Who are you?"...

"Maybe. Tell me who you are and we'll see."...

"How did you get this number?"...

"No, he's not."...

In the lounge, the man in the armchair was forced to look to the door as his stooge came to it phone in hand. He put a palm over the receiver.

"Boss, it's some guy. 'Says he has some information you'd be interested in. 'Want me to tell him to get lost?"

There was a pause, then the man in the armchair spoke in his own, deeper and slightly more matured Italian dialect.

"No, I'll take it."

The other man nodded his curly, jet black hair flopping around. He then left his boss to some perceived privacy. Picking up the phone that rested on the table beside him the mob boss of the Tagliano Family received the call.

"Hello?"

The voice that came through to him was unknown. He did not recognize it in the slightest, so was inclined to put the phone down, however something kept him listening.

"Donato Tagliano?"

"What's it to you?"

"It's a whole lot."

"Who the hell is this?" Again, the man was tempted to hang up, but held on.

"Someone who wants rid of Ray Bentley. Just like you."

The man froze. Processing what the caller had said was more difficult than it should have been. He leaned forward, engaged.

145

"What's this about?"

"He killed your brother and your nephew. He's crippling your organization. Surely you want him in the ground?"

"More than anything," the man said through gritted teeth. "Just what have you got against him?" He stood up and walked over to the window. Pulling back the curtains his dark eyes stared out onto the grounds to the north of his property. Nothing but a guard having a smoke.

"Let's just say there's a lot of bad blood. 'You want to know who was behind the incident at Helix Hotel? Meet me. Venice Beach, near the Venice monument. Look for a bench dedicated to the memory of Charles Ryan. Don't come later than twelve P.M."

"Wa..." The caller hung up before the man could reply. He looked at the receiver for a moment and then put the phone on its cradle.

"Who was that?" The gangster with the curly hair was standing in the doorway with his arms folded.

"Nobody. Keep your nose in your own ass, Slip. Take a spot check on the grounds."

The man called Slip looked put out and obviously wanted to stay in the house. Nights had begun to get rather cold of late.

"Now," the man in the bathrobe ordered firmly and with a look of incredulity. With a quiet sigh, Slip slipped away and a second later the man heard the front door shut with a thud. He sat down in the armchair and reached for the glass of whisky only to realize he had drained it.

A photograph rested in a gold frame on the side table, depicting two middle-aged gangsters engaged in an arm wrestle over a table with other men in suits all around. Luga Tagliano's expression was one of little effort with a hint of amusement. His brother's was one of much effort trying to disguise itself under confidently gritted teeth. The photograph walked a borderline between making the man want to smile and want to cry. Picking it up and running a finger over the glass that protected the precious memory, he let out a harsh breath from his nostrils. Ma had been expected. She had been ill for years and had been comatose for at least two of them, but his brother...

It wasn't over.

Somehow...

Someway...

Ray Bentley was going to get it.

CHAPTER TWENTY-FOUR
DONATO TAGLIANO

It was a dreary day that promised warmer temperatures than the previous one, but still failed to tempt those who didn't have an unhealthy obsession with fresh air to take a walk across Venice Beach. A soft wind carried litter with it and the waves were calmer than they should have been as they lapped against the shore. A couple who were presumably on vacation took pictures of the Venice monument. The scene was picturesque.

Donato Tagliano was a man who was moving into his mid-sixties. His brother's gray hair had taken up residence on Donato's head at a young age, but his face had fewer wrinkles than his sibling's had featured before his untimely death, and rightly so. *He* had after all been killed at the ripe age of seventy-one. At present the new Godfather was wearing a long, dark gray coat with an almost identically colored suit beneath. A burnished gold tie was the only thing that even mildly stood out. As he stared down at the bench dedicated to Charles Ryan, he thought about his brother and wondered about erecting a bench in his honor. That would have made him smile. He would have loved that. He would have laughed and observed that Donato was a soft fool and then granted him a grateful look. That was...

If he was still alive.

He had started to wonder whether it was wise to come to a meeting with someone he didn't know without any form of guard. He guessed he had made that decision based on the fact that it didn't really matter to him anymore. If death wanted him then it could stop pussyfooting around and take him in the open.

With this in mind he sat down and checked his Rolex watch. 11:55. He was always fashionably early. It gave him some time to think. To prepare. To wonder who on earth this son of a bitch was; however, he was denied thought on the subject because before he could consider it a man sat down next to him.

About to say something, he stopped himself. 'Had to be sure it was the right guy. The man was wearing a relatively unworn jacket, but that didn't tell him anything. He had a tidy husk of blonde hair and green eyes. Was it him? He looked to be in his late twenties or early thirties.

There were a few moments of silence, then the man with the blonde hair spoke.

"Did you come alone?"

Donato immediately recognized the voice. So it was him. He had suspected as much.

"I didn't hear that particular request over the phone," he muttered.

"I didn't request it. I'm just curious."

"Yes. Now what's this all about? Who are you?"

"Dean Cottrell. I worked for Red Dawn before they decided I was no longer necessary."

Donato chuckled for a brief second. It was a guttural, from-the-throat noise.

"Oh, so that's what this is. You wanna get revenge and you think I want the same thing."

"I don't think. I know."

His reply was simple and strangely annoying. The guy clearly had his wits about him, with an understanding of the human mind because he could tell that the strongest thing burning in Donato's psyche was a desire to gaze upon Ray Bentley's lifeless corpse in a dimension that wasn't his wildest dream. Wanting to steer the conversation away from the potentially painful subject of his dearly departed brother, Donato said the first thing that came to him.

"You shot up his deal with the triads."

"Yep. It would be in everyone's best interest to keep the Red Dawn brittle and without backup. Assault on your warehouses should ease slightly."

"Well, I guess I have a lot to thank you for, but what I don't understand is with Ray and his brother dead in your sights why they weren't on the coroner's list."

Dean considered this and gave the man a dry smile.

"I want Ray to suffer. His make or break deal just got vanquished. He's not going to be too happy. Killing him is my final goal, but why not make him feel it?" he said nastily.

Donato concluded that the guy was a serious nutcase and was not to be fucked with.

"Alright. Let's get down to it. You obviously didn't call me here for no good reason. What's your angle, Dean?"

"On a business level, I've crippled him and he still doesn't know who I am. Now... it gets personal."

The mob boss liked where this was going. Dean Cottrell knew how Ray operated. He was an ex-inside source and he wanted to hurt his former boss. Who would have thought that out of nowhere the man who had the potential to be the Tagliano Family's saving grace would have come from the very organization that was trying to destroy them?

"What did you have in mind?" he asked a bit more enthusiastically than he intended to. 'Couldn't be too hasty. His brother had always analyzed what was on the table before putting down his chips and he hoped to follow that example.

"He killed your brother. I need your help to kill his."

Thomas Bentley. Donato knew very little where Ray's brother was concerned other than the fact that they were partners in crime and that Thomas had definite connections to corrupt weapons contractors and black market dealers.

"Thomas Bentley is the driving force behind Ray's stockpile of imported weapons. Getting rid of him is key if we want the Red Dawn to cave."

"And you know where to do away with the bastard?"

"Thomas operates outside of the Holden Tower. The zoo in the Lake Arrowhead region is his hub. He stockpiles arms behind closed doors. In some senses it's the perfect cover."

"So what's this got to do with me?"

"Not only do we have a common goal, but I'm looking for something specific that I could no more get legally than from any weapons peddler."

"Oh, yeah? What's that?"

Dean pulled something from a pocket inside his jacket. It was a folded piece of paper. He handed it to Donato who opened it and read the words in pencil at the top.

"Remote detonated Semtex. It's used for licensed commercial demolition and military applications. I need two bombs." Dean had considered procuring the required explosives from Big Bob now that he and the shifty gun salesmen were sort of friends, but he would need the old mobster at his side in the end, and had felt it best to ask him instead.

Donato gave Dean a strange look, making further judgments. He knew his stuff. 'Probably former armed forces.

"I'll see what I can do." He put it into his pocket, and they both stared out at the ocean not too far away. A father was walking his very young son over the beach. At one point, the child fell and then was lifted onto strong shoulders. Dean wondered whether Yuki would ever want kids. He had a feeling she would and he would comply very willingly with the request if it was ever made. At that moment, being a father, walking his own kid across the beach seemed like a distant reward. Something so tranquil and wonderful. Was it possible? Not with Ray Bentley still alive. After the business was taken care of he would marry Yuki and maybe work legitimately. He wanted to forget crime. He had served it and how was he repaid? Almost getting blown apart.

Fuck crime. Fuck it all.

"Do you really think we can bring them down?" asked Donato. His rationality had him doubting.

Dean looked at him and the old man noticed a sadness in his eyes. The same sadness he had seen in Luga's eyes when ma had died.

"We work together, I don't see why not. Ray's just another man."

Donato nodded and kind of half-smiled. He had decided that Dean was a friend. Friends were something he had been far too short on as of late. He held out an aging hand.

"Donnie."

Dean took it and they shook firmly.

"Let's get it done."

CHAPTER TWENTY-FIVE
RAY'S PROMISE

"Fifty thousand. They drive hard deal. What are your orders?"

Thomas had never found Cheo's Mexican beat down of the English language annoying up until now. The greasy mustached security man looked more out of place than a flamingo in his office. He rested his chin on his hands and considered.

"Fuck 'em," he said finally. Cheo did a double take.

"Fuck 'em. They won't bargain then tell them to go elsewhere. Go and trade their shit for some rice for all I care. I gave 'em the numbers and said we could negotiate. Fifty-fucking-thousand is not what I call negotiating."

Cheo nodded and left the office, closing the door quietly behind him. It had been a hard day at the zoo; luckily it was coming to an end. Thomas looked down at his bandaged left hand. It sent shooting pains up his arm whenever he knocked it against something, but so far he had been able to put up with it.

Going over to the window he opened the blinds revealing the scene they obscured. The loading area was thankfully starting to become more organized. The crates of what Thomas referred to as his '*useless shit*' that consisted of everything to do with the actual zoo, had been given a section of the floor and for now, were staying put. The loading shutter door was open and one of Thomas's men was driving (albeit badly) a forklift into the bay carrying a wooden crate. One of the other goons, Marty, was directing the forklift by backpedaling away from it and making 'come on' hand gestures. When the vehicle was inside, he quickly made a stop signal. This proved foolish, as the forklift desisted suddenly and the crate slid off and crashed down onto the floor. Its front end snapped off and four navy colored drums rolled out with intent to cause havoc.

"Oh, shit!" exclaimed Marty, who ran forward to stop them rolling any further.

Thomas scowled and threw open the door to his office, coming out onto the top step that led up to it from the floor. No wonder these dropouts couldn't find real jobs.

"What the fuck do you think you're doing?! Do you know what that shit is?!" he yelled, pointing menacingly.

Marty looked down at the barrel and saw the orange diamond symbol that represented explosives. Written on the drum in stenciled lettering was the word 'Nitromethane'. Marty didn't pretend to be no chemist or physician or whatever, but he knew that was bad. Thomas continued to yell at them both.

"If that shit went up in here, they'd be scraping you two screw-ups off of the walls with a fucking shovel!"

"Sorry, boss. Dipshit here can carry stuff, but it's probably fair to say he drives like a fucking retard." Marty shot the man in the forklift a nasty smile. He shrunk at the criticism.

Thomas knew Marty quite well, and the little shit often pissed him off. He was about nineteen white as paper and thought he was some sort of gangsta with his cap and his wife beater and his cheap sneaks and his pierced ear and his shitty attitude.

"Well, if you're finally through getting hit by parked cars, pick that crap up and get it stored, Marty. If not, then I'll gladly come down there and kick your ass." Thomas went back into his office and slammed the door.

The youth frowned huffily then turned to hear the forklift driver chuckling. He made a cell phone imitation with the pinkie and thumb of his left hand and walked towards him.

"Yo, dipshit! It's my grandma! Wants to know if you need any help driving that thing!"

Dipshit's face fell immediately.

Still seething, Thomas seated himself in his office chair again and started to fill out some forms that were crying out for the tip of his pen. He was just lucky he was right handed otherwise he might not get anything done at all and that would be severely inconvenient. Some time passed and then the phone on his desk rang.

"Hello?"

"It's me. 'Need you down in the hold for a second," came the voice of a middle-aged man in his ear.

"Horace my man. What's the problem?"

"Just another order mismatch."

"Okay, I'm on my way." Thomas hung up and, as if eager to be away from the tedious paperwork, exited his office and headed for the heavy, steel doors some way down the hall from the loading bay. A wide set of steps led down to a well-lit space that housed the fruits of Thomas's labor.

Rows of tables lined up like soldiers ironically were home to hundreds of weapons. Not a surface was free. Against the far wall in cheap, wooden racks were more guns. Small crates, both wooden and metal were piled up to the ceiling in some areas. Many were labeled with a certain caliber and then in big, red letters 'AMMUNITION' while others had numbers which were only decipherable by someone with the inventory list. A few barrels of volatile chemicals were set aside on the far left.

Only three people were down there at this time. Horace, who served as Thomas's weapons expert and two of his underpaid stooges who were checking over assault rifles and no doubt wondering if mom's basement would ever be considered a cool place to live.

Thomas knew a lot about firearms, but it paid to have someone who knew close to every gun back to front, which is why he had hired an expert. Horace was wearing his usual dark green duffel coat and with good cause. It had to be kept reasonably cold down in the weapons hold for practical reasons. The man with a bristly goatee, a bald patch and some cheap glasses turned to greet him with a nod before explaining his predicament to his superior.

"See, here on the form it says 'A total of twenty Winchester 1300 Defenders."

He was right. The form on the clipboard in front of him didn't lie. Thomas looked at the shotguns lined up on the table and knew immediately that there were less than twenty.

"Now, we only have sixteen. That's four shotguns gone walkabout. I don't understand it," Horace said, scratching his head. Thomas bit his lip awkwardly.

"'You wanna give 'em a call?" he asked.

"Well, I don't know. 'You think I should?"

"Yeah, I'll get the contact number for you ASAP. We'll get onto it."

"Yeah. Goddamn Colombians. The fuckers can't even count," the older gentleman pulled a cigarette from a pocket on his duffel coat and lit it. Thomas wondered whether to let it slide, however decided against it. He had to be tough on these morons or they'd never learn. With little visible hesitation he pulled the smoke from Horace's mouth and dropped it to the floor crushing it under his clean, black shoes. His expert gave him a worried look.

"No cigarettes in here. You know the rules. You take that shit outside." Thomas turned and left.

On his way back to his office he noticed that Marty and the other man were still gathering the barrels into a corner and as per usual the kid's craving for a toke had overcome his capacity to learn. A joint quivered between his lips as the men dumped the fourth barrel with the rest of them. Thomas was close to hitting the roof now. It seemed like everyone he worked with that wasn't his brother was either mentally unstable or mentally retarded.

"What the fuck are you doing now!" he yelled, walking over. Marty prepared himself for another grilling, but with Thomas, you could never prepare enough. After ripping the joint from his mouth and putting it out with a harsh stamp, the message seemed to go through.

"Oh, shit. Yeah. Explosive. I forgot. I think these barrels should be labeled more clearly."

That was the last thing Thomas needed. Some grade-A fuck-up giving him a suggestion. The shit was printed on the side of the Goddamn thing!

"Well, is this clear enough? You are a fucking moron!" Thomas snarled, indicating the stenciled warning on the drum. He turned on his heels and trudged up the stairs that led to his office before slamming the door. He couldn't wait until next month, when he could fire every single one of these tools. According to Ray they could then pay actual professionals to work the zoo and all of the current staff would have to start sending their résumés to Walmart.

Taking a seat again he couldn't gather up enough will to continue with his paperwork. Instead, he stared at it and thought about his brother.

Screw the triads. Ray would find a way around it. He had always been the one with enough ambition to pull both of them through all those years. God, to him it seemed like a lifetime had passed since he had waved goodbye to his fucked up older brother who hated the way everything worked and said hello to his fucked up older brother who was going to do something about it.

It was a time around late fall, when winter was closing in, and leaves were blown carelessly around by light wind and raked up into piles for children to play in. Four months since Ray had been expelled from their previous school and they had both been sent to one that they hated even more. Ray hadn't been getting good grades. He would never stay in a class for more than ten minutes. His father scolded him for it, but his younger brother saw no hurt in his eyes when it happened. They sat together on a wall outside school. Only the final dregs of children with late parents were left hanging around. Suddenly, Ray spoke. His words shook with some unknown energy.

"I'm gonna get 'em, Tom. I'm gonna show 'em all."

At his age, Thomas hadn't quite interpreted this correctly and thought that Ray was going to kick the crap out of another kid for saying something about him. They had always been close, Ray and Thomas. They consoled each other like the last two people on earth.

'To Hell and back' had been one of Ray's old phrases he had stolen from a movie, to tell his brother that no matter what happened, they were the only ones who would look out for each other, and they'd do that regardless of the situation. Anybody else was just out to hurt them in the end. That was one of the reasons Thomas had reached out a hand to hold his brother's shoulder in comfort, but Ray had grabbed him by the wrist before he could. It was a solid move that didn't even require him to look at his brother. Only afterwards did he turn his head. His grip was firm and borderline painful.

"They can't break us down, Tom. Not anyone. Not dad. Not the teachers. Not even the fucking police. I'll show 'em, Tom. I'll show 'em they don't know who they're fucking with." Ray's voice was a *harsh growl that Thomas had heard very few times before. The grip on his wrist really started to hurt.*

"Ray, you're hurting me."

He ignored Thomas and leaned forward his eyes blazing with concentrated will the fire fueled by so many things that he hated about his life, about the system, about those around him.

"Me and you, Tom. To Hell and back. We'll get those fuckers. You and me. We'll make 'em wish they were dead. I've got a good idea where to start. We'll show 'em, Tom. We'll have this fucking city and we'll get every last one. I promise"

His wrist had not retained the mark left by Ray's death grip, but for some reason, whenever Ray got angry about something, he felt it burn. Such careless memories. He really did hate to reminisce.

"We'll have this fucking city and we'll get every last one. I promise"

To an extent Thomas knew more about Ray's ambitions than Valentino or anyone else did, yet his brother's motives were still an enigma even to him. The crime was all within the realms of regular conversation. Making more money. Expanding into other states. Getting rid of opposing gangs. It would seem that Ray had achieved his goal or at least it lay within the next couple of years, but Thomas always felt there was more to what Ray had told him all those years ago. His final ultimatum. One goal he desired above all else and one that he would keep even from his brother until he felt it was within reach. Whatever it was, it was an ambition that Thomas would support.

Side by side until death.

To Hell and back.

CHAPTER TWENTY-SIX
ALONE IN THE APARTMENT

Setting down shopping bags, Yuki turned and shut the door behind her securing both of the locks. Dean had always been keen on drilling her about that. It was rather late now. Semi-dark. The color of deep seawater had settled over L.A. and had smeared the clouds in a mysteriously uninviting blue. Yuki's friends at work had been interrogating her about the wedding, asking her questions like when she was picking out a dress, where would the venue be, who was going to be a bridesmaid: the basic stuff when it came to the announcement of matrimony.

She put the cartons of orange juice into the refrigerator and hit the message button on the landline.

"You have... no messages," the voice said in a monotone.

Yuki sighed. She was the only one who answered messages on the landline. In fact, she was the only one that got called save the occasional reminder from the landlord that could be picked up by either of them.

She really did hope he called her tonight.

The previous night she had received no contact and had restrained herself from calling him. He had said he was helping the business out of a serious jam and she figured he might not appreciate her pestering him. That was just the way she thought. It had been the expectation of her from an early age that she should cater to the needs of others *especially* her partner. Her father had been surprisingly supportive over the phone when she told him she was set to marry the American boyfriend she had mentioned the last time they spoke. Part of her kind of felt sorry for the old man. He hadn't been around too much when Yuki was a girl and she did resent him slightly for that; however, he was all alone now. Yuki's mother's death had taken everything from him and now, his time was running out. Loneliness may have been the only reason he called, but Yuki appreciated it all the same. He, of course, would not be at the wedding. He scarcely ever left the hospital.

Gliding over to the window she pulled up one of the blinds and took a glance down at the street. Not much was happening in the area, bar some old man walking his dog. The sky wasn't looking very friendly. So far, small showers had permeated the long nights and that was all, however as the days dragged on a storm came closer and closer. It could be tomorrow or the next day and Yuki wasn't happy about it. Bad weather was one of her least favorite things. It ranked right up there with long periods where she went to bed alone.

In other words, things weren't too good at the moment.

The letter she opened from the comfort of the couch offered no joy either. Just something from work. She tossed it aside and rested the letter opener on the arm. The television set provided only minimal entertainment as usual. Jay Leno was ranting on about something or other.

"But, seriously, folks. I love Los Angeles. If you need a good read, you just turn to the obituaries and the only thing higher than the housing cost is the crime rate."

The showman's crowd was amused, but Yuki could already feel her eyelids getting heavy. It had been a draining and lengthy day, but like a cruel puppet master there was no way fate would allow her the solace granted by sleep. Just as she was beginning to doze the phone started to ring.

She sat bolt upright just at the point where Jay's audience burst into hysterics. Shaken and now fully awake, she was quick to mute the crowd and answer the phone.

"Hello?"

"Yuki, it's me." Dean's voice was a little scrambled, but it was definitely him.

"Hey."

"I was just checking up on you. How was your day?"

"Nothing out of the ordinary. Tiring to say the least. You still haven't fixed the fuse box. 'Lights keep cutting out here."

There was a raspy chuckle from the other end of the connection and a shuffling sound then Dean said, "I'll get to it as soon as I get back. Listen, sorry for not calling yesterday. Things have been really busy here. The company's nosedived some more. I've got a lot of problems that I need to figure out, but I think I've found someone who's going to help me."

"That's good," Yuki replied. She turned away still holding the phone. "How's your boss?"

There was a small moment of hesitation in which Yuki suspected her fiancé to tell her that he had cut and run or something similar.

"I haven't spoken to him in person for a while, but right now, I expect he's at his fancy desk drinking scotch and telling people that things are going fine."

"Oh, that kind of guy, huh?"

"Yeah. This one's a real slippery bastard. He'll lie to anyone."

"So, where are you now?"

"Now? 'Middle of Goddamn nowhere. Halfway to Sacramento. 'Gotta try and convince an investor he has no future setting up a

162

department store in Weymouth." There was another small chuckle from Dean and Yuki smiled with him.

"Dean... when are you coming home?"

There was a long pause. It was depressing. It seemed Dean had not wanted her to ask because he honestly didn't know.

"Look, I'm sorry for dropping this on you so suddenly. I couldn't have been less prepared and it's a terrible time." He sounded genuine. "I know I'm always making things up to you, but I promise I *will* make this up to you. I am coming back and when I do things will be different."

Yuki tried hard to believe him it sounded like something Dean really wanted, but would never happen.

"That's hard to believe sometimes." She couldn't believe she had just said that, yet she had.

"Yuki, I know I've screwed up. Just give me time and I swear to God, this is all going to go away."

Feeling guilty for doubting her love she made sure her next statement was as true as it could be.

"Okay. I love you."

"And I love you too. So much."

Dean hung up.

Silence.

Yuki put the phone down and gave a long sigh. At least he had called. He would come back. She doubted whether things with him would ever change, but as long as he came back she was happy.

Sleep was difficult even when wrapped in her bed sheet. She would toss and turn still wide awake. Trying to convince herself that she would eventually just fall into a slumberous state was difficult. Rolling over on the mattress she was forced to take a good, long look at a photograph of her and Dean sitting on a stone wall by one of L.A.'s finest beaches. That had been one of the best days of her life.

163

It was only a week before Dean began to get completely tied down by his occupation, whatever that was. Looking at the picture gave her an unsettled feeling. A feeling that was possibly similar to the one that a twin would feel when the other twin died. Whatever was going on in Dean's world was bad. He was worried and scared about something, but he was also angry. More angry than he had ever been. She felt it in the way he replied when she had questioned his promise. There was something in his tone that hadn't been evident to her until after the call had ended. It was amazing how she knew this. She hadn't processed it consciously, but her subconscious had picked it up with ease.

Yuki shivered. She wished she knew what was happening because she was pretty damn sure there was more to it than what Dean had told her. Could it have anything to do with all the killings that were going on in L.A. at the moment? Had one of Dean's colleague's been murdered? Had his boss killed someone? Had he?

Yuki's mind reached a point of frenzy, forcing her to breathe deeply and gather her thoughts. Now was time for sleeping not forming conspiracy theories about her fiancé. She loved him. He loved her. If he said there was something that he needed to fix before they could continue to pursue a life together then that was what was going to happen. There was nothing more to it.

CHAPTER TWENTY-SEVEN
STORM WARNING

In his motel room Dean listened intently to the portable radio beside his bed.

"Last night we avoided the downpour, but now it looks as if tonight will be the flashpoint with thundery showers moving over Los Angeles throughout the evening. People are advised not to use poorly maintained roads…"

Dean had been counting on a rainy night and a full-blown storm would definitely turn events to his advantage. 'No doubt with the poor visibility, accidents would draw police attention to urban centers. If gunshots went off at a zoo - who would hear them? It was completely isolated.

He pulled out his Beretta and took a long, hard look at the gun's slender form. It had yet to be fired and was fully loaded. The weapon clicked as he cocked it, and then he proceeded to place it back inside his jacket. He was thinking about killing Thomas, trying to remember every word the man had ever said to him, but it had all blurred together and faded into obscurity. He could no longer make sense of all those death certificates he had signed in the Red Dawn's name. Was this how it would always be from now on? Traveling in secret with reckless abandon, all consequence folded in on itself, bleeding moments from his past? What good were all those thoughts anyway? He didn't need them to exact justice. All he needed was this gun.

Dean's suit had been dry cleaned the previous day and now hung crisply from his figure. Standing up he straightened his crimson tie.

He would wait until later before justifying why he felt it appropriate for him to be wearing the trademark dress code of the people he was endeavoring to destroy.

It was now three-thirty-three and with the storm just starting to collect, the clouds were readying themselves, high above in the sky. Time to leave.

With the Tagliano home address on a piece of paper in his jacket pocket he locked his motel room and slipped into his car. His keys rotated in the ignition and the BMW pulled out of the parking lot.

The house of Donato Tagliano (or Donnie as he had informally introduced himself) was just how Dean had expected it. Luxurious, yet admirably diminutive.

Climbing out of his car, Dean was greeted by a man with curly, black hair who spoke in an accent typical to traditional mafia goons. He could have easily been Joe Pesci's less reputable cousin.

"Mr. Tagliano's in the dining hall. Drinks are prepared. Let me show you inside."

From what Dean could tell the guy was rather stiff and probably cautious of the new arrival. He didn't blame him.

The interior of the house was very traditional with a burgundy theme. The wallpaper had an embossed pattern that looked like rolling waves and the walls themselves were decorated with various oil paintings. In fact, it felt dangerously close to home for Dean who had once walked hallways of similar design. Perhaps all the mob bosses used the same catalog.

He was led into a dining hall that followed the feel of the rest of the house. A glass table separated him from the man he had come to see. Donnie was impeccably dressed for the occasion and greeted Dean warmly.

"Dean. 'So glad you could make it to my humble abode and on time too," he said through a smile.

166

"I try not to make a habit of being late." Dean sat down. A glass of wine had been laid out for him and he was glad to take a long swig of it.

"Do you have what I need?" he asked.

"Yeah, I 'got what you asked for." Donnie clicked his fingers and a man who had been standing at the edge of the room by the French doors that looked out onto patio and then out to sea, came closer and pulled a duffel bag up onto the table. He then unzipped it and withdrew two, rectangular, yellow blocks.

"Semtex. Nasty fucking explosive. Two receivers and of course, the detonator."

The detonator looked like a gun with the top half removed, leaving only the grip and trigger. All of the items were slid in Dean's direction and he turned each component over in his hands.

"I assume you know how to use it."

Dean nodded.

"Just where did you learn so much about explosives anyway?" Donnie asked casually.

Dean didn't dignify it with a response. He retained the belief that the less people knew about him, the better.

"This is perfect."

"So, what's your plan?"

"My plan?" Dean looked up. "My plan is simple. Tonight, the cradle falls. Storm surge washes out L.A. It's almost too coincidental. I'm going to the zoo, after dark. I'm going to kill Thomas and anyone who gets in my way. I know the rough layout of the place. Thomas keeps his guns, ammunition and other crap in a cement room halfway underground. I'll destroy Ray's assets and his contact with the arms supply."

"But what about the guards? Thomas is bound to have security on an operation of that size."

"Oh he does, but I have the element of surprise. I'll let the storm cover my tracks."

Donnie had formulated many opinions and theories on Dean Cottrell since their first meeting. The one that intrigued him most was that Dean appeared to be someone who was currently living a life devoted to this vendetta. Whatever Ray Bentley had done to him, it had affected him badly. His eyes were full of callous intent. It was the same callous intent that Donnie had seen in his own reflection after he had found out that his brother and nephew were dead, however the mobster was much older than Dean and the years had increased his capacity for patience. He was just lucky that his opportunity for revenge had materialized in this strange character, because he wasn't capable of enacting his own counterblow at present. The syndicate was really struggling with the yakuza and the Red Dawn tearing chunks off at either end. He and Dean had the same motives, the same thought processes, but Dean had the drive and was in the position to act on his feelings. It was quite likely that if the ballsy (and possibly foolish) killer carried out what he had planned, he would not return to the heart of L.A. the next morning, or ever. Not that the Tagliano Godfather cared all that much. Dean was inconsequential in the end. If he did, by some miracle, manage to put an end to Thomas Bentley's dealings, then celebrations all around, although Donnie and his consultants weren't holding their breath. It was a crazy plan.

"You 'got a piece, I presume."

"Yep. She's fully loaded and hasn't been fired."

"Then you're all set?"

Dean downed the last of his wine and then dragged the duffel bag over to where he was sitting and packed his equipment into it.

"When this is over and done with, Ray will be stumbling around in the dark. He and Thomas are closer than cola and ice. With his weapon supply a smoldering pile of debris, he'll most likely stop to review the playing field. This should give you enough time to try and recapture your assets or at least bolster the defenses on what you have left, but killing Thomas is by no means the last step in my plan. I will come back. I'll have to. Valentino, the brains behind the operation, will probably try to drive Red Dawn forward even if his boss seizes up. You'll have some time; however you'll have to work fast."

"Thanks for the heads up."

Dean stood up duffel bag in hand and got ready to leave.

"Dean?" Donnie called after him as he began to walk away.

"What?" he replied distantly.

"What exactly did they do to you?"

Dean felt a shiver run down his spine. Cramp set in around his stomach area. Without turning and with a serene tone he replied, "Ray thought I'd run his job. A suicide job. Man, was I a fool. Ray killed me alright, but only the part that worked for him. Now, what I 'got left is coming back to take everything."

Dean walked away and out of the front entrance.

Moments later Donnie heard the slam of a car door and then the telltale sound of an engine starting up.

"He's a strange one, isn't he?" said the man with the curly hair.

"I don't know. There's something about him I just can't get to grips with... but I like him. He's got spunk."

"'You think it'll work? One man versus all of Thomas's personal guard?"

"It's not unheard of. We'll just have to wait and see." Donnie stood up from his seated position and turned to look out of the French doors.

The sea was calm like a familiar dog waiting for some great event to rouse it from the collected quietude. Everything was as real as it always had been. The gray suits that had to be cleansed of a gun smoke bouquet. The disconnection with death that had to be overcome. The gracious and fragile scenery that had to push back against the city's sin and corruption running through every subway, blowing through every street and sitting in mental solitude, wearing monogrammed bathrobes and sipping the liquor of true destitution. This was the reality of the room and the reality inside his head. Dean was another gear in the grand machine that was always active, always shaking the ground.

Still, the sea was calm.

The calm before the storm. When it hit, the waves would turn ugly.

'Better not come far enough up the shore to damage my house' Donnie thought quietly.

Everything bar numbers was in Dean's favor, although usually, numbers counted a whole lot. It would all hang on how skilled Dean was. He was obviously good with a rifle, but at closer range? Maybe...

Maybe. He certainly had the guts.

CHAPTER TWENTY-EIGHT
DARK CLOUDS OVER LOS ANGELES

It was as if a creature of immense magnitude had descended upon Los Angeles that night. The cloud formations were violent. The wind blew astringent and merciless. Only those who had great need to be out wandered the streets. No area was safe from the shadow. Papers flapped in the gale like vultures and all food stands had their metal screens pulled down. Those who were out and had made a sensible choice carried large umbrellas and prepared for the barrage of rain, while those who were more foolish were walking with great speed, eager to get to their destination before the pelting began.

Unlike some showers the one that fell that night began softly and turned murderous at a slow rate with the drops becoming larger and the force of the downpour becoming heavier. Rain streaked the windows and filled the drains. Potholes became shimmering puddles wracked by constant rippling and the night air became cold very suddenly. Much colder than had been predicted. The lightning started at around ten. Blue and purple cracks in the clouds like fault lines in the smoky dispersion that showed the heart of the beast within. Antennas received some attention from the streaking incandescence, but the worst thing about the storm was the continuous boom of the thunder like cannon shots.

The rhythmic sliding sound of the M5's windshield wipers made the atmosphere within Dean's car an uncomfortable one. The road ahead of him was deserted. Trees and badly maintained hedgerows lined it and rainwater slicked its surface. Thunder like the roaring of some enraged animal was perfectly audible, and visibility was poor just as he had predicted. The radio had given him updates on a serious traffic collision that had occurred on the Barstow Freeway not too long ago (fulfilling his prophecy of the distraction the weather would create). An expression of cogitation showed that he was still thinking about the task at hand. Things were going perfectly so far. Nothing had occurred to slow him down. No road works, no washed out dips, no engine failure, nothing. The path ahead was clear. He knew what he had to do.

With no warning Dean could have detected with his distracted mind, Duran Duran began putting their own soundtrack to the plot in motion with '*Hold Back The Rain*'. He found it at least mildly relevant in its title; however the beat was far too positive for the massacre he was mentally planning out. Turning the stereo off, he left only the stale taste of his own emotions in the air. Everything else had been sucked out of the car by the storm caterwauling above.

The feeling in Dean's head at that moment was confusing, but at the same time, definable. He was forcing himself to block off any kind of fear. Fear of being killed. Fear of giving away the secret that he was still alive. Fear of coming face-to-face with Thomas again. He had to get rid of those thoughts or he would talk himself out of it using statistics like the fact that Thomas probably had over thirty men around him. Thoughts like that wouldn't help. He was going to carry this out and he was going to succeed.

His handgun sat inside his jacket. It wasn't silenced. Dean had seen no need for that. Even if he broke out with a Gatling gun in this weather it would probably go unnoticed.

Rain blurred the surroundings until a flash of luminous electricity ignited the image of his destination.

Dead ahead a few miles, give or take.

He was taking the side entrance as he always did. Hopefully, the beefy individual with the beanie would still be guarding the gate. He would most likely find it difficult to snap Dean in two once he had a bullet in his head.

Dean had already decided that anyone was collateral. They were employed by Thomas. He would kill them without a second thought.

After all, he would expect no less from them. This invoked a sly smile from the driver of the M5 who, though lumbered with some unavoidable insecurity was surprisingly confident in his own skill. That was another thing Thomas would have against him. He had numbers, but how well would they fare against an ex-special forces soldier turned hitman? Thomas could hand out as many weapons as he liked. It didn't mean his underpaid, undereducated thugs would use them well.

After this job was done, he would leave things to simmer, take time lying low, and then he would go back to Yuki quickly, before taking things to the next level. Some personal contact would convince her that he was still committed. God, he was an asshole. He wouldn't be surprised if she failed to stick around. It must have seemed to her that Dean was being an unreliable son of a bitch without one thought for what she wanted. He immediately stopped thinking about this. That wasn't the mindset he needed. He needed to think reactively. He needed to think about how much pain he wanted to put Thomas Bentley through tonight. He needed to visualize Ray receiving the news and falling to his knees, a broken man. Heck, he was even putting serious thought into coming clean to Ray in a phone call and telling him how his brother had begged for death and how Dean had been all too happy to oblige. It wouldn't be the smartest move, although the satisfaction it would give him would be pure ecstasy.

Dean gripped the steering wheel tightly. He was going to enjoy this.

The guard on duty at the side entrance to the zoo was leaning up against the wall in his beanie and slacks. He had thought himself clever leaning against the wall. The angle of the downpour meant that it provided some shelter from the wet. He might have been cold, but at least he didn't have to haul things around like the rest of the zoo's operants.

He was surprised when headlights penetrated the darkness and a car pulled up in front of him. He recognized it from somewhere, but couldn't quite remember where. His memory skills weren't the best. God damn it, he knew that car from somewhere. Was this guy a regular? These thoughts went through the thickset man's mind, hidden from view by an icy expression of boredom that held no motivation even in the smallest amount. Though he knew the car was familiar, he did not know it was friendly. Thomas had given him no heads up about an arrival and anyone who turned up at the premises unannounced was to be treated with extreme caution. That was what Thomas had told him.

Dean got out of his car and was immediately soaked. He didn't care. More thunder rumbled. He started to come around the vehicle which helpfully obscured the big thug's view as the new arrival reached into his jacket and pulled out his gun.

The same brainless fucker that had been there last time. It would be interesting to see whether the brute would say anything before Dean planted one between his eyes.

He didn't.

The guy still had his tree trunk arms folded when Dean raised the Beretta and shot him in the head. He fell backwards and then into a position that bums often use to rest against subway walls, only he wasn't playing a saxophone or asking for quarters. After a few seconds, some repulsive mass seemed to crawl out of the hole in the back of his head and hit the concrete like dropped lasagna.

That was it. The first one down. No going back now. He could have killed someone more worthwhile with the first bullet, but it would suffice. At least the first had been a kill shot. He had two extra clips tucked into his pants, and the explosives were also on his person. The only thing left to do now was to open the steel gate and enter what would soon become a warzone. With a deep breath he entered the familiar compound. He was in Thomas's world now.

Inside the exterior walls of the zoo, things were very much the same as on the outside. Darkness made everything look like a half-faded scene from a movie and the enclosures loomed over the pathways as shadowed edifices. Under normal circumstances, the zoo had been an unfriendly environment, yet entering the place now felt like a departure from the land of the living.

174

Dean walked across the rain-slicked pathway, past cages of different sizes, making his way to the light source in the middle of the zoo, the main building where Thomas's underlings were probably sorting through guns. It didn't take long to encounter more guards. Two men sat on a division fence that cordoned off a sharp drop into a pool of water. They didn't see Dean come striding out of the darkness towards them. One was too preoccupied trying to light a cigarette in the rain and the other was laughing at some recent joke.

The first round hit the cigarette man in the chest and sent him backwards off the fence, where he crashed through the surface of the pool into frosty water. The other guard jumped off in immediate reflex and pulled out a gun. Dean nailed him twice before he could get off a shot and he went to ground with a pathetic cry of pain as his lungs collapsed.

The killer lowered his gun. Two more dead. Thomas was going to have to do better than that if he wanted to get out alive.

Footsteps sounded close by, just audible over the weather. In automatic response Dean took cover beside an enclosure.

Thomas's chief of security, Cheo, came running up a small flight of stone steps. He had been close when the gunshots had sounded and even then, he had been unsure of what he had heard. A man lay on the floor by a fence in front of him.

"Chekov?" he said loudly. Under a brown jacket he was wearing his usual creamy shirt.

From his sheltered position, Dean watched as Thomas's stooge walked over to the downed form with an air of caution.

"Barnes? What is now going on?" His Mexican accent was hoarser than when Dean had last heard it, but it could have just been a result of the moment of panic. Bending down, Cheo rolled the body over and saw the two holes in the black thug's chest.

His reaction was quick. He was upright again in a flash, holding a pistol with both hands, aiming it around him and grunting in frustration and concern. He was aiming the gun at all the pathways that converged at the watery enclosure, but he failed to see Dean hiding in the shadows. Slowly, and still keeping his gun on the

175

darkness, Cheo pulled a yellow walkie-talkie off of a clip on his belt buckle and raised it to his face...

That was when a bullet ripped through his collar bone, sending him flying backwards where he impacted the wet concrete and his walkie-talkie flew over the fence and into the water below.

CHAPTER TWENTY-NINE
AT THE ZOO WITH DESTRUCTION IN MIND

Cheo lay panting on the floor. He could barely grip his gun so it was pointless for his attacker to come close and kick it away from him breaking one of his fingers in the process. The gunshot wound was bleeding badly now. He winced in pain, but couldn't find the energy to yell for help. He just grunted repetitively.

Who?

He looked up and his eyes widened in horrified shock.

"No." His voice did not raise itself beyond a whisper.

"How are you alive?"

The pistol came into Cheo's view its black barrel aimed directly down at his face.

"Fantasma." Cheo's last, Spanish exclamation was greeted with a gunshot.

Inside the loading area, the air was cold due to the wide open door. A shipment had been dropped off half an hour ago and using forklifts, Thomas's men were still ferrying the crates inside. Thomas himself was on the floor, overseeing things. He wasn't going to let his peons slack off just because of a little rain. Their schedule was already packed enough without setbacks, so he had instructed them to bundle up and shut up. The only members of his team not dressed appropriately against the weather outside were the doltish ones, such as Marty, who favored looking cool over preventing hypothermia.

Damn, he needed better employees.

"Back it up and this time don't drop it dipshit," Thomas's aforementioned, white cap-wearing goon said to the forklift driver entering the space.

Their boss was certainly prepared. His jacket hung around him and kept him pretty warm. Plus, he hadn't had to go outside which was a bonus as his hair remained glossy and dry.

The faint banging sounds he heard were unsettling to say the least. Part of him said thunder and part of him said no. They were quiet, but the weather was muffling them so that explained it. If Thomas had been standing a foot further away from the door he probably wouldn't have noticed them at all. It was all background noise. He wasn't the only one who registered them. A few of the thugs gave the torrentially assaulted view that the open loading entrance granted them a worried look, then returned to what they were doing. After all, they weren't paid to think.

Horace, who had been standing right beside the door, must have seen the look on Thomas's face because he came over and stood next to him. They were both looking out at the rain.

"'You hear that?" he asked.

"Yeah." Thomas didn't afford him a look, but pulled out his walkie-talkie. His henchman, Cheo, was doing a sweep of the grounds, as per his orders.

"Cheo, come in."

There was no reply.

"Cheo, we've just heard some weird noises from the north. 'You got anything?"

Still, Cheo failed to come back on his end.

"Cheo? Is there anyone out there? 'Anyone got Cheo?"

Nothing.

"Could the rain be scrambling the waves?" asked Horace, who knew nothing about walkie-talkies.

"I don't like it," Thomas said simply. He turned to look at all the people who were supposedly working hard.

Some were stacking crates, some were checking content with clipboards in hand and two were operating forklifts. Marty was scribbling what he thought were 'killer rhymes' on the inside of his wrist.

"Everyone stop!" Thomas yelled.

His men were quick to obey. All the eyes were on him. For a moment he considered whether stopping work was really necessary, but he wasn't going to let this go. The business was just too unpredictable to attribute such noises to violent weather and if he was truthful, the recent attempted hit by the yakuza had spooked him.

"Something's going on and we're going out." There were a few sighs and curses, but Thomas shut them all up quickly.

"Hey! You wanna whine; fill out an application for JC Penny. If not and you haven't got a piece, head down to the hold and get one. You three, go with Horace and you guys come with me. The rest of you, in pairs. Shoot on sight." Thomas took out his Colt Delta Elite and cocked it.

His men obviously had mixed feelings. Some were excited at the thought of killing something, while others were pissed off at having to go out in the rain. Horace and a few others headed off to the hold before Marty came over to Thomas with a pained look on his face. The idiot was still wearing a wife-beater.

"Boss, I'm shakin' as it is, yo, and it's raining out there. Do I gotta go?"

"Jesus Christ Marty. I knew you fucked up at school and failed the ACT five times, but this is an instruction even you can understand. Unless you want me to give you a slap you'll get the fuck out there," Thomas said firmly with a hint of a nasty smirk. He then pulled out his Maglite and turned on the beam. A gang of men were already assembled to go with him and they all went out into the rain together Thomas carrying a new, annoyed scowl as his hair fell flat on his head under the force of the driving vertical tide.

"I failed it four times," Marty muttered before pulling out two Mini-Uzi's that he had tucked into the back of his pants. "And the third time I was high, so that didn't even count."

The rain outside fell like a sheet, blanketing everything except the night's black embrace. Marty groaned.

"Whoever this fucker is, I'm gonna bust a cap in his ass."

"Shut the fuck up Marty," someone behind him said. Grimacing he left with three other armed goons.

The hunt was on.

Dean had chosen a slightly less trodden route to the main building.

After all, 'no reason to give himself more trouble than he needed. The path he now traversed was lined on both sides by high hedges and ran to a small set of steps a few paces ahead.

He was prepared for anything, so when two figures appeared from a conjoining path on the left at the top of the steps, they stood little chance. Luck actually dictated that the one in a sleeveless denim jacket over a hooded sweatshirt looked the opposite way. The young man behind him didn't notice Dean either before it was too late.

"Nothing. There's fuck all out here," were the first goon's last words as he turned around to face Dean.

He was shot in the stomach and slipped backwards on the wet concrete, cracking his back on the steps and tumbling into an inelegant position. Before the other man could react a second bullet blew off half of his jaw and sent him flailing into a bush.

Dean continued. His Beretta 92 held ten rounds, so he was now down to two bullets in his current clip. This was all too easy in some respects. Dean regarded a lot of things with that internal statement.

Meanwhile, Thomas and his gang were all rotating stupidly in the rain.

"Where the fuck did that come from?" asked one of the men.

"'You mind shutting up so I can hear, dickwad?" Thomas shone his flashlight into an enclosure and cursed the rain. He was now sure something was up. 'No doubt about it.

The aquatic gunfire was beating down heavily like a drum roll. Dean pressed his back against the west wall of the central structure then turned the corner sharply his gun raised and ready to shoot, but nobody was there. The entrance to the greenhouse was completely unguarded.

Still alert to anything Dean slipped through the plastic strips and edged around the pathway that led through the jungle. When he came out on the other end he suppressed feelings of relief. Thomas, in all his idiocy, hadn't left anyone guarding the heavy doors that allowed access to the hold. The entrance creaked slightly more than Dean would have wanted it to, but didn't appear to give him away. He still had his gun raised as he descended the steps, however the room was devoid of life.

Tables, covered with guns. Crates and barrels stacked up on every spare inch of floor that wasn't a gangway. The Red Dawn were amassing so much weaponry that a room the size of a large bank lobby felt like a broom closet.

Dean pulled up his shirt to reveal the detonator along with the two yellow blocks of Semtex, taped to his chest. He ripped them off and winced at the pinching sensation. The two receivers were deep in his pocket.

This was it. He had made it to the epicenter of Ray's gun supply and he had the means to destroy it. Several stacked barrels of nitromethane sat against the far wall. Ironically, Thomas was kind of asking for what was going to happen next.

Dean put one block of Semtex at the foot of some piled ammunition crates and the other in the gap between the stacked barrels. The place would go up like the Hindenburg as soon as the bombs were detonated. The two receivers slid effortlessly into the doughy Semtex and Dean primed them by twisting the caps which began to glow.

"Okay, Thomas. This time you get to see the explosion you piece of shit," he muttered. Putting the detonation trigger down on one of the tables, Dean took a good look at all the guns. It would be foolish not to leave with at least one. The Winchester Defenders looked good. Eight shell capacity. Dean looked one over. Perfect. He pumped it with one strong arm and then holstered his pistol giving the shotgun his full grip. Not forgetting to slip the detonator inside his jacket, he left the hold.

Deciding that the way he had chosen to gain entry to the building was also the best exit he came out of the greenhouse and then followed the path back, but before he could round the corner an armed unit of men appeared ahead of him.

The duffel-clad Horace armed with a Winchester of his own was taken by surprise as a shotgun blast blew apart his midsection and sent him flying backwards. Not only that, but some of the tiny projectiles that exploded from the shell rebounded off of the man's gun and traveled deep into the head of one of his companions killing him instantly.

BANG!

BANG!

The other men were felled before they could even attempt to return fire, sizable chunks of their flesh sticking in the shrubbery. Dean didn't have time to stick around and look at the mess with disgust, so he continued on, leaving red footprints from the pooling blood he had been forced to walk through. Kicking off a piece of someone's cheek that had also stuck to his shoe, he climbed a few more sets of steps, getting as far away from the building as he felt necessary. Overhead, the sound of the vexed clouds throbbed heavy and hot. It was as if the environment itself was waiting with baited breath.

The time had come. Dean stood looking over a stone barrier at the building. The detonator was in one hand. His shotgun dangled loosely from the other. It was similar to when he had had to fire the first flurry of bullets into the room at the Helix Hotel.

Now or never.

Dean squeezed the trigger...

CHAPTER THIRTY
NIGHTFIGHT

Thomas Bentley and his group of six men were standing looking at Cheo's body, a soaked lump with a warped face. Suddenly, they were roused from their staring by three shotgun blasts faint in the night. The men were now spread thinly by the aquatic enclosure and Thomas was shining his Maglite everywhere to reveal the shadows. Cheo was dead. So were two others. Was the hulk Thomas always put on the side door dead too? Probably. Those gunshots didn't sound good either. He was having vague thoughts of getting back to his office and calling Ray. They were under attack from someone. Someone who had yet to show themselves.

These thoughts left him when an intolerably deafening boom that could not have been mistaken for thunder by anyone close by, permeated the noise of the weather.

The central building of the zoo exploded with brilliant orange light and flames. It was unreal how the brickwork warped and then was blown apart. Every pane of glass on the greenhouse shattered at once as a second sun appeared, a mushroom topped with black smoke and flanked by blue, cloud-like columns of heat that rose up until they almost touched the sky. Everyone felt the force of the explosion push at them.

Thomas glazed over.

Debris...

Flaming debris fired upwards and rained down like the aftermath of fireworks. Thomas was only shaken from his shocked state when a chunk of scorched concrete came hurtling in their direction. The man a few feet from where he was standing lost his head and a section of his upper chest as the thing collided with him and he flew backwards as if blown by an almighty wind.

Thomas's face was splashed with red, but he didn't care. He walked forward with purpose.

"NOOOOO!!! FUUUCK!!!" he screamed falling to his knees. It was gone. The hold had gone up.

"NO! FUCK! FUCK! FUCK!" Thomas was on the verge of tearing his hair out or at least shooting one of his men. He stood up and watched the flames start to shrink under the stiff force of the rain. There was an abhorrent smell like burning plastic that made Thomas's eyes sting.

He turned to his men. It was gone.

A few of them backed away a step. Their boss' wet hair fell over his forehead giving him the appearance of an escaped mental patient. Thomas spat out some rainwater.

"Come on!" Determined to find the culprit, he started to run towards the rubble of his precious cargo. His men followed.

Everything was going wrong. How could things go this wrong? How in hell could a situation go from fine, minus bad weather, to a disaster of cataclysmic proportions? Whoever was responsible for this was going to pay dearly. Thomas was going to make sure of that.

Dean was currently engaged in a firefight with a team of four goons. He was under cover behind a pillar, but they were blasting him with an array of guns. He had somehow managed to find himself in a platform area with a pillar-supported shelter on one side. The open space was covered with single stacks of crates that towered like giant chess pieces. A wide set of stone steps led down off of the platform and south, however Dean just couldn't get to them. His shotgun had been run dry and he unleashed the remaining rounds left in his Beretta clip. Two of his attackers were killed and Dean dodged fire from what sounded like an M4. He reloaded listening closely to quick footsteps interspersed with shouting and splashing. Haze from the explosion was thick in the air even through the rain as was the sound of somebody coughing out the vapors.

"Where is he?" enquired a Jamaican voice.

"Behind the pillars. We 'got him trapped!"

There were more footsteps which Dean didn't doubt were the men spreading themselves. The two remaining thugs now had backup and his current position wouldn't cut it.

Running to another pillar he was glad no gunshots chased him. He looked up just in time to see a man in a soaked cowboy hat perched on the roof of an adjacent building with a hunting rifle trained on him. Dean got off a shot first and the gunman tumbled off of the structure and hit the ground with a wet thud.

The rain had eased slightly; however, this provided little calm. Lightning still flashed every twenty seconds.

"Use the crates!" yelled the Jamaican voice.

"Yo, Bruno! Get some cover!"

Dean took a swift glance at the setup. One man was hiding behind the pillar on the far side where Dean had come from. He was obvious, because the stupid sucker had his gun hand up in the air just in view. There was shadowy movement between the crate stacks as the other men took up positions.

Dean had no idea how many people were there now, but more would come given time. He had to be fast. Sending a very accurate gunshot to the man behind the pillar, Dean ducked back behind his own cover to avoid fire from some automatic weapon.

"Aaah, fuck! My fucking hand!" the man wailed falling on his ass in a puddle. Dean's bullet had gone all the way through his palm and blown the top off of his middle finger.

"Aaah! Shit!"

"Take him out!" came the Jamaican voice once again.

In one expeditious move, Dean passed from the pillar to behind one of the crate stacks. Whirling around it with his gun raised, his barrel came into fleshy contact with a bald man's temple. He fired without hesitation blowing the guy's brains out and all over the ground. It was automatic like a mechanical function fuelled by the hatred and thrill in his soul. His bloodthirsty psyche carried out the steps of each execution without error. When the destruction and death reached maximum intensity, everything became meaningless.

It was like shooting deer or playing a video game. It was just that easy.

There were loud curses and someone got into a position that allowed them to fire upon him.

He ran to the next source of cover.

There he stood, only ten feet from a black assailant with dreadlocks who had a Winchester aimed right at his heart. However, before the blast could reach its target, a second man came between them. The projectiles from the shell obliterated his chest and Dean caught the man under the arms and then fired over his shoulder, taking out the one who he suspected was the Jamaican. He dropped the body and snuffed out another goon that tried to take him by surprise.

In a weird way this was becoming fun for him. He hadn't done this since Afghanistan and without any real refresher course; he was back into his own again. How interesting.

A large man with a Calico 960 strafed Dean's position with automatic fire and he was forced to take cover again. After some return fire that missed, a single round found its victim. The automatic siege stopped and the man fell against the side of a crate pile, limp.

Dean wanted that gun. Nice, light, and fast-firing.

To get to the weapon he had to cross a threshold between some stacks and as he went for it he was immediately prompted to take cover again as a barrage of repetitive gunfire was sent his way. He wasn't going to get to that Calico unless he took his marker out, but that would be no trouble. Another one of Thomas's nameless stooges was no trouble at all.

He noticed no movement from anywhere now. All the other bodies were lifeless, even that belonging to the man Dean had shot in the hand. His buddy's had probably put him out of his misery or he had gone into shock.

Suddenly, there was one of those annoying voices you hear from wannabe gangstas.

"Look man, I ain't fuckin' playin'. Drop the gun or I'm gonna fuck your shit up, ite?"

Dean didn't reply. Instead, he decided to be crafty and try to get around the back of the last thug. Unfortunately, things didn't exactly go to plan. Dean came out from behind the crates on the other side of the platform; gun raised and so did the remaining goon.

He was lanky and wearing a wife-beater that had been turned gray by the rain. In his hands were two Mini-Uzi's held on their sides.

Neither fired.

How could they? It was a stalemate.

Marty was shaking in the cold, yet kept his guns unwaveringly trained on this new adversary. He sure didn't recognize the punk, but that didn't matter. He had the advantage because he held his guns sideways. Instant kill shot! Now he had this foo in a tricky situation. Now Marty had *him* on the ropes.

The thug gave Dean a visceral stare from below his white cap, then spoke.

"You ain't goin' nowhere, playa! Drop the piece or I'm gonna put some serious pain..."

Distracted by inconsequential dialogue, Marty could only have feelings of surprise as the 9x19 Parabellum round hit him directly in the chest. In one involuntary muscle spasm his hands flew up and he sent a few rounds high into the sky as his body arced backwards and he fell, tumbling over and over down the stone steps behind. The shot didn't kill him immediately. Even the violent fall didn't kill him immediately. It was when he got to the foot of the stairs and his head flipped up and made messy contact with a low wall. That was when he perished.

Dean trembled. He really had taken a gamble there and it had paid off. All of a sudden, the vile fumes from the building he had demolished got to him and he doubled over, coughing up something into his elbow. Looking down his eyes widened at the sight of blood and something yellow. The air was clearly toxic this close to the site of the destruction. He needed to put some distance between himself and the smoke. Whatever Thomas' nest egg of poisons had contained, it wasn't doing him any good.

187

Holstering his pistol, he returned to the corpse that cradled the Calico submachine gun in limp hands. With the compact, yet deadly little weapon in hand, Dean set off down the steps.

Marty's body now lay in a pool of watery crimson, as did his fallen comrades. The rain was picking up again. Thomas wouldn't send out hunting parties and not go out himself. That just wasn't Thomas. He was out in the rain somewhere and Dean was going to find him.

CHAPTER THIRTY-ONE
PENULTIMATE RAGE

A firefight had broken out somewhere close to the central building.

Thomas and his remaining men were heading straight there. They had hoped to make it in one piece, but as they reached the rope bridge they came under assault. It extended across a deep ravine with one side acting as a majestic waterfall into the pool below. On the other side elephant statues provided good cover and whoever was shooting at them knew this well enough. All of the men ducked behind walls on reflex.

Dean stopped firing. The men had taken cover too quickly for him to kill any of them which was an annoyance. Thomas was with them. His distinctive snarling face, his dark jacket, his jet black hair, he was here and he was about to meet his end.

One of the goons took a few potshots and the mystery assailant responded by putting a lucky bullet through his head. He fell backwards and Thomas swore under his breath. A young guy was right next to him with a pistol in his shaking grip, his fear as pungent as chopped garlic. He was quite obviously a pussy not cut out for this and the other men were cookie-cutter morons you could have found in any sleazy back alley, however one had an AK-74 which would prove advantageous.

Negotiation seemed to be a prudent option in Thomas's eyes at that moment. He signaled for his men to stay down.

"Hey!" he shouted. There was another crackle from the electric storm overhead.

Dean remained crouched the Calico vertical almost touching his face. The deceitful shitbag was actually going to try and negotiate. God, he couldn't wait to kill him.

"Hey, Asshole! What're you doing? What do you want?" There was a small pause. "What is this?"

Dean wanted to reply, but there was nothing to say at that moment. This was all about action. Words were meaningless now and Thomas would find they were useless as weapons.

"You killed my man, Cheo. You blew up my fucking building! What the fuck for, huh? Is this about Taiki? Who are you?!" Thomas's words became a bitter scream, still there was no reply.

That did it. His question ignored, he would finish this the old-fashioned way. He made a hand signal telling two of his men to approach slowly and the one with the automatic to lay down some cover if required.

Dean took a fleeting look at what was going on. They were trying to come over. The stupid fucks were trying to come to him. Thomas really was desperate. Before the men even got halfway across the bridge, Dean opened fire again with the Calico. A few stray rounds cut into the second man's head and neck, but most of the fire was received by the first who fell sideways, his lifeless, fat body supported by the rope of the bridge which promptly snapped under the strain. The man freefell and hit the lagoon below with a splash.

Dean took cover again as a third gunman laid down heavy automatic fire on his position poking holes in the statue and spraying the area with wet dust. The opportunity to remove him too was taken, unfortunately it was a risky move and this time Dean wasn't so lucky. A round hit his right shoulder making him cry out, however he did put a few rounds into his attacker's chest causing him to flail in agony and accidentally spray gunfire towards Thomas. Naturally, always fixated on self-preservation, Thomas threw his final asset in front of him as a human shield and it saved his life. In anger he immediately took a few lazy shots with his Delta Elite none of which hit anything fleshy.

All of his men were dead. Just him and whoever this son of a bitch was.

"Fuck!" he yelled, shoving the corpse of the young man away from him. He tensed himself, looking down at the glassy eyes which now stared into his own. With a grunt of disgust he pushed the head to the side with his gun if only to avoid the creepy, soulless gaze. Dean himself actually managed to refrain from cursing as he fingered around the wound he had sustained. A few tears scorched his retina and more lightning ripped across the sky. It was painful. Dean had sustained two gunshots in his life before now and the pain never became familiar. Luckily, it was the only ailment that he suffered as the harsh rain had finally diluted most of the poison from the air and his lungs no longer felt knotted with the presence of Thomas's chemical stockpile.

He gritted his teeth and squeezed the grip on his Calico tightly.

Thomas could have more men, although Dean had a feeling he didn't. He was all alone. That was just how Dean wanted him. He wanted to witness the shock and horror on Thomas's face when he saw the bullet come flying at him from a gun held by a dead man.

On the other side of the bridge the last breather had had enough. If this fucker wanted to play hardball - then so be it. Thomas stepped out into the line of fire looking at the bridge ahead with his Delta pointed in the direction where he knew his antagonist lay. His men may have shot like Stevie Wonder, but he sure as shit didn't. His bravado was about the only thing reassuring him at the moment. The rest of him was shaking with fear. Thomas had never been shot before and he didn't want to add it to his list of experiences. Even so, he bit down and edged forward.

"Alright then motherfucker, you wanna fuck with me? Then come on!" Thomas released the valve on his rage for a moment.

It was at the halfway point that the figure leapt out from his cover and Thomas fired too late. The bullet missed. He was quick to right himself, but something made him stop.

At the same time Dean fired with his own gun. Nothing happened. The weapon just clicked. The sick and horrible feeling in his stomach rushed to his throat. He had run the weapon dry.

Thomas stared wide eyed his Delta's aim slightly off. Things slowed down.

It couldn't be. The man standing before him in a soaked black suit with a red tie blowing in the wind looked a bit like... just a bit like... Cottrell. It was impossible of course. It was someone who shared a similar face. Not just similar, the exact features. His blonde hair was dripping and flat and he stared out through those familiar, predatory, green eyes. There was a darkness to them, something that had made Thomas feel uneasy whenever the two had met. No one else had eyes like that, leaving only one conclusion. Thomas almost screamed, but stifled it. The realization stopped his heart dead.

"That's impossible," he croaked. His voice was weak and vulnerable.

There was no time to draw his Beretta and Dean knew it. He lunged for Thomas in a flying football tackle dropping his useless Calico. Without preparation Thomas fell like a sack of potatoes not even putting up a fight.

There was a gunshot, but no sensation of pain indicated it had flown uselessly up into the air.

They fell - no rope to stop them.

Thomas slipped from Dean's grasp. They continued to fall.

The next thing Dean felt was the crunch of hitting a rather shallow part of the lagoon and damn near breaking his ribs. A dull throbbing started in his head and things got darker. The sound of thunder and the crashing water were nothing but echoes.

The other man who had taken the plunge wasn't so lucky. He made messy contact with the jagged, rocky face of the falls and finally released his scream as the part of his leg just below the kneecap was torn open. He tumbled lost his grip on the gun and landed with a splash.

Dean remembered a lot of things in that moment. He remembered all the men he had killed after exiting his car. He remembered talking to Donnie Tagliano and drinking wine. He remembered his dream. He remembered everything.

That was when he rolled over onto his back. No, he didn't do it himself. Someone else was doing it for him.

192

To see Thomas's face contorted with the combined agony from his leg injury and the built up rage that had started with finding Cheo's body was to stare into the face of the devil.

Dean couldn't think about reaching for his gun. He couldn't think at all. Thomas punched him in the face, dead on, right in the nose, fracturing it. He then came close to killing his prey with a hard blow to the temple. He punched Dean again in the jaw and then again in the nose until the damaged head was leaking red stuff from almost every opening. Water cascaded from his face onto the fallen one man army, as did an ocean froth of saliva from his twisted mouth. He stopped the punching suddenly and looked at the man's bruised face. It was him alright. The fucker had somehow survived the bomb.

"You piece of shit!" He thumped Dean hard in his already damaged ribs. Thomas was currently in a cat-like position over Dean and was every bit as threatening as a wild animal.

"I don't know how you survived, but I'm gonna make you wish you hadn't!" Thomas continued to yell and raised a fist to silence Dean once and for all.

He was ready for it. If Thomas hit the right place Dean's skull would crack open on the uneven surface he was laying on. This was it. He had failed. Thomas was going to kill him here and now.

No.

He wouldn't accept that. Not in a million fucking years.

At that moment the delirious rage that had been simmering for days came out of Dean, and he did something he wouldn't have considered doing in any other situation. He grabbed Thomas's shredded shin and drove his thumb right into the exposed flesh.

"AAAAAAAAAAAAAAAAAAAAAHHHHHHHHHHHHHHHHHHHHHHHH!!!" Thomas's howls didn't seem to end. His whole body shook violently and he couldn't finish Dean off. The agony was too much. Excruciating pain so unbearable he lost control of all his bodily functions. He fell sideways off of Dean twitching and the man, who just seconds ago had been the underdog, now had the upper hand. Dean looked to his left and saw a Maglite lying in the water. It had fallen from Thomas's belt when he fell and now it was in Dean's hands. A smooth, black tube of metal and a deadly weapon. With an undeniable position of power, he crawled onto Thomas and dealt a blow that cracked a cheek bone and glanced off the nose, breaking it. The screaming stopped as his victim was forced to spit out a mouthful of blood.

WHACK!

WHACK!

WHACK!

Each hit was as brutal as the previous. Thomas felt the Maglite dent his malleable skull a little more each time as Dean continued to hit him on every side of his face. Two of his teeth were knocked out. One of his eyes lost vision completely and started bleeding. He was covered in sticky red.

"Please," he coughed, but Dean could only hear the driving rain urging him on. He didn't notice the look in Thomas's eyes. The defeated look of a man who was begging for his life, the look his brother had seen after every time Thomas had gotten beaten up. His tongue had become more venomous over the years, but when all the talk had vanished, he hadn't changed that much at all. His own pathetic nature might have prompted mercy in any other situation, but Dean was blind to it. All he saw was the maniac who had helped destroy his life and for that man, there would be no redemption but death. Dean grabbed his collar and yelled into his face.

"Words of wisdom, Tom! Next time you fuck someone over and leave 'em for dead, MAKE SURE THEY'RE REALLY DEAD!"

WHAAAACK!

Dean's final blow slowed before it impacted, but only in his mind. Thomas's eyes widened impossibly as his head lolled to the right and he fell silent.

The flashlight fell into the water.

Thomas was dead.

Even so, nothing had changed. The rage was still inside Dean's soul, burning hot like swallowed fire. He would have thought killing Thomas might ease it. Instead he was still stuck, as angry as ever. He thumped his victim in the chest twice and then broke down completely. Soaking wet with a bullet in his shoulder, Dean started to cry out uncontrollably, his psyche unable to take the strain a second

194

longer. This was what they had done to him. It was their fault. They had reduced him to this. These fuckers! He slugged Thomas hard again. The body didn't react. Doing half the job wasn't going to make anything better. To put an end to this insanity, he had to get them all.

Ray was next on his list. *He* was the true heart of the betrayal, giving the final say on who the organization could afford to lose. His brother had been little more than a convenient, blunt instrument. A coward, hiding behind his hired scum and although Ray's particular variety of hired scum were paid better and dressed nicer, they would fall just the same.

Overhead, the storm began to settle.

CHAPTER THIRTY-TWO
GUILT COCKTAIL

It was starting to get late at the Holden Tower, yet still; the place was home to quite a few breathers. In the bar that was an introduction to the third floor, Williams was slouched on a stool downing a fourth Manhattan. Those who walked by regarded him as a nasty spill. The fact that he was lonely, depressed and possibly guilty was worsened by the fact that Bert (the bartender) had decided that instead of one of his usual, soft melodies that often hinted an oriental theme, the song about one being the loneliest number would be more fitting for the occasion and Williams was becoming increasingly suspicious that the man was deliberately pissing him off.

"Bert, turn that shit off!" he half-yelled.

Bert obeyed, but openly chuckled to himself.

Asshole.

Williams sighed and looked at his empty glass.

"And you can get me another Manhattan too." His tone was obviously one of extreme annoyance. He was already low enough and the last thing he needed was Bert's apparently hilarious social commentary.

"I'm sorry. 'Couldn't help myself." Again, Bert was chuckling. He set a fifth Manhattan down in front of his customer and leaned on the bar. There was a moment of silence between them.

"Where's my cherry?" Williams asked, looking disapprovingly at the drink.

"We're all out of cherries."

"Jesus, you 'gotta be the worst fucking barman in the world," he said, putting more alcohol into his system.

"What's the problem Williams, huh? I haven't seen you knocking them back like that since you screwed up that job in Toronto."

Williams was set to give Bert one of those 'shut up' stares, but instead found himself opening up completely thanks to the intoxication. He was a talker, and couldn't keep everything he was feeling bottled up any longer.

"I just can't believe Dean's gone. I fucking knew that guy you know?"

Bert noticed the telltale slur to Williams' voice. Manhattan's weren't all he had had that night.

"Yeah. 'Gonna miss him and his money. 'Heard he got caught in a blast. 'That true?"

"Not just any fucking blast. Ray sent him in with a fucking timer strapped to his chest. They stabbed him in the back." Williams glanced over at the table where he and Dean had sat and had a conversation mere days ago. It was an enigma wrapped in a conundrum with no real answers. Talking to Thomas hadn't helped at all.

"Listen, Williams. In this business a whole lot of people are going to fall down around you. Dean was a fifth wheel and got chosen for the op. It's how it goes." Thomas Bentley stood in front of Williams after he had demanded to know what the hell had happened to Dean. It had been a setup with no exit plan, a suicide mission.

"Why him? He did everything you fucking asked, Tom!"

"Hey!" Thomas's voice instantly raised and the snarling; weapon-stockpiling maniac was right in his face with those pearly white teeth. "I decide who goes and who stays, not you! You do what I tell you, understand?!"

Williams hated it when people reminded him that he worked for them. He hadn't really cared for Thomas too much in the first place, but at that moment, he wanted to kill him. He wanted to wrap his hands around the man's neck and snap it like an injured bird's. Such barbarism wasn't alien to him.

"You could go far Williams. You've got the eyes for it, but that fucking attitude of yours has to curl up and die because I ain't gonna vouch for you if Ray thinks we can afford to lose someone else." The look in Thomas's eyes was one that Williams knew all too well. The look of someone who didn't like him. It was a look that told him that whatever they did from now on was pure business. Thomas gave the orders and Williams followed them. If he didn't play by the rules then his boss wouldn't lose sleep over having him taken care of.

"It's the craziest shit I 'ever heard. He didn't put a foot out of line Bert. Not one fucking toe. Heck, I was in most ways a worse employee than him!"

"Well, he must have been disposable. The boys upstairs 'got a whole damn list of people they could stand to lose," said Bert.

"What does that mean for me? What if one day I'm carrying that bomb?"

Giving a heavy shrug Bert started to clean out a selection of glasses.

"Oh, God, Bert. I'm a waste of skin. I pissed my life away and now... I 'got no friends."

"Come on! You've got friends," Bert said encouragingly.

"Like who?"

"Well... Huan over there. He's your friend."

Now feeling very drunk he followed Bert's pointing finger. The Chinese man in the cloakroom hatch waved and flashed a cheesy grin.

Williams, with both eyebrows raised, turned back to Bert.

"I'm not holding out much hope. Aren't you my friend Bert?"

"Umm... well, how about those guys over there." Again the barman was pointing. This time, he was trying to indicate two men sitting in a fretwork booth. The first was a tall individual with a shaven head and an old scar down his left cheek. The other was Kruge who now had shiny flecks of metal embedded in the flesh of his right cheek, put there by the explosion at the Starcross motel. They were a perfect pair.

Once more, Williams turned back around with despondent eyes.

He wasn't quite sure why he felt so shitty. He couldn't have prevented what had happened. He hadn't known until it was already too late. It was a strange feeling that crawled all over him like a plague of carnivorous locusts and it wasn't even related to all the alcohol he had consumed that night. Strangely, it felt a whole lot like guilt. God, if only he could get a set of crosshairs on Thomas's head and then pull the trigger with a big fucking smile on his face.

Bert noticed that Williams had zoned out and gave him a tap on the arm.

"You need to treat yourself more often Williams. You think too much. Go to the movies once in a while, maybe rent out a porno. I know girls on film always cheer me up. I mean, look on the bright side. At least it wasn't you. I'd hedge my bets on them promoting you any time now."

"You 'gotta be joking. That asshole over there with the scar, he's on Ray's personal staff now. He drove the fucking van on Dean's last mission. A driver got put up before me. Looking at things realistically I'd hedge *my* bets on them getting rid of me next."

Someone passed through the bar on their way to the elevator and Bert straightened up and called out to him.

"Hey, Nolan. Why not stop by for a drink, huh?"

"Not with your prices, douchebag," the man replied with a heavy voice.

"Fine." Bert seemed embarrassed and made to continue his conversation with someone too wasted to care about prices.

"I don't know Bert. Dean and I were like best buds. He's irreplaceable. 'Even took a trip to Vegas last year and now he's just... gone. I 'got no real friends now. All the guys I hang out with are douchebags."

"Well, I'm not a douchebag."

Narrowing his slightly bloodshot eyes, Williams looked up at Bert.

"That guy just called you a douchebag man."

The burly bartender went quiet and turned to do something, leaving the drunk patron alone with his thoughts

The whole thing was so screwed up; Williams just hated to even think about it.

He had had this steady career for a while now and with no other prospects, he wouldn't be able to leave. Why had he chosen this stupid job? He couldn't even complain to a union. He should have just tried to get contracted by the yakuza. At least they followed a code of respect, to some degree.

Williams rubbed the dry skin from his face. He would have to journey home soon, but in this damn weather he would exhaust every excuse not to, before heading down to the parking garage.

He raised his glass in the air and looked up to the ceiling.

"This one's for you, buddy. You're killing angels now." The rest of the Manhattan slipped down his throat.

CHAPTER THIRTY-THREE
LOSSES

News of the night's events reached the Holden Tower the next morning. The massacre at the zoo out near Lake Arrowhead came before a list of traffic collisions that had also occurred that night. Details in the report were sketchy, but luckily for Valentino, he had somebody down at the scene of the crime. He was currently taking a phone call from one of the lower level employees that he had bumped up to Ray's personal staff. A tall guy with a big scar on his face.

"Sir, somehow the main building exploded. All of the ammo and shit must've gone up. The good news is it probably incinerated anything linking back to us."

"Okay." Valentino accepted the good news. That was one of the main things that had been worrying him. "Any signs as to who might have pulled off this stunt?"

"Nothing I can see, sir. 'Huge amount of casualties though. It's a bloodbath."

Valentino knew what the man was going to say next. The tone of voice gave it away. 'Gave away the fact that he was trying to get Valentino ready for the really bad news. The husky mobster screwed up his face in preparation.

"There's something else too, sir. Ray's brother is one of the deceased."

That knocked the wind out of Valentino even though he had prepared for it. Thomas was dead. Never mind how the fuck Ray was going to react to that. What about the weapons supply? What the hell were they going to do now?!

201

"Alright. Vessup, you stay on this. Keep it low. See if you can't get some more information from the bacon patrol down there."

"'Got it."

He hung up and rubbed his forehead, but managed to restrain himself from crouching down in despair. He was stronger than that.

The business had taken heavy losses before now and it would be a cold day in Hell when he let the death of someone like Thomas Bentley break him. However, the situation was still a dire one. The question he couldn't shake was, who could have pulled off something like that and not leave a trace of their presence? If the yakuza were trying to make up for lost ground, then they were doing a swell job of it.

The worst part was no doubt just about to come. He now had to walk through those double doors and tell Ray that his brother had been wasted.

Valentino brushed down his suit to keep any creases in line and then turned to Ray's office and entered, closing the doors behind him. Ray was drinking a glass of scotch at an unusually early hour, but these days it wasn't so unusual anymore. He had his back to Valentino, staring at the picture behind his desk. Inside the fish tank the yellow beauties stared out at the individual none of them remembered in morbid expectance. The mob boss turned revealing a set of slightly sunken eyes. He looked greasier and more disheveled than usual.

"What news from the front? Did you reach my brother?"

A sort of half-smile appeared on Ray's face for a second. He had most likely started drinking upon hearing the news that his weapons supply had been attacked. The blows just kept coming. First the deal with the triads and then this. Ray wasn't a happy man and Valentino wished there was a way of just not telling him. Thomas and Ray were brothers if ever he had seen them with each other till the end, born from the same womb, possibly cut from a different cloth than that of their parents, but definitely the same one as each other.

"Ray..." he choked. He couldn't complete the sentence. His mouth had gone dry. Fucking Thomas. 'Had to go and die and put him in this shitty mess of a situation.

"What?" Ray sipped at his scotch.

"Ray… someone with a lot of balls was messing with us last night. No survivors. Thomas… He didn't make it. He's dead."

Like a corpse over time, Valentino's voice dried out completely. Like a corpse over time, the color in Ray Bentley's face left the premises. The glass of scotch seemed to fall in slow motion. At foot level the carpet prevented it from smashing; however the amber liquid spilled out regardless and darkened a patch of the floor. Ray stood completely still to the point of being statuesque. It was unfamiliar the atmosphere that filled the room like water, but at the same time, seemed to suck everything out of it. It really was as if time had stopped completely and it was just the two men who had thoughts at that moment.

"Get out," Ray said finally.

Valentino didn't hang around for the obligatory, louder order. He left.

Ray was still fixed on the spot like some depressive art student's sculpture, perhaps a tribute to struggling crime lords. It was too late to try and keep face and Ray didn't want to. Tears were already running wild down his cheeks. His lips quivered and then it came.

The break.

Ray let out a harsh whimper and turned his head away from where Valentino had been standing. It couldn't be true. It just couldn't be. There was no way. He leaned up against his desk and fell to his knees.

"Tom! Fuck!" he got out through clenched teeth. He had lost his other half, his brother, his friend. The only one who would ever understand. He was gone. Through all of those painfully long years of hurt. The troubles at home, the troubles at school, their whole shitty back-story, it had always been Ray and Thomas, to Hell and back.

"Tom! How the fuck could you die on me!" he yelled in rage. He stood up and grabbed the crystal decanter of scotch and ran a few paces before hurling it at the opposing wall. It disintegrated on impact with a mighty shatter that marked the surface in more ways than one.

He pounded a fist on his desk. Images and memories flashed before him. Seeing Thomas after he had been beaten up at some young age. A cold day in the late autumnal season just him and his brother sitting on a static teeter totter. Then there was Thomas at the age that Ray had last seen him. He nodded slowly, encouraging the natural grief. This was despair. The feeling of not being able to get air into his lungs overcame Ray, and he was forced to breathe heavily as if he were suffering an asthma attack. He would have to compose himself soon.

Valentino would want orders and Ray was curious as to whether this meant that his dream was finished.

Outside the organization's no.3 was standing with his back to a wall. He anticipated that Ray would have a breakdown and then pull himself together before calling him back in. Besides, there was nowhere else to go.

"Valentino. Get in here," came the loud voice.

Valentino obeyed and entered Ray's office for the second time. He took a quick glance at all the broken glass on the floor and the big splatter on the wall. Yep. Ray had definitely flipped out. The guy was now sat in his chair behind his desk. He had been quick to remove any trace of upset from his face, but his bloodshot eyes betrayed him.

"Valentino, my good friend, my all-knowing advisor. Are we screwed?" His question was simple with less interest than it should have contained.

"No. Whoever did this wanted to get rid of all the stocked weapons. There was an explosion and in short we think any ties to us are ashes, but I wouldn't be too shocked if cops come asking you questions. Thomas was your brother after all and this isn't looking like an accident."

"'Police can ask all the damn questions they like. 'Doesn't mean they're gonna get any answers."

Valentino figured that it had been the scotch decanter that Ray had thrown at the wall in anger as it was missing from his desk.

"That's good," his boss concluded. "I want my brother's body."

"Of course."

"Now, go 'get me some more scotch. I must have drunk it all." The voice was so distant, it might as well have been a radio signal from Pluto.

"Sure thing Ray, I'm sorry for your loss." Valentino left and Ray was alone once again.

The yakuza were responsible for this travesty. 'No doubt about it. Burning his deal with the triads hadn't been enough. They had come back for seconds and this time, they had taken so much more than was necessary to slow the Red Dawn. Slow it, but not stop it. Ray wouldn't stop for anything. In fact he would gain momentum. If the Japanese wanted a war, then a war they would fucking get. That was what Thomas would have wanted. Just because he was dead didn't mean Ray wouldn't keep his promise. They would pay. Every last one of them.

But he still had trouble believing it. His brother was dead.

His brother and the word 'dead' didn't belong in the same sentence and yet there they were. Thomas Bentley. His brother. Dead. The last stretch was up to him. The last push for victory.

He got up and walked to the window. In a blatant display of lost sanity he put a cold hand to the glass and spoke to the city below.

"I see you. Laugh it up you Japanese cocksuckers. I'm gonna hit you so hard your ancestors are gonna shit themselves. That goes for everyone. Before this thing is over the skies are gonna turn red and it'll all be mine! That's a fucking guarantee."

That day, more of the Ray that had existed all those years ago died away and the new man grew stronger. The rage got stronger. He was more dangerous than ever. Nothing could hold him back.

CHAPTER THIRTY-FOUR
THE WARRIOR RETURNING ALIVE

"**W**ell, I'll be damned. He got it done."

Donato Tagliano was watching the news coverage of the zoo massacre. The death toll was at twenty-seven and holding, but firemen were sifting through the wreckage of a destroyed building. Dean had got the bombs into the place and had managed to detonate them. He had also gunned down a small army. Whether or not Thomas Bentley or Dean himself were among the dead, had yet to be discovered. At present, many of Donnie's goons were in the lounge with him. His right-hand man, Slip, was sitting next to him on the couch providing commentary.

"Tricky bastard. 'You think he could have gotten out?"

"It's always a possibility," Donnie replied.

The announcer on the television continued to report.

"*While police refuse to give out the names of any of the victims, they do believe that all of the deceased were involved in a massive gun smuggling operation and have put the massacre down to gang violence. When asked whether this latest development could be related to a general increase in statewide violence due to organized crime, the police department refused to comment.*"

Behind the couch one of Donnie's men came into the room with a pleased smile on his face.

"Sir."

Donnie turned where he was sitting.

"What?"

"You have a visitor."

Wearing a new, gray suit, and with a subtly pleased gleam in his eyes, Dean took a few paces forward and came into view. Everyone stared. There was silence. Even the news announcer seemed to shut up for a few seconds.

Donnie laughed and then stood up and came around the couch, hands outstretched.

"Dean." He gave him a friendly hug and then shook his shoulders and turned to his right-hand.

"'See? Dependability. 'Had a feeling you had balls kid. Come into the dining area. We'll talk. Monte, get us some wine. How about it?"

A tall member of Donnie's assembly nodded and walked off in another direction while the mob boss himself led Dean into the beautiful dining hall. They sat in the same positions that they had taken up on their last encounter.

"My God. 'Was thinking I might not see you again, but here you are. Twenty-seven men dead in your wake. 'Thomas Bentley among them?" Donnie's mood was chipper and his beaming expression was a harsh contrast to how he had been recently. A shell of the man he once was, now rejuvenated.

"Oh, he's dead alright," Dean said with newfound vigor.

"You really are something else. You kill the bastard, blow up the place and return alive. Few men are that committed or that skilled."
Dean could tell that Donnie was pleased with him. He had in all likelihood expected Dean to die in the face of insurmountable odds.

With a bit of know-how Dean had removed the bullet from his own shoulder and had the wound sealed for now, but one of the things he would need from Donnie would be someone with some real medical knowledge.

"Donnie, I got hit last night. I 'got a bullet wound I need someone to take a look at."

"No problem. I can get a doctor here in fifteen minutes. 'Knew nobody could come out of something like that without so much as one mark."

One of Donnie's men set down two wine glasses and filled them to the brim. The triumphant killer was glad to get some alcohol inside of him. He had decided against going to the liquor store last night with the round in his shoulder and all.

After a doctor had been requested Dean and his partner in crime talked while they waited, mainly about the specifics of what Red Dawn were currently doing.

Time passed.

The doctor was an elderly gentleman who was doing a fine job of patching Dean's laceration properly as he sat in the lounge. It wasn't the best location for such a procedure, but the bullet hadn't done any permanent damage. Dean winced as a stitch was pulled tight.

"'You think cops will find links to Ray at the zoo?" asked Donnie.

"No. It'll have all been in Thomas's office. The explosion was bigger than I anticipated. It's probably all been destroyed."

Donnie looked at the red carpet sadly.

"No matter though. We don't want Ray to die in prison."

At this, Donnie lightened up immediately.

"'Shouldn't be too concerned about any police involvement at the moment anyway. After Orion got wasted the fuckers probably have enough on their plate."

"True." Dean winced again as his injury was messed with.

"There. All done. You're lucky the guy that shot you was either badly trained or had learning difficulties. No permanent damage at all, but I'd recommend staying out of action for a while. The wound might hurt for some time." The doctor's voice was grating and dusty. Dean had a notion that the man had held a license for a short while and probably had it revoked for performing some questionable operations. Even so, he was grateful.

"Thanks."

"All in a day's work. I must say though, the removal of the bullet and the short term patch work you did yourself was pretty textbook. 'You ever a paramedic, or in the army maybe?"

Dean drew in some breath sharply and smiled.

"Good guess. 'Seems so long ago when I served."

The man nodded with his mouth slightly open and said, "thought so," before giving Donnie a soft nod and picking up his things to leave.

Dean put his shirt back on and winced for the third or fourth time in minor discomfort. He was just lucky the round hadn't hit something more vital. His shoulder would heal, but he guessed the scar would serve as a permanent reminder of this chapter in his life.

"Okay then, you're oiled and ready to go minus some downtime. What's our next move?"

"You're a stand-in Godfather and you're asking me what our next move is?" Dean chuckled, and Donnie returned it then sat himself down in his usual armchair.

"Dean, before you came along I was considering closing down, and heading to Hawaii. You're the one who wants to keep things going and you've proven you've got the balls for it."

"I guess so. Well, I'm considering giving Ray a call sometime soon to give my condolences, but I'll take the doc's advice about staying out of action for a while. You should work on finding an ally in all of this. Ray's hitting organized crime all over L.A. I'm sure you can locate some people who want him in the ground."

Donnie nodded like men who are getting old do, but with a youthful grin. That was something Dean had noticed from the get-go. This relic from the days when gangsters were more respectable was a man most likely in his mid-sixties; however that didn't stop him from possessing a touch of upstart criminal spark.

"Alright. I'll see if the Gambino Family is willing to make an arrangement, after all that's happened. If that falls through I'll get in touch with some of the local gangs. Ray's scratching the surface of the underground. He picked off two dealers and cleaned out a large crack den of the Caligula persuasion a couple of days ago."

"Okay. I'm going to head back to my motel. You have the number you need to reach me." With everything said that needed to be said, Dean left the Tagliano house and as he drove his car down the streets of Los Angeles past everyday citizens. He resisted a strong urge to head straight to his apartment and what resided there. Instead, he tried to think of Ray Bentley's breakdown. Killing his brother should be enough to show the bastard that he'd fucked with the wrong guy. He gripped the steering wheel. He wanted to hear Ray's voice now more than ever. To hear whether it had changed. To hear his reaction when he found out who was really behind the death of his beloved sibling.

CHAPTER THIRTY-FIVE
REVELATION AND THREAT

Finishing up another glass of JD was a challenge, but Dean just about managed it. He was not yet ready to define himself as 'drunk as a skunk', however the eyes he was aiming at the phone had definitely taken an off-color pigment. Once or twice he had reached for it and then withdrawn.

Dean had an incredible knack for remembering numbers very quickly and Williams had once given him a direct link to Ray's office in case of some grand emergency like knowing the place was about to be attacked. Finally, after some very long deliberation under the dreamy influence of Lady Liquor he felt ready to do it.

He wiped some residue from his chin and swallowed an acrid taste, cramming it way down inside. 'Had to be professional about it. This was scary stuff. He was about to call Ray Bentley, *the* Ray Bentley and give him the biggest shock of his life. This was it.

In his office, that hovered as a static domain of consideration on the city skyline, Ray Bentley leafed through a few pages of linear notes.

He was not alone in the room. The yellow tangs swam carelessly in the blue euphoria that was water at perfect temperature and another much larger fish was standing in the darkest recess of the room, his animalistic eyes penetrated the shadows like something from a horror movie. The shark that was Lysander Shades, had taken up residence in the office earlier in the day for a long talk with his employer and after they had finished he hadn't respected the cue to leave. It was now nine P.M., and still, he stood there unmoving like a bad stain on the wall.

Ray grimaced and resented not being alone, but for some reason he couldn't bring himself to ask Shades to leave. He couldn't bring himself to do much at the moment. News of his brother's death had taken almost everything from him.

He had one last phone call to make that night and now felt like the time to make it. His hand reached for the landline, but before he could touch it the phone lit up and rang loudly. Recoiling at the abruptness of it Ray was quick to recover himself. He picked it up.

"Hello?"

There was a long pause where Ray could only hear harsh breathing. The possibility of a prank call came to mind instantly, but Ray wasn't listed in any phone book.

"Hello?"

This time, the answer was alarmingly immediate.

"How are things on your end, Ray? I'm guessing not too good."

Ray stood up and thanks to cordless technology, was able to venture as far from his desk as he pleased. The message coming down the line was slightly fragmented and the caller didn't sound all-there, but Ray knew that tone from somewhere... That voice belonged to someone he recognized. That in itself wasn't too disturbing, but something deep in the man's head was telling him it wasn't a voice he wanted to hear.

"Who is this?"

Shades looked directly at Ray and took a step out of the shadows. He had the same resentful, gaunt face that he had always had except this time, interest was holding his expression.

"You know the problem with a bomb is that it's too unreliable."

Ray wanted to put the phone down, but found himself compelled to identify the caller.

"'Not in the mood for bullshit today, pal. Wrong guy to call. Do you even know who you're talking to? I'm not the kind of guy to mess around. If you wanna tell me your name then maybe..." He was rudely interrupted.

"Ray, I wouldn't expect you to remember every man you've killed, but I thought the ones you stabbed in the back would remain a little clearer in your mind."

Ray's eyes enlarged, his lungs briefly emptied of their contents. He knew where the voice was from, and the conclusion was impossible. Dean Cottrell. For some reason he had retained the name of the gullible S.O.B who had made the organization's brief victory over the yakuza possible, but he was as dead as Kennedy. There was no way he was calling from beyond the grave.

"Are you getting warm yet, Ray? Do you know who this is?"

As impossible as it was he was now sure the voice belonged to Dean Cottrell. Either that or someone was doing a damn fine impression.

"I'll take the silence as a yes. 'Seems strange talking to a dead man, huh? I guess now you know that some mistakes can come back to get you. Your brother sure as hell does."

Something inside Ray shattered at the mention of his brother, and he started to feel a white hot pain in his chest, melting the frozen lake of shock in his mind. He hadn't put everything together yet, but he knew enough to deduce that he was speaking to his brother's killer.

"Dean."

"Yeah. Surprise." The caller's tone was full of visceral hate. Ray could practically taste it.

"Dean. Dean Cottrell." Ray actually chuckled slightly. "The thing is, you can't be Dean, because Dean's dead."

"You're right Ray. Dean is dead, but that didn't stop him from beating the shit out of your pussy-ass brother."

Rage from a steadily tensing mouth was wiped with a sleeve in an attempt to restore calm.

"So, you really are Dean? I don't believe it. You survived the explosion and now you're on some sort of fucked up revenge mission?"

"That's about the size of it."

Ray really did have trouble believing it. How in hell could Dean have survived? Valentino had planned everything down to the finest detail, but the voice was definitely that of the supposedly dead assassin. The flammable pain inside Ray finally became unbearable and he clenched his fists almost to the point where the phone broke in his hand. His next words were serious and lethal.

"You're so dead 'you don't even know it."

"That's an empty threat, but you wouldn't believe how much I can fuck with you now Ray. I mean, I make a big mess of that triad pow-wow and now your brother's on ice. Who's next?"

"Nobody's next because I'm going to hunt you down and kill you and everything you hold dear. That is a promise."

"You don't sound too thrilled about this whole thing boss. What's the matter? 'Annoyed you can't fuck your brother anymore?"

The rage that jolted through Ray at that second was like a full-blown electric shock.

"SHUT THE FUCK UP! I WILL FUCKING KILL YOU, 'YOU UNDERSTAND?! I WILL PUT YOU IN THE GROUND, DEAN!"

"Was that your scary phone voice? That was pretty good. I'm shaking here."

"You fucking should be. I'm gonna cut off your fucking legs you piece of shit. When I find you I'm gonna skin you down to the bone. I'm gonna rip off your dick and shove it down your throat. I'm gonna kill you so slow you're gonna beg me to end it."

"Yada, yada, yada, Ray. I love you too."

"And don't even think you're going to get another chance to put a bullet in me like at that hotel. I have you marked now and I'm going to find you one way or another."

"Well, in the meantime, watch your back 'cos I'm coming for you. You won't know when, but I'm going to turn Red Dawn into a smoking pile of shit and then I'm gonna take you out."

"You can't even contemplate it. I am fucking untouchable! 'You got that?!"

"Not in your wildest dreams, you son of a bitch. Enjoy your funeral." The caller hung up, and hollow silence was all that was left.

Ray stood speechless. His face was as red as ketchup and a single, stupid tear that could not be attributed to a single emotion, had found a route down his left cheek.

214

Shades stood staring at him.

"Get Valentino here now," Ray growled, and Shades didn't hesitate.

He left the room.

Ray was so maddened by the phone conversation; he was just about ready give his new scotch decanter a date with the wall.

Valentino had a shit-load of explaining to do.

Dean put on his jacket. He was checking out. Another couple of nights in a different motel. That was what he had planned, just in case Ray found some way of tracing the call.

Not long now. Not long until he proved to his former boss that he wasn't joking. The phone call was nothing in terms of gratification when compared to the thought of killing Ray.

Not long now.

CHAPTER THIRTY-SIX
VALENTINO

The way Valentino saw it, Ray was at his angriest at this moment. It was late, but instead of the usual unsettling, blue light of the fish tank illuminating the room, Ray had all of the lights on. Even so, it was still unsettling.

Shades was against the near wall with his arms folded and Valentino couldn't help but think he was there only to observe Ray's anger as if the plight of others genuinely amused him. That in itself wasn't too hard to believe. Behind his desk, Ray was pacing. A half-emptied glass of scotch sat on his workspace. He raised a hand to his face and rubbed his mouth area as he spoke.

"This is really fucking something, huh? I mean, how does shit like this happen?"

Valentino opened his mouth to reply, but he was cut off.

"Don't answer that. Just tell me in short what the hell went wrong."

"Dean somehow figured out the bomb was going to wipe him out early and got away. I think..." He was cut off again.

"You said the plan was fool proof!" his boss yelled.

Valentino got a clear view of Ray's bloodshot eyes.

"You said that I had nothing to worry about! NOW I 'GOT THIS GUY WHO YOU WERE SUPPOSED TO GET RID OF, FUCKING EVERYTHING UP!"

"Dean obviously wasn't a fool. I couldn't predict exact events, Ray. These things happen..."

"Tell my brother that! You fucked up, Valentino. This one is on your head. Shades and everyone else did their part!"

His boss was closer now. Much closer than Valentino would have liked, but he didn't back away. Ray could have his tantrum, yet at the end of the day he would have to face the fact that his brother was dead and that things weren't looking good at the moment.

"Ray. I know you're upset, but you can't blame this on me. Your brother chose Cottrell for the op. Thomas was the one who supplied the bomb which didn't have enough yield for the desired effect. Thomas was..."

Ray hit him. Out of nowhere, Valentino received a solid blow to the right side of his face that sent him to ground. Things didn't go blurry and his hearing wasn't impaired. He just felt a lot of pain.

"DON'T YOU FUCKING SAY HIS NAME!!! It was you who failed! You're my expert!"

Valentino, supporting himself on one arm, wiped some blood from the corner of his lip and looked up at Ray's maddened expression. It was then that he realized his life was in danger. It was at that point that the things he had denied came to him. The man before him wasn't right in the head. Valentino had believed he could tone Ray down to be a rational criminal, but that was impossible. The guy was beyond help. Whatever his angle was, it wasn't to make money. He wanted something else and he didn't care who he had to get rid of to achieve it.

The reaction to the hard stares the two men gave each other from different heights was a second, slightly lighter punch from Ray which invoked a lot of swearing from Valentino.

"I really tried, you know? But things just keep going wrong." Ray was momentarily distracted by his yellow fish and unknown thoughts, so with a burning desire to show him that his latest scapegoat wasn't just a big guy with know-how, the victim of the assault dealt a blow to his boss' leg that immediately made it go dead. He stumbled backwards grabbing a chair for support. Valentino was on his feet in a second and was ready to land a second good blow, but there was one thing he had forgotten.

A hand grabbed him roughly by his shoulder and turned him around, before a second punched him in the gut making him bend forward. His legs were then knocked from under him by an

217

effectively mastered sweeper kick. Again, Valentino was sent to ground and then before he could even register what had happened, his head was brought to bear as his new attacker grabbed him by the hair.

He breathed heavily. Shades had a blade to his cheek.

"Fuck! Motherfuck!" yelled Ray, holding his leg. He came over and brutally slugged Valentino in the chest. Any harder and he might have broken the man's sternum. The fact that his blow didn't seem to warrant anything more from the moron than a heavy moan only served to anger him more.

Ray walked over to his desk with a limp and took down the rest of his scotch. There was a long moment of very little noise where Valentino tried to recover his energy before his boss was ready to scold him again.

"You blew it, asshole," he said scornfully. There was another long pause, and Ray turned to look out of the window.

"Do you know why we're called the Red Dawn, Valentino?"

"Because you're a commie bastard... Ah, fuck!" Shades cut into the skin of Valentino's cheek, just enough to hurt.

"Humor's cheap, Valentino. No. It's because me and Tom... we didn't have the easiest time growing up. I went down the wrong path and he followed me."

The two men were now eyeing each other and when Ray realized that Shades was also looking at him from under furrowed brows, he turned back to the city of night.

"I told Tom I was going to change things. I was going to show those fuckers that we weren't going to just lie down and die. I said I was going to take this fucking city. I said I was going to paint the dawn red with the blood of everyone who could hurt us."

Ray's eyes, though fixed on the night were crazed. His words were powerful and Valentino instantly recognized them as words of a madman.

"I made a promise and I'm going to stick to it. I don't need you or anybody else!" Ray came over once more to the one he held responsible for his loss. "I'll get rid of the scum in this city and I'll dismantle this corrupt excuse for a fucking government and then

218

everything in L.A. is going to run through me. Who knows where from there, huh? Worse men have made senators. Worse men have made presidents."

Valentino was close to laughter, however couldn't quite muster it. He had been right all along. Ray was out of his Goddamn mind and even if it was the last thing he ever did he was going to make sure the bastard knew it.

"You know, Ray. I always thought there was something off about you. The way you handled things, the way you talked. I convinced myself that maybe you did have an unhappy childhood and maybe you were a little keen, but now I know the truth..."

Ray's left eye flickered out of time with the other as his head dipped towards Valentino, eager to hear the man's divine wisdom that he couldn't give two shits about.

"You're fucking nuts!" Valentino spat. "I can't believe I led your schemes for so long. You're not a criminal. You're a maniac." He prepared for another blow, but it didn't come. Ray just took a few steps back and looked harshly at Shades.

"Kill him," he ordered.

Shades was about to obey when Valentino started to talk again.

"He'll kill you too Shades! He'll see all of us burn before he goes for any real power!"

Shades hesitated. He wasn't sure why. Instead of taking the fat fool's life he just stared at his boss as if looking for guidance.

"What are you waiting for? Do it!"

"He stabbed Cottrell in the back and now he's getting rid of the one person who's got him all this way. Think about it! You don't mean shit to him!"

Shades' gaze flicked between his boss and Valentino. Was he really considering what the man was saying?

"His brother's dead. He has no friends to turn to. This whole thing is gonna collapse. 'You wanna be inside when it does? Self-preservation, Shades! It's rule number one! Are you going to leave yourself in the hands of this crazy son of a bitch?!"

"KILL HIM NOW!!!"

Valentino's pupils dilated...

His mouth hung open...

In one movement and with a grunt of effort, Shades had driven the knife into the back of his head right up to the hilt. He fell forward and hit the carpet on his front while his killer stood looking down at him.

The assassin's breathing was heavy and he looked more unfastidious than ever. The longest silence took hold until Ray gave a final order.

"Get someone up here to take this out."

"Sure thing, boss," replied Shades in an unenthusiastic tone. Before he reached the door, Ray called to him sharply.

"Shades?"

"What?"

"'Guess the cat's out of the bag. You tell nobody. My brother would have wanted this. I always had a plan in mind and it was always the same. To take it as far as it would go. If you want to bow out, now's the time. If not, then I have to warn you. I'm looking at consecutive crimes against God and country." Ray wiped his lips and Shades considered the statement, all the while looking at the body of Valentino.

He came back into the heart of the room, knelt down and yanked the blade out of the head holding it grudgingly in his hand as he turned to leave.

"If I may, boss. I left *God* behind when my daddy pumped buckshots through his head."

BANG! BANG! BANG!

Lysander Shades wouldn't forget that noise for as long as he lived. He would never forget the crooked cops who had driven his father to take his life. He would never forget the cruddy childhood that he suspected was a whole lot more fucked up than even Ray could imagine.

Shades shot his boss a cold look of agreement.

"And I fucking hate this country."

220

CHAPTER THIRTY-SEVEN
INSOMNIA

The day that followed Dean's relatively drunken phone call was a slow one. All he could really remember from it was that he had stayed in his new motel room the whole time, recovering from a hangover. At night, things had faded to black at around eight. The next day was much the same, except Dean no longer felt that acidic burn all the way down to his stomach and he had in fact, been out on a couple of errands that included picking up his suit from the dry cleaners.

It was now approaching nine thirty, and he was trying to fall into a deep sleep, however on this particular night it just wasn't happening. Every attempt he made to clutch at the possible solace of the night's rest ended in the most vexing failure. Now he lay spread-eagled on his bed, the red neon of the vacancy sign drifting in through his window. Consciousness plagued him. He sat up and let his legs fall over the end of the bed.

He had called Yuki that day and told her that if things went according to plan, he would be back with her by Wednesday, in three days time at the latest. That had improved her slightly upset tone.

Dean looked at his bare feet and remembered when they had been militarily booted all those years ago. He had just achieved SFC/E-7

Having gone in for the 18X enlistment option at nineteen, he effectively bypassed a lot of the normal requirements for joining. The direct recruitment program had a high wash-out rate (88% for his age group), which Dean was driven enough not to fall victim to. It was the crowning achievement of his life and ironically, it had ended life as he knew it. The memories from before he was submerged in the military were so painful to him, he liked to think that he had erased them completely. Instead of going back to those dark days, he skipped ahead to better times.

Once inside the machine, he had made a name for himself as an exceptional soldier, naturally gifted in the art of killing. They had said that execution was in his blood and rumor had it that on some occasions, officers had fought over him. It didn't take long however for restlessness to set in. Eventually, he wanted out. Knowing that the best chance of slipping away without too much of a scene laid in the commanding officer he had the best relationship with, he had arranged a talk. At that point, Dean had vague notions of going into engineering. Little did he know that fate would have him back killing people in no time. Regardless, the day he made it clear that he was leaving was one that had always stuck in his mind for some reason. Maybe because it was then that he started working against the system instead of for it.

"I'm sorry, sir. It's just not what I want anymore."

Dean Cottrell stood in slack, military clothing in front of a desk where a man in his early forties sat surveying him with disappointment in his eyes.

Colonel Fischer was an individual for whom Dean had great respect and even if he did hit the roof, Dean would still give him that respect because he genuinely deserved it.

"I'm looking at these papers Cottrell and it just doesn't add up for me. Why?"

"The force has been good to me sir, but it just isn't what I want to do with my life."

"Cottrell, your knowledge of advanced weaponry is outstanding. Your hand-to-hand combat skills exceed all expectations. You look down a scope and they've already counted it as a kill. Not to mention, your report from Captain Moss in Afghanistan was exemplary and I still tell people about that ROBIN SAGE. You could go far, son." Fischer was hunched forward and had his glasses low on the bridge of his nose.

With his hands clasped behind his back, Dean straightened himself to an extent that was almost painful. He had been prepared for that argument. It was a good reason to stay, but he had given all that was required of him and more. It was time to go.

"Sir, your praise is of great inspiration to me, however, I've been thinking long and hard about this decision and my mind is made up."

Fischer let out a sigh and leaned back in his chair. He removed his glasses and played with the forms on his desk.

"I always had you down as someone who knew his own mind. It's a shame. A mighty shame, but I'll respect your wishes. I'll have it all filed by Monday. If you need recommendations for any careers in law enforcement or other areas of the armed forces, I'll be happy to spend the time to make you look good and if you ever find yourself in some trouble, don't hesitate to call."

"Thank you, sir."

Dean smiled. God, if Fischer knew what kind of trouble Dean was in now, dwelling in the criminal underground with more murders to his name than he had ever wanted, pissing off a maniac and working with a mob boss.

He stood up and walked over to the window, pulling back the curtain just enough so that he could see outside. The hum of the neon sign was close like a large fly buzzing in his ear. On the nearby street a few people were loitering. A group of five men, who Dean suspected were gang members just from their attire, were sitting on the sidewalk rolling joints.

All of a sudden the heat in the room got to him. He had put the heater on earlier in the day. Then the warmth had been a blessing, but now it was the most likely cause of his insomnia.

After grabbing a pack of cigarettes from the machine by the front desk he went outside and withdrew one throwing the rest of the pack into a dumpster. Dean's history with tobacco wasn't very complicated. At seventeen he had done half a year of it and then had decided to quit, which he had found easy. He just stopped smoking them. The last smoke he had had was at the age of twenty-seven and it had been a single indulgence. At the most isolated of moments he would feel a strange craving and would grant himself no more than one. This time it was the same. With a misplaced sense of relief Dean leant against the motel wall facing the parking lot and satiated his habit. Unfortunately, the relief was soon balanced and then outweighed by the growing sting of weakness that grew with each puff, so what happened next might have been for the best.

He hadn't even gotten halfway through the cigarette when something kicked off on the other side of the street. A middle-aged woman passed the gang members on the sidewalk and they began to harass her. That was just who they were. People who couldn't mind their own goddamn business. Even walking past guys like that was a crime.

"Hey, honey. 'You lookin' for something?" one said. From the way he talked Dean guessed this was a Hispanic gang. She ignored him and walked on, but the gang members were now on their feet.

"Why 'you walk away from me, huh?" The lead followed her. There were some more shouts that Dean couldn't quite make out and then it happened. The woman was grabbed from behind and pushed against a wall. Dean knew exactly what was about to take place as the woman cried out for help.

Rape was something that Dean detested. He could abide the murder of jerk-off mobsters almost all the time, but rape of anyone was something he regarded with the most visceral reaction.

He dropped his cigarette and crushed it into the ground with his foot. In all honesty, he thought it might be the last he would ever have.

He had never attempted anything like this before, and he really didn't consider himself a vigilante, but with everything that was going on, he didn't give a shit. Someone had to stand up to bottom feeders like this and in the end, if he was forced to kill all of them, he wouldn't care.

He stalked across the parking lot. His gun was in his room in the top drawer of his bedside table, but he didn't need it. 'Hand-to-hand combat skills that exceeded all expectations' after all.

As he crossed the street a gang member who had been hanging back turned to greet him. Just as Dean had suspected, the gang was of the Latino persuasion.

"'You want something, homes?" he snapped.

He obviously had no idea what was coming next because Dean caught a surprised look on his face, before his fist made contact with it. The man fell to ground as his compadres turned to the intrusion.

"What the fuck?!" One withdrew a switchblade just as another lunged to punch Dean in the stomach. He dodged the blow and kneed the man in the face before flipping him onto his back in an unspecified martial arts move. They were far too easy. Just like Thomas's goons at the zoo, they knew nothing. With an inexperienced stab attempt the man with the knife made his move, but Dean stopped him short by grabbing his wrist and then kicking him hard in the ankle. There was a cracking sound and Dean suspected he had either broken it or come very close. The thug was crippled into a kneeling position whereupon his own knife was forced down into his kneecap. This of course, triggered a barrage of screaming and foreign curses that flew up into the night air. Sensing another man coming from behind, Dean launched a devastating back kick that sent him flying to the pavement with a crunching, wet slap.

Four of the assailants were now on the floor grunting and cursing. The guy who had taken the first blow got up and made a run for it. Dean didn't stop him. Realizing he had a situation on his hands the lead gang member left his screaming victim for a second and pulled a gun from his jacket, however before he could fire the strange vigilante had joint control of his hand and with some twisting broke the man's fingers in the trigger space.

"AAAH! FUCK!"

Dean then blindsided him with a hard fist for the finisher.

Injured, the men ran after their fleeing colleague, the one with the knife in his leg, limping a short way behind.

Turning, Dean saw the woman was gone. She had taken her chance to run. Good for her. Weirdly enough, that had felt somewhat satisfying.

Throwing the gun into the same dumpster as his cigarettes he went to bed. Maybe now he could sleep.

CHAPTER THIRTY-EIGHT
THE FUNERAL

Murdock's funeral home was a small affair that Ray was rather pleased with. The hall was lined on either side with chairs and sported the traditional aisle running down the middle. Up front a closed casket rested on a platform in front of a curtain. At the podium a rather portly man was speaking to the congregation that consisted of both men and women.

Strangely enough, Ray Bentley was sat a whole three rows back with Shades on his right and he was currently trying to ignore the minister's rehearsed eulogy while admiring the classy décor of the place. What the fat, old preacher said meant nothing to him and never would. His parents had liked the Church. He hated his parents. Therefore, he de facto hated the Church.

"Thomas was taken from us before his time and God and only God can pass judgment on he who hath taken life. Christ shares our pain, He shares our suffering and He shares our memories of Thomas. He tells us not to mourn for the death of our dearly beloved, but to celebrate the life that he led."

Murdock's was a service that many criminal families used to send off their departed members and if the man was still convincing himself that only God could pass judgment then he really was one body short of a burial. Trying to distract himself from his own anger, he wondered just how Catholic this whole thing was. Didn't Catholics oppose cremation? It saved money. Did Catholics approve of saving money? Was that in the Bible? These redundant questions weren't enough to lift Ray out of his seat and away from what was actually going on.

On a table that was set aside from the casket a small array of red roses surrounded a framed photograph of Thomas Bentley. He was smiling with perfect teeth and had his hair just the way Ray remembered it. A poorly disciplined tear rolled down the surviving brother's face. He flicked it away quickly.

"Thomas leaves behind his friends. He leaves behind all those that looked up to him and respected him, but most tragically he leaves behind his brother Ray, who holds him forever in his heart. We now request that all those who would like to make one final remembrance, please step forward."

A couple of men on the front row who had worked very closely with Thomas stood up and walked to the table. A soft violin symphony played in the background as the men accompanied by one woman clad in black, laid red roses beside the picture. Ray knew none of them very well and if he had possessed the energy he would have excluded them all. None of them knew Thomas like he did. Their tears were all as fake as God's supposed love. They were all snakes who had the disrespect to show up here of all places...

Ray calmed himself when he realized he was clenching the chair fabric tightly in one hand. It was now his time to rise. He had felt safe away from the front row, but the pain he had to face was inevitable. With a slow, begrudging ascent, he was on his feet and ready to make the long journey. The journey he had dreaded his entire life. The journey where he would have to walk to the box that contained his brothers' body. It was difficult to bear.

A red rose, just bloomed hung from his clasped fingers. He ignored the table and stood at the foot of the casket for a few seconds while the other people took their seats. With a strained arch of his back he leaned in over the casket and put the rose down on top of the name plate, before whispering softly to his brother.

"This thing'll never be over. Not until I say so." With a glance at the funeral director Ray walked slowly back to his seat.

"We now commit Thomas's body to the flame from where he will be delivered into God's grace, for dust you are and dust you shall return."

The casket started to recede into the curtain and then it disappeared from view. There was a yellow light and the sound of burning.

Ray turned his head and spoke to Shades while the funeral director continued to speak.

"I need you to find someone."

Shades listened intently.

"Find our best guy to track down this son of a bitch and take everything from him." In that moment Ray's voice even scared his most violent henchman.

In a tone that gave his boss assurance, the assassin replied in his Southern dialect.

"I think I have just the right man for the job."

"Good."

There was a pause.

"And, Shades, if you fuck this up... I'll kill you," Ray said bluntly. Behind the curtain, Thomas burned. It was exactly the sendoff he would have wanted, and it contrasted pretty badly to what had become of Ray's organizer. *His* body had been driven to a remote location near the county line and buried. Very few people would ever learn of what had happened to Valentino. That was no better than what he deserved.

While Ray was thinking deeply about two lives that had come to an end very abruptly, the subject couldn't have been further from Shades' mind because when it came down to it he really didn't give a shit. He hadn't liked Thomas from the get-go. The guy had come across as a suck up and an asshole and if he had been Shades' brother, then he would have been left behind long ago. Valentino was someone Shades had had a little more respect for, but he would never have said that he liked the guy. Despite this his last words still echoed in the mind of Ray's wingman.

"Are you going to leave yourself in the hands of this crazy son of a bitch?!"

Valentino was wrong. He made a mistake and he had gotten killed for it. He was a guy who made a mistake. Shades didn't make mistakes. He was too good for that to ever occur. If Ray wanted Cottrell dead ASAP then Shades would call the particular specialist he had in mind, later that day. The man in question was also someone who didn't make mistakes. Someone precise. Someone who got the job done.

Shades eyeballed the funeral director who was quoting something from a Bible. Beside him Ray grimaced, mulling things over in his tortured mind. Thomas was really dead. This was his funeral. He was still having trouble accepting the fact. Dean Cottrell was the one who had caused all of this. Every problem Ray was facing was down to him. He clenched his fists tightly and wondered how one man could cause so much trouble. One man who was supposed to be dead.

The service finished and the congregation disbanded.

230

Just as Ray was leaving Miles (protection racketeer extraordinaire) stopped him and started a conversation. With Valentino gone he was wondering what the hell Ray was planning on doing next.

"I'm not sure, but I think we're going to have to move things along faster. I want to start clamping down on small-time gangs"

"What about the larger crime families, the yakuza?"

"We'll get rid of them too. Don't worry about it, Miles. I 'got some things in the works right now. I'll storm this city when the flags are all blowing our way."

"Are you sure that's wise? I mean without the triads or your brother's weapon supply, the organization isn't looking too good."

Ray looked at the shorter man with contempt. Couldn't he see the big picture? Couldn't he see the vision?

"Miles, the plan from the start was to grow as rapidly as we could. Setbacks aren't going to stop me. The element of surprise is our advantage. We can do this. I can do this."

Leaving his crony with a puzzled look on his face Ray headed back to his sedan and climbed inside.

Miles had always thought that the organization would be run better if Valentino was the top dog. Of course, he had never let this thought exit his own mind, and even in there it was shy and didn't come out of hiding very often. Now that Valentino had inexplicably vanished, he had only Ray to trust. Whatever happened, he would get through it alive. He always did. Miles had wormed his way through the woodwork of many crime syndicates in and out of state. He wasn't sure whether Ray was a visionary with a hidden agenda, or a lunatic with nothing to lose. Either way the man had ambition. Sometimes in the criminal world that was all you needed.

CHAPTER THIRTY-NINE
GET THE JOB DONE

There was a definite crack in the air as the knife drove itself halfway through the cork board. Shades, frozen in a post-throw stance with one leg forward, half crouching and his throwing arm outstretched, breathed heavily and stood straight. The knife was about two inches off the bull's-eye of the board.

On the fifteenth floor resided a canteen area along with a fitness facility that if the Holden Tower had been a legitimate corporate HQ would not have existed. Weights and other gym-typical equipment were scattered throughout the more open level of the building. One room was a soundproof box for the live discharge of weapons to targets and in this room alone with his thoughts, Shades was perfecting his knife art.

He pulled another from about his person and took aim before drawing the blade back and launching it through the air. This hit was even less close to perfection, roughly three and a half inches from the bull's-eye.

He grimaced and stalked over to the mark. With a disturbingly violent effort he ripped both the knives from the board he was working on and retraced his steps back to the white line. It was very early in the morning, and for Shades to be overexerting himself at this time on a Wednesday wasn't an otherworldly occurrence. Solace granted him the time that he enjoyed most.

What happened next would have struck fear into the victim, had it been a person. There was a harsh and animalistic grunt as Shades whirled around at the same time pulling two knives from the inside of his suit jacket. The first was sent spinning tip over tail towards the target and after a second turn, Shades sent the other one cruising on its horizontal axis.

CRACK! CRACK!

The knives were just above and under the center by about half an inch.

Their owner smiled as he corrected his posture. That was better.

Before he could approach to withdraw them, his cell phone started up with its simple and repetitive beeping. He answered it immediately.

"Hello?"

The voice that came through on the other end was what could only be described as *'upper-class American'*. It was a rare, but existent way of speaking that somehow managed to be both eloquent and cold. The tone reflected the man's years of experience.

"Mr. Shades. You requested that I update you on my progress."

It was him. The man Shades had selected for the job of striking back at Dean Cottrell in the most sadistic, most methodically perfect way possible. Why the hell he always addressed those he knew by their formal title was beyond Shades. The fucker certainly wasn't low-rank.

"Go ahead." Without conscious thought, Shades began to pace the length of the room behind the white line.

"Your man is quite the ghost. He isn't listed in any public records that I could find and very few men have that to their credit. I should know. I am one."

"That doesn't surprise me. The guy's got brains. Former military"

"I can tell. I can't find a car registered to him or even a birth record. I expect he had the means to get rid of it all. There might be something on a more official network, but nothing I can get a hold of at this time."

"So you have nothing?" Shades started to get annoyed. If this guy couldn't find Dean Cottrell's Achilles then nobody could. "I gave you an assignment! It's pretty darn simple! Find out everything you can about Dean Cottrell, and get rid of him!"

"If I may, I didn't say I had nothing."

There was long silence in which Shades rubbed the area around his mouth where he could just about feel the warning signs of stubble. He would have to get rid of that immediately.

"Go on," he said.

"It took some digging, but with help from a few contacts I ran across a piece of information regarding Mr. Cottrell quite by accident. It seems just because a man is smart and deadly doesn't mean he's not human. Mr. Cottrell is currently in a serious relationship with a certain Ms. Yuki Nakamura working for a local company called Neeson Affiliates."

"And from there you got an address." Shades allowed a smile to flicker onto his face like an old light bulb.

"Exactly. In fact, they're planning to marry soon. You said Mr. Bentley wanted me to deal a blow to him that he would never forget?"

"Yes."

"Well, Vincent Vitrelli once told me that there are about five ways to kill a man. I'm familiar with at least three of them."

Shades was borderline laughing. He crouched slightly as the smile reached his ears and was followed by a satisfied and wicked chuckle. It didn't matter that he had no idea who Vincent Vitrelli was.

"This is too perfect," he exclaimed.

"I concur. Would you like me to proceed with what I have planned, tonight?"

Now trying to stifle his enthusiasm at just how clean the situation was, Shades stood tall and turned on his heels.

"Of course I want you to proceed."

"Then I'll have it done before tomorrow."

Suddenly becoming serious again, Shades let one last warning pass through the phone from his lips.

"But just remember this. I want you to get the job done as cleanly as possible. If by some catastrophe you manage to fuck this up and Ray plays the blame game... I swear to God, I'll take you down with me."

He hung up and allowed himself to smile again. His eyes were drawn to the knives still stuck deep in the target board. He cocked his head and walked over pulling them out and inspecting the blades. The impacts hadn't dulled them in the slightest. Still sharp enough to penetrate a skull as long as the required amount of force was used.

Shades had always been a natural with accuracy. Star pitcher for his little league team if he recalled correctly. Knife throwing was something he had always wanted to learn how to do and when his life of innocence left him, he had taken up the art and had never stopped practicing. Not a week went by when he didn't. The whole concept of it was so attractive, he even found himself gaining physical stimulation when he used knives. Guns were all well and good, but it was just too easy and predictable. You aimed a gun, you shot, the bullet hit where you aimed, and that was that. Knives required more skill. More class. They were his obsession and it had been too long since the last time he had used them.

As soon as Cottrell was dealt with Shades could get back to doing some serious work. For some reason that Shades suspected was Valentino-related, Ray was shy on trusting him at the moment. All that would change once the problem had been handled. Then the Red Dawn could continue on its grand journey. Shades doubted most of Ray's ambitious dreams, but the man had such a raw desire for power that if he set his mind to taking the city, then he would probably get it in the end. He just had the drive needed for that kind of goal. Shades didn't doubt that his boss was a few hosannas short of second coming, but most successful people were.

Looking hard at one of his knives he told himself he had chosen the right man to carry out Ray's task. Red Dawn employed four men on the level of this guy and they all worked off-site. This one was the most dependable and Shades had complete faith in him.

How hard could it be to use a woman as leverage? Love was the ultimate inspiration to weakness after all. He himself would have had no problem with it, but this guy was paid for these kinds of situations. The right man for the job. 'No doubt about it.

CHAPTER FORTY
THE INTRUDER

It was approaching ten to ten in the evening outside of a reasonably well-kept apartment complex in the farthest reaches of Westlake, before you hit Downtown. The area had undergone total redevelopment some years ago and was now a little more upmarket than it had been previously.

A black Lincoln sat across the street from the parking lot. Its windows were tinted with a charcoal screen to stop those outside from having a clear view of the driver, not that anyone was looking in anyway. In fact, the streets seemed rather deserted tonight.

Inside, a suppressor was being twisted onto a Llama M-87. With the component fitted, the gun was deposited inside a dark suit jacket and its owner breathed a quiet sigh onto the glass as he looked out at the building. It was always cold inside the car. The driver had an aversion to the heat, and the air conditioning was permanently set to max. Looking down at his watch, he decided that the time had finally come. He opened the door of the vehicle, stepping out into the night air. Moonlight hit the front of his car just as he looked over its top, towards the apartment block.

The figure in question was just over six feet tall. His face represented a man in his mid-thirties who showed very few signs of heading for forty, eyes full of injected, dull gray instead of that sparkling kind you sometimes get. His hair was short and black and ran forward to a small, spiked fringe in regimented lines. With his red tie blowing in the wind and his black, leather gloves sheathing experienced hands he walked across the road towards the location. His finger paused for a moment over the bell for twenty-three. That was the man's way. He considered every move, always sought a better route. If he rang the bell for Cottrell's fiancée, she would have the opportunity to question him and it was a distinct possibility that Dean had warned her about strangers. Turning up straight at her door would be less expected and provide a better opportunity to execute his plan.

He hit the bell for number two and before long; the scarred intercom panel fizzed into life.

"Who the hell is it?" The man's voice was one that belonged to an obvious smoker. It was choked and old. Considering his words carefully, the stranger spoke.

"Good evening, sir. I'm from Vista International Insurance Brokers. Sorry to disturb you, but my company are launching an investigation into your landlord. This apartment block may have been involved in an insurance scam pertaining to him."

"Well, I ain't the landlord, so what the hell do you wanna speak to me for?"

"No sir, you misunderstand. You're in no trouble at all. We are launching an enquiry and I need to ask you a few questions," the stranger countered. He stood silent, waiting. Everything he had just said was a steaming pile of bullshit. Hopefully the man's sense of smell had been dulled by his habit. Heck, he didn't even know if Vista International Insurance Brokers insured apartment blocks. The pause wasn't very encouraging, but eventually there was a heavy sigh and the owner of number two replied.

"Okay, hold on."

There was a buzz and the door opened. That had been exceptionally easy. People were far too gullible in today's world.

The man stepped inside and took note of the brick walls and every other detail his eyes surveyed in the lobby. The elevator to his right was decorated with a yellow 'OUT OF ORDER' sign, so the man headed up a set of stairs to the second floor. The hallway stretched down to the next set of steps and standing outside an open door in a bathrobe and some hastily applied old-man pants stood the owner of number two.

Putting on a fake smile the stranger walked towards him with an offered hand. The owner took it, and scanned his new acquaintance.

"Thank you so much for your time sir. May I have your name?"

"Troy," he replied. Troy was pushing sixty at least and had a pair of thick-rimmed glasses on a long nose. The assumption had been dead on. The smell of tobacco ash hung around him like a garland of dead roses.

"Do you live alone?"

"Yes."

"How long have you been living here, approximately?"

"That'd be about four years and I'll tell you now, I ain't seen or heard anything fishy when it comes to Mr. Welch."

The man's eyes flickered as he stored the information.

"That's what I expected, sir. Mr. Welch has a prior rap sheet of felonies. He's an experienced conman."

Aware of time, the man looked further down the hall past Troy. By his judgment, apartment twenty-three would be on the third floor.

"How much did he cheat you for?"

"Fifty-eight thousand," replied the man with little concentration. Troy tut-tutted and turned back into his apartment

"Well, it's like I say. Nothing fishy about Welch. Not to my recollection anyway, but…"

Something very hard cracked him on the back of his neck. He let out a weak yelp and almost fell forward, but was immediately pushed up against the wall adjacent to his door.

The stranger had landed a skilful chop to the top of Troy's spinal cord with enough force to momentarily paralyze him. With him now up against the wall the aggressor elbowed his heart area with even more force. Troy managed to cry out, but it was immediately stifled by a gloved hand clamped over his mouth. He went into cardiac arrest almost immediately. After that, he was allowed to fall to the floor.

Being old and a smoker was never a good combination, especially when you received serious trauma to the chest area. The assailant kicked Troy's legs out of the way and shut the door to the apartment.

With one look around to see if anyone had heard anything, he continued down the hall and up the stairs. The corridor above was identical and door number twenty-three was just a step away.

Once, the man had killed politicians and the like and mundane tasks such as this bored him. He felt like an inferior silhouette of his true self when executing these easy terminations. Looking up at the ceiling for a brief moment, he cursed his former boss for saddling him with this sorry excuse for an organization. This wasn't even worth his time or skill and he hated conversing over the phone with that moronic, hick lapdog Ray kept. It was all like one big joke of a bad dream he couldn't wake up from.

Yuki had been expecting Dean back the whole night. Usually, she would have been in bed by now because she got up early, however Dean had called her that day and said he would be returning late, so when there was loud knocking she couldn't help but rush to the door. It had two locks and a chain. The evidence of Dean's security

240

complex. She guessed it was just his way of saying he cared about her.

She undid the first lock on impulse and then stopped, thinking she should probably check just to be on the safe side. Bringing her left eye to the peephole she smiled and then displayed a concerned countenance. The suit immediately told her it was Dean, but when her brain registered the face she saw it was someone else.

Who? She had never seen him before in her life, so what was he doing knocking on her door at ten P.M.? Cautiously she undid the other lock and began to open the door with the chain still barring access to the room and this time she was thankful to have put it on.

The man on the other side knew people very well. He found them fascinating. The way their little minds worked. Someone who meant her harm might have tried to gain her trust and ease her insecurity. Not him though. The key to having someone in the palm of your hand was fear. Fear was what put people off balance and he was an expert in creating it.

Wondering whether the man had something to do with Dean's work due to his attire, Yuki opened the door. Without any warning, one of the scariest things that had ever happened to her, happened. A gloved hand shot through the gap preventing her from closing the door and a heavy weight was thrown against it. She tried frantically to shut it, crying out in shock, but she could hear the chain start to come loose with the second blow. She screamed and fled from the door running for the phone. There was a third and final thud as the chain was pulled from the wall and the intruder gained access to the room. He slammed the door behind him and came charging at Yuki, who had the phone in her hands. There was no time to dial the number. That was the most petrifying thing about those fleeting seconds, the fact that she knew there was no time. Her eyes flashed with horror and her heart clenched like a convulsion-fueled fist when he withdrew from his jacket the one thing she had been dreading for the last two seconds and pressed it to her head as his free hand closed around her throat in a cold grip

"Drop it. There's a good girl," the intruder whispered.

CHAPTER FORTY-ONE
NOTHING EVER CHANGES

Dean's reflection stared back at him from the bathroom mirror of his motel hideaway. He threw more water over his features before going back into the room that was now devoid of any trace of him. Just his brown, khaki jacket sitting on the bed, ready to go over his informal attire. For him the suit was only part of his vendetta. Yuki wouldn't see him in it again.

He was just about to put the jacket on when his cell phone announced that somebody was calling him. Pulling it out from inside the jacket he checked the caller ID. A smile immediately found a place on his lips. He answered it.

"Hey, I'm almost there. I should be about fifteen minutes max', okay?"

The voice that came from the phone was something that shocked Dean to his core. It was the voice of a man and not anybody he knew.

"Mr. Cottrell. Forgive me, but I felt that using your landline was the most appropriate option."

"Who the fuck is this?" Dean tried to mask the fear creeping into his voice with a scathing tone. Who the hell did the voice belong to and what were they doing in his apartment? A feeling of dread took hold with that last thought.

"I wish to speak to you in person if you aren't busy. Come home and we can work this whole thing out."

"Where's Yuki?" Choler was rising in his voice and he was almost surprised to find he was locking the door to his room and pulling the jacket on unconsciously.

"She's with me and you have no need to worry. She is unharmed. Whether it stays that way is up to you."

As Dean stalked down the corridor and threw the key onto the desk in front of the motel manager he heard something awful. There was screaming, slightly muffled in the background.

He pushed open the door and jogged to his car, climbing in and slamming the door.

"I swear to God if you touch her you're gonna regret it." The engine was already up and running. Dean skidded the car around in the parking lot then put the pedal to the metal. How had this happened and more importantly, how had it happened so fast? This guy had to be Red Dawn. How had they found the link from him to her? Dean slammed his free hand on the wheel and turned a corner.

"The situation you find yourself in is very simple so I think threats of violence you are in no position to back up can be skipped, hmm? Come to your apartment... alone, or I'll put a bullet in her head." The man on the other end of the phone hung up.

"GODDAMNIT!" Dean yelled throwing the phone into the passenger seat. He put on more speed, exceeding city limits, but road safety couldn't have been further from his mind.

The car lurched to a halt and Dean stepped out. He had made the journey in just less than ten minutes.

Opening the trunk, he equipped himself with his Beretta and locked the vehicle. Wasting no time he thundered up the stairs of the apartment block to his door. It was busted, forced from the outside.

Petrified by what he might see beyond it, his shaking hand reached out and gripped the handle.

One thing that Dean was good at was being able to pick up scents and he detected the smell of fine wine as the scene opened up for him. It took him a while to register what was actually playing out in the room. Two figures sat on the couch. Yuki was on the right.

It was just as he had suspected. Red Dawn. The man's attire gave him away instantly. The red tie. The black suit. He was a little older than Dean and had a handgun pressed against Yuki's temple, a wine glass in his free hand.

"Slowly," the man said calmly. "Don't try anything funny. Shut the door."

Powerless, Dean took a step forward and closed the door behind him. He had his own gun loosely trained on the intruder, but he knew that the chances of being able to shoot him before he put a bullet through Yuki were slim.

"That's it. Now, throw the piece to the right"

Dean stiffened. Dropping the gun would be suicide, but what other option was there? Begrudgingly, he threw it aside. The weapon slid across the floor and under a wooden cabinet, causing him to wince and realize that he was now completely helpless and both he and Yuki were at the mercy of this stranger.

He stared hard into the eyes of the intruder and was greeted with a sly smile which made his blood boil. Yuki's hands were bound by a plastic tie and she looked to be extremely distressed.

"Dean..." she said quietly and Dean couldn't even process how shaken she sounded. Why had he done this to her? That was the thought that gripped him then. How could he have done this to the woman he loved?

The man on the couch took no notice.

"You know Mr. Cottrell, very few men have good taste in wine, but I'm glad to say you're a natural. I hope you don't mind. I helped myself to this bottle of Silver Oak."

Noticing the bottle by the side of the couch, Dean watched the strange individual swill the dark, red liquid around in his glass. In fact he minded very much. He detested the presence of the stranger. The fact that he had helped himself to his wine was a travesty, not to mention everything else he was doing.

"Oh, please forgive me. Introductions. Quinn. Frank Quinn and yes, I work for your ex-employer."

"Leave her out of it. This is between me and whoever that bastard puts in my way," Dean said through gritted teeth. Quinn regarded him with amusement.

"Well, I guess that would be me, but I'm afraid I can't just let her go. Mr. Bentley was very specific. I have my orders. You understand." The statement seemed oddly robotic, the human element of the man's cold intent displayed only by the way he lazily stroked the gun's barrel against his captive's head.

While the intruder was talking to Dean, he was distracted from Yuki who was trying to figure a way out of the situation. The man had bound her hands roughly and placed her on the couch, but other than that he had been quite passive. She didn't know whether that was good or bad, but right now, he was concentrating on Dean and that left it up to her to save them both. Whoever Frank Quinn was he intended to kill them at the end of this. She had figured out that much.

Something caught her eye. Tucked down between the cushion and the arm of the couch was the letter opener she had used a few days ago. Unlike a knife its edges were about as sharp as a yard stick, but its pointed end provided the only weapon within easy reach.

Slowly, she moved her hands down towards it and tightened her grip on the handle.

"You know you caused this. You have nobody to blame but yourself."

"I caused this?! Ray tried to kill me!" Dean exploded. Quinn reflexively tightened his grip on the gun he had at Yuki's head.

"Mr. Cottrell you didn't work at Olive Garden. You can't just lose your shit when you get fired from a criminal organization. You could have just walked away, moved somewhere else, but, no you had to go and kill Mr. Bentley's brother. Now he's pissed and now I've got to waste my time cleaning up this mess."

"She hasn't done anything. Kill me," Dean pleaded.

"Not possible. 'You know what I do? I'm the guy they call in when things start to get serious. This is serious Mr. Cottrell and serious has collateral."

"Please... I'm begging you. Let her go." A tear had found its way to the corner of Dean's lip and his voice was whispery, floating like tissue paper on the thick tension of the space.

"You're going to die here, Dean Cottrell. You cheated death once, but when your number's up, your number's up. Nothing ever changes. You still die..."

Just then, the lights went out.

CHAPTER FORTY-TWO
STRUCK DOWN

Bad wiring issues in the fuse box, which Dean had forever been meaning to fix, took action at a moment that seemed all too advantageous and darkness fell over everything. For those last few seconds it was a very tangible thing, death; in the apartment, with the stranger and the gun; himself about to be shot, helpless to stop it; Yuki to follow shortly after. It suddenly became real; the black and white comic of his life so far, full of cliché occurrences and violence that seemed detached. It was all abruptly filled with color and became the real world; the real world in which he could die and there would be no escape. After all, Quinn wasn't one of Thomas's thugs. He wouldn't miss a kill shot...

But now, at this moment, the game had changed.

"What the fuck?" came Quinn's voice notched with surprise rather than panic.

The lights flickered back into existence and that was when Yuki took her chance. The letter opener she had discreetly acquired was driven all the way up to the hilt into Quinn's thigh and his uncalculated gunshot flew just past her face, close enough for her to feel its heat.

"AAAAAHHHHH! FUCK!" Quinn yelled. Somehow the wine remained in his glass despite his convulsions of pain.

Knowing this was his only opportunity Dean rushed forward past the T.V. and leapt at Quinn, who had no time to react. There was another silenced bullet that flew into the wall as the couch tipped backwards and both men were thrown off and down the two steps behind. The wine stained Quinn's shirt and his gun slid away from him, under the coffee table. Dean got in one punch before his quarry landed an expert kneecap blow to his stomach. Cursing, he fell sideways and Quinn sat up, grabbing the letter opener in his leg and pulling it out with a slicing sound.

"AAAAAHHHHH! SHIT! BITCH!"

Judging by the amount of blood that dribbled forth, the aforementioned bitch had hit a fairly substantial blood vessel, but had just missed his femoral. Before he could consider anything else Dean got up on his knees and punched Quinn in the jaw, sending him down into an uncomfortable position and all the while one thing was running through the hitman's head. How the hell was this happening? Quinn had never been in such a situation. He was perfect. Nobody was ever able to fight back. How was this happening and where was his gun?

Dean hit the assailant again breaking his nose, but with some effort Quinn wrestled him away and slammed his head into the floor. The room was in chaos, full of grunts and impact noises and for Dean, who was now trying to stabilize his spiraling vision; nothing was in focus for more than a second.

Yuki had dived to the floor as soon as Dean had come rushing towards the couch, but she was up now and managed to grab a vase from the display cabinet. Her hands were still bound; however she had enough movement in them to manipulate the ornament. The violent stranger was too busy with Dean to notice her until she smashed the thing right over his head. It didn't bother her that it had been a present from her grandmother. The cries of pain from Quinn were worth it. Unfortunately, it didn't hurt him as much as she had expected. With a hard kick he sent her reeling backwards, where she tripped on the steps and fell flat on her back.

"You fucking whore! I'm gonna gut you like a..." Quinn snarled, up and advancing towards her, but before he could take more than a step, Dean was upon him. Using newfound, adrenaline-fueled strength he grabbed Quinn's suit jacket and with epic force, threw him around and into the display case, which stood half a foot taller than him. Crying out in surprise he fell to the floor and then only heard the creaking of the huge object behind him, before the entire cabinet toppled forward onto his twisted form in a symphony of snapping wood and smashing glass.

"Get the fuck out of my apartment," Dean said in intrepid conclusion.

Yuki was leant up against the marble kitchen worktop and he immediately went to her. Kneeling, he checked her over.

"Are you alright? Did he cut you anywhere?"

"No," she replied, but he could see it in her face that she was in pain. "Who is he, Dean? Why did he want you dead?" she demanded answers and Dean couldn't give them to her. Just then there was a loud bang from the felled cabinet, and Dean decided he couldn't take any risks.

"I need my gun," he said aloud and walked towards the front of the apartment.

Yuki stood up and screamed as a hand smashed through the back of the display cabinet and Quinn managed to haul himself from the debris. He was a wreck, torn up, punctured by shards of carpentry, his nose mashed into an unrecognizable mass and as he crawled like a cockroach in its death throes towards the coffee table where his dropped weapon resided, what had to have been close to a few pints of blood dripped from his destroyed figure.

"DEAN, SHOOT HIM!" she yelled.

Dean dived to the floor and reached for his tossed gun that lay under the small cupboard.

On the other side of the room Quinn was on his feet the pistol in hand and a maniacal flash in his bloodshot eyes. It was now inevitable that he was going to die from blood loss, but he was still running like some demonic machine hell bent on killing everything in its sights. He pointed the gun at Yuki and she screamed one more time.

That was when a bullet flew through his neck with a loud bang and the sound of splattering bodily fluids.

Quinn still fired. Dean's effort was brave, but not fast enough. A round soared across the room and found its way into Yuki's chest. She went to ground.

Dean fired continually putting all his energy into the task of making sure Quinn didn't get off a second shot. All the while some sound he did not intend to create issued from the hollows of his open mouth. A strange, animalistic roar of defiance in the face of the reality. The reality that his fiancée had just been shot.

Convulsing, the attacker gradually started to fall backwards. More blood seemed to issue from each wound as bullets ripped through his stomach, his chest and his shoulders. The glass coffee table shattered under his weight as he fell back onto it and with his legs draped over the frame, his head rested on its side and his last breath escaped him.

He had failed.

Dean dropped the gun (having stood there for several seconds, pulling the trigger of a now empty weapon) and ran to Yuki. Tears, bruises, and blood stained his face. He brushed her hair from her still beautiful visage and looked at the gunshot wound realizing it was bad. She was losing a lot of blood. Her eyes stared up at him full of shock and disbelief as he cradled her and refused to accept that she was dying.

"Don't die. Please don't die. I can't live without you," he whispered. His features were tensed, and his teeth were gritted in reaction to the fact that he could hear in her breath the blood scaling the inside of her throat. She went stiff in his arms.

"No. No. No! Wake up! Wake up!" He shook her, but she did not stir. She just stared up at him with vacant eyes. What happened next was a blur of sobs and protests on Dean's part. How had he allowed this to happen? Why had he left her vulnerable? It was his fault. He might as well have pulled the trigger himself. There was so much he could have done to prevent it. He could have got her out of Los Angeles as soon as Red Dawn became a threat, but he hadn't. He hadn't done a damn thing! These thoughts circulated in Dean's mind and as they did, a new one began to surface.

The gunfire would have been heard. His rational mind took over on autopilot as a survival mechanism. He realized he didn't have much time to flee the premises. In a hurry he grabbed everything he wanted and needed, including the picture of himself and Yuki together and his laptop, among other personal effects. Dean almost broke down halfway to the door, but just about made it. Before he could leave, he kissed his dead fiancée on the forehead and hugged her one last time.

"I'm sorry," he whispered. Tears fell from his face onto her and with all the power he could muster he pulled himself away and fled not forgetting his gun.

There was nothing he could do. He couldn't wait there and hold her until the cops arrived. That would be stupid. He was distraught, torn up inside, but not stupid.

It was so strange. He wanted to stay, but his legs just walked him away as if they had a mind of their own. He left his dead lover in the worst way possible. He left her as the killer he was. He had left her as a cold, heartless professional and though the other half of him pleaded and begged and longed to stay, the man he had become took over regardless. Dean had granted that man too much power and now, as the figure he barely recognized carried the broken shell of Yuki's fiancé into the cold of the outside world, he knew that it was all he was. He had become that man.

His car pulled out of the parking lot and he was still crying as he sped down the street not paying attention to where he was going. It was a moment of pure agony. His professionalism finally shut off and left him in the pit of his own despair as a final kiss of pain. One last bitter gift from the burning hole in his heart. His soul mate had been killed. The Dean Cottrell who could love, who could care... was dead.

In that instant his bloodshot eyes narrowed and he gripped the wheel tight enough for it to hurt. It was an instant that would last an eternity.

He was going to kill Ray if it was the last thing he ever did and Heaven help anyone who tried to stop him.

CHAPTER FORTY-THREE
A BROKEN MAN

One of Donnie's guards was thinking about reaching for a cigarette when a BMW pulled into the drive. It was fair enough he supposed. He was planning on quitting anyway. The driver's identity became apparent when he got close enough and ground to a halt. He climbed out and started to grunt loudly as if in pain.

"'Little late to be visiting, isn't it, Mr. Cottrell?"

"I need to see Donnie," Dean said in a voice unlike his own. It seemed distant and possibly injured. For some reason the guard felt unable to say no and led Dean inside the house before going to wake his boss.

"They killed her Donnie. They killed her."

Dean sat opposite the now wide awake Donnie who eyed him with some sympathy. Now he knew. Now he knew that the feeling of being betrayed was nothing to the lust for vengeance that comes after the murder of a loved one. Dean's eyes were a crimson color and tear marks tracked his cheeks. He looked more disheveled than he had done at any other meeting they had had and Donnie couldn't blame him. He hadn't known much about his mysterious friend on a personal level and the fact that he had had a fiancée came as more than a surprise.

"He killed her and I couldn't stop him."

Donnie shuffled uneasily in his bathrobe.

"Where do you live, Dean?" he asked calmly. The battered face in front of him smiled weakly as if it had been reminded of some pleasant memory.

"A small apartment. Westlake. I could afford better, but it was all we needed. It was nice."

"How did it..."

"Happen? How did it happen?! That's what you want to know?!" Dean was raising his voice in anger, but it was evidently a symptom of how shaken he was, so Donnie only punished him with a stern look. "He got into the apartment. He had her at gunpoint. 'Told me if I didn't come to meet him there, he'd kill her. I should have known he was going to kill us both anyway, but all I could think about was getting her out of danger."

"Who was at the apartment, Dean?"

"When I got there one of Ray's fucking hitmen was sitting on my Goddamn couch. Ray sent him after me and he used her to get what he wanted." There was a long moment of silence. "And he shot her."

Dean's face drained of its color even further. His eyes seemed to empty. Donnie really didn't want to watch it. He hated to see it. He had despised seeing that same face in the mirror the night he had found out what had become of his brother and nephew.

"I got my gun in my hand and I tried to stop him. I aimed for his head and I missed... I fucking missed. I was just shooting madly. I couldn't focus. I shot him over and over again, but it was too late." His head lowered, and he began to weep uncontrollably. It was an incredibly unnatural thing for him to do as he hadn't cried like that at all in his adult life, but now he had lost everything. The urge to let something out was overpowering. Everything gone with one bullet.

Reduced to nothing, save his unquenchable thirst for retribution and the fact that he was still alive.

"We 'gotta go after him, Donnie. Right now."

"No, Dean. We need to strengthen ourselves. Gambino are still in denial. We 'gotta find someone else."

"Fuck someone else! I'll kill him myself!"

This would have been the moment where Donnie would expect the man to start throwing furniture into walls, but he just shouted from where he was sitting, still as stiff as a corpse.

"Dean, you killed his brother. You killed the guy in your apartment. He's scared, Dean. He's scared that you're gonna ruin it all for him. We 'got him on the ropes. Let's not fuck it up now."

"He's taken everything from me." Dean hissed.

"And he's taken everything from me too!"

The silence that followed seemed to swallow them both. Their eyes made contact and Dean noticed that Donnie's face was pained. The sign that he was thinking of something very bad.

"We 'got nothing but what we are. The only thing he can take away now is our lives and that is one thing I ain't going to let that son of a bitch have, so keep it together. You can grieve after things have been dealt with and Ray Bentley appears in the obituaries. Until then... I'm a mob boss, and you're a killer. Nothing more, nothing less because those are the only two people who are going to be able to take Ray out."

This was exactly what Dean would have said had he been the one trying to pull himself from the brink of destruction. He was still smart. He still had the mobility and position to keep one step ahead. If he let himself break down he was only giving Ray what he wanted.

"Look, Dean. Stay here tonight. I 'got spare rooms and I don't want you in some trashy motel. Tomorrow we can talk logistics."

Dean knew that a night of absolutely zero sleep awaited him, but there was no other alternative. He had to lie down. He was completely exhausted. The grapple with Quinn in the apartment had taken all of his energy, and even if he couldn't find solace in sleep, resting was a much preferable option to sitting in an armchair and wasting away.

He noticed nothing much about the room he 'rested' in that night. Every aspect of his being that wasn't essential to basic bodily functions was in a comatose state, and he was far beyond being able to take in details. He was far beyond being able to take in anything. There was no focus in any view and not a single aspect of what had happened that didn't fill him with affliction. As predicted most of the night was spent staring through blurred lenses at a white ceiling, however, in the end he managed to fall into a shallow sleep. His aversion to sleep before was based upon a desire not to lose consciousness because he knew that bad dreams would accompany it. They did. Dean's few hours in the dark were haunted by fragmented images. Drinking himself to death with Williams during a trip to Vegas was probably a highlight, but was far outweighed by the burning smell left after the Starcross Motel explosion the feeling of cold water soaking into his skin as he beat Thomas Bentley's skull to a bloody pulp and then the voice of the stranger…

"You're going to die here, Dean Cottrell."

The significance was brooding and impossible to decipher with any true certainty. Had Quinn really meant that Dean was going to die in the apartment? He had certainly been planning to conclude the night with that, but what if he had meant something else. Not that Dean was going to die in any specific location, but that he was going to die in this world that he had plunged himself into. The dance with death that never ended. The trap that was always ready to snap closed. He was going to be killed doing what he did best. If Quinn had meant this, then Dean couldn't argue. He wouldn't be surprised if he got himself killed going after Ray. This risk however, would not stop him.

CHAPTER FORTY-FOUR
CELEBRATORY PLAN

"One and only rebel child, from a family, meek and mild.
My mama seemed to know what lay in store.
Despite all my Sunday learning,
Towards the bad, I kept on turning.
Till mama couldn't hold me anymore."

Merle Haggard sang it Southern style over the radio in the office Shades called his own.

On a fixture constructed of clinical steel sat his television set which suddenly announced the morning news. Shades immediately flicked the portable radio off and listened intently. He had failed to get hold of Quinn an hour before so he guessed the man wanted Shades to see it on the news.

"Hello and good morning. It's nine A.M. in Los Angeles and last night more violence gripped the city as police were called in response to gunshots at an apartment complex in Westlake. Police arrived on the scene and immediately closed off the premises. Though resistant to giving out details, police have confirmed that both a man and a woman have been found dead with the suspect on the loose. An elderly resident in the same building is reported to have also died after suffering a heart attack, possibly due to the gunshots."

Shades shut the television set off as the reporter began to discuss stock value for Lyman Kershaw and turned away from it. What happened next was out of the ordinary for him. He crouched slightly and with one hand balled into a fist made a typical victory gesture coupled with a pleased smile; much like a nine year old might wear after winning a soccer match. Ray would have to be informed at once. This was too good.

He shut the door behind him and walked with pace down the hallway at the same time pulling his cell phone from his suit jacket. He hit a few numbers, and the device rang in his ear.

"Pick up, pick up," he said quickly, but the ringing ended with an offer to leave a message after the beep. "Frank, I told you to leave your damn phone on. Great work. You saved both our necks there. I'll have the money wired to your account this afternoon. Enjoy your day."

He slipped the phone back into his pocket and turned a couple of corners before he was faced with the two white doors. He opened both of them and stepped inside Ray's office, an air of heroic ascendancy accompanying his presence. Unfortunately his boss wasn't there. His chair was vacant and a half-finished glass of scotch rested on his desk. Coming around the large table Shades wondered when he would be back. Now Dean was out of the picture maybe things could get back to normal.

When Ray finally did arrive at the office he was surprised to find Shades sitting in his chair. The henchman's smug expression became more annoying every time he saw it.

"What the fuck do you think you're doing?" he asked, closing the doors behind him.

"Waiting for you, boss." Shades got up, and Ray could tell from the shit-eating grin on his face that he had news he perceived as
260

good. This pleased Ray because he knew that Shades could only have one piece of news he would care about.

"Dean Cottrell is no more," Shades said sweepingly.

Ray was hit by a tsunami of intense relief. Cottrell was dead. It was a shame his brother wasn't here to enjoy the moment.

"Fucking excellent," the lead mobster said, apparently admiring his yellow tangs. Shades knew he was really containing his delight.

"Not only that, but my man got rid of his significant other in the process."

"What?" Ray turned.

"Dean had a fiancée. She's dead too."

After a small pause, Ray's grin broadened and he actually started to laugh. Shades couldn't stop himself from doing the same. They both had to lean against each other to stop themselves from collapsing at one point.

"Fucking excellent!" He shook Shades lightly. "I knew I could count on you Shades. I fucking knew it!" Ray let go of him and swallowed the probably now vile-tasting half-glass of scotch and filled it along with another, from the crystal decanter. He handed one to his henchman and raised his own.

"A toast! To us being the most badass criminals of all-fucking-time!" He downed most of his glass and Shades managed to knock back a third before realizing why he preferred vodka or JD. "We fucking own this city, Shades!" Ray walked over to the window behind the table and spread his arms like he was accepting some divine power. Forcing himself to take down another third, Shades stepped closer.

"It's ours for the taking. Nobody messes with the Red Dawn. Nobody! Or you get capped." Ray slammed his glass down on his table, and Shades couldn't help but notice a vicious and possibly crazy flare in his eyes. 'Probably a little early for the man to be

261

drinking. He put away the rest of his scotch like the hardened expert he was and came around to Shades, shaking his finger at him.

"This is it. The big time. I got word from Pally down at personnel that membership is both quantitative and qualitatitive."

Shades ignored the fact that his boss had used one too many 'it's in qualitative. It was obvious he meant that he had a shitload of people coming through the ranks and most of them were mentally competent.

"This Sunday... we're going to fucking sweep the board! Major attacks against gangs all over L.A. I want Caligula wiped out. I want the pressure we're putting on the yakuza to increase tenfold. If it meets on a regular basis I couldn't give a shit if it's a parenting skills group, we hit it fast and hard. The Gambino warehouses in San Pedro, all of it."

If Ray was serious then Shades really hoped he knew what he was doing. A major attack... this Sunday? Jesus.

"Are you sure that's a good move, boss?"

"Of course I'm fucking sure."

"But Valentino would have..."

"I don't give a shit what that fat fucker would have done!"

Shades made a peaceful gesture with both of his hands.

"Valentino couldn't see the big picture. He couldn't understand the plan because he was raised on that Italian, tread-lightly bullshit. The reason we got this far is because we didn't play by the rules... Because we took risks." Ray poked Shades in the chest "Let's quit dickin' around, huh?" Ray took a seat behind his desk and picked up his phone to make a call while Shades slunk off down the corridor.

On the upside he would get to return to taking down more scumbags and cops, but he definitely felt uneasy about Ray's over-enthusiastic plan. It didn't sound like he had thought about it at all. He shook the feeling. It all came down to the fact that he had been out of action for a while. He just needed to be in the right mindset. He needed to let his lust for carnage intensify to the point of frenzy before unleashing it upon those who stood in his way. When that happened, no one would stand a chance.

For about a minute, Shades began to think of something that hadn't occurred to him before. Why had Dean been sent on a suicide mission? There were a hundred different ways that Ray could have done the job without killing Dean. Thomas must have been overwhelmingly uneasy about the promising sharpshooter. 'Too bad that had blown up in his face. Shades smirked.

Whatever. It wasn't his business. Things were different for him. It wasn't like he had anything to lose.

*Mama Tried, written and performed by Merle Haggard (1968) is the property of Capitol Records.

CHAPTER FORTY-FIVE
WADE HARRINGTON, FBI

FLASH! A crime scene photographer got another shot.

The sergeant in charge of the scene shook his head disapprovingly and warded off the urge to go for a Jack in the Box. One of the other officers came up behind him and tried to up his credit by making conversation.

"What a mess," he said.

"'That your two bits worth, Lacros?'"

The sergeant hated little ass-lickers like Lacros, but there were people he hated more and coincidentally they turned up not fifteen seconds later.

Upon entering the hall the lead cop saw two men in gray suits coming down the corridor towards him. A low-level officer barring their way was silenced by a badge. As they continued towards the apartment the sergeant felt ready to tell them to fuck off. Of course, he didn't.

"'You in charge?'" asked the first man. He was taller than his partner with graying hair that had once been light brown. The other indication of his age was some slight wrinkling around the corners of his mouth, but other than that, his skin was quite well-kept. The only extra noticeable features were his rich, hazel eyes and an upper jaw that preceded the lower just slightly more than was usual.

"'Sure am. Sergeant Nicks. What are you guys doing here?" he replied as politely as he could manage. Again, the man pulled out the badge inside his I.D.

"Wade Harrington, FBI. This is my partner, Boris Shalhoub."

Despite his name, Boris Shalhoub didn't look in the slightest bit foreign. He was a little younger and pale skinned with blonde hair that hung lower than Harrington's, down to the shoulders. The man was also shorter with a wider girth and a big face, complete with those cheeks you just want to slap.

"And since when did FBI have anything to do with this?"

"Since I arrived," said Harrington stepping inside the apartment followed by his partner. That threw the sergeant. He had said it in a way that lazily asserted himself as top dog, but didn't rub anyone's face in it.

"Woah," Harrington said nonchalantly. The room was a complete wreck. The couch was on its back and there was a huge display cabinet on the floor that looked as if the Hulk had burst through from the inside.

Harrington immediately noticed a bullet hole in the ceiling near the kitchen area and one in the near wall. The bodies came second.

As he stepped down onto the middle level of the apartment he took in the corpse of a female lying against the kitchen counter and a male lying in the broken frame of a coffee table towards the rear. Two officers stood on the far side of the room and some CSI was taking photos from different angles.

"So, we got two bodies, male and female," Harrington announced. Shalhoub went to a door on the left and reported that the bedroom was clean.

"Okay. The action all happened here then. Sergeant, could you fill us in?"

Reluctantly the sergeant granted Harrington's request as he paced around the room with his hands in the pockets of his jacket.

"Neighbors reported gunshots 'around ten twenty. Police arrive and find two stiffs. Nobody else."

"Are they the owners of the apartment?" asked Shalhoub, pulling out a notepad and pen.

"The owners are Yuki Nakamura and Dean Cottrell. Some residents knew Nakamura, but Cottrell never spoke to any of them. We have limited information on both, but we can confirm that the female is Nakamura. She had an ID in the bedroom. We're still trying to acquire a picture of Cottrell."

"Well, if that's the girl and this is Cottrell, then we 'got a double homicide from an outside source. Any extra information? Who were they? Occupation, parents?" Harrington knelt down by the body of the male corpse, observing the bullet wounds.

"Yuki Nakamura worked for a small office firm in Westlake called Neeson Affiliates. They handle paperwork pertaining to accounting contracts. She was originally from Japan. Mother dead and father being treated for kidney failure back home. Dean Cottrell is more of a mystery. Literally the only things I could find on this guy were minor details and a military record that we should have soon. After he was discharged on his own terms, he became a total ghost. I can't get a driver's license on him, but neighbors say he took a car to wherever he worked most mornings. Oh, and get this. They were supposed to be married soon. She was his fiancée."

"Huh," Harrington made an interested noise as he eyed the silenced pistol clenched in the dead man's hands. Peculiar.

"Cause of death?"

"The guy from the obvious, multiple gunshot wounds. The girl received one to the chest."

Harrington stood up and looked in the direction of the sergeant. He was playing it through in his head, how things might have gone.

"Assuming our man here is Cottrell then I would guess our suspect forced his way through the door judging by the state of the frame with intent to shoot them both. There was a struggle, Dean put up a fight and it ended with him and his fiancée dead."

"Nice observations," said the sergeant, with a hint of sarcasm. Just then another officer came into the apartment with a print-out.

"Sir, I pulled Cottrell's military photograph."

Harrington was over to the other side of the room in seconds.

"Not our guy," he said after a fleeting look at the dark blonde individual in the photo. "So, who's John Doe?"

Now downstairs looking at the body of a much older man, Harrington was again crouched down. There were no visible wounds whatsoever. He rolled the body slightly checking him over.

"Why was it assumed this guy had a spontaneous heart attack?"

"Our coroner took a good guess from what he had to go on. Troy Marlin, army veteran, suffered three previous attacks, no visible wounds and the fact that there were loud gunshots pointed him to the most likely C.O.D. We're moving him out soon."

"Was the coroner retarded?"

The sergeant looked Harrington dead in the face and scowled. He didn't like this guy. Not one bit.

"Look at the bruising here on the back of the neck." Harrington pointed out the black and purple marks under a lifted patch of hair. "This was a homicide."

"How do you come to that conclusion?" asked the sergeant as Harrington stood up.

"It's a professional's method. A sharp blow to the back of the neck and then a deep impact to the chest can bring on an attack in a second with someone in this condition. I can smell the smoke in here and our killer probably did too. Back upstairs."

Before they could head back to the main crime scene another officer updated them in the hallway.

"Sir, the car outside you asked us to access," he said

"What did you find?"

"That's just it, sir. Nothing. No spare tire, no jack, no candy wrappers. The vehicle isn't officially registered and the only thing we found was a cell phone in the glove compartment."

"Where is it?" cut in Harrington, imposing himself on the conversation.

"Sir, there's a problem with it. Ryder tried to access it without a password and it shut itself off. It won't even turn on now. 'Could have been rigged."

"Tell me you're joking. What kind of people have you got working this scene, Nicks?"

Now the sergeant was starting to get annoyed. This guy was a total prick.

"L.A.'s finest," he said in an indignant manner.

"Not fine enough," said Harrington all too quickly before heading upstairs. Shalhoub followed and with a threatening look at the officer, the sergeant did too.

"Okay, new theory. Nakamura and one other that could or could not have been Cottrell, were in the apartment. This guy over here is our killer." Harrington pointed out the dead man in the room. "He uses Marlin to gain access to the building, kills him and then comes up here and forces his way into the apartment. There's a struggle, the place looks like shit, and then judging by where our female victim is, John Doe gets a shot at her and is then mowed down by our second individual who proceeds to flee the scene. Ballistics should verify."

"How can you be sure he's the killer?" Through the long theory, the sergeant had pinpointed Harrington's dialect to Arkansas or somewhere close.

"Silenced pistol. It's a classic for mob hitmen. I'll bet the car outside is his along with the rigged cell."

"Good deduction," said Shalhoub, writing something else in his notepad.

"Woah, hold on. Mob? What do they have to do with this?"

"This whole scene has got mob written all over it. You might have read about the massacre at the Helix Hotel. We found two, disparate groups dead there. Some triads wanted in New York, and men in black suits and red ties, members of a shadowy syndicate we've been tracking for a while now. Coincidence, I think not." All three regarded the deceased man and his distinctive attire. Nicks pulled some gum from his pocket and began to chew on it.

"If this was a mafia job, the mayor is not going to be happy, the governor even less so. These fuckers are out of control," he said.

Wade turned to him and wondered about his integrity. The police had lost all credibility in Los Angeles, and in the Bureau, working with them came with its own warning label. When they weren't covering for their political paymasters, they were covering for the syndicates.

"The crime industry has never been under control, Nicks. That's the whole point."

CHAPTER FORTY-SIX
A DAY WITHOUT DANGER

Breakfast had already been served at the table when Dean stumbled in. Prior to that he had been lying in his bed reflecting, cursing, and at times crying. Now he set it as his task not to let those feelings surface this morning. One of Donnie's men had fetched him some clothes from the back of his car. Something that he had taken from the apartment.

In a bowl was some kind of flake cereal.

"Here he is. Take a seat, Dean."

Not trying in the slightest to fight off the hospitality Dean sat down and grabbed the bottle of fresh milk from the center of the table and poured it all over his cereal, watching it fall through the cracks and fill up from the base of the bowl. If there was one physical thing that was definitely wrong with him, it was hunger. He started eating right away and detected a hint of fruit (possibly strawberry flavoring) in the flakes. It was good.

The only other people in the room were two faceless goons, and they weren't permitted to sit. Dean noticed one outside the French doors as well, doing a round of the perimeter. It was possible his ability to pick out details was returning to him, but it all felt too soon. It hadn't even been twenty-four hours.

He looked at his fingers and turned them over as if searching for something. Donnie eyed him with concern.

"I had her blood on my hands," Dean said quietly. His host didn't reply for a few seconds and continued to take in more cereal. He was genuinely worried that the shock had been too much for Dean. Sure he didn't know him that well, but they were both in the same boat. Dean had the crazy ambition and Donnie had the means. They needed each other if they wanted to get rid of Red Dawn, and with Dean now looking his hands over with Lady Macbeth's horrified eyes, things didn't seem too positive.

"Dean, you're suffering from post-traumatic fuck-up disorder."

"It's my fault. I should never have called him. Fuck! It's all my fault." Dean's hands were now balled into threatening fists on the table.

Yet again Donnie was feeling sorry for him.

"None of this is your fault Dean. The blood is on Ray Bentley's hands, and you know I can relate. I felt guilty after my brother was found. Maybe if I had gone with them. Maybe if I had tried to talk them out of it, but it was a last ditch attempt to stop yakuza from taking over."

"And how close were you to your brother, huh?"

"This fucking close." Donnie put his thumb and forefinger together. "We honored family. Your family is your life. Now he's gone and there's nothing left for me. Nothing left but an ambition to get past all this and start over."

That was something that seemed all too distant for Dean. How could you start again with nothing to build on? Yuki had been his fresh start and Ray had taken that away. He'd taken everything.

Dean found himself unconsciously eating and within moments, his importunate hunger had cleaned the bowl.

"Come on, let's go outside. 'Sea's terrific at this hour." Donnie opened the French doors with vigor and led Dean out onto a well-kept, fenced-off deck.

He was right.

Leaning on the metal barrier, it was one of the best views of the Pacific Dean had ever seen. Almost ethereal. Somewhere out on the ocean there always seemed to be a boat no matter what time of day it was. A large, luxury yacht was cutting up the view of the horizon as the two men watched and Dean picked out five people on board. One was yelling something in anticipation. He couldn't help but smile at the thought of their enjoyment. They were young and free with the world to explore. Dean, though not in possession of such luxuries was happy for them. The sun was on its upward arcing journey and the rolling tide glistened spectacularly. It reminded him of the picture in the trunk of his car. The picture of him and Yuki at the beach and how it had looked just as it did now, except much brighter. Just beautiful.

"I love this view. It beats every view from L.A. that I've ever experienced. It's awe-inspiring to see the towers against the skyline during the late evening and to see the blurred lines of traffic heading down the four-o-five, but this…. It's simple, you know? The ocean. 'Never gets old."

What Donnie said made Dean feel very strange. It wasn't depression and it wasn't joy. It was kind of a surreal expectation. He could touch that view. One day. He had a long road to travel down, but one day he could taste the air out there and feel the wind.

"This one time I couldn't sleep. I just came out here and watched the moon in this kind of purple haze of night where you could just see the dissolving crack of dawn at the vanishing point. The ocean was almost glowing." Donnie watched the yacht gain distance with sad eyes.

"What are we going to do? 'Seems like he holds all the aces now," Dean said negatively.

"He doesn't hold all of them. He's alone and he'll slip up. He wants power Dean. I know it, and he can't get that until he's got rid of everyone in L.A. who can stop him. That is where we're going to hit him. When we find allies who want him gone, we can make it happen."

It made sense.

Dean just wondered what kind of allies they could find who were willing to take on Red Dawn plus, with Valentino behind the wheel of the organization he felt it unlikely that a catastrophic mistake would be made. Now with Ray moving into the big league he was going to be all the more difficult to kill.

"To the shore, Dean. It's a long way, but if you don't even try to swim you might as well be dead. Don't give it up just yet."

Dean cursed himself for letting Ray live at the Helix Hotel. He should have killed them all there and if he had done, then Yuki would still be alive. He felt so responsible for her death that it had started to make him feel physically ill. A tear found a crack in his right eye to escape through and he blinked it away. Yuki was watching him from beyond. He genuinely felt that. He had never been a devout Christian. He didn't even know if he believed in anything anymore, but somewhere his fiancée was still present, still smiling, still waiting for him to come home. He really did hope she was in a better place.

The only way to repent for what he had done was to remove Ray from the picture once and for all. Thomas was already a faded memory thanks to him and now Dean could only expect to go through all of Valentino's recycled mobsters and at some point, Shades as well. He had no quarrel there. Valentino had headed the engineering of Dean's planned demise and Shades was a soulless assassin much like himself. If Dean could kill people whose crimes ranged from petty street peddling to pirate broadcasting, then ridding L.A. of Ray's enforcers would be a pleasure. This was at last a thought that gave Dean a new sense of aspiration. He had already burnt Ray by killing his brother, and if the megalomaniac thought he could get himself out of the line of fire that easily, then he was gravely mistaken. It didn't matter who Ray threw at him, he would end it and draw the final curtain. Just him and Ray. The inevitable face off.

His time would come. Eventually.

CHAPTER FORTY-SEVEN
FRAGMENTED EVIDENCE

In a spacious FBI analysis room, Wade Harrington threw his suit jacket onto a hook and strolled down some plastic steps to the main area where a glass board was a permanent fixture.

Boris was in an office chair half hidden by a cubicle to the left. A tall, black woman called Janice was leafing through photographs and clips of information all laid out over a transparent table, and another agent, DeFeo, was just entering with a piping hot coffee. Wade Harrington wasn't one to start slow and finish last, so without any kind of a warning other than his team's knowledge of him he went straight into building his case.

"Alright, people. Let's get on this. Boris, first event, recent weeks." Boris was on his feet and edging around the board with his hands in his pockets.

"The mob boss of the Tagliano Family is murdered, but isn't found until a few days later. It was likely the work of a rival gang."

"Another one bites the dust," Wade quipped.

Janice stuck a picture of a Japanese man dead at a desk, onto the board and said, "Kyoichi Yoshikuni is shot through the head with a sniper rifle while in his office at UBS Electronics. He's suspected of having worked for the yakuza."

"Good. Next."

"Five people, two still unidentified, are shot dead in a room above the Misty Drink night club. One of the deceased, Ryosuke Motobuchi, was a suspected member of the yakuza. Another of Taiki's stooges," said DeFeo, who was roughly in his thirties with dark blonde hair and a serious face. Janice stuck up corresponding pictures and wrote notes.

"Then, Starcross Motel is laid waste leaving many high-ranking yakuza members dead after an explosion, as well as a number of police officers including Chief Orion," Boris continued. Harrington then took things further in the timeline himself.

"After that, Helix gets hit hard by someone with long range, automatic weaponry. We find bodies of New York triads including notorious figure, Jun Heng, and mystery men in black suits and red ties. Cameras in the hotel were not of sufficient quality for us to pick out the faces we needed... figures."

DeFeo winced as he sipped heated coffee and then realized he was being targeted by Wade's wandering eyes.

"Oh... then the washout occurs and somebody racks up a body count of more than twenty armed men at the zoo. Evidence suggests it was a cover for a gun smuggling operation."

Janice put up more photographs of assorted carnage, one of which was a gruesome depiction of Thomas' face, which was only just recognizable when compared to older photos of the man.

"Exactly, and that brings us to the present. John Doe, in a black suit and red tie, pays a visit to an apartment complex in Westlake and ends up killing two people, including one of the apartment owners, Yuki Nakamura, whose fiancé Dean Cottrell is still unaccounted for."

That was it. Everything was up. His whole case connected by colored arrows. This was all linked. He knew it. Crime was on a huge increase and these events were fueling it. With his hand supporting his chin, he started to think while Boris and DeFeo watched intently. That was when Janice added some fresh information to the mix.

"There's something else. A resident of the apartment block said in his report that Dean usually wore a black suit and red tie when he left in the morning, presumably heading for work."

That was a real curveball for Wade, who went into an even deeper state of contemplation as he stared at the photographs on the board. Uniforms? Assassinations? Why? What did it all mean? Dean's military profile photograph revealed a man whose eyes let on nothing.

None of it made sense. Writing names down below the timeline he ringed them and joined them.

"Dean Cottrell... John Doe... The goons at the Helix Hotel. They're all involved in a group, mob activity. John Doe tries to kill Cottrell and his fiancée. Why?"

"Disagreements within crime syndicates aren't uncommon. Maybe Dean did something wrong?" commented Boris.

"Yeah, but why do it like this instead of getting some nobody to shoot him while he was on the job? John Doe was a professional. You can tell. The silencer, the inducement of a heart attack, the rigged wiper cell and the empty car. I'd say Dean did a little more than something wrong."

"John Doe wasn't professional enough to keep himself from getting killed though."

"That's something else. 'Means Dean wasn't a novice either and the events prior have to be linked, right?"

"Not necessarily..."

"Look, I got a report from New York about Jun Heng and the triads, the guys we found dead at the Helix hotel. A week prior to Heng taking a flight here, a massive shootout in NY between triads and yakuza leaves Heng's younger brother dead. Look what's happening here. Yoshikuni and Motobuchi and Taiki were all members of the yakuza taken out in L.A. recently. The red ties, presumably based here, meet with the triads, and both are at war with yakuza. That is no coincidence. The meeting was an alliance attempt. Whoever shot it up was trying to stop it taking place."

"That could have been yakuza. They have intel' collection rats everywhere." DeFeo liked where this was going. Damn, Harrington was good at deciphering facts.

"Yakuza aren't renowned for sending snipers in. 'Not their style. This would have been executed by a long range, automatic, scoped weapon. Yoshikuni and the poker game attendees all executed using a sniper rifle. There was that kid too. What was his name?" Wade clicked his fingers repeatedly until DeFeo remembered Jake Bentwood's name. There was a long period of deep though where Wade tried to make a connection.

"Wait…" Wade turned swiftly to Boris with the look of someone who had felt the light bulb turn on.

"Cottrell's military file. Something I read in it." He snapped his fingers. "What did the commander compliment him on in his report?"

Boris fumbled through the files on the desk in his cubicle and produced a brown folder. His eyes scanned a page and then he looked up with a similar, knowing look.

"Exceptional sharpshooting skills."

"That's it! Dean Cottrell assassinated these individuals for the red ties."

"That part still makes little sense," cut in DeFeo. "His Special Forces report is excellent. Why would he leave it to join the mob?"

"That's unimportant."

"But if Cottrell was boasting enough headshots to fill a cereal bowl, then why would they want him dead?"

"That's what I'm trying to figure out. What about the zoo?"

"Though completely scorched, we found a shitload of weapons and traces of explosives. The operation was covered by an innocent exterior. Whoever was running the show was stockpiling weapons in the hundreds." Janice reported.

"Thomas Bentley."

"What?"

"Thomas Bentley was the target here. Chances are he was running the show."

"Why do you think he was at the head?" hoping that Harrington's explanation would be based on more than a hunch, DeFeo continued drinking his coffee.

"The thugs at the zoo received gunshots. Thomas had his skull caved in with a Maglite. This was personal. What've we got on Ray Bentley, the brother?"

"Nothing much. He was a deadbeat at school. Acts of violence and such, but I've got no criminal charges."

"'Not good enough. I want more. Look into Ray, he's a loose end. At the zoo we've got reason to believe it was a single individual with the odds against him. You have to be pretty skilled to pull that off. Special Forces skilled."

DeFeo laughed uneasily. "That's a bit of a reach, isn't it?"

"I got pretty far on reaches, Jack."

"It doesn't make sense though. It doesn't explain why red ties would want Cottrell dead."

"Well, what if Thomas was affiliated with red ties, huh? He had to be supplying the weapons to someone."

"Then you have the same problem. Why would Cottrell want to launch an attack on the red ties if he was an oiled part of their machine?"

There was a long silence where Wade continued to scan over the photographs looking for something, but with the current evidence, a single assumption had to be made.

"They did something to him or he betrayed them to another gang."

Wade's colleagues regarded him with skepticism.

"Cottrell was responsible for the attack on the Helix Hotel. Red ties were operating in conjunction with Bentley. It all comes down to the one guy we can't find!" The man had gone into obsessive rant mode and the rest of the team was used to it. When Wade Harrington thought he was right, he knew he was right. In fact, nine times out of ten he actually was right, which is why he often had more say than the special agent-in-charge. Wade could have been the SAC if he had wanted to be, but that would have meant taking on a lot of paperwork at the expense of real action, and if there was one thing that Wade had a penchant for, it was action.

"I want nothing released to the papers. We keep a low profile on this one. Dig deeper into Dean. The man must have some kind of electronic record besides this damn military file. I want Ray Bentley grilled. Men who grow up together do illegal shit they don't want anyone to find out about together. Let's move people!"

The office began to rage with activity and Wade trotted off to equip himself with some caffeine. He was going to nail this case just like every other case and then maybe he could be credited with putting a halt to the crime wave that was seeping under every door in L.A.

He had been working for the FBI longer than he cared to remember and much like Cottrell had exceeded expectations within Special Forces, Wade Harrington had exceeded expectations within the Bureau. It was only by his own volition that he wasn't part of the high command, but then again, his work was in some ways more important than theirs. When it came to getting down in the mud on the most high profile cases, they called on Wade Harrington because he had a deserved legacy and right now, the syndicate rivalry in L.A. was becoming a crisis. The side project he was working on would need to be put on hold for a while. He simply couldn't take his eye off the ball with the body count rising as dramatically as it was. At least he had a lead. With every second that passed, the supervisory special agent became surer of it. Dean Cottrell was the key to everything.

CHAPTER FORTY-EIGHT
THE SEARCH FOR AN ALLY

It was a dreary Saturday when Dean and Donnie had a truly business related conversation. Dean himself had taken a couple of walks along the beach at night, trying to release the guilt from within, trying to convince himself that the root cause was Ray, but when it came down to it Dean had had the choice not to work for Thomas. He had chosen to take up the career as a professional killer after breaking onto the scene of the criminal underworld straight from Special Forces. It all came back to him. Yuki would have been better never knowing that he existed.

Now he was knocking back a glass of wine while Donnie talked to him over the table on the deck. As usual, two goons stood with their hands in front of them, unmoving and ever-watchful. Both the yakuza and the Red Dawn were very real threats, every second of the day, so the mob boss had 'round the clock protection. Donnie had no fear of being outside, although why he had decided to talk out on the deck, under the gray clouds, was anyone's guess.

"I'm pushing on the Gambinos, but the Godfather, Sergio. He's a fucking monkfish. Ray hasn't messed with him yet, so he seems to think they can operate side by side. He's blindfolding himself, wrinkly old bastard. I've tried everywhere, Dean. Nobody wants to shoot themselves in the foot by picking a fight with Red Dawn and my numbers are dwindling."

"I don't understand. Ray is wiping yakuza off the map along with you. Why do these people think he'll let them stay on his turf?"

"It's an age-old human condition my friend. Denial. There are gangs in this city that together could challenge Ray, but they aren't going to risk their numbers until he bites into their bruschetta you know?"

"What about the yakuza themselves?"

"Keep dreaming. A lot of bad history there. Luga knocked off their Japanese boss' son during a visit here. That's part of the reason they want us all dead."

Dean nodded and looked out onto the choppy sea. He was in full black getup today. Even his moderately priced sunglasses were black. Obviously he didn't need them with the current weather, but he didn't much like the thought of anyone peering into his soul today, even Donnie, who lit himself a cigar and puffed on it with a thoughtful look on his face.

"I always had a fallback option, but you aren't going to like it."

Dean raised an eyebrow. He couldn't guess who Donnie had in mind. He wasn't amazingly well acquainted with small gangs in L.A., but right now, he would take whoever he could get.

"Who?" he asked.

"There's a museum in Inglewood. 'Museum of Historical Art. Pretty standard, right? Well, a year back skinhead gangs pushed forward and set up shop in Inglewood for a new onslaught on a newly arrived mass of Mexican immigrants. Now, you might think that with it being Inglewood and all, that these guys would have gotten kicked out immediately, but that's not how the story goes."

Donnie took a second to vent the tobacco smoke from his mouth before continuing. "You see, whereas the skinheads were once a ragtag shamble of warring factions, they've changed. They're working together now and they're more dangerous than ever. Their L.A. operations centralize at the museum."

Dean saw where this was going and he didn't like it. Regardless, he allowed a small and discomforted smile to form on his lips.

"You want to use neo-Nazis as your cavalry?"

"No. They aren't Nazis. There's a distinct difference. These guys are hardcore nationalist scumbags with a mean streak."

"Whatever. You want to bring them on board?"

"We have limited options, Dean. I want nothing to do with them after this is over, but if we don't find someone who can see that Ray is planning to cut down all the other pieces in L.A., then we're finished. I wouldn't give us another week." He was serious. Deadly serious. Dean could see the logic, but were skinheads the answer? He really doubted it.

"Donnie, you're Italian-American. What makes you think these fuckers are going to even listen to you?"

"They're not. They're going to listen to you."

Dean's heart stopped for a brief second. Had he just said what Dean thought he had said, or was the wine too strong?

"Excuse me?"

"I want you to go to Inglewood tomorrow... late. Walk in with that confident swagger of yours and tell them you want to speak to Brandon Goddard. He's the brains behind the operation. You tell him that you're a representative of many of the other gangs in Los Angeles and that you wish to inform him that Red Dawn are going to challenge his weapon and drug dealings."

"That's ridiculous Donnie. It's too far."

"They're just guns Dean. Nothing more."

"Why me?"

"Because you said you wanted to be the one to up the pressure on Ray. If this falls through I don't know where else to turn. Plus, you have a history of getting the impossible done."

Considering, Dean swilled the dregs around in the bottom of the wine glass. So this was what it had come down to. Having to resort to skinheads in order to get his revenge on Red Dawn? Dean slid his now emptied glass across the table a short way and gave Donnie a look of lethal seriousness.

"Anything to bring Ray down. I'll do it."

"Dean. Understand that I never wanted it to come as far as it has. We're beyond the threshold now, you and I. There is no turning back... and there may be no way forward if this fails."

Dean stood up. It was approaching late evening according to one of the goons' wristwatch. He trusted it as his only source of time reference. The clouded sky offered no indication.

"I'll find a way," he said and then went inside leaving Donnie to finish his own wine, by himself.

Throwing his full weight on the comfortable bed, Dean continued to choke down the phony prescription pills Donnie had given him to combat his depression. He didn't want to trust himself to drugs, but felt if he didn't he might do something reckless and stupid.

The room was dim, with the atmosphere of a derelict space shuttle. Things moved slowly and there was a loneliness that stabbed at the nerves with every muscular twitch. He felt tired when he shouldn't have. It was odd, but he felt like that a lot of the time now. Like he was running down and approaching empty. His dream last night had reflected these feelings. Sprinting down what looked like a hospital corridor with the lights behind him being extinguished one by one. He supposed it was a common dream, like falling. Falling endlessly.

The mirror on the room's dressing table called to him and he pulled himself up taking off his sunglasses. He wanted to see if he looked like shit. Heavy footfalls on a carpeted floor and his hot breath. The ceiling lived in the reflection and to see his own he pulled the mirror's angle down.

His ears rushed with the sudden pounding of dread and distant screams. The cold features of Lysander Shades stared back at him, his eyes more freezing than a collected blizzard and his mouth curved down into a warning frown.

Unable to control his movements Dean fell backwards onto the floor with a thump and a startled cacophony of shallow breathing. For a while he sat there regaining the air that had vacated his lungs faster than a Tokyo-bound bullet train. Hours seemed to pass and then he managed to face the reflection again, except this time it was mercifully his own. He didn't look good at all, but that came as no surprise. Water filled his eyes, and he looked on the brink of a complete nervous breakdown. He refused to crack. That only happened to psychotics. He wasn't psychotic, but the face that now regarded him with a pathetic and pleading expression, was that of someone who was losing their grip on reality.

Dean pounded a fist onto the dresser and let out a frightened mumble. Each tear that fell from his face was filled with the fear that Dean's physical state was not all he needed to worry about.

"I'm losing my mind," he said in fragmented bubbles of speech. Darkness was all he could feel around him.

He was alone.

CHAPTER FORTY-NINE
RAY GIVES THE ORDER

"**W**ell, I'm afraid we don't have time to find someone who gives a shit. Get it done." Shades hung up his cell and pocketed it as he strode confidently down the crimson walled hallway. The Holden Tower was alive with activity. Not a floor was empty. Ray had been right. The organization's population had doubled, maybe even tripled since Shades had taken up his position at Ray's side.

"Mr. Shades!" A young member (most likely one of Ray's many errand boys) began treading softly behind Shades like a dog at heel. "I found you the best driver we 'got. Vessup. He's keen and ready to go, sir."

"That's good. Now run along, and get me a Pepsi. I can't work when I'm thirsty, boy."

"Of course." The kid turned off at the next junction and Shades swung open the guarded, white doors ahead.

With newfound confidence and perhaps a little arrogance, he burst into the room with his cockiest walk. Ray was standing at his window staring into space and turned to greet his employee.

"Boss, you sure were right. Pally's divided our boys up and they're approaching key gang installations around L.A. as we speak. All that remains is for you to give the order."

Ray made one of those lip movements indicating consideration and then reached his hand into a glass bowl of pretzels on the table.

Chewing on two, he flicked another one between the fingers of his left hand and shot Shades a sly grin. If there was a night that would define his future, this would be it.

The pieces were set up and his soldiers were in position to begin the chess game. The 'pawns' would fall quickly and easily. Ray had focused a huge amount of firepower in the direction of smaller gangs. Once they were out of the way the entire weight of the Red Dawn could be put onto targets like the 'queen', the yakuza, who would be forced to withdraw. Ray considered the 'king' to be the Gambino Family, who still thought they would remain untouched. They had assets he wanted badly. If he was honest, Ray didn't expect much of a fight from Tagliano's remaining, paltry force.

Damn, he really hoped this whole thing wasn't a misjudgment. Of course it wasn't. *He* had thought of it. His instincts had never led him astray before.

"Fight or flight? The decision that divides us all... But what am I, huh?"

"Sir, you're all the things leading up to dangerous."

"Dangerous?" Ray's smile widened. "Shades... I'm positively lethal." A moment of decision.

"Do it," he said calmly and then crushed the final pretzel between his teeth. Shades nodded with a satisfied smirk, thinking about plunging a knife into flesh. He could hardly contain the growing excitement about what lay ahead and the jubilation was clear in his eyes.

Ray walked slowly towards his desk, looking happier than he had ever been. He was standing on the crest of ultimate control. Nothing would stop the shift. L.A. was going to change. The game was about to begin.

Shades found his way to the parking floor and the Pepsi he had requested was being held by a goon behind the last black van leaving the parking lot tonight. He checked both of his Desert Eagles to make sure they were loaded and then tucked them into the back of his pants.

Taking the soda and opening it he surveyed the people that would be accompanying him to the destination tonight. No less than fifteen armed thugs in the black suits and red ties of the business. Even that jarhead Kruge was in the trademark attire. The driver was out of rank, wearing a long, onyx trench coat. A similarly dark beanie slipped over his shaven head and a long scar running down his face told Shades that he had the intimidation factor, not that he would need it as a driver.

"What have we got?" asked Shades through deep swigs of carbonated go-juice.

"We set up a sniper at the location. He reports that the area's quiet. Nobody suspects a thing." The driver's voice was grainy Canadian.

Considering this, Shades gave them the nod of approval to get going. The van started up and Shades climbed in beside the driver. There was the solid slamming of the rear doors and then the van pulled an excellent quarter reverse, before setting off up the ramp and out onto the streets.

The person Shades was calling took a while to pick up and when he finally did his tone was full of tension and exhaustion.

"What? Do we have the go ahead?"

"Pally, we are green. Launch now and don't fuck it up." The conversation was quick, however so was everything tonight. It would have to be. Speed. That was the key element according to Ray. Hit them hard and fast.

He took an almighty mouthful of Pepsi and wiped his chin with his sleeve. This was it. The moment of truth. It had been a crazy couple of weeks, but Shades had made it this far and knew he could take it further.

The van pulled 'round a corner and then paused at some lights.

All over Los Angeles, hell was about to be unleashed on the criminal underworld. Gangs all over the city would be counting in profits from their drug dealings. The yakuza would be packing illegal goods into their stolen trucks. The Gambino goons guarding their warehouses would be smoking and playing blackjack. All were unaware that they were going to come under attack very shortly.

Even though the plan sounded good Shades couldn't help but feel slightly apprehensive. Red Dawn's vast numbers had been divided well and despite the setback with weapons they were all armed. However, the task of dealing a blow to organized crime on this scale had been attempted very few times before and had a zero percent success rating. Shades started to have second thoughts about his chosen destination tonight. He had said that he wanted to aid the onslaught on one of the smaller organizations, so that they could be wiped out quickly and then attacks on larger targets could be bolstered with increased speed. That was the plan, but whether it would work out exactly how he had said it would was all down to infinite variables.

The driver of the van was thirty-nine year old, Victor Vessup and he wasn't even close to being apprehensive. He had slavish faith in Ray Bentley due to his desire to speed to the top of the criminal world. Coming in as someone with great driving prowess was something that had given him a head start and now he wanted to successfully provide transportation for Ray's top man which would hopefully gain him some credit. He guessed that many of the other people on his level were hoping the same thing.

The vehicle was now heading through South Los Angeles at some speed. A very light and misty drizzle came and went, but other than that it was just dark. Even so, the driver had no trouble on the road. Not the smallest slip. He overtook cars with unneeded precision and Shades wondered if the man might deserve a promotion after tonight.

Turning, Shades slid open a panel to reveal the back of the van separated by steel plates and a grilled window. It really was amazing how many people the vehicles could carry. They looked bigger from the inside.

"Okay, boys. What're we packing?"

A man with a shaven head and thick sunglasses replied.

"Handguns across the board. Three shotguns and an AK. 'Didn't think we'd need much else."

"'Sounds good. Now, when we head inside, we're gonna firestorm the place. Right through the front door all guns blazing. I call it the element of 'what the fuck just happened?'"

"You 'got it, sir."

Shades shut the panel and relaxed in his seat. The driver shot him a look of what he supposed was reassurance.

"After this we'll head to San Pedro, 'slaughter some eyeties. I think the guys on the yakuza aren't gonna have too much trouble. Their hierarchy's in chaos."

"No problem," replied Vessup, with no indication that it made any difference to him.

Shades sighed heavily and finished off his Pepsi before doing something that would only amuse him. He took a knife from inside his jacket and shoved it all the way through the can.

The driver's eyebrows furrowed as if he was watching something quite bizarre, but he quickly went back to staring at the road. Shades observed the impaled can for a while. The thrill he was about to procure was already starting to stimulate him. Blood was rushing like a wild river through his veins to ever part of his body. Death was on its way.

Shades smiled to himself as the van continued on its journey to Inglewood.

CHAPTER FIFTY
THE MUSEUM OF HISTORICAL ART

Nothing much was happening in Inglewood at that moment. It was almost nine and the streets were nearly deserted.

The Museum of Historical Art stood like a looming, stone monster against the clouded and inky sky. Though defaced in some places with graffiti it was actually rather architecturally impressive for a small museum. A wide set of stone steps ran up to two old-fashioned, wooden doors (an indication that it hadn't been updated in the last few decades). The traditional pillars defended its face by supporting a stone crafted shelter. The surfaces of its form were cracked and brittle, but they had stood the test of time. From its exterior it just seemed like a soon to be demolished or renovated resting place for old relics, but no outsider could guess what the museum was used for over the long nights.

One person didn't need to guess. He knew.

Dean Cottrell pulled up in his BMW and was about to park when he decided that he would rather travel a little further down the road just in case. He would have to be quick about this (not that he wanted it to last long). Inglewood was notorious for its car thieves and the area looked decidedly rough. It was full of closed down shop fronts and Dean guessed that the skinheads had claimed this area as their own.

Standing at the foot of the steps that led up to the doors he took in a deep breath. The cold air stung him and he felt an involuntary need to reach for the Beretta holstered inside his jacket. He had to stay cool.

"Check your shit at the door, Dean," he whispered. With one, agonizing step he began to make the journey. When he got to the door he gave it three hard knocks. There were voices from inside then suddenly a hatch in the right door, guarded by steel bars, opened revealing the face of someone no older than eighteen.

"Yeah?" he said rudely.

"I'd like to speak with Brandon Goddard. Business related."

The face eyed Dean up from the smart suit to the shoes and then back to the face. He definitely wasn't some crackhead. Unsure, the man who was really still a boy turned from the hatch and there was more talking. A minute passed. The sky grew a little darker. Eventually, an older face appeared this one about thirty.

"What's your business with Goddard?"

"That's between me and him," Dean said firmly. The man scowled at this then someone else distracted him. Dean could hear somebody saying, "Boss says, let him in."

Dean smiled inwardly. That had been easier than he had expected.

The inside of the museum looked a lot better than the outside. The main lobby was surrounded by a balcony with stairs leading up to it on the right. Glass displays littered the area and three pillars stood in front of the elevated walkway at the back. A wide hallway ran left into another section of the museum and a set of double doors sat against the far wall. Roaming the floor were the very literal kind of skinheads. No hair, most of them big and brooding. He had expected nothing less. There were about five on the balcony above and maybe eight on the floor.

Dean was approached by a middle-aged man in a puke-green colored jacket, who boasted a perfect smile and unlike some of the others, his baldness worked in his favor to some degree. He offered out his hand and Dean took it, though he wasn't sure why this one was being so friendly.

"You got a name, suit?"

"My name's unimportant." Dean wasn't in the mood to explain himself to the stooge. He needed to get straight to the point. "I'm here to warn you about a gang in L.A. who you could find yourself under attack from in the next few weeks. 'Need to discuss a possible allied front with Mr. Goddard."

The enforcer nodded his head and had a look on his face that represented serious contemplation.

"Ah. Big league stuff." He grinned. "Usually you guys announce yourselves. He's up the stairs, first door and please don't try anything funny. We have been known to get pretty violent when the opportunity arises."

This was possibly one of the last things Dean had expected. To just be told where he needed to go. They hadn't even checked him for a weapon. What kind of establishment was this? He wasn't convinced it was any kind of trap. Regardless, it all felt like he had been expected.

Skinheads shot him odd glances as he walked up to the balcony. It was extremely unusual and the eyes upon him instilled a sense of primal unease. Maybe they knew something was up and had been counting on someone to come and bail them out. He suspected it would all be revealed when Goddard made his appearance. A single door separated him from the man he had come to see. He swallowed softly, knocked once and entered.

The office was felicitous. A rectangular space, two windows with big, parted curtains, a small amount of fake art decorating the walls and at a desk at the far end was the guy presumably running things. He wasn't at all what Dean had expected. He wasn't even a skinhead. A mass of curly, blonde hair on a rather stout gentleman in suspenders and thick-rimmed glasses. Two other men were in the room, both shaven. One stood with his back to the first window and the other was right next to Dean, at the closing door.

"Alright, let's be quick. What do you want?"

Goddard certainly didn't sound pleased to see him. He stopped writing on the paper before him and stood up, an American flag forming a cliché backdrop.

Dean stepped forward. The two skinheads regarded him with cautious eyes embodying an aura of unfriendly. Typical. They expected him to feel uneasy, but he knew they were just a conglomeration of high-class rednecks.

"I have a feeling you already know."

Goddard regarded Dean with some suspicion then seemed to relax and even smile.

"You think we might be interested in playing some team games. It was kind of predictable. Crime goes through the roof and some big shot thinks they can get a handle on it by taking control of the little men. We just want to get the message across that you assholes don't scare us. We're huge now." Goddard obviously had an overinflated opinion of himself, but that usually indicated some sort of hidden insecurity. He would undoubtedly crumble if Dean put him under any real threat. It was all about psychology. Dean had studied the topic due to his belief that becoming successful in the criminal world involved more than being a crack shot with an intimidating stare.

"Don't flatter yourself." Dean placed his hands behind his back and walked over to a piece of art hanging on the wall. Goddard's face lost its colorful edge and before he could regain his footing his new acquaintance continued.

"I didn't come here to take control of your small-time operation. I came as an envoy of the other gangs in Los Angeles."

"Who the fuck do you think you are? You don't know our operation. You don't know what we're about. You're just some prick in a suit."

"Well, if I'm just some prick in a suit then I guess you have no interest in the fact that a major player is about to wipe you from Inglewood for good."

The only thing that stirred was the soft breathing of the room's occupants. Dean turned his head and gave Goddard one of those *'that's right, you're fucked'* smiles.

"The Red Dawn is looking to take L.A. by force. They've already instigated wars with the yakuza and the Tagliano Family. Their agenda is to control all criminal enterprises in Los Angeles and that includes yours."

"How the fuck do you know all this?"

"I have strategic contacts," Dean lied. Mentioning a big syndicate was scary to people like this.

"I'm just a messenger, Mr. Goddard. Other gangs know what I've told you. It's up to you what you're going to do about it."

"What makes you think I give a shit or believe you for that matter? Mafia issues don't affect me. They don't fuck with us, we don't fuck with them."

"The game is changing!" Turning suddenly, Dean stalked back to where he had been standing originally. "The guy running this show is a lunatic. The rise in crime is his doing. He doesn't care how small you are. If you're turning a profit from drugs and guns, he'll wipe you out and replace you."

Some light caught Goddard's specs as he adjusted them and gave Dean a bitter stare. The thought processes were close to visible. He was considering the enormity (and reliability) of the information that had been thrown in his direction.

"If people don't start coming together to tackle this guy, then L.A. is going to belong to one man. That's not what I want. 'Bad for business. The cops aren't going to do anything because we're scum. I'm not offering an alliance. I'm offering survival. A lot more than you deserve."

"What, you think you're better than me?" Goddard said indignantly.

"I know I am."

"Oh, yeah? You're not the only one with big fish to fry, you fucking corporate dropout. While you're having your little turf wars we're defending the country against the real scum. There is a takeover going on my friend and it ain't just in L.A. It's the whole Goddamn country. We're the reason you're not swimming in Spics right now so show me some fucking respect, faggot."

"Do you really think you're solving problems? You deal and smuggle and all the rest so don't even try and bring up that American crusade bullshit. You're in this for profit. These jackasses might be easy to fool, but I see right through you." The two men stared each other down and Dean became aware that these guys weren't going to be of any use. "You know what? This was a waste of time. Maybe I should put you out of your misery before Ray Bentley does."

Guns were trained on Dean almost instantaneously as he pulled out his Beretta and got a lock on Goddard's head. Once again silence took hold. He eyeballed the two skinheads wielding cheap Bernardelli copies while Goddard smiled apologetically.

"'Not going to happen. We've come too far to get stopped by you or anyone else."

Beyond the windows, across the back alleys of Inglewood, a rifle sat completely still. In the dust covered, concrete room that had once been part of some chain store, now boarded up and closed, Williams was looking down the scope of his weapon. An AI Covert with a conventional, green paint job. It had been slightly revamped with a marginally shorter stock and a custom scope. He altered some settings for a better focus and made sure he was correctly positioned. Through the two windows he had a view of a skinhead standing at the door, one with his back to the window, and also a large man at the desk. The two goons had their guns on someone, but whoever it was remained out of view.

Getting his head in the game was tough with the wandering mind recent events had gifted him with, but he eventually entered what he referred to as his Zen of execution. He was a sniper and he had his marks. Williams took in a shallow breath that tasted of dust and depression.

The others wouldn't be much longer.

CHAPTER FIFTY-ONE
ALL HELL BREAKS LOOSE

Indrawn breath. This was it. They were going to shoot him. There was no point asking himself why he hadn't played it smarter, because he would then have to face that tiny part of him that wanted to die. It wasn't a conscious suicide, it was just a victory for the side of his mind ravaged by guilt and suffering, torn to shreds by the thoughts of the woman he had killed through his own thirst for vengeance and for what? His wounded pride? The sting of betrayal that was a mere itch compared to the sickening torture he endured now? If Shakespeare had written his life story then this would be the tragic hero's end. Just like Hamlet, his pursuit of justice underlined with his own, deserved death...

But it didn't happen. Dean would later wonder whether the timing was fate or somebody watching over him. Gunshots erupted inside the museum. There were curses of surprise from the main hall: smashing sounds; bullets hitting stone; people crying out.

The two skinheads were momentarily distracted as was Goddard, who again adjusted his specs.

"What the hell is going on!" he yelled.

The man with his back to the window suddenly went flying forward along with a company of shattered glass. He hit the deck, dead. Confused, the other skinhead just stared around aimlessly for a second, before his gray matter was spread across the wall like a

Jackson Pollock painting. He collapsed in a heap. His messiah then received two gunshots to the chest and went down, dragging the items on his desk with him.

Dean stood, his gun still pointing at where Goddard had been. They were dead. Shot by someone on the outside. There were no explanations Dean could conjure up at that moment in time. He had been ready to die and then he just... hadn't.

For the moment he was frozen, listening to ruckus of the shootout close by, repeated sounds of bullets leaving the chamber, shouts mixed in with it all, muffled by the noise, but existent.

"HE'LL BE IN THE OFFICE!" someone yelled. Dean heard the door burst open and the clicks of cocking guns. He was still unable to move, partly because he couldn't fathom what was going on and partly because he was too busy silently cursing death for toying with him.

"DROP IT!"

Dean thought of the cops immediately. How unlikely that both of their visits would coincide. He obediently dropped his Beretta 92 and turned. What he saw confounded him. A bald gentleman, gun in hand, made a tactical walk to the wall space between the windows his weapon trained on Dean the whole time, but the other man that stood with his Beretta 87 Target Cheetah (in all its long-barreled glory), was recognizable.

A well-toned individual with short, spiked, blonde hair, cheap, black sunglasses covering his eyes and flecks of metal shrapnel embedded in nasty scar tissue on the right side of his face. Kruge's expression was at first one of disbelief and then a small smile started to flicker.

"Dean Cottrell," came the voice that sounded as if it was chewing gravel.

Dean had wondered whether Kruge had died at the Starcross Motel. Obviously not.

"I heard you're supposed to be dead," he said stupidly and sent a chuckle in the direction of his colleague.

Dean took a few steps backwards and replied, "Don't believe everything you hear. Nice face by the way." In spite of the snide remark, Kruge continued to leer victoriously as if this was some kind of one-up over the elite.

Williams pulled his eye back from the scope. He stopped dead.

He had to double and then triple check before he could be sure of what he was seeing. Unless he really had been beating his liver too much recently, he was seeing Dean Cottrell. He had just moved! There he was! Dean Cottrell... the deceased... was standing in view of the window in the black suit and red tie he had last been seen in. Was Williams seeing a ghost? If he was then why did Kruge have a gun trained on a ghost? It was ridiculous. How could Dean be alive? He was supposed to be a blackened corpse, maybe not all in one piece, buried in a cemetery that Williams had felt too guilty to look for.

A solitary tear began to form in his eye. He couldn't stop it. Damn! Why was Dean messing with him like this?! He grabbed his head with his free hand in an attempt to fend off a migraine, but the pain came on in waves. Somehow, Dean was alive. He didn't have time to contemplate how that was possible. All he knew was that he wouldn't let his friend get killed again. Thomas would have a hard time scolding him now that the bastard was dead.

Williams realized at that moment that he was done. This just wasn't fun anymore. He was going to pick up his shit from HQ and never look back. Maybe think about that bar job in Tel Aviv.

Right now however he was going to do what felt right. The crosshairs settled on Kruge.

"Goddard's dead. 'Shame. We wanted to talk to him a little before we blew his fucking head off. This is ten times better though."

"Fuck you, Kruge," Dean said bluntly. He was ignored.

"You know Ray or Shades probably want to do you themselves, but this is an opportunity I ain't gonna let pass." Kruge was ready to shoot and yet again Dean was powerless in the hands of another individual. The fact that a sniper had saved his life from the grip of the skinheads had been a miracle and he hadn't expected it to come again however nothing these days went how he expected it to.

There was a bloody splash that burst out from Kruge's chest as a bullet clipped his heart. He fell backwards, a shocked 'O' on his lips. What was presumably a muscle spasm made him fire his Target Cheetah. The weapon packed quite a punch and caught the second man in the stomach as Kruge fell onto his back, splattering the wallpaper with blood and sending him to the floor.

This was too strange, but Dean wasn't going to freeze up again. Somebody was watching out for him. He snatched up his Beretta and went for the door. Gunfire still raged outside.

Williams left his rifle and ran for it. Something told him he wouldn't need a gun like that wherever he was going. He had to get back to the Holden Tower and quietly erase himself from the place. He had a bad feeling the whole house of cards was about to come crashing down and he didn't want his details found by the inevitable fed investigation that would follow. Dean could handle himself now and if he was still as dangerous as ever, then the Red Dawn was in trouble.

Kicking open the door, Dean immediately sighted a red tie wearing figure ascending the stairs towards him. He nailed him in the head with a bullet, sending him back down again.

The noise was tremendous, unbelievable.

On the balcony Dean took up position behind one of the huge pillars where a skinhead was taking cover. The man took a few badly aimed shots and ducked back to avoid getting massacred by automatic fire.

"HOW MANY?!" Dean shouted over the gunshots. The man looked at him in confusion.

"YOU'RE HELPING US?!"

"I HAVE NO CHOICE!"

"I'LL SEE!" He did a full turn onto the open balcony and shot down at moving targets with his pistol. Dean saw his squinting eyes counting, but he wasn't allowed to finish as a knife smashed right into his forehead, making his skull loll backwards. For a brief second, he was actually looking at Dean, the blade sticking out of his head like some perverse horn. Then, his whole body fell over the railing and hit the floor below.

It was one of the most jaw-dropping things that Dean had ever seen. It had come out of nowhere and could mean only one thing. Shades.

Dean grabbed a hold of the pillar and jumped over the balcony, using the structure as both cover and a ridiculously wide fireman's pole. As he touched down he immediately saw some skinheads fly backwards under the combined force of two shotguns and took their attackers out with a couple of well-placed rounds.

Bullets skated towards him, but missed.

He was now sharing cover with the puke-jacket thug and another skinhead who were shouting at each other.

"FRIENDS OF YOURS?!" the leader yelled when he saw Dean.

"EX FRIENDS!" retorted Dean who proceeded to fire some unlucky shots in the direction of his attackers.

On the other side of the room Shades was having a hard time believing what he had just seen. He was taking cover behind a display case.

BANG!

Another individual became the victim of his Desert Eagles, but the shot was lazy due to his distraction. Still he was trying to make sense of it. The man had looked like Dean Cottrell. 'Had 'looked a hell of a lot like him, yet it was impossible. Dean Cottrell was dead. It had been on the news... But who else would be in Red Dawn attire and shooting at them? He guessed he would have to find out the hard way. The way he liked it.

Dean watched the other skinhead jump out to let off a few rounds with a submachine gun, but a knife slammed into his chest sending him backwards to the wall and then to the floor.

"WE'RE FUCKING LOSING!" Puke-Jacket was now pissed to the point of suicidal frenzy. He made the same move and fired an AK at the enemy. Surprisingly he managed to take down another two before something caught him below the jaw. He took cover again, but Dean knew it was over for him. He could only watch as the man squeezed the bullet hole in his neck that was pumping out blood all over his poorly designed jacket. There was a moment where their eyes met and Dean saw the lack of understanding in the fading pupils. He hadn't been ready to die. He just didn't get it.

Another skinhead fell from the balcony with a scream and crashed down through a glass display. Dean watched a second get mowed down by Red Dawn moments later. Some reinforcements arrived from a door on the second level; however he knew they wouldn't last long.

A few more wide shots emptied Dean's Beretta. He was out. Not expecting violence tonight he hadn't brought extra clips. He could have grabbed the dropped AK, but the chances of him taking down the whole squad, including Shades in this environment, was minimal at best. The most skilled of people knew when to run.

Risking getting shot, Dean launched himself through the doors on the far wall looking for an exit. Bullets followed, but they were aimed with lousy precision.

He found himself running down a hallway lined with colorful abstractions and threw his useless Beretta to the ground. It had served him well, but its life was at an end. Another set of doors stood at the end of the gallery and he charged through them. The next room was a work of art in itself. A truly respectable area. The clearly signed, double doors of a fire exit lay on the other side of the circular room. Pillars ran all the way around it with a space between them and the walls to act as a pathway for admirers of the paintings that resided there. The central area was expansive and above it was an ornate ceiling fresco of a dragon surrounded by rocks. He really wished he had more time to admire it, but he was undoubtedly being pursued. He had to leave now.

Unfortunately, fate would not allow him to escape so easily. The fire exit would not open. No matter how hard he pushed on the bar it was like the doors were chained shut on the outside. Typical skinheads. Poor at gunfights and even poorer at health and safety. OSHA would not be impressed.

CRACK!

Dean felt the movement of the air cause his hair to shiver. He turned his head and caught his reflection in the blade of the throwing knife, now embedded in the door, three inches from his head.

The entrance he had come through slammed shut.

CHAPTER FIFTY-TWO
SHADES OF RED

Dean turned slowly on the spot, fear all over his face. He couldn't stop the undeniable feeling of terror that came at that moment. This was it. He was dead. The lack of a functional fire escape had caused his death. Ironic, as the lack of a functional window had almost killed him at the Starcross Motel.

Shades had his back to him. Two knives were held tightly in his hands. He violently nailed them both through the woodwork at the top of the entrance doors, sealing them shut.

Dean had known that he would have to face down Shades at some point, but this situation was far from faultless. His exit was gone and he was unarmed. Shades on the other hand, had all the advantages one could be blessed with. He was now strutting towards Dean dual Desert Eagles at his sides with barrels up. The look on his face was one of indrawn uncertainty.

Surely Shades knew he wasn't dead.

A disturbingly calm chuckle passed the armed man's lips and he stopped in the center of the room.

"Dean, I am having a really hard time with this. You look far too well for a dead man."

Okay, so he didn't know. That was a revelation. Dean stood completely still his hands balled into defiant fists.

"Where's Quinn?" A hint of worry crept into Shades' voice as he remembered the fact that he hadn't spoken to Quinn since before the apartment hit.

"Dead," replied Dean quickly, and the veil was lifted. Shades realized that the dead man at the apartment hadn't been Dean. At first, he scowled at the thought of what Ray was going to do when he found out that his brother's killer was still alive, but then he realized that that fact would soon become fiction. He had Dean exactly where he wanted him. His trademark sly smile took hold and he let out another snigger.

"Very good, Dean. I underestimated you." The killer's gratification was evident in his sharp tone that cut to the nerves like bourbon down an open throat. "This is just too perfect! You see, if Ray found out you hadn't been killed, he would in all likelihood want me dead." Shades gestured at his chest with one of his guns before training them both on Dean. "Now by the grace of some divine power, I have the chance to end this... here and now."

God, the man spoke like a true redneck. Dean was half listening and half running over his possible options.

"That little peach of yours, Dean. Your fiancée."

Now he had Dean's full attention. His fists clenched even harder and his teeth grated.

"I'm so goshdarn sorry for what happened there. She must have meant a lot to you. Ray really does employ some vile individuals, doesn't he? 'Never had oriental myself." He licked his lips. "I hear they're as tight as a drum though." Shades gave a full on laugh of amusement at the powerlessness of his prey. This was what he lived for. The torment of others. The rush it gave him, the sense of power... it was unlike anything else.

Dean closed his eyes with a sense of hopelessness. He was going to die at the hands of this venomous and hateworthy man. It was an ending he felt undeserving of. Shades' laughter died to a heavy breath.

"Allow me to do you a favor, Dean. You can see your fiancée again when you're in the ground."

Just as the assassin was about to put an end to his problem, the cold eyes of his target widened and his teeth formed a defiant smirk. Was he... laughing?

"That's just what I would expect from Ray's little bitch. Come on, Shades, shoot me. I don't have a gun and you're too much of a pussy to end this like a man."

"What?" Shades hissed. Nobody had called him a pussy since his childhood. Nobody had ever dared.

"You heard me, trailer trash. Shoot me or fight me like a man. What's it gonna be?" It looked like Dean's psychological manipulation was working perfectly for a while, but Shades wasn't born yesterday and after some consideration, his frown turned into an accepting smile and his eyes closed. He pulled his guns back to his sides and then dropped them to the floor.

"I'll come halfway," he said conclusively. There was the sound of metal against metal as both of his hands reached into his jacket and withdrew two, silver blades.

With no solid plan in mind Dean ran to the nearest pillar for cover. Both of the blades dug into the wall that he left in his wake. His breathing was heavy. He was in no way ready for this. 'No shame in trying though. He ran to the next pillar and a third knife missed him by an inch. He practically felt the heat of its movement.

"Wooh! You were right, Dean! This is a fucking rush!" Shades couldn't wait to kill this son of a bitch. After the pussy accusation, he was considering cutting out his prey's tongue.

Dean made another run from pillar to pillar. The knives flew in his direction with great force and were only just too slow. Shades could pull them from his jacket at speed and throw them within a second. It wasn't long before he would make contact. Ray's enforcer crouched slightly and did some knife tricks with his hands, flipping them over in the air and such, all the while, a big smile adorned his face.

Making a grunt of effort, Dean dived for the next pillar. The knife caught the support and stuck just like its brothers, but inflicted no pain. Dean could see the door, a pillar away. What the hell was he going to do when he got there though? Shades had nailed it shut. Using unknown telepathic powers, Shades seemed to read his mind.

"Thinking about the door, Dean? Go ahead. If you feel lucky enough."

Wincing at the sound of his attacker's laughter Dean went for the next pillar, but Shades anticipated the move, and a knife just missed his face. A spinning blur that caused him to fall back on his ass and quickly pull his legs out of the line of fire as the knife buried itself into a Monet replica.

"Face it, Dean! There's only one way out of here! You can't win!"

Dean refused to accept that. He hadn't come this far to die. Fuck that.

Tensing his legs and preparing them to move again, Dean listened to the sound of approaching footsteps. With shocking speed, Shades had him in sight again. He was standing to his left with a knife ready. Dean ran for it, backtracking. The blade missed and rebounded off the wall hitting the floor with a clatter. Unfazed, Shades stalked back to the middle of the room.

"Hiding is a coward's tactic, Dean! I have a feeling this ain't gonna end well for you."

"Don't count on it," Dean said, before running for the next pillar.

"JUST DIE!!!" roared Shades.

There was a sudden lightning bolt of pain that turned Dean's whole world red. He skidded behind cover again. He had been hit. Daring himself to look, he stared at the knife driven into his right arm. It was an agonizing intrusion and a deep cut that felt like it had reached the bone.

"Ah, ha! Direct, fucking hit! I've got plenty more, Dean! Show that face of yours, and I'll mess it up worse than Thomas's."

With eyes watering from the sweat and pain on his face, Dean pulled at the knife and let out a harsh scream as it exited him. He held it in his hands that were now the residence of crimson streams and saw himself reflected. Disheveled, wounded, yet still determined.

"I've got a fucking knife, you son of a whore!" he yelled in frustration, but he only managed to provoke more laughter.

"I'm crappin' my pants and you know what? My mama probably was a whore. She left when I was two years old and my daddy wasn't exactly the picky type."

It was all so useless. Dean had a blade, but he couldn't do anything with it. He could probably put up a good fight at close range, however he hadn't thrown one in years and even then it had only been one time. Then again, what other options did he have? It was his last and only hope. Shades was no doubt ready to pick him off as soon as he went for another pillar. He was probably assuming he would continue to backtrack, so Dean could maybe surprise him by double backtracking. Even that was a reach. He cursed himself. He should have picked up that AK just in case. Why was he making such stupid decisions of late?

"I'm waiting, Dean!" All of a sudden there was an uncontrolled burst of anger that appeared to stem from nothing. "DON'T MAKE ME FUCKING WAIT!!!"

Dean took a deep breath. Another moment of truth. It had been the same when Thomas had been punching him in the face at the bottom of the ravine and the same when he had scrambled for his gun to the noise of Quinn breaking through the back of the display cabinet. It was a will to live. If you didn't have it, you might as well kiss your ass goodbye.

A grunt of frustration. The energy required to propel Dean's diving jump into the threshold. The will and accuracy required to send the knife spinning through the air. The noise of obvious shock as Shades changed his footing. His own throw that sent a second projectile spinning through the air...

Dean pulled out a flying leap that would have been applauded by any action movie enthusiast, and Shades' knife failed on its mission. It skimmed his thigh as he descended to ground, (ready to let his shoulder take most of the impact) and then ruined another piece of art.

Surprisingly, Shades actually saw Dean's knife come spinning towards him like a helicopter blade. His eyes widened comically at the sight of the gleaming metal and then he lost sight of it...

It sunk deep into his windpipe, halfway to the hilt. The other knife in Shades' hand clattered to the floor, and he gagged on the object that choked him. Blood poured out down his suit and onto the floor.

He fell to his knees, his eyes still wide with the notion of mortality. Blood was literally gushing from the wound and he could feel it filtering through his lungs. It was impossible. One inexperienced nobody with one knife against an expert with a whole fucking armory! Physics dictated it impossible. At one point Shades seemed to attempt to remove the blade, but as soon as he touched it his gargled scream became louder and more torturous than ever. His vision went darker and he saw Dean get to his feet and stalk towards him.

Much like Quinn, he was in too much shock to contemplate his death. There were too many questions as to why is had happened. He had come to a point in his life where his invincibility had become part of his reality, yet now all illusions were slipping away like fleeting seconds and the sound he dreaded rose up among the towering buildings of the city. It came to him from every street corner, every bland office and every shade of sky he had killed under. It even came to him from the distant Yellowhammer State, that sound that's echo had never truly faded. The sound of a car door slamming. The sound of a gunshot.

Probably just as shocked as the victim of the blow, Dean stood and watched Shades on his knees. The man's hands were now covered in blood and his eyes stared up at Dean, pleading. It wasn't conscious. Shades didn't know how to beg. It was his body's reaction to being at the mercy of another. It didn't want to die. He made this kind of screeching sound, which told Dean that his ability to breathe would soon disappear if blood loss didn't take hold first.

"Goodnight, asshole," Dean said with hatred and conviction. He could have sworn that Shades' eyes almost popped out as Dean stepped back and launched a side kick his way. The knife was forced in up to the hilt and Shades fell back and hit the floor with a kind of dreamlike slowness.

He twitched once and then died.

No tears for Lysander Shades. No sense of remorse. Not anymore. He was relieved of the clips tucked into the front of his pants before Dean acquired the two Desert Eagles. The dead man's tie was ripped off and wrapped around the knife wound he had caused. Time was of the essence. There was more killing to be done.

Blowing away the top of the doors Shades had sealed, Dean was allowed to exit. He burst back into the atrium. Four Red Dawn men were the only ones standing. They were huddled together kicking the

313

bodies of skinheads and laughing about their superiority. All were gunned down before they could even raise their weapons. He wasn't sure where he was going next, but he would figure it out.

As he stepped over the countless, massacred bodies, a skinhead (miraculously still alive) crawled out from behind a display case. One of Shades' knives was sticking out of his back and he had gunshot wounds to boot. He wasn't going to last much longer.

"Help..." he whispered, grabbing Dean's leg and trying to look as pathetic as possible.

As Dean had already concluded, he hated both of the factions that had taken part in this slaughter. They could all go to Hell.

Not at all bothered whether or not he hit the head accurately, he took aim.

CHAPTER FIFTY-THREE
UNFINISHED BUSINESS AT THE HOLDEN TOWER

Nobody had stolen Dean's BMW. It was still parked where he had left it. Tucking both of the Desert Eagles into the back of his pants he sprinted to it, unlocked the door and climbed inside. The headlights came on. Dean pulled out into the middle of the street and began to speed away, leaving nothing but destruction in his wake, as usual.

Not too far behind, another set of lights came on and the sound of a heavy engine ripped through the cold night as a second vehicle started to tail the fleeing car.

Images flashed by on the street outside the BMW's windows as if Dean was trapped inside a zoetrope. He didn't even have to look to know what was being depicted in the scenes. Dead people. When had there ever been anything else? Knowing Yuki would be among them he distracted himself from the apparition, nailing his focus to the road ahead.

Dean gained speed as he reached the edge of Leimert Park and made a beeline for Downtown where Donnie was to meet him. The picture box around his car finally began to fade and he was allowed respite from the ghosts that haunted him. This wasn't the end of all that would happen that night however. The museum had only been the opening act.

When he looked out of his window towards the east, an explosion tore the sky apart in the distance. It looked like it was coming from Pico Rivera, but Dean couldn't say for sure that it wasn't further than that. What the hell was going on tonight?! The whole city was going to shit. He put more pressure on the accelerator. Heavy traffic was still absent where he was and he wanted to be as far away from Inglewood as possible. The ordeal there hadn't been clean and consequently, Dean didn't want to stick around.

The BMW hit Downtown in no time at all and that was when his tail made its move. He didn't pay a huge amount of attention as the big, black van pulled up alongside. It wasn't exactly the rarest occurrence in the world.

Victor Vessup wasn't too sure of what he was doing, but he knew that Dean wasn't an ally. He was an enemy. An enemy that was supposedly dead. Getting rid of him would cast Vessup in a favorable light once this night was over. Reaching back and pushing the van to its max speed, he got a hold of the Franchi SPAS 12 he had hidden there. One of the things he prided himself on was being able to drive pretty well while concentrating on other tasks. He pumped the gun and that was what got him noticed.

Dean leaned left just in time as the shotgun blast was fired into the car, smashing the window and showering him with glass.

"WHAT THE FUCK?!" Dean exclaimed in shock. He then acted on reflex.

Vessup was forced to put a hand back on the wheel as he was rammed from the side and his second shot only left a selection of nasty holes in the car's door. It was one fast van for sure. Dean didn't know how it was keeping up with the BMW.

This time it was him who received a nudge, and his car almost went hurtling into a chain link fence, but stabilized at the last minute.

This really was the icing on the fucking cake. Every five minutes somebody was trying to kill him!

The traffic was heavier now and Dean did his best to stop the van getting into the right lane. Unfortunately for him, the driver was unbelievably good at weaving in and out of oncoming vehicles. Horns filled the air. For some reason he decided that an attack from the rear would be just as effective and pulled into the spot behind Dean. They were still breaking the road safety laws on so many levels, but Dean was more concerned with his own welfare at that particular moment. He jolted in his seat as he was shunted from behind and heard his back end fold in on itself. Luckily, he was wearing a seatbelt. If he hadn't been, that could have been the end.

There was another blast from the shotgun and the rear screen was shattered, shredding some of the leather interior. Another shot made sure that whoever sat in the seat behind Dean next would not be resting their head.

That was it. Now he was pissed. Nobody fucked with his car.

"Okay, motherfucker. You wanna fuck with me, huh?!" With some driving power Dean edged forward and then performed a criminal skid into oncoming traffic, rounded a jeep and then went back into his lane.

In the van Vessup was reloading his shotgun while trying to maintain control. It was difficult, but manageable and it wasn't long before there was that grating pump sound again. He took aim and fired at Dean's rear right tire. He missed.

Dean wiped some more sweat from his brow. Up ahead there was an underpass, supported by concrete pillars. It was his opportunity.

He pulled a hard right once again, thrusting himself into cars going in the opposite direction, but this time, Vessup followed. There was another poorly aimed shotgun blast that sent a random car skidding into a fire hydrant.

The bridge was upon them.

Dean weaved around an RV and back into the right lane and as he had planned his pursuer made a fatal mistake.

He tried to get around the RV and chase Dean until the bitter end, but he didn't have the velocity. At the speed he was going he was unable to stop or go fast enough to clear the divide. The van slammed into the pillar support of the bridge and the whole vehicle crumpled around it like a can being crushed against a railing. A flurry of sparks and flying metal was all that horrified drivers got. No explosion, just a good, old-fashioned head-on collision.

There was no way the driver survived.

Dean continued, an emotionless expression on his face.

As he looked down a side street he caught a glimpse of an overturned police car on fire and cops shooting at a target further down the road. Chaos had gripped Los Angeles and Dean was about to find out why. His cell phone in the glove compartment started to ring and he immediately answered it after it informed him that Donnie was the caller.

"Donnie! What the hell is going on?! The city's gone nuts!"

"Dean! You have to listen to me because I got a lot to say and not a lot of time to say it. Forget the skinheads."

"'Already did."

"Ray has really lost his shit. He launched a city-wide attack on gangs everywhere. The yakuza are having three way shootouts with his men and the cops. He's blowing the Gambino warehouses near the docks to shit. Are you hearing me, Dean?!"

"Yeah, but I don't get it. Why would he do it? Valentino wouldn't..." Dean stopped mid-sentence and remembered the sweaty figure of Valentino the last time he had seen him, rubbing his hot face with a handkerchief. The jigsaw finally completed itself.

"Dean?!"

"He must have killed Valentino. He must have blamed him for everything. The dumb shit is running things on his own terms, now."

"'Makes sense, but you have to listen, okay? Gambino are launching an attack on the Holden Tower and we're with them. The bulk of Red Dawn are in firefights with yakuza reinforcements. We're going to storm his HQ. I want you here!"

"What about cops?" Dean asked, apprehensively.

"They've got more than they can handle. Did you hear me? There are fucking wars in the streets and some disgruntled employee set fire to the Strickler building. Can you believe it? Just get your ass over here. We're going to fucking back the rat into his last corner."

"I'll be there; Donnie, but not to help you. This is something I have to get done myself."

"Wait, Dean, you..."

Pocketing the phone Dean put himself on course for the Holden Tower. The final showdown was about to commence and Dean wasn't going to miss it for the world. Then he had an idea. He pulled out his cell phone again and started punching in numbers.

In the Holden Tower, Miles was informing Ray of how their city-wide assault was going. Ray himself was standing beside his desk, scotch in hand.

"The Gambino assets are ash in the wind, but it's not all good news. 'Yakuza are really putting up a fight. We lost contact with all the teams tackling Caligula and the drug barons, but I see fires coming from their direction."

Ray heard something Valentino had said echo in his head and he smiled at the memory of an old, dead friend.

"Rome wasn't built in a day, huh?" He laughed. "They must have been fucking amateurs."

Miles raised an eyebrow.

"What about Shades?" asked Ray.

"I haven't managed to get a hold of him."

Ray considered. The likelihood of Shades being dead was minimal. He doubted it. Everything was going according to plan. He had a fight on his hands, but he was certain that by the end of it, Red Dawn would be the only syndicate left standing.

The phone on his desk started ringing and he answered it immediately, wondering if it would deliver more good news.

"Hello?"

"Hey there, beautiful. 'You miss me?"

Miles was alarmed by the sudden change of Ray's features. He went very red and his jaw locked up.

"Dean... you're dead," he said with laughable uncertainty. This wasn't happening again. There was no way this was happening again!

"Yeah, well, I guess some of us have a few extra lives under our belts."

"HOW THE FUCK ARE YOU STILL BREATHING!!!" Ray's outburst of rage was so pure; Miles and Dean could practically taste it. The caller then took on a darker tone of voice.

"That's unimportant Ray. I'd be more worried about myself if I were you because any second now you're getting a visit from some friends of mine and you better pray they get to you before I do."

"You're bluffing. I'm untouchable. That is unless you have a chopper you're gonna fly up here. You don't think I'm stupid enough to not leave myself some protection, do you? I've got guys on almost every floor."

"Then I'll be sure to enjoy killing each and every one of them. I'm coming for you, motherfucker, and you better believe it. Nothing is going to stop me finding you, especially not that hillbilly piece of shit who's lying in a pool of his own blood right now. Your time's up! 'You hear me, Ray! I'M COMING TO KILL YOU! And don't bother calling me back because I've got nothing to say to you." The voice cut out.

"MOTHERFUCKER!!!" Ray threw the phone at the wall hard enough to break it and then grabbed the glass bowl of pretzels and threw that too. Miles was shocked to say the least. In a violent show of fury his boss toppled chairs and cursed repeatedly.

"THIS FUCKING CITY IS MINE!!!" he yelled at the city view he had from his window, that now showed the extent of the damage he had caused.

Helicopters were scouring the sky. Floors of the Strickler building as well as others, were issuing smoke and flame. The scene that Miles gazed upon was one that could be compared to Nero watching his empire burn all around him. Fortunately they were in the safety of the Holden Tower. This thought was followed by the shuddering aftershock of an explosion from somewhere far below and the sound of gunfire ricocheting through the ventilation system. Miles knew what this meant. He looked to his boss, who slowly turned to the sounds. The situation was unmistakable. They were under attack. Luckily, Pally had indeed left a good number of men at home in anticipation of this happening. Hostile forces couldn't get all the way up to the office. Not a chance in the world.

CHAPTER FIFTY-FOUR
RETURN OF THE BETRAYED

Two guards stood listening in the underground parking lot of the Holden Tower. The shorter of the two was rolling a cigarette from one corner of his lips to the other. Gunfire and other assorted sounds of destruction were coming from one floor up and both men just stared.

"'You think we should go and help out?" asked the bigger man.

"Hey, I'd rather be down here where it's quiet than up there where all hell's breaking loose."

"Well, that's how it goes around here. Just another day. Welcome to Planet Earth." The men were suddenly ignited by car headlights.

It was coming down the ramp at such speed that when it hit the bottom, sparks flew out from its front end making messy contact with the ground. It didn't slow, and they didn't have time to move. The BMW crashed headlong into both of them and they went flying over its roof and onto the concrete behind. The car pulled to an immediate stop and Dean climbed out, not bothering to check the two men. They were dead.

"I'll want your insurance info when I get back," he remarked snidely.

He discarded the half-empty magazines of Shades' Desert Eagles and gave them each a new clip. He wanted to go up there, floor by floor, as prepared as he could possibly be.

The elevator was waiting for him and as soon as the doors were open he stepped inside and turned to face the closing gap.

On the third floor, Bert the barman was watching three men in Red Dawn attire having a conversation about blowing people away. A few others were sat in the fretwork booths. He sure was glad some people had been dispatched to handle whatever was happening at ground level. Unfortunately, he should have been worrying about what was about to happen on the third floor.

The elevator doors opened without attracting too much attention. At least not until the occupant stepped out and opened fire with dual pistols. The three gentlemen in the middle of the room were sent floundering as they were gunned down. None managed to fire back. The closest one got was pulling out his own handgun. Bert ducked for cover behind the bar as bottled and glasses in the rack above shattered, raining glass down upon his head. A man in one of the booths got ready to take out the new arrival with his Colt, but before he could, he was shot in the head through the fretwork. Another two laid down some fire from the left side, yet the booths provided little cover and they were both dispatched with a few quick shots. At the end of the room someone burst in through the double doors packing a suppressor fitted P90, but the attacker was too quick and shot him twice in the chest with his left hand Desert Eagle. The gun went off making short work of the surrounding booths as the man hit the floor.

Bert heard the sound of a clip being replaced and also his own heart pounding against his rib cage. He couldn't die now. He was in his prime for Christ's sake! There was the sound of crunchy footsteps and then someone said, "Get up," in a cold voice.

Hands raised, Bert stood up slowly. At first, he didn't recognize the face, but it came to him after a few seconds, and Dean smiled at his realization.

"Dean? Is that you?"

He had his left hand pistol away, but the right one was primed to put a bullet through Bert's head and from the look on Dean's face, so was he.

Bodies and bloodstains littered the bar. He had massacred everyone. Bert wasn't the type of guy to try and make too much sense of things, so with the knowledge that he would be pleading for his life he tried to persuade Dean not to kill him.

"Dean, now you're a smart guy. You know that out of everyone in this building if there is one man who is the least responsible for what happened to you, it's me."

"'You strapped?" Dean asked casually tilting his pistol slightly. Bert gave a fleeting look at the sawed-off shotgun clipped to the underside of the bar.

"Of course not. I'm a fucking barman." He wasn't sure why he was deceiving Dean though maybe something inside him was saying that he could take the undead son of a bitch down when he went to continue his rampage. That thought was dashed when Dean's free hand shot forward violently. He had an iron grip on the shotgun behind the bar and it came free into his grasp as he brought it over the surface.

Bert went white. His hands remained up.

Still with the pistol on the barman Dean looked the shotgun over and then with a little throw, changed his grip on it so that he was ready to shoot.

"Dean, I swear I had no idea that was even there."

"DIE, MOTHERFUCKER!!!" came an Asian voice along with a sliding metal sound. The cloakroom's hatch shutter was pushed up and Huan stood there with an Uzi ready to blow Dean away. Bert was hopeful, but he should have known better.

Dean's shotgun hand flicked in the direction of Huan and without even looking he sent forth a blast that knocked the man backwards and splattered many coats with red. The end of the gun issued wispy smoke, and Bert couldn't help but bask in the sheer thrill of it all. Sure, his life was in danger, but this was the kind of shit you only saw once. It was too bad he didn't see much more. Dean flipped the shotgun in mid air and took hold of the guarded barrel. He then cracked Bert on the side of the head with it, hard enough to knock him out cold.

Discarding the weapon he tucked his other Desert Eagle into his pants. It was time to grab something heavier. The P90 was a beautiful weapon, black, with the bullets visible inside the box magazine on the top. It felt good to hold and the next scumbag Dean encountered was going to be the victim of its lethality. He held it firmly and before he left, grabbed the pair of black shades that the carrier had been wearing. Now he was ready to kick some ass.

Another man armed with a P90 was coming down the steps to investigate, when the double doors opened and he was shot to shit. He fell forward and tumbled past Dean as he ascended. Another one tried as well just as unsuccessfully.

The disco area that Dean entered next was an expansive room covering two levels. At the far end a staircase led up to a balcony that ran along the right side of the room. The ground was open to the dance floor as well as a DJ podium in the corner. Dean took it that only those three men had heard the gunfire downstairs over the loud, almost oppressive music.

Bee Gees. 'Stayin' Alive'.

How fitting.

Nobody noticed Dean. They were too busy making asses of themselves so he was happy to put them out of their misery.

325

The music didn't stop. It continued while Dean gunned down the first row of people and then was forced to take cover behind a tiled pillar. Even when they danced, everyone in Red Dawn was packing. There were screams and shouts and curses and cries of pain, all quite comical when combined with the Bee Gees' track. Dean shot out another few who were standing their ground, not ignoring the ones fleeing up the stairs. Some heavy fire sent many of them tumbling down again.

From what Dean could see he had two girls with revolvers over near the left speakers. Somebody with a pump action was using the stairs as cover and a few more were crouched by the walls.

First, Dean forced the shotgun connoisseur to take cover with a few bursts then took out a gaggle of men in the corner who then fell all over each other. Dean hadn't killed a woman in a long time, but these ones were skanks, call girls paid to service murderers. He killed them both.

The DJ, who looked to Dean like a wannabe pimp with his furry hat and coat, withdrew two Micro-Uzis from within his garb and from the cover of the podium, started lighting up the dance floor with them. The flashing bulbs and lasers were still making a show of the situation.

Dean wasn't going to be able to take out the DJ without some quick thinking. On the side of the room where he had entered, what looked like an industrial smoke machine was humming away. It would prove a necessary distraction.

A well placed burst had catastrophic results and smoke started pouring into the room at an alarming rate.

"I CAN'T SEE NOTHING!" the DJ yelled.

In the confusion Dean managed to take out four men who had decided the dance floor wasn't their final resting place and had started to get to their feet. The whole thing was like a macabre 70's night. Blood was all over the glowing panels of floor which gave the room a satanic glow whenever they lit up.

Dean considered his next move then realized that these fools didn't deserve his serious killing style. Williams had once said to make fun of situations to take the edge off so just as Stallone or Seagal would have done, Dean discarded the almost spent P90 and withdrew his acquired Desert Eagles. He was ready to do it.

Visibility was completely obscured on left side of the dance floor and the smoke was creeping slowly across the open space. The man taking cover behind the podium squinted into the obscurity.

"Shit," he hissed, his Micro-Uzi's ready to blast anyone who stepped from the vapors, but Dean didn't step from the vapors.

To the DJ's horror and dismay a figure came sliding across the floor on his side, propelled by the momentum of a leap, using the blood to combat friction. Dean fired his dual pistols until the right one was spent. The DJ was downed, his luxurious coat bullet-ridden and looking like something from an animal abuse awareness campaign.

His whole sliding idea had worked even better than Dean had thought. He was still sliding. Gunshot victims lay all around as he left an impressive trail in the red behind him. In fact, he got all the way to the stairs before his kinetic energy would carry him no further. When the man with the shotgun tried to shoot him under the steps, Dean grabbed the weapon and smashed his face in with the butt.

He stood up now with one side of his suit darker than the other. A Middle-Eastern man on the stairs was ready to shoot him, however Dean capped him in the leg before he could fire and he fell on his backside, shooting the ceiling. When he tried to actually nail the intruder properly he found he was out of ammo. Dean grabbed his head and threw him down to the foot of the stairs where five or six more bodies lay.

With confident hands he reloaded both of the Desert Eagles as he reached the top of the stairs and found that it wasn't over yet. Another man with a P90 started to shoot at him but was a lousy shot and allowed Dean to put a bullet between his eyes. The second man, with some kind of automatic pistol, Dean nailed in the leg. While he collapsed to a crouching stance and cursed the air, Dean offhandedly walked up to him and pushed him over the balcony where he joined many of the other corpses with a loud snap.

That was the disco cleared.

In all honesty this was quite liberating for him. He had dreamed of doing this at the end of all things and here he was, living the dream. He reached yet another set of doors at the far end and took one last look back at the carnage as the Bee Gees faded away. How could he resist?

"Now, that's murder on the dance floor." He smiled broadly.

Ray Bentley wasn't far away now and taking out these fucks was a repayment to Donnie for all the help.

It really was killing time.

CHAPTER FIFTY-FIVE
THE UNSTOPPABLE APPROACHES

Gambino and Tagliano forces were pushing up a stairwell to the second floor. There had been a wall of heavy defenses on the first and a lot of hiding behind desks, but now they were making some serious progress.

In most respects both the gangs were interchangeable. Most of the men had the traditional, greasy, black hair and snappy suits.

"WHERE THE FUCK ARE THEY COMING FROM?!!!" shouted a Red Dawn goon before he fell to automatic fire at the top of the stairs.

All the while armed with a Glock, Donnie was thinking about what crazy shit Dean might be pulling at this very second. He knew this place. He knew the interior. He was surely going to be able to advance more quickly than them if he was in the building already. He just hoped the kid didn't get himself killed. Whether he liked it or not he felt some responsibility for Dean, like a son he had never had... or a brother he had never lost.

With no intention of getting himself killed Dean was in fact advancing very quickly. There had been a few guys, who had fortified a hallway with upturned canteen tables, but after some heavy fire from a G36 he had picked up from a dead man, it fell through, and the defenders found themselves full of lead.

329

He was now traversing a long corridor towards where he knew the second bar to be. 'No doubt they would be prepared for him there too. With the powerful G36 in his hand though, he was ready to take on anything Ray wanted to throw at him.

As he had predicted, as soon as he opened the door a poor shot from a Winchester blew apart a section of the wall. He dodged right with remarkable speed and put out bullets in the direction of some suits at the tables ahead. Flipping another table to use as cover Dean could feel the heat of gunfire and the powerful booming of the Winchester as he protected himself. What was it with barmen and shotguns? Within minutes, Dean took down most of the defenders as they reloaded.

The barman still held firm as a cold silence gripped the place.

"You know what? I could use something to take the edge off." Dean said, checking his gun over.

"Oh, yeah. What'll it be?" the barman sneered.

"You, on ice."

There was a pre-death cry from the man as Dean jumped up and unloaded his gun. The man crashed to the ground, his Winchester rattling on the far end of the bar among shards of glass. Dean emptied the G36 into an injured goon on the floor and discarded it.

A few more skanks in revealing dresses were huddled against a pool table, making worried noises.

"Please! Please don't kill us. We're just call girls. We don't even work here!" sobbed one.

Dean really didn't have any intention of killing unarmed women so just gave them a simple message, "Get the fuck out."

He then walked past the bar to the next set of doors, calculating in his head how much longer it would be before Ray was in his sights. His ear reacted with a twitch as he heard the distinct clicking of a revolver being pulled out of a holster.

Whirling around, Dean snatched a bottled of Jack Daniels that was on the bar and hurled it in the direction of the girls. The one who was actually armed received the blow directly to her face and was sent to the floor with smashed glass and alcohol covering her features. All of the prostitutes were now withdrawing weapons and Dean really couldn't find any reason not to kill them. In a surprising show of skill, the Winchester on the bar flipped butt over barrel in the air until Dean held the trigger and the combined force of a shotgun blast and repeated shots from his Desert Eagle turned the women into a pile of sparkling fabric and bloody flesh. Now he just had to get away before their pimp came to collect. Deciding that the Winchester was a decent ally to have in the confined hallways he took it with him.

At that exact moment in time Wade Harrington was in one of the Bureau SUV's. Boris was driving, and they were now stopped at a set of traffic lights, unable to move when they needed to. All the while distress calls came in over the radio with annoying frequency.

"Request backup in Echo Park, Lake Shore Avenue. 246's in progress. Repeat. Backup needed. Lake Shore Avenue, over"

"187 in Beverly Crest. In pursuit, over"

"Unit 2, reroute to Little Tokyo, over"

"TC on West Olympic Boulevard. It's an unmarked, black van, over"

"Fire Service has control of the Strickler Building, over"

"This whole city is crazy," Boris said, moving to switch off the radio.

"No, leave it on. Let's head for Little Tokyo." Wade leaned back and took a sip of his coffee.

The lights turned green, but still, movement was slow. Roadblocks had been set up at some points and many streets were still the venue of shootouts. They hadn't rounded two blocks before the radio came to life again.

"We have reported gunshots at the Holden Tower. Can we get a unit over there?"

Wade's brain started to click and he paused mid-swallow.

"Wait. The Holden Tower?"

Boris gave him a confused glance.

"Yeah?"

"Where did you say Ray Bentley worked?" asked Wade and then it clicked with Boris too.

"The Holden Tower."

"Right, let's get rolling. Drive on the sidewalk if you have to, just get us there. GODDAMN IT!"

Rubbing his head in frustration and wondering where he had gone wrong, Ray couldn't deal with Miles and his whining. Also in the room now was some goon Ray didn't even recognize and a big guy called Gimble who had been involved in operation Heavy Storm.

As if nothing was wrong at all, the yellow tangs continued to swim back and forth in the tank. Ray watched them with the eyes of a drug addict. He was so tired and beaten down that he might as well have been. For now, only the scotch was stopping him from totally losing it.

"I knew this was a fucking stupid idea. Look what we 'got now, all hell coming for us! What have you done?!"

"WHAT THE FUCK IS THAT SUPPOSED TO MEAN, MILES?!!!" Ray yelled brutally. All of a sudden he realized what a useless asset the old fucker was. He was standing there in his cheap suit with an aluminum bat gripped between his petrified fingers. God, Ray hated him so much.

"It means this is all your fault! You've killed us all! Valentino wouldn't have been so fucking brainless."

Unable to control himself, Ray snatched the pistol from the nameless goon's hands and shot Miles twice in the chest. The bat clattered on the floor. With a moan that could be better attributed to a stomach ache than to a gunshot, his colleague collapsed and died. Trying not to even consider whether that had been a wise move, Ray handed the gun back. He was sick of not getting his own way! Why was this shit happening?!

"Sir, if it's Dean comin' for us, then I think maybe I 'got an idea," said Gimble.

With a shocked look on his face Ray turned to the huge henchman who had never spoken before, but had just invaded the room's quiet with his rich, baritone voice.

"Sorry. What?" Ray said indignantly. Gimble didn't have time to reply.

"You have an idea?" he turned to the other goon, "'You hear that, this guy has an idea. Well that's great, but next time, remember that for you, having ideas should be filed away with all the other shit you suck at, like reading... and writing." He said the last part slowly as if he were talking to a five year old. "I don't pay you to come up with ideas you big, Samoan shithead. I pay you to look big and scary. Don't forget it."

"The way I see it, right now, you're running out of options." Gimble raised his voice with newfound confidence, and Ray was too drained to yell at him again.

"Dean's best friend, Williams, can be used as leverage. He's two floors down, puking in a sink; with a face that says he's gonna run. We can use him as a bargaining chip."

"That idea fucking sucks," retorted Ray.

333

Just then, the walkie-talkie on the other guy's belt started to say something that couldn't be understood. He answered.

"What?"

"We've got a big fucking problem down here! I'm on the thirteenth floor and someone is breaking through. We aren't going to last much longer, 'you hear?!"

There was then a loud bang from the walkie and some shots.

"What the fuck?!" came the voice before it was silenced. The goon tossed the communication device aside and held his gun tightly.

"It's him," Ray said conclusively. He didn't sound angry anymore, just pathetic. Gimble couldn't help but feel sorry for him. He had lost everything on one stupid move.

"It's Dean. He's coming."

"What should we do?" asked Gimble.

"Okay, I have an idea. New plan. Go and get Harry Williams. Bring him here. Tell him we need to discuss his redundancy package. If he refuses, shoot out his kneecaps and drag him."

"Sure thing," the large enforcer replied, wondering what would happen if he slowly strangled Ray when all this was over.

It was a nice thought.

CHAPTER FIFTY-SIX
RAY'S LAST REFUGE

Dean's journey after the final bar showdown was relatively easy. Some of the floors seemed completely deserted which told him many of the rats had decided to abandon the sinking ship. By the time he reached the forty-first floor he had a new, fully loaded Winchester in hand and of course, his trusty Desert Eagles. He didn't know this floor very well at all, but he knew that Ray's office was on it.

Opening a random door he encountered no less than ten, armed Red Dawn thugs advancing up a staircase.

"Grenade!" the lead suit yelled, pulling the pin on an M67 fragmentation grenade and throwing it towards Dean who casually shut the door on the flying explosive.

"Ah, shit."

The door that Dean was now walking away from was blown off its hinges in a fireball as the men behind were violently torn apart and cremated.

So, Ray had people on the lookout for him. It mattered not. He wasn't trying to blend in or perform a sneak attack. He was kicking down the front gates and not letting go of the trigger until they were all dead.

Within a few minutes of hunting, Dean found himself in a hallway that ended in two, big white doors which were without doubt the doors to Ray's office. Only an idiot like him would want such a recherché entrance to his personal space. Unfortunately, two men with Ruger MP9s were guarding it, and started to fire at Dean as soon as he came into view. One of them however, found a Winchester 1200 flying in his direction. Reflexively he dropped the Ruger and caught the weapon with the barrel pointing down. Unable to get a good grip he triggered it accidentally and ended up blowing off his own foot. Going down in a symphony of shrieks his partner was distracted long enough for Dean to gun him down and then finish off his partner with the Desert Eagles.

This was it. He was here. He could sense Ray behind those doors. Dean threw the black sunglasses to the floor. The final showdown was about to begin.

This was it. He was here. Ray could sense him behind those doors.

Under his desk an M4 with an under-barrel grenade launcher that wasn't loaded was fixed to the wood. Ray disengaged it and held it loosely. He was ready.

Dean kicked open the doors and came in with both Desert Eagles raised, taking in every detail of the scene and unconsciously figuring out how it could play to his advantage. Points of interest included; a dead body on the floor surrounded by a pool of blood, an idle guard by the window and Ray himself armed with an assault rifle, hiding behind two other individuals. Some big goon that Dean recognized from somewhere, and there on the floor with his hands tied, was a disheveled-looking Williams.

"Don't shoot, Dean! Don't do anything stupid, man. Back in Inglewood? That was me! I saved your life. I had nothing to do with the shit that went down."

Typical Williams. Always concerned with his own welfare.

The situation was moderately dire, but not unworkable. Gimble had what could have been one of the smallest pistols ever made, aimed at Williams' head, but Dean's Desert Eagles were trained on everyone at the same time, it seemed.

He cursed himself for not reloading before he entered. Rookie mistake. He had no idea how many rounds were in each gun. Hopefully more than two.

Spilt pretzels crunched under his feet.

"Good to see you again, Dean. I was starting to think you weren't gonna show," quipped Ray, the M4 quivering in his hands.

"Why would I miss the chance to kill you, Ray?"

This made Dean's former boss laugh halfheartedly.

"Check the situation, Dean. Your friend here had no idea about the plan to kill you. He's innocent in all this. Unless you want him to die tonight, drop the guns."

"And what then, Ray. You're boxed in. They're all coming for you and you know it. You aren't getting out of here alive."

Ray took an uncertain step back. It was strange to see Dean in the flesh again. Not as strange as that first time hearing him over the phone, but it was still weird. Twice now he had been killed and twice now he had come back. He was covered in blood. It was all over his hands. There was splatter on the left side of his face and for some reason, part of his suit appeared to have been dipped in it. Then again it wasn't as if Ray was the poster boy for sanity. His hair was a lot messier than usual. His tie was wrinkled and his shoes weren't shining anymore.

Dean stared him down. Things had finally come to bear. Him and Ray in the same room together. Both had killed somebody close to the other. Both had killing the other in mind, but only one could have what he desired.

Though Ray was in the power position in that closed location, if you looked at the big picture, he was in a very vulnerable state. He wasn't prepared to take on a situation like this and come out on top. Dean was just too good at turning the tables and Ray had no backup plan in place.

"Drop the guns or I will kill the last person who gives a shit about you, understand?"

Dean's eyes connected with Williams', and then Ray's and back to Williams'. He gave him a sly wink and Williams returned with one of those *you wouldn't* looks.

Gimble wasn't concentrating much. He never concentrated on anything much. Dean saw this as an opportunity to take a leap of faith. He screwed the hostage negotiation rulebook and shot Gimble in the head...

Ray received a spattering of blood and the giant of a man who had been killed didn't even twitch. He just kind of toppled to the floor like a felled tree.

After that, several things happened at the same time.

Yelling something inaudible, Ray stepped forward and pulled the trigger on his M4. It didn't fire. Meanwhile, Dean dived left behind the table, firing as he fell through the air. The right hand Desert Eagle he had aimed at Ray was empty and clicked defiantly, but the left hand gun managed to nail the second goon through the neck and then the chest before it was spent.

"FUCK!" Ray had forgotten the damn safety. A rudimentary error. Instead of righting it he didn't think he had time and made a run for the desk. Dean watched as a section of the wall where the fish tank was situated swung open for him, and he disappeared.

On the floor, Dean checked the clips in his pants. He had one left. Tossing one of the empty guns he reloaded the other and stood up. Williams was on his side now, struggling to break his bonds.

"Hey, man! Give me some help here. Dean, where are you going? Dean!"

Dean ignored him and picked up the aluminum bat on the floor next to the body that had been still when he entered the room.

Ray was going down, right now. He could run all he liked, but Dean was going to kill him and he hoped that Ray knew it.

Not amazingly far from the Holden Tower, Wade Harrington was slamming his fists onto the dashboard. The traffic simply wasn't moving. Everything was at a standstill. Boris hammered the horn a few times, but it was no use. In fact, it provoked the man driving the Ford in front to lean out of his window and shout an obscenity at them. Not one to back down, Wade opened his own and shook a threatening fist.

"Hey, asshole! Get your shitbox out of the road! We're the damn Bureau!"

"It's just not moving!" Boris exclaimed.

Wade had had enough of this. Why, when the big break he had been waiting for came along, did the city fall into a state of unprecedented chaos? SWAT had been called into some areas because gangs had been sparked into an all out storm. Robberies, stabbings, shootings. It was a mess and Wade was sure that the Holden Tower was at the center of it all.

"'You know what? Forget it. Somebody has to get to the bottom of this." Wade, being the heroic, can-do kind of guy that he was, climbed out of the car and got onto the sidewalk pulling his gun out and cocking it.

"Where the hell are you going?" asked Boris through the window.

"Stay here. I'm going in on foot. If I'm right about this, Ray Bentley has a big role to play in all of this. He might make a run for it." Wade started to run down the sidewalk through the noise of horns and shouting.

"Wait! We found nothing on him!" Boris yelled after him.

He turned, now running backwards and replied, "Guilty until proven innocent!" With surprising speed, Wade disappeared into the night.

CHAPTER FIFTY-SEVEN
WE DESTROYED EACH OTHER

With tentativeness, the swing door disguised as a wall opened.

Dean looked up a set of eight metal steps. At the top of them the light was dim and threatening. Ray was nowhere to be seen. It was just like him to install a hidden passage.

Refusing to stop now Dean mounted the steps and walked slowly up to the hidden area. On the right the fish tank was completely open. Inside, the yellow tangs swam dispassionately around. They wouldn't help him find Ray. The whole place was a mess of grated walkways, a maze of pumps and generators and other machines that pertained to things like air conditioning and heating. The only sources of illumination were flashing lights amidst the tangled cables and air ducts.

Ray was here. Somewhere.

Edging even more cautiously now, Dean made his way down the walkway in front, keeping the Desert Eagle pointed everywhere that Ray might be hiding. There was a low, surreal hum in the air, along with the smell of a renovated home clinging to the steel plates and pipes that flanked Dean's approach. Ray couldn't run anywhere here. There was no chopper on the roof to save him. He had to face everything he had done. Of course he wasn't going to go without a fight.

Behind a large, steel pump with plastic tubing running off of it Ray flicked the safety off. His hands were sweaty and felt almost numb. He wouldn't admit that he was scared, because that wasn't how his mind worked. He had been backed into a corner, but he had the odds on his side. Dean had some pistols, and he had an assault rifle. Plus, Dean was looking for him. In Ray's mind this gave him the upper hand because Dean had to walk the dark walkways while Ray could lie in wait ready to open fire. The M4 was close to his chest. His breathing was heavy. Somewhere, somebody was walking slowly. It was a huge shock that Dean had actually made good on his threat. The fucker really had determination. Ray could give him that. He peered 'round the machine, his vision divided by the piping. He was close. Thoughts of Thomas encouraging him kept Ray going. Dean had killed all he had. If Ray was dying tonight he was taking Dean with him.

Appearing from the shadow, the man who had ruined everything crossed the threshold from the entrance walkway and Ray opened fire relentlessly.

Dean ducked back behind some pipes after letting a shot fly in the direction of his attacker.

He wasn't hit.

"You're a lousy shot, Ray!" he shouted, his voice echoing in the vacuous darkness.

He checked where Ray had been, but he was gone. Just empty casings. There was a second walkway heading back the way they had come, while the other exit routes didn't look manageable thanks to spider webs of wiring. Turning to face the path Dean took a deep breath. He gripped the aluminum bat in his free hand, hoping that if they ended up fighting in close combat he would have a serious edge.

The ingress he was on ran all the way back to the open fish tank and was divided on the left from another gangway by steam conduits and power terminals.

Movement, sharp and quick behind the machinery was followed by rapid gunfire. It caught an electricity cable that disconnected and fell to the floor, sparks shooting out venomously. For a second he wondered whether he was about to be electrocuted, but it appeared the grating wasn't a conductor. He got off two shots and then Ray disappeared again into the shadows.

Uninjured, Dean found a break in the divide and stepped through to where Ray had been. He was about to head down the new walkway when a figure in a crouched position about sixteen yards ahead started shooting at him before taking cover behind some sort of air purifier. Dean took a similar form of shelter where he was and took five shots, none of which hit anything.

Both men were in the same area now, backs against the environment with the knowledge of where the other was. Dean had one bullet left. This was harder than he had thought it would be.

"Dean! What the hell are you doing, huh? This is ridiculous. Let's talk about this." Ray didn't say it with any hint of sarcasm, but he didn't sound serious either.

"It's over, Ray. You've lost."

Ray's eyebrows furrowed. He hated people telling him he had lost worse than losing itself.

"Hey, Dean. I'm sorry about your fiancée. Was she good?"

There was a pause.

"Yeah... She was." Not amazingly perturbed, Dean smiled at the mention of her. "How was your brother?"

"MOTHERFUCKER!!!" Ray let loose with the assault rifle again and Dean sent his last shot in response. It failed to hit its mark. He was now unarmed. Just great.

"How many bullets 'you got left, Ray? How many before you've got nothing to hide behind and I kick your ass?"

"You try it, you crazy son of a bitch." Ray was sweating badly now. A few drops had ventured to the corner of his lips. It just wasn't fair. He had had it all. At one moment in time it had all been his. Where had he gone wrong?

"Alright! You win!" Ray shouted. "You've taken everything, Dean. I've got nothing! Even in my worst nightmares I couldn't have guessed you would get this far. My brother, my victory, everything... But you can say the same." And at that single moment of revelation, Ray's eyes widened and he said possibly the most truthful thing he had ever said. "We destroyed each other." It was hard to believe he had lost everything. Valentino came to mind. He remembered being on a train with him, and they were both wearing those conspicuous sunglasses, joking and playing poker, talking about their plans for the business. A tear ran down Ray's face. His life had come to an end. This was the final curtain. Out of the darkness came Dean's voice.

"No, Ray. You destroyed yourself. I just get to take your life."

Ray smiled. If he was going out then he was going out in a blaze of glory.

"Then let's do this." He held his M4 up to his face and then tactically moved out into the gangway and stalked covertly to where Dean was hiding.

He wasn't there. Ray had been ready to shoot, but Dean wasn't there. He turned, expecting to be attacked from behind, but he was alone.

"Where are you?" he whispered. The break in the divide to the previous walkway beckoned. Raising the stock of the M4 a little higher, Ray stepped through.

At first he saw nobody, but it was so dark, he wouldn't have.

A heavy blow knocked the M4 from his hands and it went skittering across the grated floor towards the fish tank, just barely avoiding the water. Ray was about to punch Dean, who was now visible, but received such a massive blow to his side that he stumbled and fell onto his back. Dean didn't have his pistol anymore. It had been emptied. Ray had played right into his trap. With a cry of frustration, Dean delivered a blow with the bat, powerful enough to break a leg.

"AAAHHH! FUCK!!!" Wincing, Ray scuttled backwards down the walkway, in the direction of the fish tank. Dean was on him before long though and this time swung the bat at his head. Things lost all focus. Ray was temporarily blinded.

WHACK!!! He felt like his head was splitting open.

WHACK!!!

With each blow, Dean vented more anger. This was what he had desired for so long. What he had done to Thomas was nothing compared to this.

"YOU SON OF A FUCKING WHORE!!!" he yelled and smashed up Ray's face even more as everything the man had done ran through Dean's mind.

The open fish tank was now directly behind Ray and for a moment, it seemed like he was going to beg for his life. There wasn't an inch of his face that wasn't red. One of his eyes was for all intents and purposes, gone, and there were tears in the skin just about everywhere. A slice so clean it looked like a knife wound ran down Ray's forehead and divided his nose all the way to the visible bone. The trauma was beyond horrific. He didn't beg though. That just wasn't how he operated.

Dean was about to smack him again when something stopped him. He just couldn't deliver the final blow. The man seemed so pathetic, the very idea was monstrous. Then he remembered holding Yuki as she died. All Ray's doing. He was at war with his conscience over whether he could take the man's life and every second he looked at the mutilated face made the decision even harder to make.

He had to do this.

Ray looked up with his one good eye and what could have been a smile appeared on his face. Even from within his disfigured mouth, his voice was still audible.

"I took her, Dean. You'll never see her again, so I still have that. Go ahead... kill me. I have nothing to live for anyway."

With what seemed like a slurred, but epic cry of rage, Dean brought the bat back and then dealt a lethal hit from the chin up. Blood shot into the air and landed in the water before Ray himself fell into it with a huge splash.

Dean breathed heavily and the tip of the bat touched the metal floor with a ping.

The victim of his fury floated in a bent over position in the water. Blood surrounded him. It was finished. Finally, Ray was laid to rest. The gap had been sealed.

"I told you I was going to get you, you son of a bitch," he panted. Dean turned away and started a slow and muscle-aching limp back down the walkway.

"AAAAAAAAAAAHHHHHHHH!!!" There was the sound of distressed water and a scream of something between anger and pain. Ray snatched the M4 from the side of the tank, where it had fallen previously. He was about to grab himself a partner for the trip to Hell.

Using the bat, Dean flicked the insulated, broken power cable on the floor towards Ray. It skated across the ground, sparking as it went, and then fell into the tank...

There was a horrid sound of surging electricity. Ray's screams got louder, and the M4 was aimed upwards as it was emptied into the ceiling. Smoke and electrical discharge ran across Ray's skin, blackening it, but Dean didn't stay to watch. He left it behind him. Now it was truly finished.

Donnie, and a large number of armed men burst into the office like a SWAT team, but no gunfire greeted them. Three individuals were dead on the floor and one was helplessly trying to wriggle free of some bonds.

"No, wait! Don't shoot, man. I'm not with them!" protested Williams in the face of all the guns pointed at him. Then, a section of the wall past the fish tank opened and Dean almost got himself shot, but Donnie told his entourage not to fire just in time.

Dean dropped the bat. He looked like shit. There was blood and dirt all over him, yet considering what he had been through, it wasn't so shocking.

"Dean. Finally. I've been looking..." Donnie stopped mid-sentence when the fish tank caught his eye. A char-grilled body floated in the water, its singular, glassy eye watching them from its blackened face. The yellow tangs floated on their sides at the water's surface.

"Holy shit," Donnie whispered. Ray Bentley looked even worse than Dean.

"Hello! Is somebody going to fucking untie me now? I 'got serious cramp!" Williams called from the floor.

"Untie him," said Dean and one of Donnie's men pulled out a flick knife to free him.

Donnie was still staring at the corpse up close, maybe expecting Ray to come to life at any second, but the body's only motion was provoked by the undulating water. You didn't get much deader than that. After a final squint of the eyes, Donnie turned away, feeling that for him... it was finished. His brother had been avenged.

"Police aren't going to be held up forever. We have a way out, Dean. 'Better get a move on," he said.

The Red Dawn's core had been destroyed. Anyone else alive would have nothing to come back to. The entire organization was crushed. It was weird, but in their lust for revenge and desire to protect what they had left, they had actually done the city a great service. Not something any of them were used to, for sure. Donnie stared into Dean's face and saw it lift and look towards him.

"It's over. He's dead." Dean sounded under the influence of something. Maybe it was just finality.

"It's really over."

The police came into Ray Bentley's office with their guns raised, but there was only one man standing. They had missed the party.

Wade Harrington surveyed the body of Ray Bentley and he had no doubt in his mind who was responsible for such a viscerally motivated murder. Already flicking the officers his badge, he tore his eyes away. With strange optimism on his face, he put his hands in his pockets and walked to the window, while the police looked over the stiffs on the floor.

The city was being brought under control once again. Most of the fires had been extinguished and many gang members were either dead or apprehended. Somewhere out there in the city, the man that Wade really wanted to speak to, was free and unquestioned. With the background noise fading around him, he whispered to the city.

"Fate catches up with everyone. Even you, Dean Cottrell. Just you wait and see."

EPILOGUE

*"**G**ood evening and welcome to the news where you are. Last night's events are finally being laid to rest as police and firefighting service bring safety back to the city. That doesn't mean that people are going to forget what happened easily. Early figures predict that no less than three hundred individuals involved in organized crime were killed during the violent gang wars that gripped the streets. That doesn't include the estimated forty men, women and even three children who were also killed due to gang violence. As of now, the cost of the damage has yet to be determined. Small protest marches have taken hold in the Downtown and South Los Angeles area with a clear message: If the police, the city, and the state government continue to fail the people with such tragic consequences, then the only choice left for them will be to leave California for good. One of the biggest shocks that came to concerned citizens early this morning was that the Holden Tower in Downtown Los Angeles may have been a cover for a massive criminal enterprise, and was possibly home to the central cause of the bloodshed. Nothing on this scale has been uncovered since the late fifties, and even though police insist that the city can now return to normal, many believe that vigilante activity may be on the rise in light of this historic crime wave. When the mayor of Los Angeles and Governor Dalton were asked whether they thought that crime levels in the city, and in the state as a whole, could finally begin to fall, they refused to comment."*

The T.V. was switched off and the reporter silenced.

God, L.A. really was a shithole.

The man set down the remote and took a short swig of JD, before lighting himself a long, Cuban cigar. Expensive, luxurious, in accordance with his tastes. The dying embers at the smoke's end glowed faintly in the extremely low lighting of the room, which if you tuned your senses in, was in constant motion.

"This kind of crap is why Nevada is a hundred times better than California. You understand what I'm saying? 'Can't even walk the streets without getting your head blown off." he said, puffing out a cloud of tobacco smog.

Sat in a shadow that was missed by the moonlight trickling in through the windows, the man's eyes could be seen, eerily peering out of the gloom at the large figure who stood in the room with him.

"Who cares? It won't affect us, will it, boss?"

"Of course not. Let the L.A. mobsters fight over their toys. It might even provide a nice distraction." The man took a quick glance out of the window at the city, miles away over the waves.

"DeBoer won't sell out. 'Guy was born with a pole up his ass. You're gonna need to take care of him. His successor should be more open to negotiation."

"You want me to do it?"

"Well, what the fuck am I paying you for? Using outside help is good for the most part, but this is important. I need someone I can trust to get the job done."

"Yeah, alright, I get it, but if I pop another one, that prick from the Gaming Commission's gonna start digging." The man's thick Australian accent served to intensify every syllable.

"Well, let him dig. I'm not worried. Our asses are covered. He won't find squat that he can convince anyone with and if the time

350

comes, then we'll just have the little weasel removed. In the meantime, do your job. Get rid of DeBoer. Make it messy."

The large figure that was the object of the order smiled and there was the sound of metal on metal as he pulled a threatening, 10.5" Laredo Bowie knife from a sheath in his belt.

"That's my specialty."

On the shifting ocean, the night boat sailed with a silent course. The fires in L.A. had been extinguished, but if the sky was inspected closely enough, it was definitely tinged with red.

Thanks to Per and Victoria,
as well as Thomas Fuller
for their encouragement, time, and support

-Regards-

Jett Harrow

6719207R00211

Printed in Great Britain
by Amazon.co.uk, Ltd.,
Marston Gate.